FOUNT AND FORTUNE

BOOK ONE OF THE EMPIRE ETERNAL DUOLOGY

MICKEY SCHOONOVER

SOMERLEN
REIGN·PUBLISHING

Version: First Edition

ISBN: 979-8-9990332-0-8 (ebook)

ISBN: 979-8-9990332-1-5 (paperback)

ISBN: 979-8-9990332-2-2 (hard cover)

Cover Design by Story Wrappers

For my mother, my first reader
and my forever champion.
For every person who leads with their heart.

ABOUT THE CONTENT

Fount and Fortune is a dystopian romantic fantasy set in a brutal dystopian world. While love and hope are central themes, the story also contains elements of grief, illness, desperation and survival, including depictions or mentions of death and injury, violence, kidnapping, torture, classism, parental death, child terminal illness, sexual assault and emotional trauma. Please read with care.

Note: *Fount and Fortune* ends on a cliffhanger, but stay tuned for Book Two, which will end with a guaranteed HEA (happily-ever-after).

PART I

HERE COMES THE RAIN AGAIN

1

EVANGELINE

*T*he armored van arrived with the dawn. I wasn't ready.

Tires crunched on gravel, and my fingers stilled at the rare sound of an engine pulling to a stop outside. I'd been knuckles-deep untangling the nest my little sister had made tying her shoes. A welcome distraction. I hadn't slept, knowing what was coming. Before the sun had risen over our little farmhouse, I'd roused Juniper from bed and helped her into her favorite dress, the cotton one our mother had embroidered with yellow chicks along the hem. She'd dug the shoes out from beneath her bed and handed them to me, a sheepish look on her face.

"I can't hold the bunny ears and twist at the same time," Juni had said, studying my fingers as I eased the laces into bows.

"You're getting real close. We'll practice more later."

My sister had started to respond, but the noise outside silenced us. Juni's gaze flicked to the curtains. Gray circles shadowed her eyes, as they often had these last few months. Her fingers found her mouth, and her teeth set to work on her nails.

"Hey, look at me, Junebug," I said, pulling her fingers free. I fished a butter cookie out of my apron and stuffed it into her hand. I wished I'd sneaked another one for myself. Cookies were my comfort food, and I could have used a little soothing, too. "I got ya. Piggyback?"

Juni clutched her cookie and nodded. When I offered her my back, she climbed aboard, snaking her arms around my neck. I handed Juni her stuffed chicken, and she tucked it between our bodies. My heart thrashed as I locked her skinny legs around my waist.

"Time to go, girls!" Pa's voice sounded down the hallway, and I clutched Juni tighter without meaning to.

"Coming!"

I wanted my feet to sink into the floorboards like quicksand, to pretend none of this was happening. But it was too late for that. Once the Guardia had realized Juni was sick and had been for months, we'd had little choice. No one came near the Conquistador's food if they were sick or ill. The only reason we hadn't been tossed outside the fortified walls of his farm was my father. Dozens of farms lay scattered across the Florida Wildlands, but El Jardín alone fed our centuries-old ruler. Pa had managed his farm for over two decades. Even so, he'd had to beg for a doctor's visit to prove his seven-year-old daughter posed no threat to the Conquistador's food supply.

Juni whispered into my ear as we stepped onto the porch. "Is it gonna hurt?"

"I don't think so," I said. In truth, I had no idea. Our midwife, Nina, handled whatever doctoring was needed on the farm as best she could. Real doctors never came to our part of the Empire.

Pa waited with Nina at the bottom of the porch steps, speaking in hushed tones. They quieted as we approached.

"Mornin', Junebug," Pa said, caressing my sister's cheek. His voice was light, almost chipper, but tension threaded his words and through his eyes. If we were ousted from our home, there was no way he could protect us in the Wildlands. The thought sent a chill down my spine.

A few yards ahead, the armored van idled between black military trucks, out of place among the sun-dappled rows of orange trees and fruit fields behind them. The vehicles were surrounded by at least a dozen Guardia dressed in crisp red-and-black uniforms. There were so many of them, much more than the usual four who conducted spot inspections of the farm. We approached the van like it was a wild animal poised to attack. Not that there was anywhere to run. Nothing was stopping the exam—not if we wanted to stay in our home, safe and protected. That was all that mattered.

A soldier knocked on the van's back door, and Juni's arms tightened around my neck. I patted her hand and made a quiet shushing noise. Her chest heaved against my spine. We'd be lucky if she didn't have a full-on breathing attack.

"Calming breaths," I whispered. My sister's breathing problems had grown worse over the last year, and over the winter months, she'd often taken to bed with blinding headaches. Mid-March's pollen blooms hadn't helped matters. There'd been a time you couldn't keep Juni indoors. She'd run barefoot around the yard, climb low-hanging branches, or follow me into the fields, pretending to be a farmworker. I missed my little shadow, even when she'd made my job harder or picked fruit before its time.

Minutes passed before the van doors flung open, releasing a whoosh of cold air and a strange humming noise. The vehicle's interior shone sterile and bright in the low morning light. Shelves lining one side were packed full to bursting with medicine bottles and strange equipment. The other side housed a large box with a hard plastic tray inside an oblong hole big enough to hold our heartiest farmworker.

A thin man stepped out of the van. His brown hair was short-cropped, and he wore black britches and a white collared shirt. He appeared to be younger than my father but older than my twenty-two years. By how much, I couldn't tell. There was no mistaking the annoyance written on his face. The Conquistador's doctor had come all the way from the Citadel, and he was not happy about it.

"Nothing like a bone-rattling ride through hostile territory to start your day," he said. "All right, let's get this over with. Bring the girl inside."

I stepped toward the vehicle, but the doctor held his hand up.

"Parents only." His glare dared me to take a step farther. Nearby, soldiers stirred, watching us.

"I want Evan," Juni said. Her arms tensed, and she buried her face in the crook of my neck. My mouth opened of its own accord, tasted the protest on my tongue. But I'd learned my lesson the hard way. I'd been brought up to follow the rules, and the one time I'd dared to open my mouth and interfere when I had no chance of changing the outcome, the Commander of the Guardia had whipped me bloody for it in front of every person I knew.

You don't argue with the Guardia, and you don't challenge the Empire, ever.

A soldier glanced my direction, and I retreated a step. It was a reflex, a flight instinct, my mind shoving sense into my muscles when my heart argued the opposite. Pa held his arms out for Juni, but she held tight.

"Let go," I said. "Pa will look after you."

My father pried Juni from my back, and her uneaten cookie fell to the ground along with her chicken. Something small and tender cracked inside of me, but I picked up Chickles and handed the stuffed animal to her. Juni clung to Pa and half buried her face in her stuffed animal, her eyes boring into mine. I stood frozen, caught in the trap of her pleading eyes.

"I won't be far," I said. "I'll come see you when it's over."

"The mother may join us," the doctor said, motioning to Nina. My father tensed, and Nina's face paled. The doctor's words were a gut-punch. He had no idea our mother had been dead for a year and half. Juni buried her face in my father's shirt, and he shushed her. Guilt twisted in my stomach.

"Go on now and get to work." Pa nodded, motioning me toward the fields, before glancing at Nina and climbing into the van. "Come on, Nina."

The van doors slammed shut, and I backed away, eager to be as far from the soldiers as possible. I had a job to do, work that could distract me from the quiet storm raging inside me.

Dominic stopped me halfway to the storage shed.

"Brought your cart," he said, offering the handle to a wagon small enough to fit through the crop rows. His hand brushed mine, and I dropped the handle. I bent to pick it up, letting my eyes wander to the van, away from his yearning eyes.

"The doctor thought your mom was my mother," I said.

"Oh...uh, sorry." He studied the hat in his hand. My straw harvesting hat.

"It's fine," I said, taking hold of my hat and retreating. "It's a comfort knowing she's with Juni."

An uncomfortable silence hung between us before Dominic spoke again. His brown eyes found mine, and he finger-combed the blond strands of his hair off his forehead. "So, I was thinking—"

"I'd better get to work." I tightened my hold on the wagon and hurried toward the strawberry fields, away from my betrothed.

For half an hour, I waded through the field of green, snapping strawberries from their stems and gathering them in my wagon. My hands moved quick. With purpose. I tried to lose myself in the doing of things, in the press of sunshine on my back, the quiet whisper of a breeze across my neck. The fields of El Jardín were my constant, the one place I could count on most things going according to plan. Where I knew what I was doing.

Where my mistakes rarely came back to haunt me.

Today I could find no solace in the fields. My eyes kept straying to the military caravan in the distance. I tried not to think about what Juni was going through. About her tiny, tired body. I tried not to think about the worst outcome, that the doctor might reckon her sickness to be a threat to the Conquistador, that we'd lose our home and end up fighting for our lives against Ferals in the Wildlands. My mind inventoried everything in that van and dared to hope for the best. Maybe the doctor had brought medicine that could heal Juni, ease her pain, and keep us in our home. His van held medicines found only in the Citadel and Florida's few other wealthy communities. We got by with herbal remedies handed down through the generations. Maybe this doctor could end Juni's suffering in a matter of hours.

Then a darker thought crossed my mind. What if we'd had a doctor at El Jardín when my mother had died? Maybe he could have saved her. Maybe he could have undone the worst mistake of my life.

More than an hour passed before the van door swung open. Nina cradled Juni on her hip and strode toward our home, the stuffed chicken dangling from her hand. Pa lingered by the van, talking to the doctor. I couldn't see his face, but his tanned arms were crossed, his body erect and tense. Dropping the last strawberry I'd picked into the wagon, I lifted my skirts and ran, threading the row of strawberries and dashing across the dirt courtyard to my house. I slowed on the stairs and caught my breath, forcing a mask of calm to settle over my face. When I found Nina tucking Juni into bed, my sister's eyes were half-closed, her body limp beneath the blankets.

"She did great," Nina said. "The doctor gave her some medicine that wore her out."

I knelt beside my sister. "I know that was hard. I'm proud of you, Junebug," I said.

"The doctor was mean." Juni's eyes lit with indignation, and she hugged Chickles to her chest. "And his *breaf* was stinky."

I wanted to smile at her mispronunciation, but her words chilled my blood.

"That man doesn't know how to treat children, was in a big hurry to leave," Nina said, moving toward the door. "Get some rest, hon. I'm going to check on your father."

I sat next to Juni and began playing with her hair. It was the only way to ease her into sleep when she was troubled. "I'm sorry he was mean to you."

Juni shrugged, then yawned. We lingered for a long while as Juni fought to stay awake.

"Evan." My name came out wrapped in another yawn.

"Hm?"

"He said he'd tie me down if I didn't stay still."

My breath hitched. I'd never hit anyone in my life, but I imagined fisting my fingers and punching that doctor square in the nose. How dare he? That man had every privilege, and he couldn't spare an ounce of compassion for a scared, sick little girl.

I cleared my throat. "He'll be gone soon, and you won't have to worry about him anymore."

"Promise?"

"Promise."

Her body relaxed and drifted into sleep. I stayed beside her until the front door opened and my father's footsteps padded across the floorboards, then I tucked Juni's blanket over her shoulders and eased her door closed behind me.

I found my father in the kitchen, hands braced on the sink. My stomach dropped. I froze in the doorway, terrified of moving forward. "Pa?"

He glanced at me. "The Guardia won't be kicking us out of

our home," he said, turning with a heavy sigh and leaning against the sink.

I should have been relieved, but the drawn look on his face said otherwise.

"What is it?"

Pa hesitated, like he was searching for the right thing to say. He shoved his fingers through his hair as his words stumbled out, awful and unchangeable. "Your sister has cancer. The doc did a bunch of tests, and he found lumps in her lungs and her head."

I sucked in a breath and crossed to him. "Can the doctor fix it?"

"No, angel—"

"But..."

I wanted to object, but there was nothing to object to.

My father wrapped his arms around me, and I stilled, fear twisting its fingers in my belly.

"He can't help her," Pa said, his voice cracking in my ear. "It's too late. He said the lump in her head is inoperable, and we have no money to pay for surgery in the first place. Nothing short of a miracle will help her now."

I stood numb in his arms, willing him to say it was all a misunderstanding, but he didn't. He kissed my forehead and grabbed his hat off the table.

"I've got to get back to work." He left without looking at me.

This couldn't be happening, not again. My father was wrong. He had to be. There had to be a way to fix this. I didn't know what that might be, but I refused to give up until I'd run through every option. I refused to let my sister die.

2

EVANGELINE

I dreamed I stood beside two Ferals as they dug a child-sized grave. I popped a mushy strawberry into my mouth, and the taste of rot shoved me awake. I blinked my eyes open in the dim, dawn light, disoriented. Tears dampened my eyes, and I wiped them away with a shaking hand. The dream had felt so real.

I'd seen a Feral once, long before Juni had been born. He'd been wading in the stream, outside a padlocked steel gate crossing the water on the farm's north wall. His hair was a matted mouse nest, his face and clothes covered in timeless layers of dirt. There'd been something off about his eyes, like something had been damaged beneath the dark, empty glare. He'd draped his arms through the bars and invited me to come outside the wall and play. His voice was grizzled and strange. And hungry, like he wanted to take a bite out of me. He couldn't get to me—I knew that—but nightmares had haunted me for years after.

I sat up in bed and shook the images from my mind. We didn't have to worry about Ferals robbing or murdering us in the Wildlands. We'd been spared that fate. But Juni? Dear God, the doctor had taken a look at her insides and declared her good as dead. The tumors must have been growing for months, spreading unseen in her little body. He'd said medicine would only prolong her life a few months, not save her, but there had to be another option, something we were overlooking. The alternative was unthinkable.

I dressed like it was any other workday and escaped into the fields, not bothering with a breakfast I couldn't stomach. Less than an hour later, Dominic wandered into the strawberry patch. There'd been a time I would have wanted nothing more. When I'd been fifteen and couldn't take my eyes off him. When I'd mapped his every muscle from afar and cherished every smile. Back then, I'd longed for him to see me, to want me, but he'd been three years older than me and too busy angling for a prized position on the farm. After a time, the crush had died out like an ember starved of air.

After my twentieth birthday, Pa had announced our betrothal without asking me. It was shortly before Mama had died, and they'd argued about it. My father wanted to keep stewardship of El Jardín in our family as it had been for generations, and a daughter marrying his trusted foreman was the logical choice. We might've been married by now, but my mother's death changed had everything.

Dominic paused in front of my cart. I was grateful for the barrier.

"I heard about Juni," he said. "Wanted to check on you."

Other workers were scattered about the field, bent to their work, but I could feel their eyes on us.

"I'm fine." I kept moving through the row, head down, eyes scouring clumps of green for the right shade of red. Putting space between us. I had no cause to be rude. The people pleaser in me wanted to welcome Dominic's kindness and knew he was trying to get to know me. But it felt calculated now that a wedding was in our future. Too small, too late. I couldn't help wondering if he wanted to marry me or if he was doing all this to please my father.

It didn't matter. All I cared about right now was Juni, about not losing another person I loved.

"I don't think you're fine," Dominic said.

I straightened, wiping sweat from my forehead, and looked at him. His eyes crinkled with concern. For me. For my family. In the end, I'd marry this man. I'd do what was expected of me. I always did. I needed to make peace with that. With him.

"I'm not," I admitted.

"I reckon no one would be. She's so young. Don't seem right, 'specially after... I mean, no kid should have to face that."

"I can't believe there's nothing we can do, but Pa says nothing short of a miracle will help her."

Dominic scoffed. "Miracles don't exist in Florida, not unless you can buy a dunk in the Conquistador's magic pond."

I stared at him, his words unearthing an old memory. Four soldiers in our kitchen, eating our food and gossiping after an inspection. Talking about Commander Nico Bane, head of the Guardia and right-hand advisor to the Conquistador.

I heard the Conquistador had Bane transported to the Fount 'cause he had pneumonia or something and his lungs were shutting down, said a soldier whose name badge had read Pickens. One of many random soldiers rotating duty at the farm. *Wouldn't go near him, though, 'cause he's a huge germaphobe, but—*

Watch your mouth, their captain had said. *The Commander hears you talking like that, you'll be wearing a mod collar for a month.*

I'd pay to see that, another soldier said. He twisted his face into a look of agony and made a zapping noise.

Pickens broke in: *As I was saying, I heard Bane walked out of the pond completely cured, healthy as a teenager.*

The Fount had cured the Commander. In seconds.

I'd never considered the possibility. The Fount was known to preserve the Conquistador's life, to make him—and anyone

13

else who could afford it—look young. The Fount's waters had kept the Conquistador alive for more than five centuries, and the rumor was he looked like a man in his twenties.

"Do you think the Fount can cure cancer?" I asked Dominic.

"That was a bad joke," he said, stepping closer, like he feared being overheard. "You know that's not an option."

Why not? My brain latched on to hope and ran with it.

"No one on this farm can afford an Immersion," Dominic said. "Don't torment yourself thinking about it."

"What if we petitioned the Conquistador?" I asked. "Our family has grown his food for centuries. He was willing to send his doctor to check Juni. Maybe he'd grant this one, small thing."

Dominic gave me a sad smile. "If she'd been contagious, you'd all be outside the walls today, Evan," he said. "We're replaceable—every one of us. There's plenty who could take our places. The Conquistador doesn't even know your name."

A blaring alarm silenced my reply. The siren meant one thing: The Guardia were at the front gate and would be at the house in minutes.

"They were just here," I said, eyes wide.

"You know how much they love springing an inspection on us. Let's go."

We left everything in the field and ran. Tardiness was a punishable offense, and you never knew what that punishment might be—a slap across the face or permanent damage. Bloodshed was always a possibility when the Guardia conducted a surprise inspection.

Workers spilled into the courtyard outside our farmhouse and fell into formation. I waited in forced stillness as the rest of my coworkers filled the dirt square. The Guardia's armored truck pulled up, so out of place here, much like the doctor's van. Our farm operated the old-fashioned way, with hands and horses, using methods passed down through generations. The

Conquistador wanted it that way, free of any invention that might compromise or pollute his food.

The soldiers spilled out of their vehicles, and Pa met them on our porch. My breath caught as I recognized one of them—Commander Bane. The same man who'd flogged me a month after my mother had died. When grief and guilt had loosed a one-word protest from my tongue. Right before his soldiers had separated a man from his hand for stealing a tangerine.

You don't steal from the Conquistador. Ever.

The Commander rarely visited the farm, but when he did, he brought trouble. More than the casual cruelty his soldiers offered. This inspection had to be perfect.

"Good morning, Commander Bane." Pa gave a short bow. His gray-speckled hair was a manhandled mess, but he bore an easy confidence, a sure command of his small part of the world. Beside him, the Commander was a stone pillar adorned with a high-collared, crisp, red military jacket, silver buttons gleaming in the sunlight. His skin was smooth and clear, unchanged by time. No one knew his age. Among the Imperial ranks, such perfection spoke of power, privilege, and utmost authority. And access to the Fount, Florida's most precious, guarded resource.

"I certainly hope so," Bane said. He surveyed the courtyard, eyes scraping across a nameless, waiting mass. An eerie quiet fell over the gathering, broken now and again by the muffled, static voices rising from the black Convo bands circling the soldiers' wrists. The musk of sweat and heat saturated the air.

"Let us begin." The Commander lifted his arms. "We are..." he began.

"The Empire Eternal," the workers murmured, dutiful and deflated.

"We are..." he said, louder, more commanding.

We replied in turn. "The Empire Eternal."

The Commander marched down the stairs, his steps clipped and precise, and began inspecting the back row. He stalked the line of workers, eyeing each individually. No one dared meet his gaze.

The silence thickened as he moved on to the line behind me. The Commander's boots crunched in the dirt, grating in my ear. Chills skittered across my skin. He prowled to the end of the row and rounded to ours. I stared at the ground as Bane drew closer, willing myself invisible. A finger brushed mine, and I nearly jumped out of my skin. Dominic's touch lingered there, like an anchor, warm against my flesh.

Bane crept toward us and halted. I choked on the breath in my throat. Sweat broke out on my back. I hadn't done anything wrong, but my body remembered the ropes around my wrists, the bite of his whip, and my heart began to hammer, pounding like a madman desperate for escape.

The Commander's gloved hand pinched my chin and raised my gaze to meet his cold eyes. His glare flicked to Dominic's hand frozen against mine, then to Dominic's face before landing back on mine. Every instinct urged me to lower my eyes, to shrink from his attention, but that would have been a horrible mistake. Bane raised a disapproving brow. I mashed my hand against my thigh, breaking contact with Dominic. The Commander smirked. Actually smirked. Despite the sweat trickling down my back, it felt like I'd been doused in ice.

Bane stepped in front of Dominic, and bile rose in my throat. Dominic's gesture had been bold and reckless, a hint of intimacy frowned upon by our community, but in the Conquistador's Empire, it was not illegal. We'd done nothing wrong.

The Commander gave Dominic a cold smile and patted him on the cheek.

"Careful," he said, so low I almost couldn't hear it. Then he punched Dominic in the stomach. Dominic let out a muffled grunt and bowed. He closed his eyes as his body absorbed the pain, and he struggled to right himself. My muscles begged to move, to help him, but I knew better. It would only make things worse, for both of us.

Bane strolled away from the workers like he hadn't a care in the world. He returned to my father's side and stood there for countless moments, staring at the crowd.

Finally, he addressed a nearby soldier. "Third row from back, second from left," he said. "The man with the blue shirt—has a rash on his neck. Get him out of here."

"Commander—"

Bane scowled with such malice that my father swallowed his words. The soldier removed someone I couldn't see from the line, and the crowd began to murmur and stir. Despite what had happened with Dominic and me, the impulse to protest surged up my throat, as it had the day the Commander flogged me.

Be still, Evangeline. My mother's voice arose in my head, smothering the impulse. God, how I missed her. I closed my eyes and pushed the uprising down.

"No, please—it's poison ivy. It's nothing." I couldn't see who was pleading, but I heard a fist smack flesh, the muffled sobs that followed.

Bane raised his fist toward the crowd, demanding silence without a word. At once, a hush fell among the crew.

"The law of El Conquistador is irrefutable. We will not tolerate any threat to our sovereign's health. Your place in this realm is a privilege, not a right. You are here at his mercy, by his grace. You have been blessed by the lives you have been granted here. You would do well to remember this. You are dismissed."

The Commander rounded on my father. "Come, Lovette. Show me the processing barn. It better be in top shape after this fiasco."

I searched for the man the Guardia took, but Dominic blocked my view.

"There's nothing you can do about him," he said.

"Are you all right?" I asked.

"Don't worry about me. Just go home, get breakfast ready in case the soldiers want to eat, and let's get them out of here before they do more damage."

"Who did we lose?" My hands balled into fists. Useless weapons with nowhere to aim.

"You have enough to worry about right now."

"Dominic, every person on this farm is family. I can't help but worry."

"It was Berto."

I felt like throwing up. Berto was somewhere in his sixties—our oldest worker. He'd never survive in the Wildlands, not if a Feral caught him.

"I know," Dominic said. "Everyone knows Berto's harmless."

But that didn't matter. Everyone knew someone would pay whenever Bane showed up.

"Better get going."

The Commander never lowered himself to eat from our kitchen, but his soldiers did. Sometimes Nina cooked for them, sometimes I did. But neither of us wanted Juni to be alone in the house with them. I sprinted across the courtyard and inside the house.

The bacon was sizzling on our wood stove by the time the soldiers filed into the kitchen. They paid me no attention as they sat at our table and waited. I brewed a fresh pot coffee in our tin percolator and gave each man a cup, then set about cracking eggs. The soldiers made jokes about our old-fashioned kitchen and lack of electricity and then moved on to gossiping like a bunch of old ladies. They'd already forgotten about the man they'd tossed outside the protection of stone walls.

I couldn't wait for them to leave.

I dished scrambled eggs, bacon, and toast onto four plates and delivered them to the soldiers. As I was sliding the last plate onto the table, a hand skimmed my backside and squeezed. I jumped and almost flipped the plate into the soldier's lap. The men burst out laughing. I stared at them like they'd lost their minds, heat and humiliation pooling in my belly.

"Easy, sweetheart," said the soldier with the roaming hand. "Just a little appreciation for such a nice breakfast."

Another soldier snorted, and they launched into another round of laughter.

I hurried from the room before I said or did something I regretted.

No one treated a woman—or anyone else—like that inside these walls. No one except the Guardia. Physical intimacies between people were forbidden in our community outside marriage, and even then, public displays were frowned upon. It was considered ungodly.

But our rules did not apply to the Guardia.

I leaned against the hallway wall and sank to the floor, my heart beating wildly. I needed to stay close in case the soldiers wanted anything else, but I was done with them. As much as I could be.

I stared at Juni's bedroom door. She would wake soon, if the siren hadn't roused her already. What would we say to her? She hadn't yet asked what the doctor had said, but she would sooner than later. How did you tell a child she was going to die? An invisible boot settled on my chest and mashed hard. It was there most days, a constant ache. Dread squatting on my heart, like something bad could happen any moment.

Now it had.

My heart began to beat an erratic song, faster and faster. My hands began to shake, and the boot...the boot crushed me with its doom. I covered my mouth as a sob choked out. I massaged my chest and stared up at the ceiling, breathing deep to calm the raging storm.

I will not break. I will not break. I will not break.

Voices from the kitchen filtered down the hall.

"I'd bid on that one if she were in the Expo, especially if she offered a consort contract."

The soldier was talking about me. It made my skin crawl.

"As if you could afford it. No woman in her right mind would let you bang her, you idiot, no matter how much you paid her. The only way you'll see the inside of an Expo is when you're on duty."

I took another deep breath as the monstrous reality dawned on me. We'd never had much, but we never wanted for much. Until now. The only thing standing between Juni and a cure was money. Enough money to get her inside the Fount. Just the kind of thing the Obligors Expo was for. It was where desperate people turned to fix their money problems. Where they indentured themselves to pay their debts. A last resort of the worst kind.

"It's on my rotation on the twenty-sixth," another soldier said. "Feel free to switch with me. I can't stand those rich, entitled assholes."

Laughter blasted from the kitchen. Something cold slithered along my spine and anchored deep within me. The Expo was held twice a year in an arena outside the gates of the Citadel, and one was coming up in less than two weeks.

Never in my dreams would I have considered giving up control of my life that way, but there it was—something I could do to help Juni. If I had the guts to do it.

If I was willing to break one of our family's biggest rules: Never go beyond the wall.

Juni's door opened, and my sister peeked through the crack. Her hair was rucked up on one side, and her face was rosy from sleep. My heart clenched. We'd lost so much in the last year and a half. Mama's death shrouded us like a storm cloud refusing to yield to the sun. And it was my fault. Juni was without a mother because of me. I'd tried to make up for it, to be there for her, like our mother would have, but it wasn't the same. Not even close.

"Whatcha doing?" Juni whispered through the door crack.

"Waiting for the soldiers to leave," I whispered back.

She crinkled her nose. "Ew."

"Yeah. Hang out in your room. I'll let you know when they're gone."

My sister nodded and shut her door.

My little bug. I would do anything to protect her. Anything to make up for what I'd taken from her. Anything to preserve what was left of our family. Now I knew what I needed to do.

3

RAFE

I knew better than to bet against Twain, and every time I scrubbed a toilet for the next year, my partner in crime would take excessive delight in reminding me. I should never have wagered he couldn't hack into the Imperial Bank.

"I'm in," Twain said, then grinned like a cat with a half-swallowed mouse. He gestured to a flat screen affixed to the wall of our home-slash-workshop. We'd named our place the Phoenix Nest honor of our shared history: We'd survived an inferno and hauled each other out of the ashes to get here. The Phoenix encompassed the top floor of a high-rise on the southern edge of the Citadel, overlooking the Atlantic Ocean and far enough from the Guardia towers to avoid prying eyes.

"Already?" I paused programming a pair of biometric gloves and peered at the screen.

"Of course," Twain said. "You lose, bro. You're on toilet duty for twelve glorious months." He pointed at me in a very unnecessary, annoying manner.

"I like to learn things the hard way."

Twain was a wizard when it came to conjuring code. When I'd bet he couldn't hack into the bank, he'd taken it as a challenge and a dare. Which meant he wouldn't give up until he'd cracked it.

Like I'd known he would.

The two of us were too much alike, and I was happy to scrub the porcelain throne if it meant we could get our fingers into the Empire's pockets. With our fake-identity business booming, Twain and I had long ago ceased breaking and entering to earn our pesos, but hacking into the bank meant we could potentially give select clients a boost. Perhaps procure ourselves a hefty raise.

"Those are account numbers?" I asked.

"Yes," Twain said, "and their balances." He palmed his fist, cracking his knuckles, as thousands of numbers filled the screen, representing accounts belonging to the Citadel's gentry.

All the men and women with power and privilege—and the money that bought it.

In the Empire of Florida, two worlds butted against each other. You had money or you didn't. Which meant you had privilege or you didn't. You had access to eternal youth or you didn't. You lived in safety behind fortified walls, or you risked your life every day in the Florida Wildlands. Money and prestige afforded you a place of luxury in the safest place in Florida, the Citadel, the shining capital of the Empire. Everyone else was expendable.

The weighted scales made our work all the more gratifying. The day we'd stolen back into the Citadel and set up shop, Twain and I had made a pact—we'd do everything we could to knock the Conq off his pedestal.

One day we'd make him pay for the damage he'd done.

Right now, that involved prying open the fingers of the Conq's iron-fisted order and letting the riffraff seep in. All it took was a new identity, one that passed for legitimate in the Imperial Prime Registry. We'd cracked the registry long ago and inserted hundreds of fake lives into the data stream. Access to the Imperial Bank and the billions of Floridian pesos deposited there had eluded us. Our clients had to gather enough funds to enter polite society. Gaining access to the bank could change countless lives.

I dropped the biogloves onto my workbench and crossed to Twain's workspace.

"Can we populate dummy accounts for clients?" I asked. We couldn't deplete real accounts without someone noticing and tracing it.

"Not quite. Right now, I can look, but I can't touch."

"Story of my life."

"It's going to take a while before we can do anything useful with this. They've got it locked down tighter than the Fount," Twain said, staring somewhere over my shoulder. His eyes journeyed to faraway places whenever he was trying to puzzle something out in his head.

I huffed. "Nothing's locked down that tight. How long do you think it will be?"

"No idea. It took me a month to get this far."

I studied the screen, a devil grin spreading on my face. I had no doubt we'd wedge our way into the system eventually, find a way to make money out of nothing.

"Twain Hedrick, you're a genius."

"Yes, I know," he said.

"You'd be charming if you weren't so humble," I said.

"*No man is free who is not master of himself,*" Twain said.

"Let me guess...Socrates?"

"Rafe, have you learned nothing? They are the immortal words of Epictetus. Greek philosopher."

"You'd also be charming if you stopped quoting dead philosophers. Tech is where it's at," I said, retreating to my workbench. Simone was due in an hour with a client, and I needed to finish programming his new identity into his biogloves and retinal mask.

"Both are important. Delighting the intellect *and* the heart makes life so much fuller," Twain said, swiveling back to his screen. He tapped his chin as his eyes raked across the display.

"Philosophies come and go," I said, plucking a bioglove off the workbench. "But you can count on the brain, on cold, hard facts and data. People, not so much. Present company excluded. The heart is an irrational beast, an unreliable narrator. Erratic, changeable, and undependable."

I positioned the glove under our coding laser, pushed a button, and started the biometric-embedding process. The laser would implant the translucent glove's skin-like fabric with our client's newly fabricated fingerprints, a unique palm-vein pattern, and DNA. The biodata was tagged to a new personal history, bank data for an account in the US that didn't exist, passport, Imperial visa for entrance to and residence in Florida, every kind of official data point he would need.

Twain glanced at me over his shoulder. "Now you sound like a philosopher. A cynical one."

"Just so you know, I'm only scrubbing toilets for six months," I said, changing the subject. The heart-versus-mind debate was an old one, and I wasn't about to rehash it.

Besides, I'm right. The mind solved problems, not the heart. I knew from experience. I was in my element whenever I was elbow-deep in a problem, picking apart options and mining solutions.

"The other six months of servitude are yours when you find a way to pickpocket the Empire's purse," I said.

"I'll take what I can get."

Forty minutes later, Simone Solano García arrived. She was the star vocalist at Joya, the Citadel's most popular nightclub. She was also the third leg of our criminal triad. Near midnight, Simone let herself into the Phoenix, still sheathed in her work attire: a sapphire silk gown, velvet cloak, and diamonds encircling her delicate neck. Simone was twenty-nine, but only her poise and acumen hinted at an age difference. She was beautiful, as awe-inducing as the crystalline night sky, and it was all natural. Not a drop of Fount water had ever touched her.

"Buenos tardes, señores," Simone said, smoke and silk adorning her voice in equal measure. As the dealmaker, she ferreted out the trustworthy clients, steered us clear of the Conq's undercovers, and ensured a smooth transaction. She gauged how much each could pay and struck the bargain. Our clients weren't oozing pesos. They needed us because our services could leapfrog them from the margins of Florida's society to the inner circle. They scraped and hustled to do whatever it took to pay the fee and establish their new lives. If successful, we benefited twofold: Clients became allies among the elites as well as repeat customers who needed to purchase new biogloves and retinal masks every two years when the old ones degraded.

"Everything ready?" Simone asked. She dropped her cloak, revealing pale brown shoulders and sleek black hair that tumbled down her back. Simone was like a sister, but it was nearly impossible to switch off her charm offensive. Perfection was her armor, coquetry her shield. Simone's flirting had no effect on me, but I couldn't say the same for Twain. She was the only woman he ever noticed, not that he would admit it. Twain waved at Simone and offered a small smile. He buried his head in his work, but I knew he was watching her. It was hopeless.

Twain was twenty-four, the same as I was, but he was years and miles from being in her realm of possibility.

"As ready as a tick on a tack," I said.

Simone choked on a laugh, letting loose an uncharacteristic snort. She pretended it didn't happen.

"Really, Rafe," she said, chock full of dignity. "Your catch-phrases need work. You've gone from bad to rock bottom. That doesn't even make sense. Maybe Twain can lend you some of his philosophy books."

"Come on." I feigned offense. "Mine are original. Anyone can memorize Plato."

Twain cleared his throat. "No one can compete with the masters, Rafe," he said. "Anyway, we've had a breakthrough—we cracked the bank."

"That's incredible," Simone said. "How?"

Twain explained what he'd done, what it might mean for our clients.

"We're a long way from being able to offer them a boost," I said.

"Doesn't matter," Simone said. "We wouldn't provide that service to this client."

"What's wrong?" Unease spread in my gut.

"Nada," she said. "I'm one hundred percent certain he's clear. There's no way he's connected to the Conquistador, but he's borderline creepy. Too eager. For someone dirt-poor, he has an outsized sense of entitlement."

"Why are we helping him?" I asked.

"He's Carlton's cousin," she said. Carlton Shires was a client who had done quite well, working his way into a chief position in the Imperial Hospital. He'd been good to us, way beyond expectations. He fed us intel whenever he heard rumors swirling around the Citadel, and they were usually spot on.

"Ah. Well, I hope you entitled him to a fee proportionate with his sense of self-worth," I said.

"Oh, sí. At least fifty percent more."

"You're too generous," I said, opening a drawer and sifting through my arsenal of disguises. No one except Simone ever saw my natural black hair and blue-gray eyes or Twain's blond hair buzzed to near baldness. We had a bloodied history with the Empire, and while the punishment for our transgressions had happened years ago, we weren't supposed to be in the Citadel. We couldn't risk anyone recognizing us.

I retrieved a brown wig, brown contact lenses, and a pair of horn-rimmed eyeglasses, while Twain plucked items from his own camouflage cabinet.

"Showtime," he said.

Fifteen minutes later, the soon-to-be Jerome Blackwell arrived at the Phoenix. His lanky form filled the door-sized view screen that showed guests on the threshold. He hummed with nervous excitement as Simone granted him entry. Blackwell had been instructed to bathe and secure a haircut, and maybe he had, but his clothes betrayed his station. He was lucky he'd made it through the pathways without getting picked up by the Guardia. His pants were stained, and his jacket draped him like a threadbare shroud. A distinct onion odor hovered about him.

Simone ushered him in like he was the Conq himself. "So good to see you again," she said. "These are my associates."

Blackwell's eyes flicked over us, then fastened onto Simone. He gorged on the sight of her, feasting like she was a prize he'd won. Twain paused his tinkering to scowl at the man, likely mulling whether to paw his eyes out. Not that I would blame him.

"Now, before we begin, there's the matter of our fees," Simone said.

"Oh, of course," Blackwell said, digging into his jacket for a wad of crumpled pesos. He offered his treasure to her, and she held her hands up, as if his money would singe her delicate flesh. Blackwell glanced at his money, confused. Simone motioned for him to give me the cash. Blackwell proffered his treasure in my vague direction, and I scooped it from his palm.

"As I mentioned before, we must make you look the part. Follow me," she said. Blackwell trailed her to the adjacent room to be fitted with a new suit and an extra set of clothes to aid his transition.

"I'm in your hands," the man said, smiling expectantly.

Twain rose from his chair, but I waved him down.

"I've got this," I said. I'd seen Simone put much more substantial men than Blackwell in their places, but she shouldn't have to. When it came to people I cared about, and there were only a few, my instinct to protect bordered on irrational. I entered the room as Simone directed Blackwell into the sizing chamber of our electronic wardrobe.

"Here, allow me," I said, moving to the control panel. Blackwell noticed me and scowled.

"Now, dear, you'll need to stand still while the chamber takes your measurements," Simone said.

The wardrobe held hundreds of pieces of clothing, half pilfered from the Imperial Laundry, one at a time over an extended period, so as not to attract attention. After growing a pile of cash, we'd transitioned to buying clothing through the black market for cheap. We had a vast collection of high-end suits, hand-beaded gowns, and assorted finery, a selection to rival the Imperial Luxe Emporium.

"This will take about thirty seconds," I said, pulling up Blackwell's profile on the chamber console. I waited as the chamber scanned his body from head to toe and an image of the man in underwear popped on a screen.

"All right, dear, now sit over there while we make the selections." Simone motioned to the far side of the room.

Blackwell ambled to a tufted chaise lounge beneath an arched floor-to-ceiling window. He lowered to the velvety fabric but froze at the sound of Simone's voice.

"No, no," she said, pointing to a straight-backed wooden chair. Blackwell righted himself cautiously, then slid into the wooden chair. Simone never showed our clients disrespect, veiled or outright. How creepy had this asshole been to her?

We experimented with Blackwell's digital likeness, clothing it with images of different ensembles from our collection. Simone was an expert at this, vetoing assorted options until she found something she considered perfect.

"That one," Simone said. She'd chosen a sleek, navy suit, a shirt of robin's egg blue, and a gray silk tie. It looked like five others we'd tabbed through, but Simone's taste was impeccable, and she was always right.

I confirmed the outfit selection, and seconds later, the suit dangled before us, swaying from a conveyor belt that ran deep into the wardrobe. Simone draped it over a nearby counter, and we repeated the process until she chose a casual, elegant set of pants, shirt, jacket, and boots. She handed Blackwell the blue suit and directed him into a changing room, while I packaged the casual suit.

When our client emerged, he was polished into a new person. Simone had chosen the perfect ensemble, one that made him appear more substantial and accentuated the blue in his eyes. He held himself more erect with the consciousness of his new skin.

"Perfecto," Simone said, drawing her hands together.

"Well done, Miss Solano," Blackwell said.

"Of course," she said, leading him back into the lab.

I met them at my workbench. "Now, your name is Jerome Blackwell, originally from New York City in the United States," I said. "These are your biogloves. They hold your new identity."

I gave Blackwell a quick rundown of the information associated with his new life. The man stretched out his fingers, eager to possess the gloves. I paused and stared at him until he had the good sense to drop his hand and continue listening.

"The gloves will meld with your hands, wrists, and forearms and become invisible." I went on, holding up a box. "These are your retinal masks—glorified contacts that provide a retinal pattern consistent with your new identity. But here's the important part: You must return every two years for new tech. After two years, these will deteriorate and be useless. Miss Solano will arrange for your visit when the time comes."

"Fascinating," Blackwell said.

"You understand the confidentiality agreement?" I asked, voice grim. "You are never to speak of our services to another person. If you expose us, we will know, and your new identity will be dismantled, the data destroyed. You revert to being Barney Garrett. If you're caught, you'll wind up in the Calabozo. You know what happens to people who end up in the Conq's dungeons—they don't come out. Ever. Don't think about trading information for freedom. We have an extensive network inside the Conquistador's palace, and our contacts have instructions to do whatever it takes to silence former clients, up to and including death."

Okay, maybe I exaggerated. We didn't have a network that extensive, but we did have a few moles and allies, and those numbers were growing. I was fairly certain none would go so far as assassination. Murder was outside our arena of comfort, but Blackwell didn't have to know that. He blanched at the warning.

"Rafe, please, you're making our client uneasy," Simone soothed, slipping into her peacemaking role whenever I tossed out the fear factor. "He fully understands the importance of keeping silent. It's to his benefit as much as ours. He wouldn't dream of informing on us."

"No, of course not," he said. "I would never."

"No, you wouldn't," she said. Point made, Simone changed the subject. "So, tell me, what are your plans as the new Mr. Blackwell?"

Blackwell's eyes lit up, like a child granted unfettered access to a candy store. "Well, I understand this season's Obligors Expo is coming up. I'm hoping to take on an Obligor, maybe an Obligor Consort if the price is right," he said, licking his lips.

Simone's eyes snapped in my direction. She'd changed the subject, right to a topic that inflamed me to the point of boiling.

I cursed under my breath.

I'd been to an Expo before. Witnessing desperate men and

women indenture their lives, sentencing themselves to years of service to the privileged citizenry turned my stomach. Knowing they had no other choice made it even worse. They either sold their servitude or languished in the Calabozo until their dying breath. The most desperate, those pleasing enough to the eye, ended up as consorts.

I was about to bodily eject Blackwell from the Phoenix when Simone shifted the subject again.

"I'm sure that's fascinating," she said, gently taking Blackwell's elbow and leading him to the door. Twain stood from his workspace and followed us.

Simone continued her instructions. "Now, you have everything you need," she said. "Remember—discretion at all times, and remember who you are. Best of luck, dear."

Blackwell snagged Simone's hand and bent to kiss it, but she finessed his touch into a handshake. His face fell, but Simone was already nudging him out the door and closing it. She slumped against the wall and sighed, wiping the remnants of Blackwell's handshake on her gown.

"Mierda," I swore.

"I think we undercharged him," Twain said.

"He's not worth getting worked up over, Rafe," Simone said.

"No more," I said. "We don't help maggots like him."

"I wouldn't worry. There's no way he can afford an Obligor," Simone said. "He could barely afford our fees."

"I don't care. We created another predator, as if there weren't enough in this city. If he's motivated, he'll find a way to get an Obligor. He's got connections among the elite already. Imagine being tethered to him for God knows how long. He's the sort who'd go for some girl offered up by her family because they couldn't afford food, and she'd be powerless to stop him from putting his hands on her. Like he was trying to do to you."

"The only reason we helped him is Carlton," Simone said.

"We can't afford to alienate him." Anger spiked her words, breaking her usual calm.

"Children…" Twain interrupted us.

Only then did I notice the hurt in Simone's dark eyes.

"We're all doing our jobs," Twain said. "Sometimes a little dirt slips in. This one couldn't be helped."

They were both right. Simone didn't deserve my ire, not one ounce.

"You're right," I said through a sigh. "Forgive me?"

She wrapped her arms around me. I stiffened. Then I remembered the hands holding me had never hurt me and never would, and I softened under their touch.

"Of course, hermano," she said.

I couldn't erase the image of Blackwell salivating over some vulnerable soul in the Obligors Expo. I'd long shunned thoughts of the Expo, knowing I was helpless to stop this ingrained institution or change it. But was I? The three of us had infiltrated the Citadel and built a home and a business right under the Conq's nose. We were slowly populating the city with allies.

I retreated from Simone's arms and caught Twain's gaze. "How do you feel about doing a little reconnaissance?"

He eyed me like I was crazy—a good brand of crazy—and pinched his lips like he was thinking hard. "A little polite-society infiltration?" he asked. "Could be fun."

"Señores, you are not going to the Expo," Simone said. "What if he's there?"

If the Conq came to the Expo, we would steer clear. We'd been doing it for years.

"We hide in plain sight," I said.

"Like we always do," Twain added.

And maybe find a way to sabotage the Conq's Expo.

4

EVANGELINE

A week passed before Juni got curious. She knew we'd been spared losing our home, but she'd yet to ask anything more. Until now.

Pa had come home from the fields and begun to wash up. I was throwing together a quick lunch of ham-and-tomato sandwiches with fresh-churned butter while Juni drew pictures at the kitchen table.

"What's wrong with me?" she asked. The pencil in her small hand never stopped moving. Her eyes stayed fixed on her picture, a chicken pen full of birds large and small. Pa and I exchanged a look.

He sat next to her at the table. "If you ask me, you're perfect, sweetheart, but if you're asking what the doctor said, that's a tough one."

Juni peered up at him, eyes wide and worried. Pa caressed her hair.

"The doc says you have something called cancer. It's these little lumps that can grow and spread in your body, making you sick."

"When am I gonna get better?"

Pa looked like he wanted to melt into his chair and disappear. "They don't have anything to fix what you have. The best thing we can do is help you feel your best. Does that make sense?"

Juni nodded, but tears were welling in her eyes. Her chest began to rise and fall in a rapid, ragged pattern. She was working up to a breathing attack. Pa's eyes darted to mine, but my hand was already moving toward the cupboard where we kept her balm.

"It's gonna be okay, Junebug," Pa said.

His words felt like a slap in the face. She wasn't going to be okay.

"Am I—" Juni's breath stuck in her lungs. "Am I...gonna die?"

"No." The lie crossed my father's lips, but not his eyes. The truth smoldered too bright to smother.

I froze. My father had lied, broken an Empire mandate with no hesitation. I couldn't believe it. But I could understand it. Right or wrong, neither of us wanted to douse the last sparks of light and hope my sister had.

Juni sucked hard for a breath, and Pa hauled her into his lap.

"Breathe, sweetheart," he said, stroking her hair. "It's going to be all right."

She fought for air, and I dropped beside her on one knee, the lid already off the jar of balm. The ointment released a strong odor, with whiffs of eucalyptus, lemon, and something earthy I couldn't place. I had no idea what Nina put in it, but the aroma made my nostrils tingle and expand.

I dipped my finger into the ointment and painted a streak beneath Juni's nose. "Breathe it in, Junebug," I said. "Slow and easy."

Tears fell down Juni's face. Pa could lie to her all he wanted, but my sister understood the one truth he'd given her—she'd never feel better, never recover the life she'd once known.

"Calming breaths. You got this."

Slowly, her breath fell back to normal, and her face sagged with exhaustion. Pa kissed her forehead.

"Good job, kiddo," he said. "Ready for some lunch?"

"I'm not hungry."

"You need to eat something, keep your strength up."

Juni tried. We watched her, like a pot about to boil over, as she ate three bites of sandwich.

"May I be excused?" she said at last.

Pa gave her permission, and she slid out of her chair and down the hallway. The door to her room clicked open and shut. My father and I stared at each other.

"You lied to her," I said.

"Keep your voice down."

"Pa, what about the Fount? She'd be healed in seconds."

"You know we can't afford that. Don't be putting ideas like that into Juni's head."

The Obligors Expo was on the tip of my tongue, but I kept it there. Pa would never let me offer myself in payment for an Immersion. Family stayed with family, and no one went outside the walls, period. The Wildlands were too risky.

"We can ask the Guardia, like we did with the doctor's exam. They sent the Conquistador's doctor. They listened once."

I sounded like a child pleading for the last cookie, but I wanted him to fight for her, to exhaust every option before he gave up.

"I did."

At that, something in me cracked. I felt it from my throat to my legs. My fingers tightened around my cup, and I closed my eyes to stop the tears from falling.

A warm hand wrapped my forearm. "I'm sorry, angel," Pa said. "We can't fix this. We can only make her as comfortable as possible with the time we have left."

I couldn't bear the acceptance in his eyes. Pushing from the table, I collected the lunch dishes.

Pa retrieved his hat and paused at the back door. "I know you want to fix things," he said. "But I'm her father. It's my job to take care of her. You need to let it go…and just be there for Juni."

I stared at the kitchen sink and said nothing. I couldn't agree with him, but I couldn't argue with him either.

The back door slammed as my father returned to life as he knew it.

But at that moment, I knew my life would never be the same. I was the only one who could fix this, and for the first time in my life, I was prepared to break every rule in my way to make it happen.

TWO NIGHTS LATER, my conviction waivered.

The house was steeped in darkness. The midnight air hung heavy and unmoving, like a breath held in check. Little hairs on my arms stood at attention, rising with the tide of goose bumps dimpling my skin. I lingered in my room, listening to sleep humming behind closed doors.

I considered chickening out. Leaving would tear apart what little we had left of our family, but if I stayed, we would lose Juni. Each choice felt like a betrayal. Pa said it was his job to protect Juni, not mine—that he was the parent, not me. But I'd mothered my little sister ever since we'd lost our own, and I was the only one who could do this. I left a note in my room to explain, but it wouldn't matter. Pa would be devastated no matter what.

I bent to pick up my rucksack, and my knees threatened to buckle. I pressed a palm to my chest. My heart thrummed hard and fast, and I breathed deep, trying to dislodge the weight squatting there. This could go wrong in so many ways. I could hear my mother saying, *If you have to think twice about something, it's probably a bad idea.*

I knew that all too well, but we couldn't have it both ways. Either I protected her or I played it safe. I already knew the answer. I would not muddle through another day with only hope and a prayer as my shield against losing Juni. Not when there was something I could do about it.

I picked up my bag and tiptoed to Juni's room. I knelt beside her in the dark. Her cheeks puffed in relaxation, making her appear younger than her seven years. I didn't want to leave her, but we were out of options. I brushed my lips on her damp forehead and stood to leave before I could change my mind.

"Evan?" Juni's voice cracked with sleep.

"Go to sleep, little bug. Everything's fine," I whispered.

"Love you more," she said. Words that crushed and filled my heart.

"Love you most," I said, my words hushed. "G'night Junebug." I eased her door closed before she could see the pack in my hand or the tears in my eyes.

I hurried outside, into the dark night. Cool air pressed against me like the hand of caution. I tugged my sweater across my chest and started walking.

The Conquistador's farm covered more than a thousand acres, but I knew the land well, and I could find the stream and its locked gate by instinct. All I had to do was avoid the patrols. If my father found out, if his patrols found me, this trek would be over before it began.

Guardia soldiers watched the perimeter and defended the main gates. Farmworkers roamed inside the farm, on the lookout for Ferals who might breach the wall. It had happened before. The Ferals had slipped past the Conquistador's men, but we'd paid the price for allowing the wild men near the Conquistador's food stock. No one wanted to disappoint our sovereign again after losing a week's rations and witnessing the beating my father had endured. It had taken two bedridden weeks for him to recover.

By the light of the half-moon, I walked fast, using the orange, lime, and papaya trees for cover. My body heated as I trod familiar ground and tried not to think about what I was doing. I'd walked for half an hour when the sound of horse hooves stilled my feet. I dropped, flattened myself to the ground, and covered my head with the hood of my sweater. The horses halted in the lime grove, one row over.

"What time is it?" It was Peter. He'd turned sixteen last month, which meant he'd started his first year of watch rotation.

"Twelve forty-five. Fifteen minutes later than the last time you asked," said Dominic.

I should have known. Dominic regularly took the midnight watch, not fully trusting others to do the job well enough. My father had chosen his foreman well. Dominic might have been young, but he was fiercely protective of the farm...and its workers.

Guilt twisted my stomach. Add Dominic to the list of people I was betraying.

Part of me was relieved. I didn't want to marry someone I didn't love. All my life, I'd witnessed the profound affection between my mother and father, the ease and depth with which they'd loved each other. That spark did not exist with Dominic. We had grown up at the same time, in the same place, but we'd never been friends, despite my teenage yearnings. I cared about Dominic and appreciated his commitment to my father. But that was all.

"Eight o'clock's my bedtime," Peter said, yawning. "I'd do anything to avoid the midnight watch."

Dominic scoffed. "Get used to it. It's part of the job. Plenty of people would be happy to take your place on this farm."

"I know. I know."

"We split off here. You go left, then circle back when you hit the wall. I'll meet you here."

A horse trotted my direction. I held my breath, praying the shadows would paint me into nothingness.

"Hey, Dom!"

The horse halted three feet from my head.

"Yeah?" Dominic replied, his voice booming.

"What if I see someone?"

"Blow the horn on your saddle and beat the hell out of them with your club."

Peter was silent before he stammered, "R-right."

Moments later, they were gone. I released a shaky breath and waited two full minutes before I pushed off the ground. I shook the dirt from my clothes and kept walking.

The night was eerily quiet. Every footfall echoed with a crunch that shouted my presence. Soon the quiet was replaced by water trickling in the distance. I followed the noise as memories of my sister poked through my concentration: Juni running barefoot into the cool water, shrieking; picnicking along the bank; reading books together. Juni in my lap, relaxed against my chest, as we watched fireflies blink alive in the golden moments between daylight and darkness. Days that had passed without a care in the world. I'd had no idea then how good we had it.

A clearing stretched next to the towering wall circling El Jardín. Kudzu and wisteria vines clung to the stone, and jagged barbs jutted from the top like a deadly crown. Dense scrub and palmettos camouflaged the lower half. The stream flowed through the only gated portion of the wall besides the farm's entrance. Once, I'd watched Pa unlock the gate to clear debris that backed water up into our fields after a week of heavy rains. That gate key now dangled like a firebrand against my chest. I was glad I wouldn't be around when my father discovered it was missing.

I paused, listening for patrols, and peered through the steel bars. Nothing stirred beyond the wall. Fishing the key out of my top, I bent toward the padlock, the angle awkward with the leather cord around my neck. My hands shook as I fumbled trying to slot the key into the hole. The bold canter of horses sounded like thunder in the distance. I flinched, and my hand jerked like the thief it was. The cord snapped. My fingers clenched the key as I dashed into the bushes and my heart tried to beat its way up my throat.

Beyond the wall, a group of soldiers waded across the stream on horseback. The men talked and laughed without a care to who might hear. This was good. Once they passed, my path would be free and clear. The soldiers sauntered away, and I waited until they were beyond earshot.

I unfurled my fingers and looked at the key in my palm. "Let's try this again," I murmured.

Dislodging myself from the greenery, I edged toward the gate. My boot slipped on a muddy patch, and the key went flying as I tried to right myself. A small splash spurted in the stream as the key disappeared beneath the water. My heart sank with it.

"No, no, no..." I waded to where I'd seen the splash. The stream was knee-deep and cold. It soaked my skirts in seconds. I peered into the current but could see nothing in the dark. I plunged my hand into the water and frantically skimmed across silt-crusted rocks for several minutes, but the key was nowhere to be found.

I trudged to the streambank and plopped to the ground, covering my face. I was such an idiot. Clumsy and foolish and a waste of breath. Another mistake. Another life in the balance.

But I couldn't give up. Not yet. I considered my options. Climbing the wall was out of the question. Sharp spikes blanketed the coping stones at the top rim, and I'd tear myself to shreds trying. I glanced at the muddy patch where my foot had slipped and squinted through the gray light, trying to make sense of it. The water came from beneath the wall.

I crawled closer, pushing behind the foliage, and felt along the stones. Erosion could be a real problem on a farm, but right now, right here, it was my best friend. Large chunks of mortar had been washed away, opening several seams. I grabbed the nearest jagged rock and started digging.

Minutes later, the first stone broke loose. I almost leapt for joy, but there was no time for that. I dug until my fingers were raw. I didn't care. If I got three more stones loose, I was certain I could push myself through to the other side.

My fingers were bleeding by the time I finished. Pain had never felt so satisfying. I listened for patrols and then shoved my backpack through the hole. I lowered myself to the ground and wrestled through the undergrowth. Tiny branches and palm fronds sliced at my face and snagged on my long braid, but I would not stop for anything. I shoved ahead until I reached the other side, then quickly replaced the stones and covered them with branches. I sat for a moment, gathering my breath. My clothes were soaked and caked with mud, my hair felt like a bird had made a hasty nest in it, and my fingers throbbed painfully.

I smiled in the darkness. I'd made it out. Now I just had to survive the Wildlands.

5

RAFE

The black-haired woman sheathed in green satin floated through the lush cabaret. Joya itself was dressed to impress as usual, with its bloodred velvet curtains, flawless white linens, and candles flickering in crystal prisms. But the old-money elegance paled in comparison to Simone. Her slender muscles shifted along her bare back as every eye in the room tracked her. She glided, unhurried, like a serpent across warm stones, luxuriating in the heat of their attention.

Twain leaned behind the bar at Joya and drank in every second of her grand entrance.

"Hey, bartender, how about a drink?" I asked.

He side-eyed me as Simone disappeared down the hall to her dressing room. "So pushy," he said. "What'll it be?"

Twain tended bar at Joya on occasion. He didn't need the money—he worked to be near Simone, though he'd never admit it. As for me, I came for the spying. Joya was perfect for keeping tabs on the gentry. I ordered a stout and relished the first fizz down my throat.

"The sculpted beard is an interesting choice," Twain said, nodding at my chin.

"You should talk. Where'd you find the man bun?"

"Hey, it's hip," he said. "You look like a villain from a silent movie."

"Your temp hair dye gave me a rash," I said. "Had to get creative."

Twain chuckled and stepped aside to take an order from a waitress. People began to filter into the bar, filling the seats before Simone's performance, the impatient ones sidling up to the bar for drinks. A man bumped into me as he made a beeline for the restroom. I didn't recognize his bulky build or long brown hair, but I knew a sleight of hand when I felt one.

I took a sip of beer as I slid my hand into my jacket pocket and withdrew the note the stranger had slipped inside: *11:10 tonight. Koi pond. Come alone.*

I grinned and tucked the note away. Simone's performance ended at ten thirty. That would give me a good thirty minutes to travel the pathways to the secluded spot.

"Everything good?" Twain was back. He passed a bowl of pub mix my way.

"Yep, we're in control and on a roll."

He scoffed. "What does that even mean?"

"Not a clue," I said, dumping a handful of mix into my mouth.

The amused look on Twain's face vanished.

"What?" I asked. It took a lot to wipe the grin off my friend's face.

The whole room bolted out of their seats and bowed their heads as the Conquistador entered the cabaret. Commander Nico Bane and a security retinue followed in his wake like an invading force.

Ice slammed down my spine, and I choked down the dry snacks ballooning in my mouth. I lowered my eyes in deference to our ruler, even as every nerve in my body urged me to run. I had to stay calm. There was no way the Conq or Bane could identify us. Twain and I had been teenagers the last time they'd seen us, and the disguises made the likelihood of recognition slim. Not impossible, but not likely.

What the hell were they doing here? It had been years since the Conq had come to Joya.

The bar manager greeted the entourage. Bane towered over the man, blocking the Conq like a shield. The Commander's spine was erect and unyielding, as if he had a pole shoved up his ass.

The manager scuttled back a step. "This is an honor indeed, sir," he said. "How may we be of service?"

Bane raised the sharp nub of his nose, sniffed like a dog, and peered at the manager, a scowl of distaste wrinkling his smooth brow. "El Conquistador wishes to use his private box, of course."

My heart clutched in my ribcage. Simone was moments from taking the stage, unaware he was here.

She would be livid.

"Of course, Commander Bane," the manager sputtered out. "The Imperial Suite is ready anytime El Conquistador wishes. We're honored he's chosen to grace us with his presence tonight."

"Then stop babbling and wasting his time."

"Of course. If you'll follow me…"

The Imperial entourage disappeared down a hallway leading to an elevated suite.

"You need to go," Twain said, his voice low. Everyone stood with their eyes frozen to the ground, waiting to be released.

"I'm not leaving you by yourself," I said. Twain couldn't leave without it looking suspicious.

"He won't recognize me. Servants are invisible to the Conquistador, but if anyone's going to recognize you, it'll be him."

"He won't," I said. I hoped. "I'm not leaving you, and I'm not walking away without listening in on the old man's conversation."

"You have a death wish? They almost succeeded the first time."

Twain glared at me out of the corner of his eye, all trace of usual flippancy gone. But I wasn't about to let this opportunity slip by. This was my first chance in years to get close to the Conq and find out what he and his minions were up to. I might discover something to use against him. Even my penchant for self-preservation took a back seat to an opportunity to erode his unending reign.

The Conq entered his box, and everyone pivoted toward the suite, bowing in acknowledgment. Bane approached the balcony railing and lifted his hands like a preacher, calling his flock to order.

"The Water holds time at bay," he began, his voice booming across the room. "Brings the ages to heel. We are…"

"The Empire Eternal!" the crowd answered in response.

"We are…" Bane repeated.

"The Empire Eternal!"

A hush settled across the room, and Bane lowered his arms. The Conq sank into a plush armchair, and the Commander took a seat across from him. Only then did the bar patrons relax and resume socializing.

I slammed the rest of my beer. "I'm going to warn Simone," I said, walking away before Twain could stop me.

I faked a path to the restroom and detoured down an empty corridor half-heartedly blocked by a *Private* sign. Around the next corner, I tapped on the door marked *Artist*.

"No visitors, dear." Simone's muffled voice penetrated the thickness between us, the irritation beneath her polite facade resonating clear as day.

"It's me."

Movement sounded from the other side, and the door

popped open. "What are you doing here?" She glanced down the hallway and ushered me inside. We rarely interacted at the club. It was a precaution, meant to keep everyone safe.

"I need to tell you something," I said. "You're not going to like it."

Concern darkened her eyes.

"He's here."

Simone's jaw clenched, and her fingers coiled into fists. Red bloomed across her cheeks.

"Don't," I said. "Don't let him get to you. He doesn't deserve it."

She inhaled a breath before speaking, but even so, her voice cracked. "What's he doing here?"

"He must have come to see you sing."

"And crush my heart again?"

The Conq had dated Simone exclusively for a year. Despite his monstrous tendencies, she'd fallen for him. But the first time she'd stood up to him had been the last. She'd tried to intervene for Twain and me, and he'd threatened her with the Calabozo. In the end, he'd tossed her aside.

"He can't break your heart because he doesn't have it anymore," I said.

"He could get me fired again."

The management had sacked Simone when the Conq stopped coming to Joya, but more customers left without her, until they'd humbly asked their favorite chanteuse back.

"It's been years," Simone said. "Why now?" The ghost of old memories clouded her eyes, and my chest tightened at the role I'd played in what happened. I owed her so much.

"I'm wondering the same thing," I said. "But I'm going to find out."

I dug into my pocket and extracted a rectangular case filled with small gadgets: a micro-camera, lock picks, laser saw—you name it. I retrieved a tiny stick pin adorned with a decorative

concave circle. It was a covert, long-range directional microphone. Once paired with an earpiece and my Convo, I could
hear conversations one hundred meters away.

"Rafe, he'll see you," Simone said.

"He won't be looking at anyone but you—trust me."

"It's not worth the risk," she said. "It's not like he's Mr.
Chatty."

"Bane's here." He'd talk to his closest advisor.

We both startled when someone pounded the door. "Five
minutes, Miss Solano."

"I'll be right there," Simone called out. I tucked the pin into
the collar of my jacket.

"Be careful, hermano," she said. "You know what he does to
spies."

"No te preocupes. I have no intention of letting him know I
still exist."

A shadow of sadness flickered in Simone's eyes. I squeezed
her hand. "Now, go out there and own the place. He's just a
customer. Nothing special."

"You're damn right about that."

I found an empty table in a shadowed corner and ordered
another beer. The waitress sauntered off, and I studied the man
sitting on the balcony. Tremors juddered through me. Eight
years had flown by since I'd been this near to him, and he
looked the same as always. He was a man frozen in time,
unchanged and un-aged. Unending. His black hair was trimmed
short and spiked in defiance of his age. He wore a suit tailored
to flaunt his lean and muscled form, and no wrinkles marred his
skin. He was five hundred and sixty-five years old, yet anyone
would mistake him for a twenty-five-year-old in the prime of
his manhood, close to my age.

I couldn't breathe. I fought the urge to rush his suite and
wrap my hands around his neck. I pictured my fingers digging
into his flesh, his face bruising purple.

Stop staring.

The text message from Twain buzzed on my Convo, shattering the tension and pulling me back from the edge. As usual. I reclined in my chair and trained my eyes on the stage, even as I fidgeted with the pin on my collar, twisting it to face the Conq's suite.

Applause thundered across the room as Simone sauntered onstage. She'd changed into a fiery gown that shimmered and swayed like it was a creature all its own. She stared straight at the Conq as if he were the only one in the room and started singing. It was the Fount song, his favorite.

"Enfold me in liquid grace, still the hands of time, with just one taste..."

Her voice rang loud and crystalline in my ear, overshadowing all other sound.

"Remake me in your sweet embrace."

A few extraneous words filtered in around her voice. The Conq was saying, "Belleza...always." Bane's words were clipped: "Don't need..."

I cursed under my breath. The microphone's position on my collar was off. It needed to be aimed more directly at the Imperial Suite. I plucked the device from my jacket as the crowd erupted in applause, drowning me in sound. I laid the microphone on the table and turned it toward the men. For several minutes, the Conq and his lackey were quiet, listening to the entertainment. I heard nothing except Simone singing. Lower this time, as if she stood at a distance, under water. Still no other voices. I was about to claw the fabric on my chair to shreds. Suddenly I heard them, loud and clear.

For twenty minutes, the Conq and Bane bantered sporadically, mostly Bane spewing small talk that would bore anyone: the state of the food on their dinner plates, the size of the waitress's breasts, the Yankees baseball game streamed from America.

After a brief pause, Bane cleared his throat. "Just received a message," he said. "They caught one."

"Not again," the Conq replied.

"Afraid so."

Before Bane could elaborate, the door swung open and a waitress ambled inside. She was blonde, dressed in a short red halter dress of crushed velvet. A golden brooch with the Conq's leonine crest was pinned to the collar. Like an animal collar, something meant to tame and subdue. Her hair was trapped in a ponytail, making her look younger than she was. Beauty and youth...the true currency of the Citadel.

The waitress presented the men with a shaky smile as she lowered two glasses of red wine to the table. Bane glowered at her, and she rushed out.

The Commander waited a beat, then continued. "Some miscreant from the Barrio tried to plant a bomb near the palace wall."

My stomach lurched. Had they captured a member of the Scythe of Thorns? I began to rethink my late-night meeting at the koi pond. Maybe it was a trap.

"Any damage?" The Conq's voice was calm as always.

"No, the Guardia caught it in time."

"Work him until he reveals his coconspirators. Where there's one rebel, there's more."

"Yes," Bane said, sniffing deeply. "They tend to breed like rats."

"I have confidence you'll extinguish any spark of defiance. Really, these idiots should know better."

Bane's reply was almost gleeful. "Anyone who so much as thinks about attacking the Empire will regret it. Painfully and publicly."

Goose bumps attacked my flesh like a tsunami, but somewhere deep inside, something shook loose, like a seed waking from a deep winter sleep.

We weren't alone. There were others who wanted to dismantle this crooked Empire.

Twain and I had known contacting the Scythe of Thorns was a risk. The nascent rebel group didn't know us and we didn't know them, but we wanted to do more than simply seed the Citadel with allies. We wanted more. I wanted more.

I wanted the Conq dethroned. Not dead, just dethroned. I wanted the tyrant to grovel in his damned dungeons and endure a life without benefit of his precious Fount. I wanted my home to be free of the cruelty and oppression that dictated people's lot, that counted bodies as expendable as paper napkins, that punished citizens for the smallest of infractions with spilled blood and final breaths. I wanted a country that counted justice and mercy as strengths and valued compassion over money and power. Maybe that was naive, but I knew we'd never get close to that ideal with this brutal dictator in power.

Someone needed to stop the bastard.

And that someone was me.

THE FIREFLIES WERE ABLAZE TONIGHT, floating in the dark forest like hundreds of fairy lights. The moon illuminated the pathway in a milky blue light. It was serene—enchanting, even—but my stomach revolted like I'd swallowed a cocktail of brambles. This clandestine meeting was the height of stupidity. After how careful we'd been all these years, meeting a stranger in the woods was akin to jumping into the abyss.

I needed to know what I was walking into.

The koi pond was half a mile away in a secluded area along one of the countless meandering pathways in the Citadel. No roads existed in the city, only walking paths. If you needed to go anywhere fast, you used the underground transpod system. Above ground, grassy parkland and thick forests were dotted with palatial mansions, sculptured towers, and intimate nooks, all designed to be one with nature.

I studied my surroundings. No one was in sight. Crickets and tree frogs hummed in cadence with the quiet dark. I stepped off the path and crept through the forest toward the pond, stopping twenty feet inside the tree line. No lights illuminated the area, but the moon outlined a shadowy figure dressed in black exercise gear. He stood motionless, studying the bright fish swimming beneath the pond's surface.

I hesitated for a moment, contemplating walking away.

"Might as well come on over," the man said.

Too late now.

I closed the distance and stood next to him, leaving an arm's length between us. He was about half a foot taller than me, with broad, muscular shoulders and dark skin beneath short-cropped black hair. He was built for destruction.

Not the same man who'd slipped the note into my pocket.

"The Scythe will reap," he said, still not looking at me. It was the first part of the code I'd been given.

"What the Conqueror sows," I replied.

"For our purposes, you may call me Rod."

"You can call me Guy."

Rod eyed me with a half smile. "I hear you're good with inventing things," he said.

I frowned. I didn't want him knowing anything about me.

"Where'd you hear that?" I asked.

"Word gets around the Sink."

Ah.

The Sink was a bustling, illegal marketplace occupying a series of caverns in an old sinkhole outside the walls of the Citadel. Twain and I frequented the Sink to support our illegal endeavors. I'd never seen this man there.

"What did you have in mind?"

"How much do you know about the electrical grid?" he

asked. His eyes dug into mine like he was mining me for every secret I owned. I resisted the pull to step back.

"Enough," I said.

"We need a device that can take down the grid. Not a bomb —nothing that messy—but something that can send a portion of the Empire into the dark ages for a while."

Something sparked inside my core. Hope or excitement or anticipation. I wasn't sure, but a smile spread across my face.

The Scythe of Thorns had a plan. Something big.

"Tell me more," I said.

6

EVANGELINE

*S*omething wet dripped onto my forehead, soft and rhythmic. I pried my eyes open. Dirt crusted my lashes, and sand peppered my tongue. The scent of wet earth plugged my nostrils. Realization dawned at once, startling me awake. This wasn't my bed, and this wasn't my home. I was three hours from El Jardín, wedged behind a cluster of palmettos in the middle of nowhere.

I'd fallen asleep in the Wildlands.

A raindrop tumbled into the corner of my eye, and I blinked. Another droplet taunted, ready to fall from a hovering palm frond. Rain pattered on the green canopy. Lightning cracked a brilliant flash in the distance and thundered loud enough to make the ground shake. I crawled from beneath the bushes, pulling my blanket and pack behind me.

What on earth had I done? The predawn rain soaked my sweater and dress, pressing cold against my hot skin. It barely registered. I was overcome by the impossibility of where I was and what I was doing. The dirt road to El Jardín lay fifty feet ahead, beckoning. Three hours and I could be home, safe and sound, easily forgiven in the rush of relief that came when something lost was suddenly found. The rule follower in me tossed guilt into my face and nudged me to go back.

I hadn't broken a rule. I'd set it on fire.

The alternative? Keep going. Walk another day and a half, dodging Ferals, chancing that I wouldn't be robbed or killed. It was far-fetched—reckless, even—but this burden had lodged in my heart. The constant darkness crushing my chest would not release me until it was done. I could not give up, not after one night in the Florida wilderness. Too much was at stake.

One road connected El Jardín to the Citadel. Following it would lead me to the walled city, but the road wasn't safe. Ferals were known to watch it, waiting to rob the rare traveler or new outcast. Last night, I'd hiked through the trees, keeping the road in sight from a distance. I'd picked through the scrub like a careful whisper, the moon illuminating my path.

Today was more difficult, each step a struggle through the brush, fueled by a few hours of crummy sleep. The rain poured steady the first hour. It tapered off as the sun rose, leaving behind a steamed breath of air, an unsettling quiet. I walked until the sun had risen high in the sky and my stomach grumbled in protest. I rested long enough for a few bites of bread and apple and continued on.

The rest of the day passed in a blur, the clinging heat constant, my senses on edge, waiting to be attacked any moment, but I never met another soul. I stopped at sunset and climbed a live oak to shelter for the night. Massive limbs sprouted from the tree, dipping to the ground and rising again. Spanish moss clung to the upper branches, swaying like ghosts in the growing dark. I settled into a cradle of branches, nestled beneath my blanket, and watched the last of the day's light snuff out while I ate a few bites of dried fish. The night came alive with a lullaby of katydids and tree frogs.

It was so peaceful, it was hard to believe danger lived in the forest. Growing up, my father had warned us about what lurked beyond the wall. He said Ferals were humans who'd lost their humanity, wild men and women who roamed the Wildlands untamed and unchecked. Rumors abounded about their origins, whether they were simply criminals banished from civilized areas for some offense against the Empire or something worse. Some said the Empire had tortured and experimented on them as prisoners until they'd lost all sense of remorse, and their impulses fed on darkness. Their minds had been destroyed, their consciences broken and reshaped into something that only depravity could sate. They stole what they needed and tortured, enslaved, or murdered for sport. All while the Empire turned a blind eye.

Ferals got nothing left to lose, and that makes 'em dangerous, Pa had said. *They'll steal everything you own and everything you are and not think twice about it.*

The image of the Feral at the gate intruded on my thoughts, his dark and damaged eyes glaring at me across time. I shivered. I had no idea how I'd made it this far without stumbling across one. It was a relief, and yet it came with an odd sense of isolation, of being unfettered in the world, more alone than I'd ever been. I tried not to think about what my family was going through back home, but it was useless. Eventually exhaustion overtook me, and I fell asleep.

A shout startled me awake, scattering a nightmare before I could remember it. I almost fell out of the tree. Beneath the bright morning sun, a long caravan of wagons, horsemen, and people packed the dirt road twenty feet away. Most wagons bore small wooden houses, while others carried supplies or people. Clutches of men, women, and children watched as a band of men subdued three others, forcing them to their knees. The cowed men wore rags and mismatched boots. Their hair was tangled, their beards long, their faces dirt crusted. They were the boogeymen my father warned us about, the monsters who haunted our dreams.

Ferals, right in front of me, in the flesh. I had no idea anyone but Ferals wandered the Wildlands, but here was an entire caravan of families moving freely about no-man's land.

A low murmur arose as a man strode to the front of the line. He was tall, with black hair skimming his shoulders and a scruff of new beard, dressed in a clean white cotton shirt rolled to the elbows and a green cargo vest. His jaw was hard, his eyes dark. He broke through the crowd and loomed over the prisoners. They exchanged words I could not hear. The Feral in the middle raised his hands in a plea and motioned frantically at his companions. The tall man ignored him and aimed a pistol at the beggar's forehead.

"No, no!" the Feral shouted. The gun fired, the explosion echoing through the trees, and the Feral pitched back, blood spraying in a hideous arc. I slammed a palm across my lips, smothering a cry, choking back bile.

The road burst into chaos. A blond Feral to the right of the dead man lunged at one of his captors. His arms circled the man's knees, lifted him off the ground and tossed him into his companions. Men fell like dominos, and the blond fled into the forest. The other Feral dashed toward my hiding spot, his captors in pursuit, bullets flying.

I ducked, and a bullet hit the tree trunk behind me, sending splinters flying. I flinched and crouched lower. The forest erupted with the snap and crunch of branches and frantic foot-falls. The chaos grew louder, drew nearer.

Below me, the Feral's breathing rasped heavy and loud. So close. I prayed no one would notice me. The man kept running, plowing through the underbrush as if it were smoke. Half a dozen men followed, shouting. They passed beneath me and kept running. I could do nothing but wait as the other travelers lingered on the road. *Who are these people?*

After a while, the men reappeared, their footsteps heavy,

unhurried, defeated. Empty-handed. The Ferals were out there, somewhere.

Great.

The men regrouped at the head of the caravan. The tall man was there, scanning the tree line as he spoke. After a few moments, he patted the back of the man next to him, and the group broke apart. Two men grabbed the dead Feral and tossed him to the side of the road. People returned to their wagons, tucked their children inside, and mounted their horses. One of the horsemen raised his arm and thrust his fist forward. The line began to move. The caravan crept past. It was long, with roughly forty wagons, supply carts, and several mounted riders.

Five horses brought up the rear. Men sat alert on four of the mounts, rifles or crossbows drawn across their laps. The fifth horse bore a body wrapped in a blanket and trussed to the saddle like a hunter's quarry. The blanket was stained red.

A shiver moved through me. I was stuck. I couldn't leave until the caravan was out of sight. Then there were the Ferals. They were out there, and I had no weapon except for a small pocketknife. How stupid I'd been, wandering the Wildlands without a proper weapon. But I couldn't sit here wasting time. I had to make it to the Citadel today. The morning was flying by, and the Expo was tonight. I sat in my perch, waiting until the forest fell into a normal rhythm. I lowered myself to the ground and began hiking.

The forest felt alive, full of eyes, but I was alone. I was almost certain.

I looked over my shoulder, scanning behind me, and tripped on a branch. My knee struck the gnarl protruding from one end. I righted myself, rubbing the tender bruise rising on my knee, and kicked the branch, then thought better of it. The stick would make a perfect club. I sheared off the dead leaves and brittle sucker limbs, then hurried on my way, clutching the stick like a rosary, counting on a miracle.

Soon I reached a forested marsh too dense for passage. The road was too vulnerable an option. Risking the marsh meant a slow, unpredictable slog and the likelihood of alligators hidden in the dark waters. Plunging deeper in the forest to hike around the marsh would set me back, but it seemed the safest way. More than an hour had passed by the time I circled the marsh and began searching for the road again. I walked fast to make up for lost time. Sweat dripped down my face as I peeled off my sweater and stuffed it in my pack. I rounded a big sycamore tree and almost ran into a man standing there.

A Feral standing there.

My instincts fired, and I hoisted my stick in front of me like a shield.

The man charged, grabbed the branch, and shoved. My spine slammed into a tree, punching my breath loose.

"Look what we have here," the Feral growled. He had me pinned. "A little lamb lost in the woods. Whatcha got in that backpack there, missy?"

The Feral was one of the escapees from the caravan. He was older than my father, judging from the crevices in his hollow cheeks and the gray streaking his dirty brown hair. He was skeletal, his muscle and fat wasted to almost nothing. His eyes were sunken and hazy, like haunted pits. A jagged grin spread inside his grimy beard, cracking crusted lips, and his breath stank like a decaying carcass, making me gag.

A knife in his hand prevented him from getting a solid hold on my stick, but the blade was too close to my chest. Pure instinct kicked in. I shoved him and twisted free. The Feral stumbled, hopping unsteady on his left leg. Blood soaked the lower leg of his britches. Maybe he'd been shot after all.

I didn't think too long on it. I ran, then lurched forward as a white-hot sting sliced my forearm. I cried out, and a body slammed me from behind, knocking me into a palmetto. I struggled out from under the Feral and stumbled to my feet, but

I wasn't fast enough. Fingers clawed my arm and swung me around.

The Feral pressed his knife to my cheek, and I froze. My chest heaved, desperate for air. Pain throbbed in my forearm where the Feral cut me. Warm blood trickled down my fingers and dripped onto the ground. The man's eyes flashed with hunger and rage. The smell of sweat, death, and dirt filled my nose.

"What will I do with you?" he whispered, his words hot in my ear. Then he laughed and growled. "What will I *not* do with you?"

Fear overcame reason. I roared at him, something guttural, deep, and primal. I grabbed his wrist, shoved the knife from my face, and kicked his wounded leg. He howled and hobbled back, giving me enough distance to swing my boot into his groin. The Feral doubled over, cradling his crotch and groaning.

I took off running. But my legs would not cooperate. They turned to jelly and buckled, tossing me to my hands and knees.

"You bitch!" the man screamed and limped after me, fast.

Despair washed through me. This man was going to track me, no matter what. He knew the woods, and I didn't. But if I died, my sister would die, and I couldn't let that happen. My hands scrabbled through the leaves and found my stick. I clutched it, my fingers sticky with blood, as the Feral fisted a clump of my hair and yanked. The pain was blinding. I screamed as he hauled me off the ground. I wheeled around and clobbered my attacker on his wounded leg.

He released me, dropped his knife, and fell to one knee, hugging his bleeding shin. "Fucking bitch!"

I swung again. The gnarl smacked the man's left temple with a sickening, fleshy thwack. He groaned and tilted sideways. His big eyes stared in disbelief and his bottom lip draped open as if he were about to object. I lashed out again, and the club bit into his ear and jaw. The man slumped over, blood dripping from his lips.

I almost stopped. But the Feral was staring at me, a weak but wild glare in his dark eyes—a promise and a threat. He'd make me suffer if he caught me. I took another swing and watched his body collapse. His eyes closed, and he lay there, unmoving.

Tremors rippled through my body, and they wouldn't stop. The stick fell from my fingers. I had no idea if I'd killed the man or not. For the moment I didn't care, or at least I tried to convince myself of that. Quaking with every step, I approached the Feral and snatched his knife. I backed away, careful, and ran. I clutched the knife with numb fingers and didn't stop until my lungs couldn't keep up.

I didn't remember the rest of the walk. The gash on my arm throbbed, and my body ached in places I'd never imagined. I was so tired, but I shoved everything out of my mind, everything but walking. One foot, then the next and the next. I stopped long enough to clean my wound in a stream, wash my blood off the Feral's knife, and put on a fresh dress. I finger-combed bits of leaves out of my hair and kept going. It was late afternoon when I reached the outskirts of the Citadel. Sweat trickled down my back, making my fresh dress stick to my skin. So much for cleaning up.

High stone walls loomed before me, magnificent yet menacing. Like even the stones thought I didn't belong there. From the shelter of the forest, I searched the city wall, looking for the one place where someone like me was allowed inside: the Imperial Arena.

It came into view further along the curve of the wall, squatting like a mini fortress next to the city rampart. The arena's high walls were a pristine white, decorated with black window casings high above the ground. Crisp red banners fluttered at the entrance, like blood on white sand. The Conquistador's lion marked each banner, its body taut, its paws stretched in mid-attack.

This was it. The point of no return.

I could still go home, and I wanted to. More than ever. My body was practically begging me to turn around. I didn't want to hand over my life for the next decade to a stranger. I wanted to be with my family and let God and the universe handle the rest. In that moment, it was too much. Too impossible.

But... But the alternative was unimaginable. I couldn't picture a life where Juni didn't exist. She was more than a little sister, more than a duty of blood. Where my mother had been my confidant and guide, Juni was my light and air. I'd failed my mother. I would not fail my sister. I would fight for her. I was the only one who could.

I stowed my knife in my bag and stepped out of the forest.

PART II

TROUBLED WATER

7

RAFE

*B*eneath the fading evening sun, the Imperial Arena teemed with pretenders—thousands of wealthy Floridians who prostrated themselves at the altar of youth, who enriched the Conq's pockets to maintain the illusion that the years they'd inhabited had not touched them.

I nudged Twain, who sat beside me reading a leather-bound copy of *Utopia.*

"You couldn't ask for a better time to commit a burglary," I said, nodding to the growing crowd.

We'd claimed seats on the left flank of the arena and watched people arrive. Several faces I knew from childhood floated by. They no longer knew me, at least not with my disguise. Their faces remained unchanged, thanks to the Fount and the requisite stack of pesos to access it. People passed us like a parade from bygone years: the bank CEO who looked like a high school wrestler, the sixty-year-old golf champion with a thick head of brown hair, the spa owner who could run a marathon at ninety-two, the blonde billionaire with a penchant for diamonds. That woman, Blythe Damling, wore the same flowing locks and flawless skin she had when I was a kid, and she was a regular at society events. She never donned the same jewelry twice. Blythe had to be pushing eighty, but she looked like a Hollywood starlet, one of many.

Imperial Arena teemed with gentlefolk armored in their finest suits and day dresses, not a gray hair or wrinkle on their pricey flesh. They schmoozed and fake-kissed like they were at a ball. No one would miss this spectacle.

Twain looked up from his book. "You never shut that brain off, do you?"

"Never. Look at them. The Citadel is empty. Everyone's here. All their homes and businesses are vacant, ripe for the picking."

The biannual Obligors Expo marked the only time these people would step foot beyond the Citadel's fortress walls. They craved the taste of danger that came from venturing outside the city, if only to the place where the Empire conducted its dirty work. They were heavily guarded while doing so, but still... Afterward, they'd retreat to the security of the Citadel. No one wanted to risk being caught in the Florida Wildlands without protection. Legends abounded about those who strayed into the Wildlands, most for the thrill of it, the bragging rights. Some were never seen again. Some returned, bruised in body and mind, warning of Ferals—depraved, soulless beings who roamed the wilderness, robbing and torturing travelers. Predators who enslaved the weak, who forced their quarry to steal and kill for them, who made a game of making their captives run for their lives.

Some of the stories were pure myth, heightened by one-upmanship. A great deal of it was true. I knew. Twain and I had survived several months out there, wandering the untamed landscape, trying—and failing—to avoid the Ferals and their brutality.

"Too bad we no longer stoop to common thievery," he said, scattering memories of a time best left buried. "We're above that now."

We were above many things now, and below still quite a few. I couldn't shake the surrealness of the moment. This had once been my life. A normal outing, a trivial thing, an entitlement. Now I recognized the perversion beneath the perfection, the flippant cruelty reserved for those unfortunate enough to be born outside of wealth and power and the casual life longevity they afforded.

I didn't belong here anymore. We didn't belong here. But maybe one day we could reshape it into a place where every-body belonged.

"I'm not above doing anything that will speed the old man's downfall," I said.

"Did you make any progress on the Wreckus?" Twain asked.

"Some, but I'm waiting on some parts from the Sink," I said. It had only been three days since I agreed to Rod's proposal to create a device that could knock out power to a chunk of the city. The Scythe planned to test it in one of the coastal cities before deploying it in the Citadel. Rod had given me a month and half to create lightning in a box. Nothing as destructive as an electromagnetic bomb, but something that could fry the infrastructure for a brief period of time. Which was good. I drew the line at creating anything with the potential for a high body count.

"I'm sure that'll cost a pretty peso," Twain said.

"You got that right," I said. "Speaking of illegal endeavors, don't get caught with that book. Someone might think you're conspiring against the tyrant."

"Maybe we should send it to him and highlight this part," Twain said, pointing to a passage about how it was better to *make such good provisions by which every man might be put in a method how to live, and so be preserved from the fatal necessity of stealing and of dying for it.*

"I doubt he'd agree," I said, scanning to make sure no one

could overhear us. "He likes his public executions way too much. That stage has more blood on it than a battlefield."

People forfeited their lives there one way or another—indenture or death. I wasn't sure which was worse. The Conq liked to make a show of it either way. Piss him off enough and he'd stage your execution in the most creative way possible, no two deaths alike. After living more than half a millennium, I supposed you got bored with the mundane. The old man was a sick bastard.

Twain studied me, his brows crinkled in concern. "What's going on? Usually I'm the voice of caution," he said. "Look, he's not here. The troops are sparse. What's got you spooked?"

I glanced to the balcony where the Conq sometimes presided over the Expo. The red leonine banners bearing his crest wafted in the breeze at the edges of his suite. Below, thousands of citizens lounged in rows of cushioned chairs arranged in a tiered semicircle around the stage. Waiters milled among the aisles, taking drink orders. The Expo was due to start in minutes, and the Conq's box remained empty.

"Nothing. I just hate this. It's pure entertainment for a bunch of bored, rich people. They can't see beyond themselves to recognize a fellow human being ransoming his life on that stage. They don't care."

"Yeah, well, short of firebombing the place, what can we do?" Twain said. "Look, we don't need to be here. Let's go."

"No, I need to be reminded why what we do is important."

"Like hell you do. You already want to throttle the Conq every time his name is mentioned. Your memory hasn't dimmed a bit, and neither has mine."

"We walk the fire together," I said.

Twain knew me better than anyone. We'd walked through hell together growing up, and the memories hovered in the periphery always, raw and insistent, even after the passing of years.

"And rise from the ashes together," he said.

The refrain was our compass, our reminder that we were in this life together. Always.

A series of delicate peals rang through the announcement system, signaling the Expo's start. Spectator voices pitched in excitement as everyone settled in their seats. To the right of the stage, the Obligors appeared, their images projected onto giant screens for everyone to see in hi-def humiliation. A line of twelve men and three women formed at the foot of the stairs leading to the stage, prodded into straightness by the Guardia. Compared to the finery in the audience, they appeared misplaced. Their clothes were worn and muted, their eyes downcast, their shoulders hunched.

A man materialized from behind the group and walked the length of Obligors, eyeing them like chattel. He wore an impeccable white linen suit that pulled taut across his tight mound of belly. Brown hair crested from his smooth forehead in a perfect, slick wave, and an earpiece connected to a thin microphone at his mouth. He pivoted theatrically to the audience, offered a smile of satisfaction, and bowed in greeting. He bounded up the stairs and commanded centerstage.

"Ladies and gentlemen, welcome to the one hundred fifty-fifth Obligors Expo. I'm Abel Preiss, your more-than-able host for the evening," the man said, his voice amplified to reach every corner of the amphitheater. "More than one hundred fifty years ago, our sovereign, maker of our Empire Eternal, abolished the appalling practice of slavery in this nation. In his wisdom and mercy, El Conquistador established the Obligors Expo to help our less-fortunate brothers and sisters—to provide them relief, an option—to pay their debts and make their paths straight. They are here by choice, ready to serve you and start anew."

I almost snorted. The Conq enslaved prisoners every day, conscripting them for his own household or for dirty work like sewers and sanitation.

On stage, Preiss paused for a polite round of applause.

"Now, a few reminders. A standard Obligor contract begins at ten years for ten thousand Floridian pesos. Length and price above the base are up for bid. Obligor Consorts begin at seven years and will be announced in advance of bidding when that is an option." He swept his arms out, giving a wide grin. "And now...let the matches begin!"

The crowd applauded as Preiss beckoned the first Obligor onstage. A guard at the foot of the stairs jabbed a middle-aged man with his rifle. The camera broadcast the man's every move, showcasing his thick cap of black-and-gray hair and blue eyes that skittered around the amphitheater. After a moment's hesitation and another vicious jab, the man shuffled forward and mounted the steps.

A change came over him as he stood next to Preiss. He lifted his head, straightened his spine, and pushed his shoulders back. His eyes gazed straight ahead, over the audience, mustering every ounce of dignity he possessed.

"Ladies and gentlemen," Preiss said, stepping forward. "I give you Mr. Charles Kremsley. He is a registered subject who hails from the Barrio. Skills include carpentry and manual labor perfect for any handyman projects around your home or office."

A subject of the Barrio. Code for a laborer living in the shabby township adjacent to the Citadel wall. Protected and better than living in the Wildlands, but not by much. At least they could earn a meager living and have a family. They gave that up when they indentured themselves at the Expo. Obligors bound themselves to their employer twenty-four seven, forever at the mercy of his whims. I'd witnessed men and women take on that yoke far too many times, the way their spirits crumbled to dust, buried in a life no longer their own.

"Let's find a match for Mr. Kremsley. Who'll help this subject of our Conquistador cleanse his debts? Who'll purchase his contract?"

Preiss bleated on, and soon a three-way bidding war broke out between a woman with orange hair and fake boobs, a man I recognized as the owner of the Imperial Collection Furniture Emporium, and Blythe Damling. The furniture salesman won, giving thirty thousand pesos for the contract, perhaps enough for Kremsley to send a pittance home to his family after his debt was settled. Once Preiss announced the winning bid, a round of polite, approving applause filled the amphitheater. Kremsley exited the stage, and his shoulders folded with every step.

Several more contracts were purchased in a series of rousing bids, each one stoking my blood to a low simmer. I clenched my fists and squirmed in my seat. This was inhumane.

How cold did you have to be to normalize shattering a person for profit?

There had to be a better way.

"Come on—let's go."

Twain's voice broke into my seething thoughts.

"What?" I stopped fidgeting and looked at him.

"You've seen enough."

I blew out a breath of frustration. Why torture myself? There was nothing I could do to stop the misery onstage. Not one thing.

Not yet.

I scratched my forehead with my thumb and sighed. "You're right," I said. I spared one final look at the stage.

The last Obligor mounted the steps, pinching her skirts, revealing a worn pair of work boots. The screen broadcast her troubled eyes skimming the arena. My heart sank. She was a slight wisp of a young woman. What the hell was she doing here?

"Oh no," Twain said. He tugged my sleeve. "Let's go."

"She barely looks old enough," I said. "She has no idea what she's getting into."

He shook his head. "She may be young, but she's an adult.

You know they don't offer kids for contract. Besides, there's nothing you can do about it, and you don't need to watch. Come on."

Twain stood halfway, but I stayed put. He sighed and sank into his chair.

Preiss extended his thick arm and beckoned the woman to his side like a proud papa. The young woman joined him and faced the crowd. Her work boots were soiled, and she wore a limp, flowered dress and baggy sweater in the humid heat. Dark circles shadowed her eyes, and fresh cuts marked her face. She held her head high, but a simple tuck of her hair betrayed her confidence.

I couldn't tear my eyes from this disaster in the making. This —this represented everything I hated about the Empire, this regime. This world that devoured people young and old for sport and profit. A beautiful and wild land filled not with people but with predators and prey.

"Ah…ladies and gentlemen, may I introduce Miss Eve Smith. She is an unregistered subject who hails from one of the sanctioned farming communities in the Wildlands. Her skills include planting, reaping, rudimentary housekeeping, sewing, and needlecraft."

A low murmur weaved through the crowd. Unregistered persons offering themselves for indenture were rare, especially ones from the Wildlands. She didn't exist in the Prime Registry. She was an unknown with no history, no way to determine the state of her mental health or if she carried disease or a criminal record. Workers in the sanctioned farms lived self-sufficiently, so how could she owe a debt to anyone of substance?

"Now, who'll give me ten thousand for her contract?" Preiss asked, his eyes surveying the crowd. Silence settled across the audience.

"Oh, come now, who'll start us off with this fine young woman?"

Still nothing. Desperation shadowed the woman's eyes as they skidded across the audience. Her fingers fidgeted with the folds of her dress and then stilled into a fist.

A guard skipped up the stairs and rushed to Preiss's side.

Take her out. Tell him to take her out of the Expo. She's got her whole life in front of her.

The guard spoke into his ear. The host smiled and leaned in close to whisper something to the woman. Her eyes darkened and she glared at him, shaking her head. Preiss laughed.

"We had an offer for an Obligor Consort contract," he announced. "The young woman respectfully declines."

Laughter rippled through the crowd, and the woman's cheeks flushed red. She tugged her sweater across her chest and straightened her spine.

At least she had some sense. Although that didn't matter. In the end, buyers got what they wanted, did what they wanted, and the Obligors lived with the consequences. The Guardia shrugged and did little to stop it.

"The contract stands on offer at ten thousand," Preiss reminded the crowd. The audience murmured, but no one made a bid. The woman shot a look at Preiss, distress burning in her eyes.

"Come now, surely someone could help this young woman," he said. "She's stronger than she looks."

Preiss snagged the woman's arm and pushed up the sleeve of her sweater to display her muscles. The woman yanked free, but not before he'd revealed a bandage wrapped around her forearm, stained with dried blood.

"Now, now," Preiss admonished. "No one likes a feisty Obligor."

"I do!" a man shouted from the audience. The crowd erupted in laughter.

"How much?" Preiss countered.

"Ten thousand pesos' worth!" the man yelled.

That voice chilled me. I followed the sound to its source. Jerome Blackwell draped in his seat, wearing the navy-blue suit I'd given him. He whispered something into the ear of the man sitting next to him and then laughed. Was his companion a benefactor? I flashed back to an image of Blackwell salivating over Simone, who'd had no trouble putting him in his place.

He would eat Eve Smith alive.

"Is that—" Twain started.

"Yes," I said through gritted teeth.

"We unleashed a monster," he said. For the first time, he sounded worried.

"Ten thousand! Excellent! Who'll top that?" Preiss said.

No one stepped up.

"Friends, we cannot let this fine young woman go at such a low price. She needs more than that."

Again, quiet.

"Looks like I get a bargain!" Blackwell crowed.

Panic blazed across the woman's face, and she turned toward Preiss, as if he would intervene. She'd find no help there.

Blackwell had said he'd do this, and I'd made it possible. I'd created another predator happy to feast on the poor and desperate. Who, no doubt, would take every advantage of this young woman, and no one would stop him.

This was my fault.

"Guess she's all mine."

Blackwell's voice dug into my chest like a pitchfork. Anything he did to that woman was on my head. I had no trouble dancing in the gray-and-black areas of the law, but I'd long ago told myself I wouldn't harm anyone who didn't deserve it.

The words came out of my mouth before I could stop them: "Twenty thousand!"

"What are you doing?" Twain hissed.

"The right thing," I hissed back. "We made that ass-wipe."

Thousands of eyes darted my way, including hers. My stomach squirmed, but I faked a dignified confidence. I wore blond hair and brown eyes today. No one would see beneath the disguise.

The woman held my gaze like a lifeline, hope rising in her eyes. My stomach twisted with nausea.

"Well done! Sir?" Preiss threw the bid back to Blackwell, who scowled and considered. Then he barked, "Thirty thousand!"

Preiss—and the woman—turned to me expectantly.

"Forty thousand."

Twain's fingers wrapped around my forearm, and his nails dug into my skin. That was a third of our savings.

"Fifty thousand," Blackwell countered before I'd finished speaking. He glared daggers at me. Did he recognize me? It was impossible.

"Sixty thousand," I said, meeting his glare in equal measure.

"We can't afford that," Twain said. "We owe money to the Sink."

We could cover sixty thousand, but not much more. Even so, he was right—we'd have trouble paying our suppliers in the black market.

I held my breath, waiting for Blackwell's response. Finally, he bristled, making a show of straightening his suit jacket. He couldn't outbid me, and he knew it. I had no idea how he could afford fifty thousand. Maybe his friend was fronting him, but it didn't matter. He couldn't win this one.

Blackwell gave a stiff bow of acquiescence, but even from this distance I could see the anger radiating from his face.

"Anyone else?" Preiss said. The audience murmured low, highly entertained by the exchange. Still, none ventured a bid.

"Done! Congratulations, sir!" he called up to me before motioning Eve Smith off the stage. A Guardia soldier escorted her out of view.

Onstage, Preiss's beaming face fell into a serious mask. He held a hand up to quiet the excited murmurs in the crowd and covered his earpiece with the other hand, listening for several long seconds. Finally, he spoke.

"Ladies and gentlemen, please keep to your seats—we have surprise for you tonight. Please stand for our sovereign, El Conquistador!"

My stomach dropped to the concrete. If the Conq was attending the Expo, why hadn't he watched from his balcony suite? Had he been here long enough to witness our bidding war? Could he have identified me?

The Conquistador strolled from the cover of the wings and commanded the edge of the stage, surveying his sycophants. He wore red-and-black military dress, and his hair was combed to perfection. The man bullied us into repeating his asinine *Empire Eternal* chant and then beckoned us to reclaim our seats. The stage fell dark, and moments later it flooded with painful light. A massive wheel stood on a pedestal centerstage. A naked man hung from its spokes, wrists and ankles splayed like a starfish. His face and body were painted with blood and bruises. My dinner roiled in my belly.

"Dear God," Twain whispered.

"Sadistic bastard."

The arena fell silent, as if the crowd feared drawing attention.

"This man is guilty of treason and attempted assassination. He will die this night for his crimes against the Empire and its citizens," the Conq said, retrieving a war hammer from a nearby table and hefting it between his hands. The handle was long, wrapped in worn leather, with a pointed spike opposite a blunt head.

"Treachery against the Empire will be paid for in blood and pain…" The Conq swung the hammer and slammed the blunt end into the man's knee. A horrid crunch echoed across the arena, followed by the prisoner's fathomless scream. Gasps echoed across the crowd.

"Commander Bane," the Conq called out, "he's yours."

The Conq's lapdog emerged from the shadows as the old man claimed his seat on a raised dais off to the side. His security detail flanked him.

Bane studied the prisoner, tossing the war hammer from one hand to the next.

The prisoner struggled to catch his breath. He drew in a lungful and spat at the Commander.

Bane smiled. And swung. The hammer crushed the man's femur. His screams mounted the air once again as his leg bent to an odd angle. Several rows ahead, a bejeweled woman puked into a champagne bucket, and people nearby guffawed.

The Expo was bad enough, but this was beyond the pale. This was evil. But no one left in the middle of one of the Conq's executions. No one looked away, not without bringing trouble on their heads.

Bane kept swinging, hitting every limb, every region of the body as the Conq watched with a cold stare. By the time he hammered the man's private parts, the prisoner had passed out and blood splattered the Commander and the floor around him.

The Conq stood from his makeshift throne and held up his hand. Bane froze mid-swing and waited. "Finish him."

Bane flipped the hammer over and buried the spiked end in the man's forehead.

Shrieks mixed with laughter filled the arena. I swallowed the bile rising in my throat. How had I once thought this was normal? How could I have considered anything this gruesome to be ordinary?

Next to me, Twain drew in a long breath and let it out slowly.

How I wished I'd heeded his suggestion to leave.

8

EVANGELINE

*I*t was done. I'd stepped across a line, and nothing could undo it. The next ten years of my life belonged to a man I'd never met. A stranger, whose nature and temper were a mystery. Any possibility of a normal future vanished in an instant. My heart drummed in my ears, in my chest, in my fingertips. I could not stop shaking.

What little I'd eaten threatened to come back up.

If only I could wash the whole Expo experience from my memory. Had my first bidder been the one who asked for the Obligor Consort contract? His lewd eyes had raked over me like he wanted to see more than what Preiss had exposed beneath my sleeve.

My new boss appeared the lesser of two evils, but looks could deceive. He could be the devil clothed in flesh for all I knew. And that was the trouble—I knew nothing about him.

After the auction, a guard dumped me in a locked room. No furniture in sight, only four brick walls and a stone floor. I stood beside the door and shuddered as the room spun. I leaned my forehead on the cold brick to steady myself. The gash on my arm throbbed. It needed stitches, but I'd tended it the best I could. I'd foraged yarrow and made a poultice to stop the bleeding, then bandaged the wound with cotton torn from my underskirt.

I slid to the cold floor and rested my head on my knees. My bones vibrated with exhaustion. My heart filled with panic, and I couldn't catch my breath.

What if he never let me leave? How would I help Juni then?

The minutes stretched long until a soldier opened the cell. I pushed myself to my feet and followed him in silence. We came to a room decorated in rich textures and thick honey-colored curtains. My employer lounged on a soft tan couch, chatting with a Guardia officer like they were old friends. His blond hair was combed into a precise cap, and a beard covered his chin. The officer wore a red military jacket and close-cropped brown hair. The men sipped from etched wineglasses, while their food debris littered delicate plates.

My escort clutched my wounded arm and forced me against the wall like a piece of furniture. I bit my lip to stifle a gasp against the pain.

The man and the official laughed over some comment I missed.

"Well, shall we get to it?" the officer asked, slapping his knee.

The blond man gave the officer a confused look. "Do forgive me, Captain Heath," he said. "I thought everything was in order. Was there an issue with the transaction?"

"Oh, no. The payment went through," Heath said. "We've instituted a new procedure I think you'll like. Something to help you keep tabs on your servant and track her if she gets…lost."

"Is that so?"

"Yes, now, Mr. Riegel, if you'll join me over here," Heath said, rising from his chair. He approached a small table near the window where a thin silver bracelet and metal cylinder lay on a white cloth. The guard dragged me to the table and held tight as Heath picked up the metal tube and offered his palm. The soldier forced my hand into the captain's and pushed up my sleeve. Heath's moist fingers latched on, and I recoiled without thinking. His hand crushed my fingers as cold terror burned through my veins, then he angled the cylinder toward the inside of my wrist.

"Wait—what are you doing?" Riegel blurted. My eyes darted to him, as if he could save me from whatever was about to happen. I knew better, but the sudden look of concern on the man's face gave me pause.

"Implanting her beacon," Heath said. Without warning, he pressed the cylinder to my skin. I gasped as the device pierced my flesh. Pressure built inside my wrist as something plunged into my arm. Pain flared orange hot beneath my skin, and I tried to pull free, but the men held me steady until Heath removed the cylinder.

"It's a subcutaneous global tracker. Should your servant decide to vacate service before the allotted time is up, you can track and retrieve her. It is also irrefutable proof that this Obligor is yours."

Riegel's cheeks reddened. His lips flattened.

My legs felt like liquid, begging to give way, but I used every ounce of stubbornness I possessed to stay upright. A bead of blood oozed on my arm from the small cut, but the lingering pain felt much bigger.

Heath continued on, addressing Riegel without once looking at me. "This is for you," he said, retrieving the silver bracelet from the table. "It attaches to your Convo, so you can determine where your Obligor is at all times."

"That's not necessary," Riegel said, not moving.

"No trouble. It's standard protocol. You've spent a great deal, and this is your insurance your investment is protected."

"I'm not concerned with losing…anything," Riegel said.

Heath held out his palm, ignoring the irritation in the man's voice. "If you'll allow me to connect this with your Convo, we can proceed."

The two stood there for several long moments before Riegel offered Heath his hand. The captain snapped the bracelet around his wrist and attached it to a black cuff already there.

"There now, see—that was painless," he said, his eyes shining with amusement. "Now the last step. We link your Obligor to your Convo."

The guard forced my arm out. Blood had begun to trickle down my wrist as another bead forced its way out of the wound.

"Mr. Riegel, if you'll place your Convo over the beacon, the system will link the two units."

Again, the man hesitated. A look of disgust pierced his eyes.

"Oh heavens, you don't have to touch it," Heath said, snickering. "Hold it above the beacon."

My cheeks flushed in humiliation.

Riegel held his wrist parallel to mine. Nothing happened.

"A bit closer," Heath said, tapping Riegel's arm. It dipped, and his wrist grazed mine, smearing the blood. He recoiled as if I'd burned him. The warm imprint of his skin lingered on mine, and it made the heat rise higher in my cheeks.

A small ting sounded, and a green light flashed on the Convo. "All done," the captain said.

Riegel brushed his wrist across his britches, as if wiping away something foul.

"You are free to go," Heath said. "Enjoy your Obligor."

Shame mixed with relief. Riegel clearly had no intention of touching me. He bore no unwanted intentions that I could see. He'd bought a workhorse, a servant—nothing more. The knot in my chest loosened, enough to feel the thorn of his contempt picking at the fragile walls of my spirit. Here stood my future: Ten years of invisibility. Ten years of scorn.

My employer exited the room without a word, and the guard

shoved me after him. I followed him as we twisted and turned down several hallways, finally exiting the building. Outside the arena, a constellation of lights from the Citadel's towering buildings blazed in the deepening night sky. They rose within the massive stone wall like mountains. I'd never seen anything like it. Moving in their shadows left me dizzy.

Riegel plowed ahead, not minding whether I was behind him or not. I hurried after him, laboring to catch my breath. Any other day, I could outrun this soft city-dweller, but this day offered no sense of normal.

The area outside the Expo arena had emptied, save for a few guards hustling stragglers home, rifles slung across their bodies. Next to the arena sat a large pavilion filled with benches on raised platforms spaced at regular intervals. Riegel joined a man leaning on one of the benches. He wore dark glasses, a brimmed hat, and a long dirty-blond ponytail. The two exchanged a wordless glance, some message passing between them that I could not make out. The friend pushed a finger to the band on his wrist, and seconds later, a panel covering the ground next to the platform slid open. A large black bean-shaped vessel rose out of the opening. The vehicle split open, revealing four chairs and a lighted panel within. The men climbed into the front seats, and Riegel punched something on the panel. The doors began to glide closed. It took me a second to realize what was happening.

Riegel was leaving me, abandoning me with no money and nowhere to go.

"Wait—what?" I rushed forward and shoved a knee into the opening, not stopping to wonder if the doors might crush me. The door slid open without touching me.

"Go home," Riegel said, staring straight ahead. He wouldn't look at me. "You don't belong here."

"I can't," I said, scrambling inside the vehicle. I pulled my bag into my lap, yanked my sweater across my chest, and crossed my arms.

"Get out," Riegel said. He still refused to look at me.

"Rafe…" The friend intervened.

"No, I will not be a part of this."

He clawed the silver circle off his cuff, the thing that tethered us together like a leash. It clicked free, and he tugged it off and threw it. The bracelet bounced off the floor and came to a rest between his feet.

"It's too late for that," his friend said. "Let's go home and think this through."

"Get out of my transpod and go home."

"No," I said. "I'm not going anywhere without my sixty thousand pesos."

"You need to go back to wherever you came from," Riegel said. "I don't give a damn about the money."

"Well, I do," I said, scowling.

"Can we have this conversation somewhere else?" the friend asked, jerking his head. Up ahead, a guard peered in our direction and started walking toward us. "We need to go."

Riegel glanced at the guard. "Dammit." He fiddled with the lighted panel, and the doors slid closed. The pod dropped back into the earth like a coffin lowered to the grave and shot forward into a dark tunnel.

How fitting. My old life was dead. I prayed I'd not thrown it away for nothing.

9

RAFE

*E*ve Smith looked like a trampled flower. Her hair, her dress, her face...everything drooped. Her eyes absorbed my living room as if she'd never stepped foot inside anything more sophisticated than a barn. She had no idea how close she'd come to ending up with a bastard like Blackwell, no clue what she'd signed up for. The sheer stupidity of the situation made me want to throw something. Again.

My world consisted of a handful of people I trusted, people who had the wit to evade the most brutal ruler on the continent, and she had no place in it. She was nothing more than a stone, chucked into the tempered glass shielding my world from disaster, and I'd done the hurling.

"You can stay the night, but you're out in the morning," I said.

"Rafe, you can't do that," Twain said.

"We have a contract," the woman said. Her lips flattened into a hard line, but she winced when she crossed her arms. "You agreed to pay me. Trust me, I will earn every peso."

"This is my home. I decide who stays and who goes. In the morning, you're outta here."

"Rafe, that's impossible," Twain said. "The Guardia inspects first-year Obligors—once within the first two weeks and again by year's end. If she isn't present at each inspection, they'll launch an investigation you want no part of. Besides, they can track her. They'll know if she leaves the Citadel. Bane's not above putting out a search party for the fun of it. They would track her down and execute her as a public demonstration."

The woman's cheeks blanched, and her eyes widened. My wall of steel buckled. Twain had the obnoxious habit of being right.

"I can't have an Obligor," I said.

"Yeah, you shouldn't, but you do. You can't change what you've done," Twain said. "Now we need to figure out how to move forward."

"There's nothing to figure out," I grumbled.

He rubbed a hand down his face. "There's plenty. Have you forgotten about your little side project?"

I closed my eyes and pressed a palm to my forehead to deaden the ache beginning to pulse there. There was a bigger picture here, and I had forgotten for a few hours. I'd lost focus, up until the point I'd bid sixty thousand pesos for *a person*. Now I'd have to find a way to cover what I owed the Sink for the Wreckus parts and finish building the device. Rod had made it clear the consequences of failure. I'd be a loose end, a vulnerability. Better off dead than risking me turning informant with what little I knew. I couldn't let that happen.

Yeah, there was plenty to figure out. First and foremost, how to get rid of the stranger in my house. I couldn't look at Eve without disgust roiling my insides, not because of her but because of what she represented.

Because of the life I'd once known.

"Bloody Conq," I said. "I refuse to live like him and every other miscreant in this city. I will not enslave someone. I will not use—"

"I am no slave," Eve said, straightening her spine. "I offered my services. You bought them. It's a called a job."

I snatched her arm and locked onto her green eyes. "You have no idea what you're into," I said.

She stood her ground, her gaze stabbing into mine. I could smell the outdoors on her—forest leaves, fresh earth, and pond water. The feel of her arm, more muscled than expected beneath the overlarge dress, caused my thoughts to hiccup. I swallowed.

"Look, you're lucky I claimed you and not one of those other bastards. But I will not—I repeat *will not*—have a slave, an Obligor, or a servant, no matter what you call it. I will not use people up and dispose of them like yesterday's garbage."

"That's not what I am, what this is."

"I don't need a servant."

The woman gritted her teeth. "Fine," she said. "Sell my contract to someone else. It doesn't matter who pays, long as I'm paid."

I released the woman more harshly than intended. She flinched, then steeled herself.

"You're not listening," I said.

"I heard every stupid word you said." Eve's cheeks flushed red, and tears rimmed her eyes, refusing to fall. "I hear what you think of me, but I don't have the luxury of walking away. You agreed to the contract. So did I. I intend to see it fulfilled."

"What the hell for?"

"That's none of your business."

"You—" Anger coiled up my throat. I shut my mouth before I said something I regretted.

Twain intervened. "Look, it's late. We're tired. We're out of our comfort zone. We're not going to hatch any solutions tonight. Let's put this on hold, get some rest, and start afresh. But first, my name is Twain Hedrick, and you are?"

He held out his hand. The woman stared at it before taking it.

"Ev—Eve. Eve Smith."

She tried to retract her hand, but he wouldn't let go.

"Your real name?" Twain said. His mouth stretched into a honeyed smile.

The woman refused to answer and tugged against his grip. Twain covered their hands with his free palm in a gentling manner.

"Your true identity is safe in this home. Secrets spoken here go no further than these walls," he said. The woman's eyes volleyed between us.

"What's his real name?" she said, nodding toward me.

Twain raised his eyebrows, impressed. I frowned. I didn't owe this woman a damn thing. She should've been thankful she was here and not suffering in Blackwell's sticky hands. I crossed my arms and kept my mouth shut.

"Come on, Rafe." Twain's scold was almost parental. If I didn't speak up, he would.

"Crawfish on a cracker, you're so annoying," I said, glaring at my friend. He snorted and waited. "Rafael Roldan."

It was the most she would get. Ever. I'd never give her my real name, my real identity. Only Twain and Simone knew that.

"Rafe, this is..." Twain gestured for the woman to speak.

Her body swayed, and she blinked, as if trying to steady herself. She sighed and said, "Evangeline Lovette."

"Beautiful name. Suits you," he said. "Now, Evangeline, how about a hot bath, some clean clothes, and a warm place to sleep?"

"I'd like that."

Twain led her to the wardrobe room, looping her arm in his like she was the queen of Spain. I stood there seething and unsettled.

Evangeline was clueless. If she'd dished out this type of insolence to any of the Citadel elite, she'd have been punished until her spirit was crushed and her tongue lost the will to argue. The entire system was disgusting, and I'd been an idiot to play a part in it. I'd been an idiot to risk my life and that of my friends over a stranger.

But...that was what we did. We helped those who needed it. We bucked against the Empire and lifted people up when we could. It was the least I could do to redeem the life I'd once known. So why was I so angry about this?

My friend's voice whispered down the hallway, low and muffled.

I knew why.

I'd let my control slip. I'd brought an unvetted stranger into our home. I'd put us on the Empire's radar. If the Guardia found out the Conquistador's own son, who'd been banished from the Citadel eight years ago, had returned, they'd come back and finish me and my friends.

In the other room, Twain secured a nightgown for our visitor and led her into the heart of our home. Water splashed noisily into the claw-foot tub inside the spare room's bathroom.

Twain reappeared and planted himself in front of me, rousing me from my trance.

"What?"

"I should be asking you that. I know you wanted to save her from Blackwell, but you can't save someone halfway," he said.

"I didn't. She's free and clear of that asshole."

"You saved her from him, but for what? To throw her out into the Wildlands? You know the odds of survival out there."

"What am I supposed to do? I can't keep her," I said.

"Obviously, but I'm not sure how you're going to undo this one," Twain said.

I thought for a minute, letting my anger ebb until a calm

came over me. The calm that came whenever I worked a problem.

"I need to find out why she became an Obligor in the first place. See if we can solve whatever problem brought her here. It may be my only way out."

A NOISE ROUSED me from half sleep. The sun was up, but it was way too early in the morning for scoundrels and reprobates like me. I'd tossed and turned all night, unable to relax with a stranger in my house. I'd locked my door, a precaution against being stabbed to death in my sleep.

The noise sounded again, somewhere in the distance. I climbed out of bed and trudged down the hallway. Evangeline stood at the stove, tipping a ladle of batter into a skillet, a tejas de almendra stuffed halfway into her mouth. From the looks of it, this woman had nosed around and unearthed my favorite almond cookies in the pantry. The audacity—making herself at home in my kitchen, with my cookies. And my cookware.

"What the hell are you doing?"

Evangeline startled, choking on the cookie and dropping the ladle onto the counter. She stepped back and eyed me like I was a Florida panther poised to strike. Her eyes were glassy, and she was swaying again. What was wrong with her?

"Who are you?" she asked, edging back.

Understanding hit me. She'd never seen my black hair and blue-gray eyes. Without my disguise, I was a stranger. But then again, so was she. So different from the person we'd brought home last night. Her nightgown revealed lean, muscular arms and accented curves previously buried beneath a frumpy dress. Her hair was clean, shiny like sunlight through honey, and tied into a long braid that draped over her shoulder. Red flushed across her cheeks and her tanned neckline—which I tried to ignore, but my eyes kept floating to her cleavage.

I shook my head to clear the distraction. Already this woman was arms-deep in my personal space. This would not do.

"The same person who brought you home last night," I answered.

"Mr. Roldan?"

Her eyes scanned my face and the rest of me. Most of which was unclothed, except for a pair of sleep pants. Her blush deepened, and she averted her eyes.

"Yes. Now what the hell are you doing in my kitchen?"

"Making breakfast," she said, ignoring me and freeing a crepe from the pan. "Crepes are my specialty. I've been making these since I was little. I can't cook all that great. I tend to burn anything that needs baking but I know the basics, and everyone loves my crepes. I can learn to cook whatever you want."

She was rambling. Not making this easy. I had no desire to argue or even deal with this. I wanted life to go back to the way it was before I'd opened my damn mouth at the Expo. There was no room for a new person in my life.

"I don't want you to learn anything," I said. "I don't need a housekeeper."

Evangeline plated two crepes and laced rows of bananas down the center of each. She wrapped the crepes around the fruit, sprinkled them with cinnamon, and extended the dish like a peace offering. I glanced at the plate but didn't take it.

"I understand," she said, pushing the plate into my hand. "But I'm here, and you might as well let me work."

She turned to the stove, but her legs buckled mid-pivot. Her hands clutched the edge of the countertop to steady herself.

"Are you all right?" I asked, setting the plate aside.

"I'm fine."

She grabbed the ladle and scooped more batter. The next

moment, her knees gave way beneath her. The ladle struck the counter, spewing batter into the air. I lunged and caught her before her head smacked granite. The hot skillet clattered to the floor, narrowly missing my leg.

"Evangeline…"

The woman's eyes fluttered, struggling to open. I held on to her to keep her from hitting the floor. Her skin was hot to the touch.

"Evan. Everyone calls me Evan," she mumbled. One hand grabbed my bicep as she struggled to right herself. Her palm was on fire. I did not like being touched. It had too often been associated with punishment or manipulation in my life. But her touch stoked an odd heat in my belly. Unwelcome, but not unpleasant.

"Sorry," she said. "Just a little dizzy."

I reached around her waist and lifted her to her feet. She tried to put space between us, but her body wobbled and her warm palm planted on my chest. Her skin on mine sent a tiny earthquake through my core. I wasn't used to being touched with any measure of intimacy. Heat rose to my chest. The moment awareness hit her, she flushed a deeper shade of red and hurried out of my arms. She turned her back, bracing herself on the counter.

I cleared my throat. "You should go lie down."

"I'm fine," she said, a little too harshly, and then softened her voice. "I'm okay. Please, enjoy your breakfast while it's hot. What would you like to drink?"

Two steps toward the refrigerator, she went down again. I caught her mid-fall and scooped her into my arms. Her eyes shuttered, and her body fell limp. Heat radiated off her, unnaturally high, impressing on my skin. Something was wrong. Very wrong.

"AVA," I said in a loud voice. The words triggered my home's Automated Voice Activator.

"How may I assist you?" a pleasant, technical female voice responded.

"AVA, turn off the stove."

"Stove off."

I shifted Evan in my arms, and her head sank into the crook of my neck. "AVA, locate Twain and wake him."

"I'm sorry—I find no *Wayne* in the system. Would you like me to add *Wayne* to the system?"

"Mierda, AVA. Don't flake out on me. AVA, locate *Twain* Hedrick and wake him."

"Twain Hedrick located." A pause, then, "Twain Hedrick contacted."

"Finally," I said, walking to the kitchen door. "AVA, send Twain Hedrick a message: *Meet me in the guest room.*"

"Message sent to Twain Hedrick."

I carried Evan to her room and laid her limp body atop her blankets. The massive bed sat inside a bay window, and early-morning sun streamed inside, illuminating her slack, rosy cheeks. I stepped back and scratched the crease in my brow. What had I gotten myself into? What if she died?

"What's going on?" Twain peered over my shoulder, wiping sleep from his eyes. "What are you doing?"

My head spun toward him. "I didn't do anything," I said.

"Why are you watching her sleep?"

I sighed in exasperation. "I'm not. She fainted in the kitchen. I think she has a fever."

"I'll get the MedScan," Twain said. He was gone before I could thank him.

I bent to pull a blanket over Evan and noticed marks on her arms. A black bruise circled her upper arm—fingerprint tattoos imprinted by force. A bandage wrapped her forearm, covering the wound she'd tried to hide at the Expo. Her face was marked with a scattering of thin cuts.

What had happened to her? I'd never bothered to ask where

she'd come from, how she'd gotten here, or why she'd offered herself as an Obligor. I'd been too focused on getting rid of her.

I eased the blanket over her and moved a stray piece of hair off her face. The Citadel was flush with beautiful women, youthful in appearance, painted and dressed in every finery available, but this woman bore none of those trappings. Her face was as clean and unadorned as the day the universe created her.

And lovely.

I retreated, shaking the thought from my head.

What would have happened if she'd been with Blackwell when she'd fainted? Would he have taken advantage of her? Considered her defective merchandise, to be returned or discarded as so many others would have? Would he have cared if she lived or died? Did I? I'd made a choice yesterday, and now I was responsible for this human being, whether I liked it or not.

"Found it." Twain offered me the small rectangular device.

"Go ahead," I said, pointing to her.

"No, no. She's all yours."

"She is *not* mine."

He shoved the device into my hand and motioned to the unconscious woman. "Even so. Stop stalling."

I pulled the blanket back and switched on the MedScan. I held the device inches above Evan's forehead and skimmed the device across the length of upper body. Results appeared on the MedScan screen: *temperature: 104, pulse: 132, respiration rate: 27 breaths per minute.* She had a fever, elevated heart rate, and rapid breathing. I showed Twain the display, but he just shrugged.

"Could be anything. Maybe the flu. Use the blood scan. See if it can identify the problem," he said.

I slid Evan's fingertip into the MedScan and pressed a button to trigger the blood scan. The device sprayed her skin with anti-septic, then drew a small blood sample. I withdrew her finger and wiped the residual blood from the end of her fingertip. Another wound to add to her list of injuries. Guilt and disgust squirmed inside me, knowing I'd played a part the last time her flesh was sliced open. A small bandage covered the cut on her wrist where Heath's tracker burrowed inside her. I should have seen to her injury last night, but Twain must have given the bandage to her. I was an ass.

In my hand, the MedScan hummed as it analyzed Evan's blood. A few moments later, the device displayed its diagnosis: *sepsis*.

Blood poisoning.

Twain and I exchanged a worried look. We'd seen this happen before. It was common in the Wildlands, where a simple cut could become damn dicey if it got infected. Where nothing stopped the slow march of death once it latched on to a body. This never happened in the Citadel.

I cradled Evan's arm in my lap and unwrapped the cloth bandage on her arm.

"Oh man." Twain inhaled sharply.

"Mierda."

A six-inch cut gaped open, partially covered by a brownish-green paste. Red rimmed the swollen skin around the gash, and streaks of red migrated from the wound. She was already in danger.

"Call Carlton. And Simone," I said.

"Shouldn't we take her to the hospital?" Twain asked.

"You want this to pop up in the system? They do an intake, and this will show up. They'll start asking questions about why a new Obligor looks like she's been in a knife fight. About her new employer. About me."

Beside me, Evan tensed. A muted sob escaped her lips, and a single tear leaked from beneath her eyelid. Without thinking, I wiped the tear from her cheek.

I glanced at Twain.

"We have to find a way to remove her from the system," I said.

He stared at me like I'd grown a second head.

My gaze fell on her. "But right now, we have to keep her alive."

10

RAFE

Simone pushed off the balcony railing and blocked my path. "Tranquilo," she said, "You need to stop pacing."

I stilled and stared into the distance.

"Carlton knows what he's doing," Twain said. He stretched across a lounge chair, eating one of my almond cookies.

Simone put her hand on my cheek. "You also need to stop feeling responsible for saving the world, hermano. That's how you got into this situation to begin with."

"I had to do something. We created Blackwell. Whoever he hurts because of his status is on us. I didn't intend to sign up for a years-long commitment."

Twain snorted. "He's already attached."

"I'm simply attached to the idea that no one dies under our roof," I said, pacing away.

Twain opened his mouth to reply, but Carlton interrupted.

"She's stabilized," he said, pulling his suit jacket on. He'd arrived dressed for work, with a dark suit and sea-green shirt that complemented his youthful brown skin. "She should be in a hospital where we can monitor her, but under the circumstances, this will have to do."

"Blood poisoning?" I asked.

"Afraid so. Pretty aggressive infection in that wound. The lash marks are old, so they aren't a concern—"

"What?" All three of us spoke.

"You didn't know?" Carlton asked, his brows creasing.

"No," I said.

"Someone flogged her, but I couldn't say when. The scars are well healed. She also has bruising along her spine, contusion on her arm, and lacerations on her face. Oh, and some burn scars on her palms. Also old."

"Who would have done that to her?" Twain said, sitting up.

"You can ask her when she wakes."

"She will wake?" he asked. All humor had drained from his face. I wasn't the only one who cared if she survived.

"With rest and medicine, she should be fine. I've cleaned and sealed the wound. She has an IV drip with the strongest antibiotics you can buy. You'll need to administer new doses daily into the IV for the next week," he said. "I'll show you how to change the IV fluids and administer the drug before I leave. I gave her some pain medication that will make her sleep for a while. Just keep an eye on her."

"I owe you, man," I said. "I can't thank you enough."

"This was the young woman you won over my cousin at the Expo, right?" Carlton asked.

"Yes." So, he had recognized me.

"Be careful. I'm afraid Barney...uh, Jerome, can be vindictive. He doesn't like to lose. I think you'll be fine because he values self-preservation above all else, but if he sees a way to retaliate, he will. I'm sorry—I should never have sent him your way."

"No, man. You've been good to us. You're not responsible for him," I said.

"I'd better go before someone starts asking where I've been."

"Carlton, one more thing. Can you remove a beacon?" I asked.

Twain cocked his eyebrow.

"I can, but not without setting off alarms."

Nodding, I thought for a moment. "Let me work on that part and get back to you."

"I'd be very interested in your findings," Carlton said, a grin crinkling his smooth cheeks. He was one of our first and most loyal clients, trusting that a couple of teenagers could work magic. And we did. Carlton had come from the bowels of the Imperial Hospital, watching and learning in anonymity as he'd cleaned up vomit and feces. After a formal education, he'd earned his place as one of the top research physicians in the Empire. He had access to information and resources beyond our wildest dreams.

Like us, he didn't care for the way the Conq treated those who could not afford his grandeur. Still, I suspected he'd sampled the Fount more than once. He must have been in his early thirties, but he looked a decade younger, the same as the day we met. Knowing him, any venture to the Fount had been motivated by science. He wanted to understand how it worked.

Simone showed him out. Twain watched as she crossed into the living room with her arm tucked into Carlton's. I felt for Twain. Carlton was a more likely suitor for Simone. But even he didn't stand a chance. Simone's heart was shuttered, her flirting an illusion. She wanted nothing to do with romance of any kind.

I leaned on the railing and stared at the ocean. Evan's mysterious past haunted me. I wanted to know the secrets beneath her wounds, what desperation had spurred her to risk bartering her life. It had become important to me. I couldn't say why. An entire epic had been etched in battle scars across Evan's body, but I couldn't decipher the language. How had she survived the Wildlands and made it to the Citadel? What wrought the fierce stubbornness that drove her to carry on, despite the pain, the exhaustion? She never complained, never backed down.

It was unfathomable.

Twain joined me at the railing. "What have you got in mind?" he asked.

"Is it possible to crack into the Prime Registry and remove evidence of our contract? Dismantle the tracking link on their end? Erase both of us from their records?"

Twain grinned. "*To the timid and hesitating, everything is impossible because it seems so.* Sir Walter Scott said that. Rafe, my friend, we are neither timid nor hesitating. You, especially. Of course it's possible."

"Possible today?"

"I'll clear my schedule." He laughed and patted my back. "Looks like you're keeping her after all."

My smile faded.

"No, Twain. I'm setting her free."

11

EVANGELINE

*A*wareness came slowly. The fog peeled back layer by layer. Sound came first, a faint hum of activity. Then light bleeding through my eyelids. The warm press of blankets. Feeling returning to my fingers and toes. Then the unpleasant throbbing in my arm. I blinked away the sleep and squinted at the morning light. How long had I been out? Everything ached, every inch felt weighted.

How did I get here?

It came to me. The kitchen. Cooking breakfast. My employer catching me. I tossed the covers aside and sat up. The motion made me woozy, and I startled at the man sleeping in a chair next to my bed, his bare feet propped on the mattress. Rafael Roldan.

I pulled the blankets to cover me. The movement sent a shock of pain up my arm, and I hissed. I spotted a clear tube tethered to my hand, held in place by a bandage. Something was piercing the skin of my hand. My stomach squirmed with nausea. The tube connected to a bag of clear liquid hanging from a metal stand. Dripping down the tube. Into my body. I clawed at the bandage covering the tube, ignoring the pain and the gray pushing at the edges of my vision.

"Hey, whoa, don't do that."

Roldan's hand covered mine, the clamp of his fingers stilling me. The thing under my skin pushed deeper into my flesh, and I gasped.

"Get this thing out of me."

"Evan, calm down."

"Take it out." I tugged my hand, but he wouldn't let go.

"Evan, stop. You're going to hurt yourself." He reached for my face with his free hand and forced me to look at him. Concern marked his face.

"It's medicine. You have blood poisoning. This saved your life."

I stopped struggling, but he didn't let go.

"You were trying to get rid of me," I said.

Roldan released my face and made a half smile, half frown that was full of pity. "Oh Evan, you thought I was trying to poison you?"

"What am I supposed to think? You don't want me around. I have no idea what you might do."

I pulled my hand free, and he let me. He smiled then, a self-satisfied, annoying grin, like I was a ninny and he was humoring me. I wanted to slap the smirk from his face. Yet if he spoke the truth, he'd saved my life, and I needed him to let me stay.

"I do not hurt people. Well, not physically anyway." His expression was open, relaxed, and there was no sign of the grumpy oaf from before. His smile made little bubbles scatter in my stomach. It was like he knew something I didn't. I didn't like it.

"Why were you sleeping here?" I asked.

His face darkened. "You were tossing in your sleep, and I was afraid you'd rip your IV out. Without that antibiotic, you might not have woken up."

A wave of dizziness rolled through me, and I braced myself to keep from tumbling over.

"Thank you, Mr. Roldan…for taking care of me."

I was humbled at what he'd done. At the fact that I needed his help. Relying on others, needing someone else was not a place of comfort.

"It's Rafael, and I have one big rule—no one dies under my roof."

"Happy I could abide. When can I remove this?"

"In a few days. Doctor's orders."

A few days? Shackled to this thing? I rubbed my forehead and buried the frustration welling inside.

"It was a pretty serious infection," he said. "You've been out for an entire day."

A long moment of silence stretched between us. He wanted to ask something but hesitated. I stared out the window, hoping he would leave.

He didn't.

"Evan, who did this to you?"

I froze, not wanting to remember. Not wanting to answer. Why did he care? I was a servant, meant to be invisible, insignificant. I wanted that barrier to stay firmly in place. He deserved an answer, though. He'd nursed me back from the brink of death.

I met his gaze as an overwhelming tiredness consumed me. I rubbed my eyes. "A Feral attacked me in the Wildlands."

Rafael's eyes widened. "You're lucky to be alive."

"I'm aware," I said, raising my bandaged arm.

"Where were you coming from?"

It was the one question I didn't want to answer. I didn't want my family connected to me, not until I had the money I needed and could find a safe way to bring Juniper to the Citadel. I'd done nothing illegal, but it felt dangerous to bring my family into this, at least until I knew what I was dealing with.

"You can answer freely. I've no love for the Conquistador or his regime. Your past is safe with me."

I had no way of knowing if that was true. It didn't matter that he'd saved my life. I couldn't gamble my family's lives on misplaced trust.

"All I can say is that I hiked through the Wildlands alone and I was attacked the day of the Expo."

I didn't want to go into details, to relive what happened. The horror was still fresh, and I wanted it buried in a dark, dusty corner of my mind.

Rafael kept probing, dragging the parts of the story out bit by bit. "Not to be indelicate," he said, "but how did you get the marks on your back? And your hands?"

Words wouldn't form in my head. I stared at him, mouth half-open. How did he know about my scars? What had he done while I'd been unconscious?

He lifted his palm to calm me. "I didn't see... That is, the doctor examined you—he found them."

A man had inspected me, touched me, and I'd had no say over it. It didn't matter that he was a doctor. I had no idea who he was. I felt naked and exposed like the day a soldier had ripped my shirt open in front of everyone I knew and Commander Bane had flogged me. Heat surged in my cheeks.

"I didn't mean to upset you," Rafael said.

"It's time I made myself useful and earned my keep," I said. "Could I have my clothes? I'd like to get dressed."

I scooted to the edge of the bed, disregarding the dark spots sparking before my eyes.

"Evan, no."

I ignored him and stretched my feet to the floor. "Where's my dress?"

"I can bring you something new to wear from the wardrobe, but you have to stay in bed."

I pushed myself to standing. Rafael stood and blocked my way. His fingers clenched and unclenched at his sides.

"The doc says you have to rest. You can't work. If we're lucky, it'll only take a week before you get your strength back. Look at you. You can barely stand without swaying."

I stood my ground, wobbly as it was. I couldn't laze around for a week and do nothing. The terms of the Obligor agreement required me to work a month before I could access any money. I needed to earn my pay. After that, I had to convince Rafael to allow me to leave long enough to get Juniper and bring her to the Citadel. I wasn't sure how I'd manage that, but I'd get to that problem when the time came. Juni was running out of time.

"I'd like the dress I wore yesterday, please."

A sound much like a growl came out of Rafael's mouth. "I'll find you a new damn dress. Now get back in bed."

This man had trampled the last of my patience and ground it to dust. Something acid stirred in my gut and hardened into steel. I met his glare and let my temper get the best of me.

"I don't want a new dress. I want mine. I can't sit here and do nothing. I don't have time to waste."

Rafael grasped my shoulders and pressed down. The rage-fueled strength holding me upright buckled, and so did I. I sank onto the bed. He stooped to meet my gaze. It reminded me of when I was little and Pa would grab my cheeks and lock eyes to make sure he had my attention.

"I don't know what the hell is wrong with you," Rafael said. His warm hands burned through my cotton nightgown. "Maybe whatever trauma you went through has fried your brain. Maybe you have a death wish. If you want so desperately to help, then stay in the damn bed."

Rafael released me and stalked away. He scratched the furrow in his brow with a thumbnail and kept muttering, but I caught words such as "stubborn," "stupid dress," and a few colorful phrases I wouldn't dare to repeat. All at once my body felt unbearably heavy, my mind numb. I was so tired. I lay down and rolled toward the window.

Behind me, Rafael sighed.

"The dress belonged to my mother. She married my father wearing it."

I didn't know why I said it. Rafael was rude and exhausting, and he didn't want me here. I didn't want him to know anything about me. Our stories, the ones that mattered, held a kind of power. They could build a bridge, or they could be a weapon aimed back at us. I didn't want to give Rafael anything he could hold against me. I'd already given him too much of my life. He couldn't have the rest.

Rafael sank into the chair. "I'm sorry," he said through a deep sigh. "I'll find out what Twain did with it."

"Thank you."

He sat quiet for several minutes. Again, I waited for him to walk out. Again, he didn't.

"I need to know something, Evan."

I didn't answer.

"Why did you sign up for the Expo? What was so important you would take your chances in the Wildlands and sell your life like this? Help me understand."

I'd stewed long on how much to tell my future employer. The Expo was a long-standing, legal tradition, one that was even encouraged—a badge of honor in the Citadel. My father, however, worked for the Conquistador. We'd never been ordered to stay on the farm, but any perceived weakness in my father's ability to manage might be frowned upon by the Guardia. You never knew what might set them off. It felt dangerous sharing our connection to the Conquistador.

And something else bothered me more: Rafael and Twain wore disguises in public and used fake names. I wasn't even sure those were their real names. These men were involved in something illegal. I had no idea if Rafael and his friends would use whatever I told them against me. I couldn't trust them, and I wasn't willing to take a chance.

"It doesn't matter," I said, voice calm. "I just need to get well and earn my payment."

Rafael released a gruff sigh. The chair scraped the floor, and he stalked out of the room, slamming the door behind him.

12

RAFE

our days had passed. Four days of learning nada about the stranger under my roof. Even Simone tried to dig for some intel under the guise of "girl time" and helping Evan get cleaned up, but the woman wouldn't budge. Evan was infuriatingly polite, stubborn and tight-lipped, which only stoked my curiosity. I was intrigued, more and more each day, much to my annoyance. So I kept my distance, except to feed and medicate her, and counted the minutes until Carlton declared her healed. I wouldn't rest until she was gone. No one belonged under my roof if I couldn't trust them.

Twain was on the cusp of erasing our Obligor contract from the Imperial databases. He'd found a way to delete it but discovered evidence that the data had been duplicated. He was on a treasure hunt to destroy the backup and prevent any other duplications. As soon as he had it, he'd delete all files, and we'd be free and clear.

"Ow!" Twain glared from his workstation.

"You felt that?"

I stared at my invention in progress and frowned. The

Tagget was designed to propel a transparent tracking beacon onto an unsuspecting person or object. At least that was the goal. The propulsion mechanism needed tweaking so a hit didn't feel like being thumped. I had yet to manage the right balance.

"You almost took my eye out," Twain said, peeling the small disc from his cheek. "Why bother with the propulsion right now? When you add the audio component, you'll have to recalibrate for the extra weight."

The idea had come from watching Heath insert a beacon under Evan's skin. My design was meant to track a target and pick up an audio feed. What intel could I get from tagging the Conq or Bane with a beacon? Enough to help the Scythe of Thorns knock the Conq off his throne? I could only hope. I'd be happy provide the spark that razed his whole shitshow to the ground.

Still, Twain had a point. My tinkering was pointless until I resolved the audio, and I couldn't work on the Wreckus until the last of my parts arrived. I'd been dabbling to distract myself, nothing more. I told him as much.

"Look, things are coming to a head," Twain said. "I'm probably within a day of figuring this out. Carlton will be here soon, and odds are he'll remove the IV. It's time to figure out when to pull the trigger on your vanishing act and map out our next moves. That's your specialty. So go, do your thing."

"Message received. I'll stop distracting you."

I left my device on the workbench and wandered into the living room. Movement on the balcony caught my attention. Evan was kneeling, her IV stand beside her, pouring water into a large pot holding a banana plant and a withered nest of unidentifiable flora. The early afternoon sun shone on her, igniting the amber in her hair. She wore the dress from the day of the Expo. It was clean and simple, out of place in the Citadel, and the sight of her in it stoked a feeling of protectiveness in my gut. A feeling that didn't belong there.

I shook it away and pushed the door open. Warm air enveloped me, and the sun brushed my cheeks. Evan startled, splashing water onto her skirt, and cradled the pitcher against her stomach as if she'd been caught stealing.

"Is this a commentary on my abilities as a plant parent?" I asked, mouth quirking.

"No, not at all," she said. "I would never... It's habit."

"The doc should be here soon."

"I'll be glad to be rid of this pole." Evan set the pitcher on a side table and peered over the railing at the ocean below. "It's so beautiful here." Her gaze swept the landscape, consuming it with a childlike wonder. "Like paradise."

She had that right, at least one level. Nothing in the world compared to the Citadel. Foreign cities were crowded, concrete mazes. The Citadel was a monument to beauty and nature. Traffic and smog didn't exist here. Our transpod system operated in underground tunnels using clean, soundless technology. Every inch of the city was designed to steal your breath and inspire awe. Each nook held a jewel: gazebos, cozy fire pits, canopied swings, flowering arches, oak-tunneled promenades, serene ponds, and countless other vignettes of staged beauty. A crystal blue river flowed through the Citadel, crowned with footbridges of wrought iron and river stone. In the center stood the crown jewel—the Conq's palace, his monument to self-indulgence and hubris.

"It's everything money and power can buy," I said, coming to stand beside her. "Paint your world as beautiful as you please. Sweep anything unbecoming outside the walls."

"I never imagined a place like this existed," Evan said. "We heard stories growing up, but your imagination can only go so far."

I looked at her, surprised at the reference to her past. She realized her error and quickly changed the subject.

"So, where's the Fount?" she asked, glancing away.

"Come," I said, taking charge of her IV pole. She followed me to the northern balcony.

"There." A castle dominated the far horizon, its white stone towers and turrets rising into the sky like something out of a medieval fairytale.

"That's the Conq's palace. He's holding the Fount captive inside his fortress, trapped behind a fifty-foot wall of stone."

"It's in the palace?"

"Surrounded by it. About one hundred or so acres of Florida wilderness are caged in the center of the palace. The Conq built his castle around it. You could see it from an airplane if the Guardia allowed planes to fly over Florida, but they don't."

"What's an airplane?"

Holy hell. Where did this woman come from?

"Well, it's like a transpod that can fly over long distances."

She shot me a look reeking of disbelief.

"Really."

Her gaze traveled to the palace, and she studied it in silence. "You've been there?" she asked after a while.

I hesitated. That was a time in my life I didn't want to remember. I'd been a different person then, in more ways than one.

"You have," she said, studying me.

I neither confirmed nor denied it. But she took my silence as confirmation.

"Have you been Immersed?"

I had to stop this.

"It was a long time ago," I said.

"How did you get inside? What was it like?"

Dammit. My carelessness had opened the floodgates. I needed to lock them down. "It's hard to describe."

Hard to explain how a place, a simple stretch of earth and water and air, could creep inside you, shake you to the core, and reform you by standing in its presence. How stepping inside the walled garden was like touching the veil of heaven. Every acre of that place was not of this world.

"I doubt that," she said.

Her words drew me out of my daze. "What?"

"Surely you could give me some idea of what it's like."

"Hold on...are you serious? After keeping silent for nearly a week, now you want to do a Q-and-A session?" Frustration swelled like a tidal wave, peaking and ready to crash down on her. "You want answers?" I asked, leaning in. "You. First."

Evan stiffened and glared at me. She reached for her IV pole and stepped away from the railing. I grabbed her wrist and pulled her to a stop.

"Don't do that again," I said. No more letting her silence slide.

"Do what?"

"Shut down. Walk away. You've been here for nearly a week, and I haven't a clue who you are."

She jerked her arm free.

"Why do you care?" she asked. "We're both hiding things. You wear disguises, use fake names. What are you hiding from? Who are you hiding from? You don't want to share your secrets —neither do I."

We scowled at each other, anger radiating between us. She had a point. I hated that she had a point. I was two seconds from telling her it didn't matter, that as long as she stayed in my home, she owed me the truth, but I was distracted by the flush of red painting her cheeks. Which infuriated me even more.

Evan waited for a response, her lips drawn into an accusatory pucker. I opened my mouth but closed it for fear I might threaten to toss her over the balcony. She wheeled around and marched off, pole clattering behind her. She came to an abrupt halt at the door.

"Evangeline, so good to see you up and about." A silken female voice wafted from the living room.

Evan stepped back, allowing Simone onto the balcony. Carlton followed close behind.

"There's my patient," the doctor said, squinting in the sunlight.

An awkward silence stretched between us.

"Did we interrupt something?" Simone asked.

"No, not at all," I said, sliding a glance at Evan. She watched Carlton with wary eyes.

"This is Carlton Shires, your doctor," Simone said.

"Pleasure to meet you, Evan," he said.

She hesitated before saying, "Nice to meet you, too."

"I think Evan's had enough of this," Simone said, pointing to the IV. "Can it be removed?"

"Let's check our patient first," Carlton said. "Evan, if you'll have a seat."

Simone gave me a knowing elbow to the ribs as he took Evan's vitals and a blood sample with the MedScan. It was uncanny how Simone could read my mood in seconds. Within a few minutes, Carlton declared Evan clean of infection.

"I'm going to give you an oral antibiotic that you'll need to take twice a day until the bottle is empty," he said. "If you have any trouble or feel sick again, let Rafe know, and I'll come back to check on you."

"Thank you, Dr. Shires," she said. "I appreciate it."

Carlton began packing the MedScan into his bag. "I brought the other supplies if you still think she needs it," he said, glancing my way.

For a moment, I drew a blank. Then I remembered. I'd asked Carlton if he could erase Evan's injuries. We didn't know the protocol for the Obligor inspection, but if the Guardia conducted a physical examination and found evidence of a flogging, it would draw unwanted attention.

"What are you talking about?" Evan asked.

"Carlton can remove the marks from your back," I said. "And possibly the burn marks on your palms."

The red on Evan's cheeks deepened, and she folded her arms across her body. Then it dawned on me. Only days before, she'd been mortified to learn she'd been examined while unconscious.

"That's not necessary," she said.

"Hear me out," I said. "There's a good reason."

"I'm fine," she said, shooting a withering scowl my direction.

"Rafe's trying to help," Simone said.

"That's not the kind of help I need," she said.

"Then what is?" I rubbed my brow in frustration and paced, knowing she wouldn't answer.

"Rafe is concerned about the Obligor inspection next week," Carlton said. "None of us knows what's involved, but if you go to the inspection with those marks, they may start asking questions. If you wish to keep your anonymity, then distinguishing marks like these are not helpful. They're dangerous."

Evan met Carlton's eyes, and then she looked to me, brows raised. I nodded in agreement.

"What do you need to do?" she asked.

"It's an easy procedure and, with anesthesia, virtually painless. We use a medical device to buff out the scars and restore your skin to normal. It will look red and may be sore for two or three days afterward, but it should be clear by inspection time if we do it today. I'll use a local anesthesia to block the pain, and I'll give you a sedative to relax. It'll probably make you sleepy and you may feel a little off or loopy. If I were at the hospital, I could induce you to sleep for the procedure, but not here."

"Loopy?" Evan asked, ignoring everything else he'd said.

"Yes, you might have trouble focusing or thinking," he said. "But it will help with the pain."

The wheels cranked in her head, spinning wildly. She was terrified of losing control, of spilling a secret.

"Evan, that doesn't matter. Getting rid of the scars is crucial. It must be done," I said.

She stewed on it for a few long moments and then rose from the chaise lounge.

"Let's get this over with," Evan said.

13

EVANGELINE

*T*he transpod tunneled through the earth like a mole. Twain drove, while I dug fingers into my seat and tried to breathe my heart into stillness. Two or three times, another transpod passed from the opposite direction, glowing faintly in the darkness, black windows masking those inside.

"You know, worrying is like paying interest on trouble before it happens," Twain said, breaking the silence. "William Ralph Inge said something like that once."

"Who?" I asked.

"Some dead guy."

"Oh."

The quiet fell again. My mind stuck on the approaching Obligor inspection. I was glad my scars were gone. All of them. I'd almost said no to removing the scars on my palms. They'd become important. A reminder to look before I leaped. To be cautious, and stop doing stupid things that got people hurt. Or killed.

Like Mama.

Grief struck me like a kick in the chest. The memory of her lying in bed, languishing in that deep, unknowing sleep—until days later, when she stopped breathing. Stopped being. I closed my eyes for a moment and drew in a breath.

"People do this all the time," Twain said at last. "We're going to be fine."

In the Citadel's unwritten rules, it was unseemly for an employer to escort his Obligor to an inspection, so they routinely sent another servant. Twain played that role. His disguise consisted of thick horn-rimmed glasses and a wig with a long black ponytail. When I'd asked why he needed a disguise, he'd offered little, saying, *It's best for everyone if no one recognizes me.* His nonanswer did nothing to ease the worry bees buzzing in my belly.

"So, you're saying I don't need to worry?" I replied.

Twain hesitated. "Worry is one of the most useless emotions on the planet. It holds no power to change the future but is a master at prolonging suffering," he said.

"Easy for you to say," I said.

"I know. I'm as tense as a cat hanging from a tree by its claws."

I spit out a laugh. A grin spread across Twain's lips and lit his eyes. It felt good to laugh, to smile without effort, even if it didn't last.

Two minutes later, we glided into an underground space filled with a scattering of transpods. We sat for a moment. Neither of us wanted to walk into a Guardia building and offer ourselves up like a sacrifice. Sitting in the dark, Twain's hand encircled mine and gave a gentle squeeze. He let go and opened the doors.

"Remember—eyes down, obedient, invisible. That's the goal," Twain said. "Avoid drawing attention."

"Got it."

An elevator carried us to the main floor of the Guardia Inspection Center. Several people waited inside the large white entry area. At the far end of the room, a red-jacketed guard manned a desk and motioned us over. Twain began to speak, but the guard silenced him.

"You, sit over there," he said, pointing to Twain. Then to me. "You, through those doors."

I glanced at Twain as if he could save me.

"Now, not later," the guard barked.

I walked past him and noticed my face floating on a glass panel in front of him. The image had been taken the day of the Expo, my face scratched and pale. The guard swiped a finger on the edge of the screen, and the image vanished. Behind him, the entrance opened, and he waved me inside.

The door slammed shut behind me. A bearded man with close-cropped hair, glasses, and a scowl motioned me forward. He held a clipboard, and his white jacket and pants blended with walls of the same hue. Stalls lined one of side of the room, flanked by guards armed with rifles. The booths were made of glass, with white trim matching the stark walls. The room smelled faintly of sweat and bleach. At the booth on the far end, a large man—one I recognized from the Expo—stooped, bare-chested, to remove his britches. His shirt and shoes rested in a pile by his feet. In the closest stall, a woman wore nothing but her underwear and bra. Her shoulders curved inward, and her arms shielded her chest. A chill needled my spine.

"You. There." The clipboard man gestured to a booth with his pen. I moved, but my feet felt like they were wading through molasses.

"Quickly," the man barked. "Clothes off, down to your undergarments. Stand in the Vita-Scan. Back to the wall, hands at your sides."

Anything he'd said after *Clothes off* hit a wall in my brain. I froze, my mind refusing to obey.

"Do not make me repeat myself," he said. One guard shifted his weapon and eyed me.

Avoid drawing attention.

I loosened the top button of my dress and stood in front of a stall. All eyes watched, including the male Obligor. I scowled at him, and he looked away.

I stared at the wall as I shed my clothes. If the Guardia intended to humiliate me, it wasn't going to happen. I'd grown to accept a certain degree of immodesty over the last two weeks, but good intentions had been at the heart of those instances. Whatever this was, it was full of dark intent. I'd play the game. I'd get through this, and it would not crush me. I had too far to go to let that happen.

"Obligors, step into the Vita-Scan," the clipboard man instructed. "Backs to the wall, palms flat on the glass behind you."

I entered the stall. My hands touched the glass, and the next instant, a tug of air sucked my palms flat against the surface. Something metallic curved around my wrists like shackles. My hands were trapped. I breathed deep through a rising panic.

"Resist the urge to move," the clipboard man said. "The less you move, the faster the scan will be over."

"What is this?" The other woman screeched like an alarm. She tugged at her bonds.

"Relax," the man drawled. "It's taking your palm print, some DNA, and a few other data points. You'll live."

I stood motionless as the machine did its work. The glass side panels reflected a subtle blade of blue light gliding up and down my backside. A needle pricked my finger, and I flinched. Seconds later, something cold and hard came from behind and grabbed my neck. Icy metal fingers wrapped my throat like they might choke me. The metal pressed against my flesh, swelling until it immobilized my head. Panic clogged my throat, and I gasped for air. My neighbors uttered frightened gasps.

"Stop!" the woman shouted. "I can't...breathe!"

"Silence!" The clipboard man growled, like we were an inconvenience to his sanity.

The woman quieted to muffled sobs.

The metal expanded like a cape over my shoulders and blanketed my upper arms. Dozens of needles stabbed the flesh on my left shoulder blade. My body begged to flee and my mouth opened to protest, but I steeled myself, burying a scream. The other woman did not. Her sobs grew to a horrifying series of shrieks. She bucked against the restraints. Her feet kicked fruitlessly.

The clipboard man retrieved a shiny metal rod from his pocket and jabbed the woman's stomach. She screamed as he held it there, her voice pitching higher until it cracked. The man pressed the rod deeper until the woman tensed and grew silent. Her body went limp.

I closed my eyes and bit my lip, trying to block out the steady drill of needles in my flesh. Long minutes later, the needles disappeared. The thing around my neck retreated. The cuffs on my wrists unlocked and vanished. I opened my eyes in time to see the clipboard man slap the unconscious woman hard across her face. She startled awake, gasping.

The man paced the length of us, eyeing each slowly from head to toe. He stopped in front of me. His gaze journeyed the length of my body before his eyes locked onto mine. Too late I remembered to lower my eyes.

"Hmmm... He'd enjoy you," the man said. One side of his mouth ticked up in a half smile. I had no clue what he meant.

"The Conquistador doesn't care for the uglies. His servants have to be lookers. You're his type," he said. He stood there for a long spell, as if playing a game of chicken, like Juni and I used to play. The first to blink lost. I knew I should avert my eyes, but meeting his gaze felt like my only defense. It was stupid. I lowered my eyes, and the man sauntered off, casually flipping through the pages on his clipboard.

"You may put your clothes on," he said.

I grabbed my dress and pulled it on. The woman rushed to

do the same. I froze, staring at her back, trying to deny what I already knew.

A heavy black tattoo marked the woman's shoulder where nothing had been before. I recognized the shape. I'd seen it before, at the Expo. A black lion in profile, pouncing on unseen prey. It was the Conquistador's mark.

We'd been branded with the Conquistador's symbol.

Like the Conquistador branded the cattle on our farm. I felt like I'd been kicked in the stomach. A fresh wave of horror washed through me, making me tremble.

"Quickly," the clipboard man said. "I don't have all day to waste on you."

I couldn't leave fast enough. I hurried to button the top of my dress, wincing as the fabric scratched against the tender tattooed spot on my shoulder.

"You'll have noticed you now bear the mark of His Excellency, El Conquistador. Though your employers bought your contract, the transaction was sanctioned through the graciousness of our Conquistador. As such, you are considered servants of the Empire, in his service, and, as always, subject to his edicts. This mark symbolizes this arrangement, honors this longstanding tradition, and serves as notice of His Excellency's greatness. Wear it with pride."

He stared at each of us, daring us to disagree. At last, he dismissed us.

"You are free to return to your new homes," he said.

I couldn't help but think of the irony. We were far from free. Had we ever been?

14

RAFE

idnight stretched across the sky with a riot of stars. I drank in the night canvas from the balcony, unable to find consolation in it. Tension thrummed beneath my skin. I'd needed a break from working on the Wreckus, a breath of fresh air to decipher why it wasn't working, but instead of puzzling out the wonky ignition component, my brain kept circling back to the gift Rod had left on my doorstep last night. A hand scythe. The message couldn't be any clearer: My Scythe of Thorns contact had discovered where I lived. He knew where to find me if things went astray. If I failed.

It wasn't just my life on the line now.

How had I let this happen?

And then there was Carlton. He'd been due to arrive after dinner, but midnight had come and gone, and he'd yet to show. Messages to his Convo had gone unanswered.

To top it off, something was wrong with Evan. Three days had passed since Twain escorted her to the Guardia Inspection Center. Three strange days. Each time we landed in the same room, she felt too close, too in my space. I couldn't relax with her around. It wasn't her fault. Evan was the most unobtrusive person within these walls. She buried herself in her work, cleaning corners and surfaces that had never seen the caress of a rag the entire time I'd lived here. When I thought she'd run out of tasks, she'd find something else to do, and she'd do it without complaint, without instruction. Without needing anything or anyone else.

But something had changed. I couldn't pick loose the threads yet, but she'd come back from the inspection somehow diminished. She'd skated across the details, mentioning the Vita-Scan and the biometric information they'd collected, but after that she'd withdrawn. I should have been glad for the distance, but I wasn't. Something dark was stirring inside her, and I longed to understand it. Something had happened, and whatever it was, it wasn't good. It reinforced the need to free both of us from this vile system—the sooner, the better.

Twain had made that possible. He'd dug to the bottom of the rabbit hole this morning. Finding Eve Smith and Adam Riegel in the Imperial Prime Registry's Obligor catalogue had been easy. Evan's description of the data the Inspection Center had collected had helped. Worming into the information warehouse had been a bit more difficult, but Twain had done it, and he'd erased all of it. Every record, original and backup, was gone. Evan and I no longer existed in the eyes of the Citadel. When the one-year follow-up arrived, the Obligor inspectors wouldn't miss Evan one bit, and there would be no crumbs leading to me. I'd called Carlton the moment I'd found out. Removing and destroying Evan's beacon was the last step.

My brain thumbed through the worst-case scenarios for Carlton's radio silence. Getting caught. The Guardia discovering he was helping us. Long ago, Twain and I had assembled two rolling trunks as go-bags if we ever had to abandon the Phoenix Nest and scuttle our operations, but I hoped that day hadn't come. Hoped it never would.

I stared at the stars for a good half hour, refereeing

warring voices in my head. I didn't regret saving Evan from Blackwell's grubby paws, but it was stupid given my history and my current endeavors. It was smart to scrub Evan from my life, but a tiny irrational part of me wanted something different. Something more. Had grown to like the puzzle that was Evan. She was strong, stubborn, and brave in a way that made me think of Twain and Simone. Of how my friends sacrificed and risked for something more than themselves. I just didn't know what that "more" was for Evan. Why she was fighting so hard.

The door alarm sounded, and my heart leapt in my throat. No one came knocking unannounced at this hour. I sprinted for the living room. The door's image screen revealed a man dressed in a black running suit with a backpack strapped over his shoulders. Carlton.

I jerked the door open and motioned him inside.

"Sorry if I woke you," Carlton said. He was out of breath, and sweat dotted his forehead.

"I was up. You run into any trouble?"

"Don't think so," he said, wiping his brow. "Sorry about the hour, but I didn't know if I'd be able to come tomorrow without someone taking notice."

"What do you mean?"

"I must be doing my job too well," Carlton said. "Someone deemed me worthy of summoning to the Conquistador's house for his monthly checkup, right as I left to come here. I'm not sure what happened to his personal physician and didn't ask. When the Conquistador wants a routine checkup in the middle of the night, you go, and you don't ask questions. He wanted to have a drink afterward. It would have been rude to decline."

"And deadly. The man likes to have his way."

"I'm not sure how much I'm on the radar now. I don't know if they're looking to replace his regular doctor or why they asked for me," he said. "They could be watching me—I don't know. I thought it best if I didn't transport here, so I came on foot. I didn't want to risk being tracked through the tunnels."

I whistled low. "That's a long way."

"Yeah, good thing I run long distance for fun," Carlton said. "Listen, I'm sorry. I can do it now or come another time, but I'm not sure when it would be."

There was no question. Wait and risk being linked to the system again through Evan's beacon, or wake her and finish this. I'd not had a chance to prep her for Carlton's visit. It would take some explaining, but it was for the best.

I pointed Carlton to the bathroom where he could wash up and went to wake Evan.

No answer came when I knocked. I eased open her door and found Evan lost in sleep, dreaming and unguarded. Her nightgown's décolletage revealed her slender neck and a narrow swell of breasts. One sleeve had fallen down her arm, baring the smooth skin of her shoulder. Her head tilted toward the window, and the bright moon bathed her face in milky dream light. For a tiny second, an ember stirred in my belly. I had the strongest urge to kiss her awake.

I almost ran from the room.

Instead, I rubbed my face and gently shook her shoulder. "Evan, wake up," I whispered.

Eyes closed, she turned her head toward my voice. A small smile pulled at the corners of her mouth.

"Hey...wake up," I repeated, giving her shoulder another small push.

Her eyes darted open, and the smile disappeared. She scooted into a sitting position. She registered my pajama pants and bare chest, and her hand rushed to push her nightgown sleeve over her shoulder. Heat rose in my cheeks.

"What's wrong?" she asked.

"Nothing. I need to tell you something. Something important."

"What?"

I'd spooked her. It was clear from the look on her face.

"Nothing bad. This is good news."

The apprehension remained.

"Carlton's here. I expected him earlier, but work kept him," I said. Her brows pinched together, not understanding.

"He's going to remove your beacon," I said, more bluntly than intended.

She flinched as if I'd snapped my fingers and woken her from a trance.

"Don't worry—the Guardia will never know. Twain erased us from the system," I said. "Come time for the yearly inspection, they'll never know you're missing."

Evan's mouth opened as if to speak, but nothing came out.

"You're free," I said. I smiled to reinforce the good news.

"What have you done?" Her voice trembled inside whispered words. Her eyes shone with tears.

"Hey, this is good," I said, sitting beside her. I placed my hand on her arm reassuringly. She stared at it.

"It means you can go home to your family. You don't have to be indentured to me or anyone else."

"No, no, no, no..." The words came out more like a moan than fully formed speech. "She'll die," she said. Or at least that was what I thought she said.

The next second, she shoved my chest. Her hands struck once, twice, a third time. She screamed, called me a murderer.

"Stop! Evan...stop. What are you talking about?"

My words inflamed her, and she lashed out with her fists. I grabbed at her wrists to stop her, but she was a tornado ripping up trees. I lost my balance and fell, pulling her with me. She landed atop me on the floor, and her forehead struck my nose. The pain made my eyes water, but I held on to her. One of her arms was pinned in the press of our bodies, and I clutched the other one, immobilizing it.

"For God's sake, talk to me."

I wanted to be mad at her. I wanted to shake some sense into her, but the brokenness in her eyes stilled me. She freed her arm and raised her hand to strike. I grabbed her wrist and flipped her over, pinning her arms to the floor. She thrashed beneath me, but I didn't budge. Evan let out a mournful growl and quieted. She closed her eyes as tears fell.

"Evan, I did this for you. For both of us. I didn't hurt anyone, and I certainly don't want to hurt you," I said. "Help me understand."

She glared at me.

"You've killed my sister." A fat tear emerged and rolled down her face, landing in her hair.

The accusation floored me. "I didn't even know you had a sister. How could I possibly do anything to hurt her?"

"You destroyed any chance I had to save her. I needed this. There's a reason I'm here. I'm here for her," Evan said. She pulled at her wrists. "Now get off me, you heartless bastard."

The name stung. I was not like that. My father was the heartless bastard. Not me. I'd spent the last decade of my life distancing myself from his legacy, his DNA. Trying to undermine his cruelty and be different. I'd been trying to help Evan.

I released her wrists and sat back, defeated, confused. Angry and tired of everything I said or did turning into a fight. Evan scrambled from beneath me and sat next to her bed. Her chest heaved and her cheeks flamed red. I rubbed my forehead in frustration.

"I needed that money," Evan said. "You had no right to keep it from me."

I looked at her. "Is that what this is about? The money?"

"Yes, I need the money for my sister. She'll die without it."

"Why didn't you say so to begin with? Why the secrecy? I'll give you the money whether you stay or not. That's not why I asked Twain to erase you from the system."

"Why would you do that?" she asked, confusion wrinkling her brow. "Why would you give me sixty thousand pesos for nothing?"

"Because I'm not a heartless bastard."

Evan's gaze dropped to her lap.

"If you'd trusted me the smallest bit, we could have resolved this a long time ago," I said.

"It's not that simple."

"Yes, it is. Haven't I done enough to prove I mean you no harm? That I want to help?"

"Your disguises and secrecy make it hard to trust anything," she said. "I have to protect my family. We could lose everything."

"That part of my life has nothing to do with your circumstances," I said, "but if you're worried about your family, then let me help. Tell me what you need, and we'll find a way to get it done without endangering you or me or anyone else."

Evan raised her face, wiping tears with the back of her hand. "Why would you do that?" she asked.

I sighed in frustration. "Does it matter?"

She stared at me, waiting.

"Haven't you realized by now? I'm not a fan of how the Empire operates. I detest a system that favors one human being at the expense of another. That indentures a large segment of society and leaves the rest to fend for their lives without the opportunity for betterment. That traffics in cruelty and brutality for entertainment and personal gain." I held her gaze. "For better or for worse, you're here. You need help. I'm not built to turn my back on that."

"I can't take your money without giving something in return," she said.

"I'll gladly give it to you if you'll tell me what you need it for."

"People don't do that."

"I do."

Evan's gaze dropped again. Her fingers knotted in her lap as she wrestled with whether to believe me. For a few long moments, I thought she would shut me out again.

"My sister's name is Juniper," she said quietly. "She's seven. She has cancer and will die if I don't do something. I need money to pay her way into the Fount. The sooner, the better. She doesn't have much time left."

I sucked in my breath. The noise made her look up abruptly.

"Dios, Evan," I said. "You're going to need more than sixty thousand pesos. It takes at least half a million pesos to drop a toe into the water."

15

EVANGELINE

A thrumming noise swelled inside my head. I couldn't focus. It would take a lifetime or more to work off half a million pesos. Juni would be long dead. Despite everything I'd done, I'd failed my sister. I'd risked my life, my future for nothing.

Rafael touched my arm. "Breathe."

I forced out a shaky breath.

"Ready?" The word startled both of us.

Carlton poked his head into the doorframe. "Sorry to interrupt, but I need to get home soon," he said. "Preferably without getting caught."

"Right," Rafael said, helping me up. The gentleness of his touch made me want to scream. This was bad.

Carlton had prepped an area in the kitchen. On the island lay a slender knife, a bowl, some square packages, a metal tube, and bandages. The doctor motioned me to a stool, and I sat, my head throbbing. Before I realized what he was doing, Carlton wiped my arm with something cold and wet and stuck me with a needle. I flinched. A tingle trickled up my arm.

"It's a local to numb the area," he said. "In a minute, I'm going to make a small incision in your arm. Is that all right?"

I nodded. It mattered little now.

"Why don't you tell me about home," Rafael said, trying to distract me.

I hesitated. Revealing what I'd worked so hard to keep secret felt wrong, but these people were taking their own risks in helping me.

"Nobody in this room is going to hurt you, Evan," he said. "I promise."

I took a deep breath and let it go. "I came from El Jardín."

Rafael's mouth dropped open.

"You know it?" I asked.

"It's the Conq's personal farm."

Carlton looked at Rafael. "How do you know that?" he asked.

"Let's just say it's not as big a secret as he thinks."

The doctor picked up the knife. "You're going to feel some pressure, but with the local, it shouldn't hurt," he said. "Let me know if it does."

"Okay." I focused on Rafael so I couldn't see him slice into my arm.

"You work at El Jardín?"

"Yeah, along with my father. My mother died eighteen months ago, and now Juni…"

I couldn't finish the thought. I didn't want to speak the words into the world again.

God, I missed my family.

"I'm sorry." He was quiet a moment before asking, "How did you get here?"

My thoughts scattered as Carlton poked around in my wrist. I closed my eyes to block it out and concentrate.

"Got it." A *tink* sounded in the quiet as the doctor dropped the beacon into a bowl. A red light on the bloodied capsule blinked rapidly. Rafael reached behind him, grabbed a pestle from a stone mortar, and crushed the capsule with it.

"We'll burn it for good measure, but this should stop it transmitting."

"I'm going to seal the incision site, bandage it, and we'll be done," Carlton said. A yawn escaped his mouth as he picked up the sealant.

"You were telling me about how you got here," Rafael prompted.

I gave him the short version of how I'd climbed through a hole in the wall and followed the road from a distance.

Rafael shook his head. "What happened to your back? Your hands?"

"I tried to stop the Guardia from hurting a friend," I said.

Carlton paused and stared at me. Rafael's eyebrows shot up.

"Yeah, they whipped me for that," I said. "As for my hands, I did that to myself."

Our mare's foaling time had been drawing close, and I'd gone to the barn to check on her before I went to bed.

"Mama told me to leave her be, that nature would take care of itself, but I'd grown up with this mare," I told Rafe. "She had white ankles, so I'd named her Bootsy. I wanted to be there for her first foal."

The mare had been having contractions, pacing and pawing the dirt and nipping at her sides. After cooing a few soothing words to calm her, I sat on a hay bale to wait for her water to break. I dozed off and woke to find Bootsy pounding her stall door, whinnying in distress. In my sleep, I'd knocked over my lantern. Flames had crackled through the loose hay on the ground and started licking the stall door.

"I didn't think. I just acted. I tried to put the fire out with my hands. Not a good idea," I said. "Once I came to my senses, I threw the horse blanket on the fire and put it out. I saved the barn."

My eyes fell to the newly unblemished palm in my lap.

"But?" Rafael said, voice soft.

"The foal died. Bootsy delivered while I slept. She trampled her baby trying to escape the fire. It was my fault."

"It was an accident."

"Which doesn't change the outcome."

"All done," Carlton said.

My arm was wrapped in gauze, and I hadn't noticed him doing it. Everything felt numb.

"I've got to go," the doctor said, stowing his materials in his backpack. Carlton touched my arm and said, "Trust Rafe. You're in good hands."

Maybe so, maybe not. I simply nodded.

Rafael walked Carlton to the door. When he returned, he held the silver bracelet Captain Health had given him on the day of the Expo, the one linking us together. He'd also put on a shirt.

"Let's have a mini bonfire on the balcony," he said, picking up the bowl with my beacon. He dropped his cuff inside as well and handed me the bowl. I slid off the stool, and it was like stepping into a puddle of grease. My knees gave out, and the room spun for an instant.

"Whoa...I got you," Rafael said, catching my arm and steadying me.

My hand had landed on his chest. Heat rushed through my belly, and for a brief flash, I wished his shirt wasn't there. My whole body reacted to the hardness of muscles beneath the fabric. I bit my lip and closed my eyes.

What is wrong with me?

I couldn't think about things like that. I gathered my senses and backed out of his touch. For a fleeting few seconds, it had felt good to feel something other than hopelessness and loss.

I cleared my throat. "Sorry."

"It's been quite a night," he said.

"Yeah."

Rafael grabbed a bottle from the cabinet and two glasses, and I followed him through the darkened house. Outside, the midnight sky stretched broad and blue black, pinpricked full of starlight. The cool air caressed every inch of my body. The skin along my arms dimpled as a shiver worked its way up my spine. Rafael loaded wood into a fire pit and touched a match to the kindling. Tiny orange flames licked upward, chasing newborn wisps of smoke. The musk of woodfire circled us.

"May I?" Rafael said, motioning to the bowl in my hands. I handed it to him, and he dumped the contents into the rising flame. The fire crackled and popped as it quietly consumed his offering.

"Good riddance," he said, striking his palms together as if washing his hands of something unpleasant. My breath hitched as I watched the beacon and the cuff dissolve in the fire. Watched the contract between us disintegrate. Watched the only plan I had to save my sister go up in flames.

I sank onto the lounge chair and covered my face. Rafael sat beside me. His palm settled on my forearm and pressed gently, uncovering my face.

"Here, drink this," he said, offering me a glass. I raised the drink to my mouth. Alcoholic fumes tingled my nose, but I drank it. My lips puckered as a rope of heat dropped to my belly, the warmth ironing out my raw edges. I swallowed another mouthful.

"Whoa—that stuff's as potent as petrol punch. A little at a time," Rafael said. He took the glass from my hand and placed it out of reach. "If Twain were here and not sleeping through all this, he'd say something witty like, 'Don't carve history into stone before it happens.' I don't know what to tell you, but there are always other choices, other options."

"Easy for you to say."

"Not really. It was learned the hard way."

I studied him, wondering what history lay behind that statement. He didn't give me the chance to ask.

"I know you were holding back with Carlton," Rafael said. "It's just you and me now. You have to tell me what's going on. Why are you worried about the Guardia?"

I fixed on the stars and thought about Pa, about how angry he must have been with me, how scared. At least I wasn't tethered to a stranger for a decade of my life anymore. I could go home.

"My father is the steward of the Conquistador's farm. He's in a position of trust. Any perceived misstep, like a runaway daughter, could be dangerous. You never know what will set off the Guardia. We can't afford for him to lose his position, to lose our home. We've—I've—pushed our luck about as far as we can go."

Rafael sat in silence so long that I glanced at him. He was staring blankly into the fire.

At last, he rubbed his face and peered at me, eyes haunted. "Dios, Evan, where did you see this going? You don't think you'll be missed?"

"We aren't prisoners, and leaving isn't illegal. The only thing I did wrong was break my father's rule and cross the wall. I planned to give the money I earned to my father so he could take my sister to the Fount. Then, I'd come back and finish my obligations here. But now it's impossible."

Rafael stood and stalked off. His hands clenched the top of his head. "You have no idea how this works, do you?"

I wrapped my arms around my stomach, trying to calm the new seed of fear burrowing inside. "What do you mean?"

"Your father would never be able to enter the Fount sanctuary, even if he had the money to pay for it. Neither would you."

"Why not?" My entire body went cold.

"The Fount is only accessible to an elite few who have the right combination of money and pedigree to fit the Conq's criteria. Servants aren't allowed. Outsiders are seriously vetted before they're permitted in the Fount. Your father would be well known inside the Citadel's power structure, and he would never pass the test."

This made no sense.

"That can't be. If not his own people, who?"

"Anyone in the world with enough money and prestige," he said. "Our wealthy neighbors in America are frequent fliers."

"So, he'll let someone from another country in but not his own people?"

"Yes."

The injustice of it was unfathomable, and it made me want to punch something or someone. The gap between the Citadel's fortunes and our farmstead's hardships was becoming clearer by the day.

I paced to the railing and fisted my hands on its rough surface. Below, the ocean danced back and forth across the sand in the darkness, unaware. Someone on the other side of that water could be healed by the Conquistador's Fount but not someone a two days' walk away in his own land. Not Juni. My plan never had any hope to begin with.

Tears forced their way to the surface for the second time that night. I wished my anger would sear them dry, but nothing would quench them this time.

I had to go home. Every minute away meant one less minute left with Juni.

"It's over, then. It was all for nothing," I said. The words cracked on my lips. An involuntary sob followed. I covered my mouth as if it would stop the next one coming.

A moment later, warm arms encircled me. Rafael's chin came to rest on my head. He said nothing, just held me. For once, I didn't care who he was—a boss or a stranger or something in between. I didn't care if I trusted him or not. I didn't even care about my father's rules of propriety. I folded my body into his and let him hold me, let the sobs come. I clung to him, and he let me unravel against him. We remained knitted together for a long time in the darkness, until my emotion was spent.

"I have to go home, before I'm too late," I said, stepping outside the circle of his warmth. Wishing I didn't have to. "If I can't save her, I won't waste more time away from her."

I left before I broke down again. I hurried to my room, where I could dissolve in private. My hand was on the door-knob when I heard his voice behind me.

"Don't leave," he said. "Give me a day or two. I can't promise anything, but I'll try to find a way."

16

RAFE

*W*hat had I been thinking? I had the perfect opportunity to send Evan home, and I'd asked her stay. I was losing my damn mind. Doubling down on recklessness.

I couldn't sleep thinking about Evan and her sister. I'd never had a sibling. My mother had died when I was young. An aneurism stole her life in a blink, and she was gone before my father could drag her body anywhere near the Fount. The spring's magic didn't include last-ditch resurrections. Dear old Papi had never remarried, never procreated again, not even little bastards. He'd had children before me, but, like my mother, they'd been too far from the Fount's help when death came calling. My birth was a rarity. That's because the Fount's twisted magic came at a cost: your fertility. It was the best form of birth control around, and people who wanted children abstained from its magical waters for at least a year. My father didn't like to forgo his regular soaks in the Fount, so frankly, I was surprised he was even able to have me. The old man had been dunked so many times, his balls had probably shriveled up completely.

My father was my only living blood relative, but Twain and Simone were more family than he'd ever been. If one of them became terminally sick, I'd raze mountains to see them healed. Didn't a seven-year-old girl deserve the same thing?

I gave up on sleep somewhere around four in the morning and trudged to the lab, powered up the computer, and began searching. I didn't know what I was looking for, only what I needed. Pesos. Lots of them. At least half a million. More, to cover my tab at the Sink. Pilfering from the Imperial Bank was still far out of reach. That left what? Good old-fashioned thievery?

Crime statistics weren't public in the Citadel, but if I had to guess, the number of burglaries perpetrated inside the city walls was so low it was virtually nonexistent. During the years Twain and I had supported ourselves through B and Es, we'd likely been the only blip on the radar. Few criminals would risk dismemberment or permanent imprisonment by raiding Citadel homes and taking its citizens' precious treasures. We'd left those risky days behind for a good reason.

And yet...what other choice was there? Evan and I both needed money—fast.

I navigated to a site I hadn't thought of in years. The Imperial Stationer. Most communication in the Citadel occurred online, but the fancy folk still organized their entertainment the old-fashioned way, with elaborate, printed invitations. Fancy soirees provided the perfect cover for burglary. Years ago, Twain had stolen the lead printer's login credentials and established remote access to his files, giving us advanced insight into the hottest events in the city. Was it possible it still worked?

I typed the credentials into the system. It quickly spat back an error message. The email contact hadn't changed, so the guy had likely wised up and changed his password. I stared at the old password: *EnchantedInvite2017*. Could it be that simple?

I typed in *EnchantedInvite2025* and hit Enter. The error

message flashed again. I added an exclamation point on the end. My finger hovered above the Enter button. If I continued to insert the wrong password, it would lock me out. I held my breath and pressed Enter. The screen displayed a spinning icon and then flashed a list of options. I was in.

For the next half hour, I snooped through the Citadel's social scene, delving through invites to a Victorian-themed costume festival complete with an illusionist, a Mexican-styled fiesta with individually crafted margaritas and a synchronized-swimming demonstration followed by salsa dance lessons, and a can-can-themed soiree complete with performers scantily clad in feathers and rhinestones. The Citadelians couldn't pass up a spectacle.

I riffled through several more invitations when a name I recognized popped up.

Blythe Damling. The elderly socialite who looked like a Hollywood starlet, who had a collection of diamonds and precious jewelry to rival the British crown jewels. I'd been in her mansion many times. I knew the layout, or at least I had, once, whenever my old man had dragged me along to social gatherings. She'd given me and Twain free rein to explore and get lost so the grown-ups could have their fun. We'd taken full advantage, helping ourselves to her liquor, her movie theater stocked with gourmet popcorn and R-rated movies, and the indoor swimming pool that was part of her bedroom suite. The woman had an entire room solely dedicated to her jewelry collection that we'd once found unlocked and unattended.

"What are you up to, Blythe?" I whispered.

The invitation read *Lose Yourself in the Garden of Eden. Taste paradise and try to resist the temptations. Clothing is optional but costumes are mandatory otherwise. Fig leaves provided upon request.*

"Perfect."

"What's perfect?" Twain stood at the door to the lab rubbing sleep from his eyes.

"What are you doing up?" I asked, glancing at the clock. It was barely five in the morning.

"You type loud. What's perfect?"

"How do you feel about a good old-fashioned heist?"

"Fuck no," he said.

Oh no. Twain never cursed, not unless he was truly upset.

"Hear me out," I said. I explained what I'd learned about Evan's situation, about a young girl in need of a miracle. About the plan I was forming even now to make that miracle a reality.

Twain listened, pacing in his pajama pants and faded T-shirt that read *I'd argue with you on principle, but I Kant.* When I finished, he stood staring at me for far too long.

"Since the moment you saw Blackwell in that arena, you've thrown every ounce of caution over the balcony," he said. "For mercy's sake, everything we've done to build this life, to fight back against the Empire, you've jeopardized without considering how it would impact me or Simone. You never even asked us."

I stared at the floor.

"You have a job—right now. The Scythe isn't going to take your being distracted as an excuse if you fail to come through for them."

I pictured the hand scythe propped against my door, pictured whose blood might spill should I fail. I closed my eyes and scrubbed a hand over my forehead. Twain was right, about all of it.

"I'm sorry," I said. I never wanted to endanger or dishonor my friends, to take for granted the people I cherished above all else, and yet this world was too much sometimes. Too much suffering, too much abuse. I knew it far too intimately, and it gnawed at me.

"Sometimes it doesn't feel like what I'm doing is enough." I glanced at Twain, taking in the hurt and frustration painted across his face. "But none of that matters if it risks you or

Simone. You are my life, my family, and there is nothing I wouldn't do to protect you," I said. "Forgive me?"

"I already have, and I always will."

I didn't deserve him.

"Look, I'm glad you rescued Evan from Blackwell, but for Plato's sake, talk to us," he said. "Let us help you without it being a last resort, and stop stoking fires."

"I can't seem to stop myself."

"So I've noticed," Twain said. "Why this one? Why now?"

I'd been pondering that very question.

"Do you remember my governess, Sumaira?" I asked. "The one who died of pneumonia when I was ten?" She'd been my nanny and tutor since I was an infant and cared for me like a mother after my own had died. She'd landed in the ICU in a coma, with a machine breathing for her.

"She used to sneak me almond cookies when Father wasn't looking," Twain said.

"My cookies, if I recall," I said, one eyebrow raised.

Twain's father had been the Commander, but Bane had betrayed Twain's dad, fabricated a story to condemn him, and climbed over his dead body to claim his place.

"I begged my father to take her to the Fount," I said. "He refused." I remembered him waiving a dismissive hand as he'd flipped the pages of his book and said, *I cannot afford to allow just anyone who wants an Immersion to use the Fount. It would destroy it. I've told you countless times how delicate it is.*

But she's not just anyone, Papi, I'd said. *She's part of our family.*

She's a servant, he'd said. *She is receiving the proper care she is due. Do not ask me again. Now go to your room and leave me in peace.*

I'd wanted to plead some more, but I'd been punished before for my insolence, paddled until I couldn't sit down for two days, and banished to my room with no electronics, no contact with friends or anyone else for three months. I'd learned the hard way that when my father said to stop asking, you stopped asking.

"I walked away that night, went to bed sulking, and she died while I slept. I let that happen," I said, recalling the warmth and security I'd felt in her care, feeling guilty for her death even now. "We had time to save her, and I failed. I'd been more concerned about my own comforts than her life."

"You were never going to change your father's mind," Twain said, sitting on a chair opposite me. "No one changes the Conquistador's mind except the Conquistador."

"Yeah, well, now I'm not asking. It's time the Fount benefitted someone who could actually use it. But getting this child into the Fount would be the riskiest con we've ever pulled, and I will do nothing without your blessing."

Twain got up, rubbed the stubble on his head, and shuffled toward the hallway. In the doorway, he offered a mischievous smile.

"I'm in. No way I'm letting you have all the fun without me."

17

EVANGELINE

$\mathcal{I}$t was hard not to stare, not to freeze and gawk at the abundance around me. The tray of crystal tumblers on my palm wobbled, and Rafael's voice sounded low in my ear: "Easy. Remember—this is nothing new for you. You've seen this type of debauchery a hundred times."

Nothing could be further from the truth. I could never have imagined anything like this.

Rafael was thirty feet away on the veranda of a massive mansion, carrying a platter of sausages wrapped in fig leaves. The tiny flesh-colored dot behind my earlobe made it possible to hear him and Twain and respond in kind. We'd disguised our features and dressed like waitstaff for this extravagant party. The male servers wore skintight leather pants and nothing else beyond a fake snake crossing their torsos and wrapping around their necks. The women in service were dressed like black butterflies, with sparkling long-sleeved tops that bared our waists, matching bottoms over sheer leggings, and tiny patterned wings on our backs. All the servants wore sparkling black masks. We were dressed for invisibility, but I felt exposed and vulnerable, even with the Conquistador's mark covered by my shirt. None of the servers had one showing.

I didn't belong here.

"This was a mistake," I whispered.

"Stick with the plan. You'll be fine."

I never should have agreed to this. Not only had I thrown a lifetime of rule-following out the window, but I was now a criminal. Breaking the Conquistador's laws, disobeying the Commandments, turning into an utter disappointment to my father if he knew what I was doing. Rafael and Twain had assured me Blythe Damling would never miss a couple of pieces of jewelry, but that didn't matter. Stealing was stealing, whether it was a tangerine or a necklace worth two million pesos. Even if we pulled off this heist, we'd still have to fake our way into the Fount. Everything seemed impossible.

A man dressed in a fig leaf and gold-chain necklace drifted by and snatched a glass from my tray without a word. My heart leapt in my chest and began tapping on my ribcage. But the disguise held. I was invisible to these people. Rafael's words came back to me.

The law doesn't serve people like your sister, he'd said. *If you want her to live, then you're going to have to get comfortable with breaking the rules. If Twain or I had the money to pay for her Immersion, we would, but we don't. There is no other way. Either we steal the means to help Juniper or she dies.*

His words were hard to swallow, but he was right, and I wasn't willing to let that happen. The more I looked around, the more I realized Rafael was right about another thing—Damling had so much money to throw around, the theft of one or two pieces of jewelry would do little harm. I could never earn enough money in my lifetime to pay for a fraction of what this party cost.

Such a waste.

Gray clouds hovered in the distance, threaded through with

spurts of silent lightning. Damling's mansion alone sprawled over three acres and was surrounded by rolling green grass and dense forest. The Garden of Eden–themed party stretched across the lawn, an extensive veranda and swimming pool, and inside the house, but there was nothing remotely biblical about it.

More than a dozen violinists sprinkled across the lawn played in unison under crystal chandeliers draped from trees in huge marble pots. Towering tree-like sculptures glowed with multicolored lights under the darkening sky. Large butterflies pulsing in bejeweled lights covered one of these structures, while another dangled with glowing red orbs like apples, and a third was adorned with rainbow-hued flowers and birds. Two unnaturally large swan lanterns floated in the pool, casting light on naked partygoers and fake water lilies. The largest tree structure sat in the center of the lawn, surrounded by roaming peacocks, baby lambs, and goats. Guests could pluck a pomegranate from its low-hanging limbs and reenact the story of the Garden of Eden.

Nearby a snake handler offered guests the chance to drape a slithering boa constrictor over their shoulders, while elsewhere scantily clad performers danced with snakes, flowers, and fire. Everywhere there were flower arrangements, food and drink like I'd never seen, and ornate couches where people could lounge or cozy up without anyone giving them a second glance. It was beautiful and breathtaking. And wholly disgusting.

"Operation Get Sloshed in full swing." This time, Twain's voice whispered in my ear. He was in the kitchen, helping prep the night's signature drink—a smoked-honey and pomegranate-muddled old-fashioned. A far cry from the simple corn whiskey some of the guys brewed on the farm. Twain was using a one-hundred-and-forty-proof whiskey, the most potent he could find. He didn't want any overly observant guests when he broke into Damling's jewel room later tonight. Rafe and I were his eyes and ears on the ground.

"It's a hit. People are passing on the champagne for it," Rafe said.

A murmur went through the guests as a woman glided onto the veranda, emerging from the mansion like a beacon at midnight. She wore a long crystal-studded gown that showed off her bare shoulders and a collar of diamonds. Red roses and vines climbed her skirts and bodice and rimmed her blonde hair like a crown. She appeared young, beautiful, and flawless, and she captured the attention of everyone around her. She waved, slow and purposeful, and the crowd applauded and cheered.

"There's our host," Rafael said.

He'd said Blythe was almost eighty, but she looked my age. It was miraculous and infuriating. Damling been Immersed in the Fount several times, and my sister couldn't even get a sprinkle to cure her illness. It was wasteful and pointless and unfair. It made me want to rob her blind. I immediately felt guilty and disgusted with myself for even thinking such a thing. My lack didn't mean she deserved her good fortune any less. Did it?

"Makes an impression, doesn't she?" Rafael said.

"Yes, she does," said a faint female voice. "So do you."

A woman with flowing red hair and a gown that looked made of dewy spiderweb plucked a sausage from Rafael's tray and trailed a red fingernail across his bare chest. I had a sudden urge to rip her fingernails out.

What was wrong with me? I wasn't a violent person, but this city and its people were messing with my head.

Rafael's muscles tensed under the woman's touch, but he smiled and cocked his head. "My thanks, mistress."

"Too bad you're not on the menu. I'm famished."

"Perhaps another sausage?" he said, sliding his tray between them.

"Another time," she said and sauntered off.

"I need a bath," Rafael muttered.

I wanted to laugh, but I couldn't shake the rabid feeling surging through me from the sight of that woman's hands on him. I turned away from Rafael, trying to focus on something else. This night already felt like a lifetime in purgatory.

Over the next two hours, guests arrived in various states of finery or undress. The music changed from sophisticated violin strings to something pounding with drums. Partygoers danced and drank themselves sloppy and lost more of their inhibitions. As the hour struck ten o'clock, Twain slipped out the service entry and made his way to an unused side of the mansion. Damling had only a scattering of security guards, most at the entrance and some on the outskirts of the property. Rafael said the security was light because crime was a rarity in the Citadel, even trespassing. The consequences were too steep. I knew that too well, and it made what we were doing even more unsettling.

"Side yard clear, starting climb," Twain whispered.

"Move into position," Rafael said.

I wandered inside the house and began roaming the hallway between the ballroom and living area, giving me a perfect view of the stairs to the master bedroom suite. My job was to alert Twain to anyone going up those stairs. Rafael stayed on the patio to monitor the grounds.

"On the roof," Twain said. "Mother of Galileo, look at this shindig. Oscar Wilde was right about nothing succeeding like excess."

"Focus, little phoenix," Rafael said.

Minutes passed as my stomach tangled in knots, sure that Twain would be caught. Hundreds of people were scattered across the lawn outside. All they had to do was look up. Twain had climbed to the roof to gain access to the balcony of Damling's bedroom, which overlooked the back lawn. Once there, he'd pick the lock and sneak inside. Only the tray in my hand stopped me from chewing on my nails.

"On the balcony," Twain said. "Everything good?"

"Good as a goat in a pile of dirty socks."

He snorted in my ear, while a man in a rose-covered suit helped himself to an old-fashioned from my tray.

"Thank you, Blythe. Door was already unlocked. Going in."

Several minutes passed. I paced as Twain began picking the lock to the jewel room. He'd described it as more of a glorified closet, but the lock was more complicated than a normal door lock. Everything was going to plan, which worried me. Nothing ever went according to plan.

Down the hallway, servants opened the double doors to the main entrance, and a murmur rippled through the crowd. A man crossed the threshold, shadowed for an instant by a brilliant flash of lightning at his back. My heart stopped. My hands shook. It was Commander Nico Bane. I forced a deep breath to steady myself.

Bane wore a crisp black suit, white shirt, tie, and shoes polished to a shine, and he was coming toward me.

He won't recognize me, I kept repeating to myself as he drew nearer. I was out of place and wearing spirals of black hair, heavy eye makeup, and a mask. I looked nothing like the young woman he'd flogged almost two years ago or the worker he'd tormented mere weeks ago. But my heart didn't care. It wanted to run.

I stood frozen as Bane plucked a tumbler from my tray and kept walking. He didn't even look at me.

Conversations had stopped. People paused whatever they were doing. All eyes tracked the Commander as he strode to the veranda, his footsteps clicking on the polished wood floors, his gaze ignoring guest and servant alike. He disappeared, and the room grew heavy with conversation and laughter once more.

"Bane's here," I half whispered, half squeaked.

"Mierda," Rafael cursed.

18

RAFE

*T*he bastard marched out on the veranda like he owned the place. Bane stood by the back doors, surveying the decadence like he wanted to snap a few necks. Wouldn't have been the first time.

The entire party seemed to sense his presence, and all eyes pivoted to him. Laughter died into murmurs and words whispered behind hands. Thunder rumbled in the void, and the wind picked up, rustling tablecloths and floral arrangements like a whip. Blythe noticed the Commander and squealed like a teenager. She hugged one of her female companions and left her circle of admirers.

Bane watched her with a look in his eyes I'd never seen before. Something hovering between hunger and possession. He waited for her to join to him, and she practically rushed to his side. Bane in lust—that was something new.

"Darling, you're late," Blythe said, pushing herself into his arms.

He swallowed his whiskey and shoved the empty glass into the hands of a nearby partygoer. "I'm never late. I always arrive when I intend to arrive."

She snuggled closer and gazed at him as if he could do no wrong. If I hadn't been terrified of being discovered by the man who'd beaten me to the brink of death as a teen, I might have puked on his shiny dress shoes. I was close enough.

"You neglected to wear a costume, my love," Blythe said, skimming a hand down Bane's impressively flat stomach. "Care to borrow a fig leaf?"

"Not even for you, sweet Blythe," he said.

Did this man actually care for another human? Twain would fall off the roof if he heard this exchange.

Blythe pushed up onto her toes and bent toward his ear, but I heard every word. "How about I take you upstairs and strip you like the bad boy you are?"

Bane grinned and grabbed her ass. He twirled her around and maneuvered her inside the veranda doors.

"I'm in!" Twain's voice sounded triumphant in my ears.

Hellfire and piss. I wandered away from listening ears.

"Bane and Blythe are headed inside," I whispered. "They're going to her bedroom. Get out of there."

"Give me a second. I'm not leaving empty-handed."

"They're going upstairs," Evan said. "You have to leave. Now."

Frantic shuffling sounds filled my ear as Twain rushed to stow his bounty.

Come on, Twain—wrap it up.

"Almost done... Oh bollocks, they're at the door. What did they do? Run?" Twain's voice was half whisper, half scream.

"Can you hide?" I asked.

"I'm in the vault. The door's closed, so unless they want to copulate among the crown jewels, I'm safe for the moment."

I wouldn't put it past them. We had to do something and do it fast. There weren't many options, and all of them were bad.

"Is there still a swimming pool next to Blythe's bedroom?"

"Yes." Twain's voice was barely audible.

"Hang tight."

I found Evan near the entrance to the ballroom. The lights had been dimmed inside, and couples were sprinkled around the room on couches, drinking or groping each other to varying degrees. A security guard blocked the stairwell to Blythe's bedroom.

"We need to create a diversion for Twain, but we've got to get upstairs first."

Evan nodded, eyes wide behind her black mask.

"There's a back way from the kitchen, but we'll need a diversion of our own. Follow me, and when you hear glass breaking, make sure everyone's watching me and then run upstairs."

She trailed me into the kitchen. A dozen caterers and bar staff worked at a twenty-foot white granite kitchen island, replenishing trays of food and drink.

"Time for a refill," I said, taking Evan's tray and placing our trays on the countertop. I left one tray dangling off the island and gave Evan a slight nod toward the service staircase. The door upstairs was likely locked, but I could make short work of that.

"Thirsty bunch," I said, leaning on the counter. The bartender huffed out a laugh but most ignored me and continued working.

"Take the empties to the dishwasher," he said, nodding to the far counter. "Over there."

"You got it." I reached for one tray and knocked the other off the counter. It crashed in a symphony of shattering crystal. All eyes darted toward the noise as glass and leftover champagne splattered the floor.

"What the hell, man?" the bartender shouted.

"Shit, I'm sorry," I said, bending to pick up glass. When I stood, Evan was gone. I dropped several shards into the waste bucket as the bartender and another man stooped to clean up my mess. I grabbed a broom, but the bartender snatched it out of my hands.

"Grab a tray and get the hell out of here," he said.

That wasn't exactly the reaction I was going for.

"Now."

I found myself in the foyer with a tray of old-fashioneds, and Evan stranded upstairs. I had to get to her. The service stairwell was out of the question now. The bartender would deck me if he saw me again. I wandered into the ballroom and surveyed the staircase from the shadows. The guard stood in his black uniform like a granite statute, his face a mask of indifference, but I was sure he'd happily body slam any intruder and go back for seconds.

I was running out of time. One of my friends was going to get caught if I didn't act soon.

"You there!" a woman's voice called from nearby. Half a dozen women lounged in a seating area to the side of the ballroom, and one of them beckoned me over. Hell and fire, I didn't have time for this.

"How may I be of service, my ladies?" I said, bowing with my tray.

"We're dying of thirst over here," said a woman in a blue gown with peacock feathers spewing from its lone sleeve.

I lowered my tray, and six manicured hands descended, taking all but two tumblers. They shooed me away like a fly. I was happy to oblige.

I had to think. How to get upstairs? I stared at my tray, eager to be rid of it, and considered my options. Then it came to me.

I squared my shoulders, lifted my chin, and marched out of the ballroom. Right past the thug guarding the staircase. I didn't get far. A gloved hand gripped my arm before my foot hit the first step. "Where do you think you're going?"

"The mistress of the house requested drinks for her and her guest," I said, gesturing toward the two remaining drinks on my tray. The guard rolled his eyes and then studied me, debating.

Finally, he released my arm. "Make it quick."

"As quick as the mistress desires," I said.

The guard scoffed and resumed his position. I hurried upstairs and found Evan waiting behind the servant's door. She jumped like she'd been caught red-handed.

"What took so long?"

"No time—come on," I said.

Twain's whisper came out of the blue: "The sounds these two are making is criminal. A slurping puppy is more discreet. Save me."

I didn't want to imagine Bane sucking face with Blythe. Or worse.

"Thanks for that unwanted visual. We're almost there. Be ready."

We crept into the pool room, and I discarded my tray. Light from Blythe's bedroom filtered through an ornate, beveled-glass door, illuminating a room that was nothing like I remembered. The swimming pool had been renovated into a hot spring and surrounded by plants and waterfalls to simulate an outdoor oasis. The air was humid and thick with the scent of jasmine.

I drew Evan close and whispered into her ear. "We're about to get caught," I said.

She jerked back and glared at me. "You've lost your mind." Tiny tremors radiated from her body. I hated doing this to her, but there was no other way.

"Trust me. We'll likely be fired, not arrested. We've got to get those two out of the room long enough for Twain to sneak out, and the distraction has to be harmless enough to keep us out of the Calabozo. That means we need to pretend we're hooking up, and it needs to look as real as possible." I unzipped my pants and yanked the waistband down enough to show some hips and lower belly.

"Whoa! Wait!" she hissed, stepping away.

"It's for show," I said, pulling her back. The heat of her skin felt electric, her trembling contagious.

Focus, Roldan. Come on.

"I'm sorry about this, but we need to get their attention, and we need to be kissing when that door opens. Is that okay with you?"

Evan was silent for a moment, her eyes wide behind the mask, but she nodded. Her pulse under my palm quickened, and my own rose in harmony to hers.

"We need to make it look real, okay?" Again, she nodded, slowly this time, like her mind was calculating her next move. Or maybe how to run.

I rubbed my forehead. I couldn't believe I was going to expose myself to Bane. The man who would have me dead. I had straightened my curls, dyed my hair a light brown with blond highlights and wore a beard. A mask covered half my face. I'd done everything I could to look nothing like the teenager he'd known, but it was still a risk. Massively foolish. But there was no other way to get Twain out of the situation I'd put him in.

I lifted the drinks off the tray and handed one to Evan. I raised my glass to her. "Here's to good luck and bad eyesight."

The whiskey sparked my tongue and warmed my throat, and I was tempted to down all of it, but I couldn't afford to lose my wits, not with Evan and Twain counting on me. Evan winced as the whiskey passed her lips, but she swallowed. I set our glasses on a table and ran my hands through Evan's hair, mussing her curls. She shivered under my touch, and it made me want to whisk her home and do it some more. But I couldn't. I wouldn't.

I drew Evan into my arms and felt my stomach dance. Her heart pounded against my chest. The heat of her bare waist seared into my skin. Her nearness was its own intoxication, and it tore me apart. The wanting terrified me. Staring into her eyes felt like walking off a ledge.

"Twain, get ready to flee," I said.

"Got it."

The sky outside was an angry bruise. A gust of wind rattled the windowpanes. Thunder boomed, shaking the walls with its aftershock. The minute the skies dropped open outside, this house would be jammed full of people. We needed to be gone before that happened.

I picked up the empty silver tray and let it fall from my fingers. The metal clattered on the tile floor like a gong in a canyon, loud enough to rattle my bones. I tightened my hold on Evan and lowered my face to hers. Time to plunge into the fire.

"Make them believe it," I whispered against her lips.

Angry footsteps pounded across carpet, and the doorknob rattled. I claimed Evan's mouth, and she melted into mine, lips soft and tremulous. One hand raked through her hair, and the other gripped her waist and pressed her tight against me. I opened my mouth and devoured her. My tongue found hers and tasted whiskey and pomegranate. Her scent filled my senses, lavender and honey and fresh air, and it shook me—the unexpectedness of it. The hunger almost felt real. Her arms were around my neck, her breasts pressed against my chest, and those brief few seconds felt like an eternity I could lose myself in.

"What the hell are you doing in here?"

The grumble of Bane's voice felt like being tossed in ice water. Lights flashed on overhead, and Evan and I parted like guilty, horny kids caught by their parents. I stepped in front of her like a shield, suddenly certain I'd miscalculated this plan.

Bane stood in the doorway—shirtless, barefoot, and frowning, a pistol dangling at his side. Murder in his eyes. Shivers ran down my spine.

"What is it, darling?" Blythe appeared over his shoulder.

"Go back to bed. I'll handle this."

Blythe laughed. "Oh, my lands, it looks like we weren't the only ones to succumb to temptation," she said. "I'm all for having a little fun, but not in my oasis. There's nothing to handle. Send them back to work and come back to bed."

Someone dashed behind the couple, and relief swelled inside me. Twain would be on the balcony in seconds and out of harm's way. Maybe this would work.

"Please forgive us, mistress," I said, fumbling to zip up my pants. "This is my fault. It won't happen again."

"It certainly won't," Bane said. "I'll have a unit take them into custody."

Evan gasped, and my heart froze. *No, no, no, this is all wrong.* I should never have underestimated Bane's cruelty. He made Jack the Ripper look like a saint.

"You will do no such thing," Blythe said. "I'll not have your Guardia ruining my party. Not over something as trivial as this."

"These miscreants are trespassing and defiling your home," he said. "I'll not stand for it."

"You're right. It's my home, and my decision. You bring your soldiers here, and it'll ruin the vibe. I'll be scandalized for months."

Keep arguing. Every moment they argued bought Twain more time. But Bane wasn't a man of compromise. If we were about to be arrested, I had to come up with a plan of escape. Once inside a Guardia transpod, we'd be doomed.

"There must be consequences, Blythe."

"Nico, half my guests are screwing on my lawn and in my swimming pool. I don't care," she said. "You two, go downstairs and get back to work. Don't let me see you again where you don't belong."

"Yes, mistress," I said. I grabbed Evan's hand and headed for the door.

"Not so fast," Bane said, pointing his gun at us.

I pushed Evan behind me.

"I'm on the roof," Twain said in my ear. "Storm's coming in fast. A big one."

Wind pounded the mansion, and lightning cracked the dark. I wanted to tell Twain to run, but all I could do was address Bane and hope he understood.

"I'm sorry, sir. Please—we meant no harm."

"Nico, you are ruining my mood," Blythe said, pushing his arm down. "If it makes you feel better, I'll call Marcus to escort them from the property and report them to the catering company."

"Fine."

Blythe summoned Marcus on her Convo, and the guard from downstairs appeared within seconds. His fists clenched the moment he saw me. At this point, I'd happily accept a punch in the face if it meant we skated clear of this debacle. Blythe gave Marcus her instructions.

"Please be discreet," she said.

Marcus clutched our arms and began dragging us to the door, but Bane stopped him. He whispered into his ear, out of Blythe's hearing but not mine. "Take them to the station. The Guardia can arrest them out of view of the guests," he said.

Marcus nodded and tugged us out of the room. No one disobeyed the Commander.

We were screwed.

The guard called for backup to assume his post and then escorted us down the servant's stairwell. In the kitchen, the bartender scowled, and his coworkers eyed us like we were contagious. They wanted nothing to do with whatever trouble we were in. Marcus prodded us out the servant's side exit and down a narrow path hidden by tall hedges. I knew exactly where he was taking us. A public transpod station outside the Damling estate, where Bane's Guardia unit would meet him and arrest us.

Lightning flashed nearby, and thunder cracked like an explosion. A heavy raindrop splatted onto my chest, and another snagged my eyelid, making me blink. The wind gusted, tossing the hedges around like a mixer. Then all hell broke loose. Rain poured from the sky, and crashing thunder chased a swift series of lightning strikes. Shouts and screams rose from rear of the house.

An alarm sounded on Marcus's wrist, followed by a voice, loud over the pounding rain: "All available security personnel to the swimming pool. Guests trapped under debris."

Marcus paused as the rain drenched the three of us. It was deadly to disobey an order from the Commander, but lives were on the line. His choice boiled down to his life or the others'.

I made the choice for him.

I ripped the fake snake from my torso and swung it. It smacked hard across the guard's face, knocking him into the hedges. I followed up with a boot to the balls. He bellowed something profane, but I didn't wait to watch him untangle himself. I grabbed Evan's hand and ran, shoving through a narrow opening in the hedges and circling back to the house. To the veranda, where bodies were running and slipping and screaming under the punishing veil of rain. I didn't want to go anywhere near the public transpod depot.

On the other side of the veranda, a swarm of security guards tried to budge the massive swan lanterns that had taken flight and landed upside down in the swimming pool, while others helped guests out of the water. Across the lawn, two of the shimmering lantern trees had toppled, and the wind had blown party debris everywhere. I pulled Evan across the patio, ripping off our masks and throwing them into the bushes, pausing long enough to grab soaking-wet clothing off lounge chairs. I ripped off Evan's angel wings and shoved a floral cape into her hands.

"Twain, status update?" I asked, pulling on a black, feathered jacket.

Nothing. Evan and I exchanged a look. Twenty feet away, Marcus rounded the corner, red with anger.

"Come on—we need to blend in," I said.

We joined a throng of soaked and wilted partygoers shoving inside the veranda doors. I pushed through the mass of people, some of whom were complaining, others who were drunk and celebrating. Outside the kitchen, I found the door to Blythe's private transpod platform. I surveyed the room to see if anyone was looking our way. I spotted Marcus in the ballroom, eyes searching the crowd, and I ushered us into the shadows. I eased the door open and nudged Evan inside.

An elevator sat next to a stairwell to the transpod platform. We took the stairs. I needed to find the service tunnel. As teens, Twain and I had become adept at sneaking around the Citadel using the vast network of service tunnels, and I was counting on the old tricks still working.

A door opened upstairs, and footsteps hit the stairs. I yanked Evan to the edge of the platform and motioned her down. We lowered ourselves to the tunnel. The footsteps grew louder. I shoved Evan into the space beneath a hovering transpod and followed her below.

Let's hope Blythe doesn't decide to go for a ride.

I waited, listening and watching. Footsteps were near now, echoing in the cavernous tunnel. Suddenly a pair of black boots dropped to the tunnel floor.

We'd been discovered.

My stomach clenched, and I thought I might shit myself. A face appeared upside down, hair dripping wet and grinning.

"Let's get the devil out of here."

"Twain, you asshole, I'm so glad to see you."

19

EVANGELINE

I couldn't stop thinking about that kiss. About what my father would have thought. Seeing what I'd done —the stealing, the revealing outfit, the kissing—would have given him a heart attack. The rules in El Jardín only permitted intimacies between married couples and never in public. Stealing was wrong by all measures. But more than anything, I couldn't stop thinking about Rafael. His hands on my skin. His fingers in my hair. The way my body had cried out for his, for more, like it had never known thirst until that moment and couldn't drink its fill. The feel of him against me had sparked a dangerous heat in my belly and lower. The taste of whiskey on our lips haunted me still. The kissing had been for show, not real, but it had felt real. The wanting was real, even now.

"Must be good, whatever you're thinking about." Simone grinned from where she was sifting through different images on the wardrobe machine. My cheeks heated, and I avoided her gaze, finding sudden interest in the late-afternoon sun seeping through the floor-to-ceiling windows. I should have been embarrassed by my performance with Rafael, by breaking the rules of propriety. By betraying the man my father had betrothed me to. I should have been ashamed for lying and stealing, but I couldn't find it in myself to be sorry for any of it. There was only immense relief. That we'd escaped, that we had the means to save Juni's life. That no one had gotten hurt.

"I'm happy we made it out safely," I lied.

"Mm-hmm."

Rafael and Twain were selling three pieces of stolen jewelry in an illegal marketplace. Twain had nabbed a diamond ring the size of a large pebble, a diamond-and-sapphire collar necklace, and a matching bracelet. They were exquisite. A treasure no one at El Jardín could ever imagine, but one that represented the cost of my sister's life.

"No…no…no." Simone kept rejecting options on the screen. She was determined to outfit me with new clothing. I'd protested—I liked my old dresses—but it was hard to argue with Simone.

"¡Perfecto!" The screen showed an image of me dressed in britches and a light blue shirt.

"Those are men's britches," I objected.

"No," she said. "These are made for women."

I wanted to tell her I never wore pants, but I'd spent an entire evening in little more than sparkling black underwear and see-through leggings. My standards were slipping fast.

Her eyes softened, and she smiled at me. "Trust me, okay?"

Half an hour later, Simone presented me with an armful of clothes and beckoned me to follow as she led the way to my room. At the door to the attached bathroom, she rummaged through her bag and handed me bottles of shampoo and conditioner. "This will wash the temp dye out of your hair, then we'll do a little maintenance."

Maintenance? I eyed her with suspicion.

"Trust, Evan. Remember?" she said, calm as ever. "Go on." She gestured toward the shower.

I did as instructed, taking time to thoroughly rinse the color from my hair. The soaps smelled like lavender mixed with honey, and I was sniffing the wet strands of my hair when I stepped back into my bedroom. Simone motioned me to a chair next to a small table. A variety of instruments and bottles lay spread across the table, including a pair of scissors.

"What's this for?"

"A small cleanup job. We need to get rid of some frizz. Please sit."

"Simone, really, this isn't necessary."

"When's the last time you had your hair cut?"

My fingers stroked the long length of my hair. My mother had been the last one to trim it. It had to have been more than two years. I couldn't remember when exactly, but the memory was as raw as if it had been yesterday. The gentleness of her fingers combing through my hair. Kissing my forehead when she finished.

"For now, I promise not to chop it off. Just cut off the dead ends."

"For now? What?"

"You'll see. Come. Sit."

I hesitated.

"Must you question everything?" A tiny crack shone in her ever-present serenity.

"Can you blame me?"

Simone laughed. "Not really. Now come on."

She motioned to the chair, and I sat. What did I have to lose? Simone was beautiful. She couldn't make me look worse than I already did. Not that it mattered.

Simone combed through my hair, releasing the tangles with tender strokes. Soon she had the scissors in hand, snipping the ends, combing through my hair, and snipping again.

"Simone, why are we doing this?" I asked.

Her fingers stopped for a moment and then began again.

"Because you need it, and I want to."

I didn't know what to say, so I didn't say anything. As she worked, my mind drifted to Rafael. Thinking of him roused little fireflies in the dark pit of my belly. I'd given him my first kiss, and even if it hadn't been real, it had been worth it.

"What's Rafael's story?" I asked. I knew so little about him. "And Twain? I know you're a singer, but I don't know much about the guys. Do they steal for a living? How did you become friends?"

"That's a lot of questions."

"I have lots more."

"I don't speak for my friends. Their story is theirs to share or not. I knew Rafe first, when I was starting out as a singer many years ago. I was a friend of the family."

"His family? Do they live here, in the Citadel?"

"His mother is dead," Simone said. Her fingers paused in my hair, and she hesitated. "His father is...estranged."

"Oh." No mother, missing father. His kindred loss moved through me like a gray cloud.

"What about Twain?" I asked.

"Also parentless. We're all orphans of some sort. We have made a family of each other."

"My mother died almost nineteen months ago," I said, the words thick in my throat. "I'm sure Rafael told you about the rest of my family."

"I'm sorry about your mother."

"I remember when Juni was born. I promised Mama I'd be a good big sister and watch out for her, always protect her. With our mother gone, I feel responsible for her," I said, my gaze falling to my lap. "In my family, we take care of each other. It's what we do. But..."

I couldn't finish it. I couldn't voice my failure.

Simone nudged my head into an erect position and resumed snipping. "Much as we want to, we can't always protect the ones we love," she said. "Too much is beyond our control."

"The voice of experience?"

Simone was quiet for a moment, her hands stilled. She sighed and stroked my hair once with her fingertips. "My parents ran out of money. They couldn't afford visits to the Fount anymore. I was born a couple of years after they'd stopped visiting the Fount. My mother was too old to be having a child. She had a heart attack during my birth and never recovered. My father drank himself to death when I was barely seventeen," she said. "By then, I'd been singing for two years and earning enough to keep our home in the Citadel. Sometimes the people you love bring misery on themselves. Sometimes other people drop misfortune on them like a brick. Sometimes it's no one's fault. Either way, you're often powerless to stop it, powerless to save them. Doesn't mean you don't still try. Doesn't mean you love them any less."

"I'm sorry about your parents, Simone. You must have felt so alone."

"I did for a while. But then I created a new family."

Rafael and Twain.

Simone punched a button on a gun-shaped device, and a high-pitched whine filled the silence. A stream of warm air shot toward my head. I flinched and leaned away.

Simone's free hand settled on my shoulder and eased me back. "Just a hair dryer. Don't worry."

My heart beat like a startled bird in a cage, but after a few moments, the steady hum, the warm air, and Simone's fingers combing my hair lulled me into a peaceful trance. I was almost sad when she finished.

Simone handed me a mirror. "Much better," she said, walking off. Behind me, I could hear her rummaging in her bag.

It *was* much better. My hair glistened, the honey-amber strands bright, wavy ribbons in the afternoon light, now tamed and silken. I couldn't stop touching it.

"Wow. Thank you," I said.

"I have one more thing for you."

"It's already too much," I said. I suddenly felt like crying. I was not an emotional person, but few people outside my parents had invested so much time and care in me. It was kind. Undeserved.

"This is for you, but it's also for Rafe's benefit," she said. She stretched out her palm to reveal a small dagger in a leather sheath. "If you're going through the Wildlands, you need protection. You and I aren't trained to fight, and we don't have time for that, so a knife will have to do. The trick is not letting anyone take it from you. Strap it to your shin under your pants. I recommend keeping it hidden and using it only in close quarters when no one sees it coming. Otherwise they'll take it and hurt you with it. Understand?"

The frightened bird in my ribcage started drumming again. I nodded.

"It's yours. Please take it." I fought to hide the tremble in my hand as I picked up the knife. Intricately carved swirls decorated the wooden haft. I slid the weapon from its sheath. The blade was four or five inches long, gleaming and spotless, with a fine razor edge. It was lightweight, but the gravity of it threatened to unbalance me.

"Thank you," I said, sliding the blade back into its sheath.

"One more thing," Simone said. One side of her mouth quirked into a grin.

"Yeah?"

"As frustrating as Rafe can be, don't use it on him."

20

RAFE

The Barrio was a stink hole hiding in plain sight—a cramped, walled borough abutting the Citadel's ramparts. The Guardia required its residents, the city's laborers, to landscape their rooftops to disguise the village from their working-elite neighbors in the Citadel. It was a concession to the doctors, lawyers, and professors whose status wasn't elevated enough to avoid living next to a veiled slum. The laborers existed one step above the Obligors. They had homes and families, but they operated like ghosts, invisible to their employers. They needed to live somewhere, and this was it.

Twain and I had been schooled in the Barrio. It'd been our home for a time, our proving grounds, the crucible through which we'd stolen back into Citadel life. I hadn't been to the Barrio for years, but here I was, pulling up raw memories like weeds, winding my way to one certain house. I hoped Cormac Vetta still lived there.

An underground tunnel served as the only entrance to the Barrio. Go one way, you'd enter the Barrio. Go the other, you'd find the Sink, if you could locate its hidden entrance. The black market was a mile's walk through a dark network of narrow tunnels. Los Reyes, the Sink bosses, had capped and camouflaged the sinkhole that created the Sink ages ago and gated other orifices. Ferals sneaking into the Sink tended to be bad for business.

Twain was in the Sink, fencing Blythe's jewels. Usually we conducted business with a man named Harley, whose network ferried contraband through subterranean passages spanning the US–Florida border. He specialized in circuitry and chips and anything related to electronics, something I needed more than ever. The task Rod had given me was becoming problematic. I was building a device that militaries spent millions of dollars developing on a larger scale. Twain had stolen as much research online as he could, but it was a challenge transmuting it for a portable device. We needed something small but powerful enough to convert stored energy into bursts capable of disabling a portion of the power grid. Not mass destruction, but mass disruption. I was close but not there yet.

This little diversion wasn't helping, but if I played my cards right, Evan and I could retrieve Juni and make it back to my workshop within a week. I'd still have two weeks left to hand over the finished product. It would be close, but I could do it. I was almost certain.

I pictured dropping that device into Rod's lap, tied up in a ribbon with the damn hand scythe he'd left as a calling card. If I didn't sink the blade into his thigh first.

I slipped into the Barrio in the late afternoon, loosely disguised with a ball cap and sunglasses. A wall of odors knocked me back: chicken dung, dirty laundry water, and sweat. I followed the dirt path between sparse shacks built with whatever materials could be scavenged: pine logs, palm fronds, corrugated tin, chunks of limestone, even mud and grass—you name it. The Barrio folk were a resourceful bunch. Vines and grasses covered the rooftops, forming the topside camouflage. Most Barrio dwellers were at work in the Citadel. The night shift was asleep or beginning to rouse for their watch. The walkways were empty. The familiarity of the place struck me, not in a good way. It felt like a homecoming, but to a place that no longer held space for me. A place hostile to its uppity neighbors.

The narrow path heightened my unease, and I surveyed the shadows for threats. Mac's home lay tucked along the outer wall of the Barrio. The squat structures were familiar, the odd crook in the pathway unforgettable, and I knew the land's cadence well enough to know something wasn't right. Eyes tagged me from dark corners, as palpable as being poked in the back.

Ahead, two figures blocked the intersecting pathway. My heart skidded, then kicked into high gear. When we were teens, these two delinquents had outpaced me in size and weight. The same held true today. A memory flashed through my mind: Me on the ground, face crushed in the dirt. The older guy, Chop, pinning me while the younger brother, Matty, kicked me. Heavy work boots connecting with my ribs. Pain so fierce it robbed me of breath. Twain finding me, helping me home.

Mac's sons hadn't liked me or Twain then, and from the look of it, that hadn't changed. Any attention their father gave us was deemed stolen from them.

"Where you think you're going?" Chop asked. A scruffy beard covered the lower half of his face, and his nose was creased from a previous break. Bulky arms crossed over his dirt-smeared overalls as he spat something brown and slimy onto the ground. It landed half an inch from my shoes. I didn't flinch.

"Thought maybe we'd outgrown this," I replied.

"You might as well turn around and go back the way you came," Chop said.

Matty raised his nose and added, "You got no business here."

"Now, there, you're wrong."

Chop lunged before the last word crossed my lips. He closed the distance faster than I thought a man his size could move. His fist slammed into my mouth. My head twirled, sending my sunglasses flying, and I staggered back. Another punch landed in my gut. I buckled into him, fighting the urge to hurl. I managed a breath and earned a nauseating nose full of sweat and onions. Chop shoved me off him. I stumbled to one knee and gulped air. I had two seconds to get my shit together, or it would be like old times. It had been years since Chop and Matty had beaten the crap out of me. I'd learned a few things since then.

"Get him, Chop!" Matty called from the sidelines, throwing air punches. "Make him bleed!"

I staggered to my feet and retreated several steps. Chop charged. I sidestepped him and punched him in the throat. Not hard enough to break his windpipe, but enough to take the piss out of him. He doubled over, gasping, and I brought my knee up into his face. I heard something snap. Chop keeled over, hitting the ground like a felled tree. He stayed there, cradling his nose, gasping as blood oozed between his fingers.

Matty hurried to his brother's side, eyes fueled with fury.

"I'm here to see Mac. I don't want to fight you," I said. My stomach throbbed and my jaw ached. I wiped blood from the corner of my mouth and spat more onto the ground.

Matty crunched his hands into fists and straightened, preparing to launch. "You was always nothing but trouble. You gonna be sorry you set foot here again," he said, advancing on me. A hand on his shoulder stopped him cold.

"That's enough, Matty," said a deep, sonorous voice. "Help your brother up and go get cleaned up. You gonna be late for your shift."

Matty glared at his father but didn't dare argue. Mac was a welcome sight, stirring a warmth I hadn't felt in a long time. The older man carried over six feet's worth of muscles, a chiseled jaw, and dimples that made him look like an old American movie star, even with his white, wavy hair. His voice hummed with a graveled harmony, like a comforting hymn. We came together in a hug.

"Neither one of m'boys was ever good at sharing."

"If I'd had a father like you, I wouldn't want to share either," I said. For the brief time I'd lived with Mac, he'd been better than a father. Like the father I wished I'd had. Patient and kind, refusing to abide any nonsense or cruelty. Mac worked as a mechanic on transpods and the underground tunnels. Everything he knew about electronics and programming, he'd taught Twain and me. We'd taken those skills and run with them. Literally. His boys couldn't grasp what he tried so hard to teach them, and they resented how easy it came to us. Last I'd heard, they were still stuck in the Citadel's basement boiler rooms.

Mac headed home, and I followed, peering over my shoulder as I went. Matty offered Chop a hand up. His brother shoved it away and glowered at me. If he had the chance, he'd repay me for putting him on the ground.

The Vetta family lived in a three-room shack built against the thirty-foot outer wall. Iron spikes and a camouflaged razor wire topped the stone barrier. Most laborers had no desire to venture beyond the wall, but some did—to hunt for food or materials or for adventure. Mac had pieced together his home with scrounged wood, stone, and palm leaves. The interior consisted of a sparse kitchen and living area and two bedrooms. The living room floor had served as Twain's and my temporary bed for almost two years.

"Been long time since we seen you around here, Rafe. What's up?"

Mac was never one for small talk. Right to the point.

"I need a vehicle. Something to get me through the Wild-lands. Fast."

"What the devil for?" His brow crinkled like he'd smelled a skunk.

"It's a long story. Probably safest if you know as little about it as possible."

"You concerned about safety, you shouldn't be going into the Wildlands," Mac said. He leaned against the kitchen table, one hand scratching his clean-shaven chin. "Remember when you first came here? You and Twain both, beaten and bloodied and starved. You'd taken a knife to the gut for Twain. If Los Reyes hadn't found you and taken pity, you'd both be dead right now."

"I know, Mac. Believe me, I know. Thus the vehicle. I don't intend on being out in the open for long," I said.

"Is it worth the risk?"

My mind skittered to Evan, to the kiss we'd shared. To the way she'd felt in my arms, entangled in my lips, to the firestorm she stoked in my core.

Mac stared at me, his eyes holding me hostage to the truth. But the truth was easy, even with a scythe hanging over my head, and it was about more than passing lust. It was worth it to see a justice done, to save the life of a child, to ensure a loving family remained whole. Dios knew how many families this empire had already torn apart. I had the chance to save one.

"Yes."

Mac waited. Waited for me to waiver or elaborate. When I didn't, he straightened and motioned me to follow. He strode into his bedroom, and I hesitated before crossing the threshold. This room had always been off-limits.

"Come on in, son, and close the door behind you," he said.

The room contained a rough-hewn chest of drawers, a lumpy bed barely big enough for two, and nothing else. Mac strolled to the end of his bed and kicked the blank plaster wall. A small cracking noise sounded, and the wall retreated a foot.

"Best close your mouth before the flies set a feast inside, son," he said. "Remember who taught you everything you know. C'mon."

Mac squeezed into the opening and disappeared. After I followed, he pushed the wall back into place, throwing the space into darkness. A moment later, light sparked as Mac flipped on a flashlight.

"Mind your step," he said, pointing down. A ladder crafted from rough wood protruded from a hole in the ground. Mac disappeared below, and I descended the shaky ladder after him.

At the bottom, we stood in a tunnel sloping into blackness. Wooden beams reinforced the dirt-carved corridor at steady intervals. Mac pushed through the darkness with his flashlight, and several minutes later, we reached the Sink. The big cavern buzzed with activity. People moved crates and bags of contraband on their backs, in carts or with utility vehicles. Mac nodded to acquaintances as we traversed the main hub and entered its recesses. Finally, we came to a room with a wide opening covered by a locked metal door. Mac withdrew a key ring from his pocket and unlocked the padlock. He slid the door open, pushing it into the ceiling with some effort. Inside stood a massive and well-equipped workshop. The beast in the center of the room stopped me in my tracks.

This was it.

A thrill of excitement burned through me.

"A UTV," I said, grinning.

The side-by-side had all-terrain wheels, four seats, a windshield, and a sturdy metal frame. I walked around it, studying it.

"Folks in the States ride these babies in the wilderness for fun," Mac said. "They got no Ferals to worry about. I've been smuggling this in piece by piece for three years, and I'm about ninety-five percent finished with it. The hardest part was converting the fuel system from gas to organic."

"It's perfect, Mac."

He had an odd mixture of pride and guilt on his face.

"What is it?" I asked. Mac lowered his gaze. The buzz inside me suddenly went cold.

"Mac, why are you building this?"

He eyed me sheepishly. "There are a few complications…"

PART III

RIPTIDE

EVANGELINE

*T*hree days had passed since Rafael had found a vehicle for the trip to El Jardín. In that time, Twain had sold Damling's jewelry to a buyer in the Sink, giving us the money needed to pay for Juni's Immersion. The next challenge was getting my sister to the Citadel, and since my father's station would bar him from taking Juni to the Fount, Rafael and I would have to fake our way inside, posing as a wealthy couple desperate to heal their sick child. One thing at a time.

Rafael had spent each day trekking to the Sink to help his friend finish building his vehicle. Yesterday he'd slept half the day and stayed up late, locked in his workshop. He'd come out long enough last night to tell me to pack and be ready to leave the next day. It had taken less than five minutes to gather my things, and then I'd wandered from room to room, unable to stop my mind from journeying a thousand directions.

This morning I woke before the sun and dressed in the outfit Simone picked out—a white linen shirt and a tan pair of britches called culottes. A thoughtful choice on her part, something between my customary skirts and her more practical pants. Sure to raise eyebrows back home, but I couldn't help but wonder why we hadn't the sense to wear them before.

Once dressed, I had little to do but wait. And pace. And clean. It was late afternoon when Rafael appeared at my door. Less than an hour later, I was in the Sink, pacing inside a large, cluttered workshop owned by his friend Mac.

I was headed home.

If everything went according to plan, we'd be sneaking inside El Jardín after nightfall. I couldn't stop shaking. We were about to go into the Wildlands. It didn't matter how brief our trip was. It was a risk.

"Will you stop pacing?" Rafael looked up from the control panel on the UTV he was working on and shot me a nasty look. The vehicle took up almost the entire floor of the workshop, crowding shelves and workbenches packed with parts and tools.

"Would it help if I hovered over your shoulder?" I glared at him. I should have kept my mouth shut. The man was risking his life taking me through the Wildlands, but my nerves got the better of me. Rafe's mouth raised in a half smile before he bent back to work.

"Almost done, darling," Mac said, patting my shoulder. "We need to work out a bug and scan Rafe's palm into the ignition."

"I appreciate you helping us," I said and began pacing again. I couldn't help it. I couldn't sit still.

"You ought to," Rafael grumbled, frowning again. "Wasn't cheap."

Mac ignored the dig and stowed our bags in a compartment beneath the back seat. Guilt twisted my stomach. I'd overheard Rafael ranting about the cost to Twain. Mac had built the UTV for someone named Luther, one of the Sink's bosses. We had to return the UTV undamaged before the end of the month. Failure to do so would land both Mac and Rafael in deep trouble since Luther didn't sound like the forgiving type. In exchange, Rafael had agreed to break into the Citadel's Prime

Registry and reassign Mac's sons to better jobs. I didn't know why that made him angry, only that it did, and I'd never be able to erase that debt.

"Got it," Rafael said, stretching his arms in triumph. His khaki shirt pulled taut over his muscled chest, reminding me of how his bare skin felt against my own. Heat rushed to my cheeks, and I averted my eyes.

Leaning into the vehicle, Rafael pushed a button and pressed his hand to a screen on the control panel. A light scanned his palm, and the panel beeped.

His eyes caught mine. "Time to go."

My knees threatened to buckle.

"Harley's at the gate, waiting for you," Mac said. "I suggest you leave as quickly as possible before anyone notices. I put a silencer on the engine, but I'm not sure how quiet it will be barreling down the tunnel."

Rafael shook Mac's hand and then drew the tall man in for a hug.

"Thanks," he whispered. Rafael released his friend, and we climbed inside the vehicle.

A massive door covered the entrance to Mac's workshop. He tugged on a rope, and the door rolled up and across the ceiling, giving way to one of the Sink's many tunnels. My stomach jolted as the UTV burst out of the workshop and turned into the tunnel. We lurched ahead, bouncing across an uneven path, headlamps scattering the darkness. My fingers gripped whatever solid metal I could find. Over the quiet hum of the motor, shouts sounded behind us, but I dared not look. Rafael's eyes flicked between the tunnel ahead and the mirror displaying whatever lay behind us. I uttered a silent prayer for safety.

The headlamps illuminated a wall in the distance. A black-bearded man waved, and Rafael slowed the vehicle as the man tugged something nearby. The wall slid to the side, revealing dimming rays of daylight. Rafael gunned the UTV forward, tossing a small pouch to the man as we sped past. The next second, we were in the Wildlands.

Warm air sang through me. Strands of hair worked loose from my ponytail and whipped around my face. It was exhilarating. Terrifying. My stomach clenched, yet I felt a quickening in my soul. Earthen scents soaked the air, and a wild beauty dressed the land, incomparable to the Citadel's manmade wonders. Despite the danger, it was oddly comforting, and I realized how much I did not belong in the fortressed city.

The UTV slipped inside a sparse pine forest, slowing to navigate the trees and flatten low shrubs. Rafael swiped his finger across a screen, and a map appeared, a red line marking a route to El Jardín.

"Not much of a secret, were we?"

"I downloaded the coordinates from the Imperial network," Rafael said. "I found the location of every guarded settlement in the Empire—the Conq's garden, the coastal communities, the ranches. I could drive you to any one of them."

"The one will do," I said.

"As the lady wishes."

We swerved through the forest. Rafael avoided the open road until we traveled beyond the sight of the Citadel's watchtowers. The sun began to fade, and the shadows stretched in the forest, cooling the air beneath the canopy. We drove in silence for about forty-five minutes before we connected with the road. Rafael stopped inside the tree line and surveyed the path in both directions. The map on the console revised our route and showed the farm about twenty miles away.

I'd be home soon. I thought about seeing Pa after being gone for weeks. Would he be angry or relieved? How would I explain Rafael? What would I tell him about the money we'd gathered for Juni's Immersion? I longed to return home more than anything, but I knew a fight lay ahead. My father would never let me leave again, especially with Juniper. I had to find a way to convince him.

"Ready to rock and rumble?" Rafael asked.

"How about we roll and ramble?"

"I take you to one heist, and you start getting all cheeky," he said, grinning. "No rambling today. We're speeding. Help me keep watch. The road looks clear, but the last thing we want to do is run into a Guardia transport."

"Or anyone else," I said.

The dirt road cut through a tunnel of wilderness. Tall pines, live oaks, elms, and magnolia trees crowded in, and springtime speckled the surrounding forest in redbud and dogwood blooms. Golden-hour light doused very branch, leaf and bud as we sped over the bumpy path mirroring the rugged route I'd hiked mere weeks ago. I shivered recalling the struggle that had been.

As the sun edged toward the western horizon, the last clutches of light shone in our eyes. I shielded my face, but it did little to help. I scanned the sides of the road, watching for any signs of a threat. After fifteen minutes, the sun beamed straight into my eyes.

I didn't see it until it was too late.

22

RAFE

I registered movement first, a blurred frisson of bodies in the tree line distorted by the sun's lowering rays. A thunderous crack reverberated as a giant pine lurched sideways, straight into our path. I stomped on the brakes and yanked the wheel to the side. Time slowed as we skidded sideways, spewing dirt and rock in a fan behind us. Evan screamed, and my heart stopped. The tree blocked the sun for a second, maybe less, and then it crashed onto the road. I stood on the brakes, but nothing could stop us. We slammed sideways into the tree, shattering the windshield. Glass pelted me, etching tiny cuts on my face and arms as the UTV careened over, teetered on two wheels, then plopped hard back onto all four wheels. My seat belt held me tight as my head whipped sideways. The engine died, and everything stopped.

Evan froze with one hand locked on the rollover bar, the other braced on the dash.

"You okay?"

She stared at me, rigid with fear. "No—I saw people in the forest. We gotta go."

"On it."

I pressed the ignition button and slapped my palm on the scan pad. Nothing happened.

"Come on!" I shouted, repeating the ignition steps.

"Going somewhere, friend?"

The voice was full of gravel. Deep and sharp-edged.

No. This couldn't happen. Not when we were this close.

"Rafe…"

It was the first time Evan had used my nickname. The sound of it on her lips made my heart hitch. I reached for her hand. She took mine and latched on so hard, it bordered on painful. I didn't mind. It was the only thing that felt solid in this moment.

I had to do something. Had to get us—get her—out of this disaster. I edged a hand toward the knife sheathed beneath my pants leg.

A filthy hand grabbed my arm.

"Don't think so," the Feral said. He was huge, dressed in dirty rags, hair matted and tangled. His eyes were wild and hungry and hooded. The sight of him dredged up dark memories.

The Feral hooked an arm around my neck. I tore at his flesh as he yanked me out of the UTV and across the felled pine. Evan screamed and held tight to my hand, but the Feral won the tug of war. He tossed me to the ground like a sack of potatoes.

"Let go!" Evan shouted.

Dios—Evan. What have I done?

I lunged, wrapped my arms around the Feral's waist, and shoved. The man simply growled, unmoved, like I was a fly taking on a horse. I grabbed his ball sack and squeezed like it was a Florida orange.

The Feral screeched and slammed a fist into my side. Breath punched loose from my lungs, and I let go. Someone grabbed me and locked my arms behind my back. My eyes skittered to where a fat, black-bearded man held Evan in a bear hug.

Six Ferals surrounded us. We were outnumbered and outmuscled.

Evan kicked and stomped the feet of her captor. She clawed his arm, leaving bloody trails on his skin. The man didn't blink. An older Feral with gray-streaked hair squared up to her, and her eyes widened like she'd seen a ghost.

"Hey, Trunk, look-it here," the gray-haired man said.

My hijacker snorted. "You're an idiot, Gator. I already seen her," he said. "I ain't blind."

Gator's dirty fingers pinched Evan's chin hard. "You don't understand. This is the bitch that left me for dead in the woods."

She shook her face free.

"That little thing almost kilt ya?" Trunk laughed, and the others joined in.

Gator frowned. "She ain't as weak as she looks." His fist came out of nowhere, punching Evan in the mouth. She cried out—a horrible, heart-rending sound—and her captor released her. She crumpled to the ground.

"I will fucking tear you apart," I roared. I thrashed at the arms holding me, and Trunk released me, shoving me for good measure. I vaulted over the tree and dropped to Evan's side. The Ferals circled us like vultures as I cradled Evan's face in my hands. Her eyes were dazed, her mouth bloody and red. It scorched my heart and dumped molten rage in my veins.

"I'm sorry..." It was a struggle to keep my words calm.

"No..." She started to speak, but hands seized my arms and dragged me away. Trunk's hold was an iron vise, and I could do nothing as Gator jerked Evan upright, as he claimed a knife from his belt. I fought against Trunk, even as I realized I was powerless to stop Gator if he wanted to drag that blade across her tender flesh. It could happen that fast. Blood cascading down her ivory blouse, her life draining away. I'd never fully understood what it meant to be responsible for another person's life until this moment. It ruined me.

Another Feral blocked my view. He was average in height and lean, with blue eyes sunken into a tanned and blond-bearded face. A newer Feral. Had to be. He had a damaged look in his eyes, like the Empire's machinations had warped his mind and purged his humanity, like the hunt was all that mattered now. But he stood with an air of authority and arrogance. His body had yet to show the signs of malnutrition and abuse that came with years of running Feral in the Wildlands. He was another life broken and cast away by the Conq's brutal games. Yet even as I recognized my father's claws in this, I had no sympathy for the asshole or his depraved partners. I wanted to murder every one of them, painfully, starting with the one who'd dared to strike Evan and put a knife to her throat.

"You're going to show us how this machine works, and then we won't cut your woman's throat," the blond man said.

"Hey, Jude, we keeping the girl?" Trunk asked.

Jude. The name of someone who'd once been a man, probably a soldier. Who was now a monster.

"Shut it," Jude said, not looking at the big man. His eyes stayed on me. "Now, show us how to start this thing."

"It requires my palm print to start the engine," I said. "You can take the vehicle, but you'll have no way to start it again."

"Then we'll take your hand with us," Jude said, cocking his mouth into a lopsided grin. "We don't mind a little blood."

The men laughed.

"Won't work. The console needs to sense body heat and a pulse to accept the palm scan. If I'm dead or if my hand is not attached, it won't start."

Jude grabbed my throat, pinching off my air. "Don't fuck with me. I'm not stupid," he growled.

I struggled to speak. "The man…who built it…programmed it for me…alone. It won't start…for anyone else."

Jude squeezed harder until my face burned red. The next second, he released me, shoving me in frustration.

"It's broken," I said, gulping for breath. "The collision damaged the engine. It won't start anyway."

He frowned, considered my words, and then punched me in the stomach. My body begged to double over, cave in, but Trunk held me firm while I gasped for air.

"I didn't say you could talk," Jude said. He paced, scratching his chin.

"Strip it," he said to his men. "Take anything you find that's not tied down. Him, too."

Trunk ripped the Convo from my arm, pocketing the only contact I had with home base. His bear paws patted my chest and dove into my pockets, coming up empty. He growled and shoved me. At least he'd overlooked the knife strapped to my ankle.

"Got this bottle here and bag of food," said a squat, fat Feral. He hoisted up the supplies we'd packed. Our other belongings were hidden in the compartment under the back seat.

"Bring it, Bear," Jude said. "And anything else you find."

Bear stalked toward Evan. "What else you got, girl?" he said. She shrank back, but there was nowhere to go.

"Back off," Gator said. "I claim this kill."

He tightened his hold on Evan, and a small gasp fell from her lips, the sound scorching my heart.

"Enough," Jude said.

Bear froze, and Gator swallowed whatever words he'd been about to spit out. Jude noticed, really noticed, Evan for the first time. He stared at her, his eyes narrowing. He drew closer and fingered a loose strand of her hair. Jude's eyes flicked to her mouth, and he wiped the blood from her lip, his thumb trailing slowly across her skin.

I lost it. I was going to bash his face until it looked like ground beef, until he stopped breathing. I yanked against Trunk's hold, willing myself free.

"Get your hands off her," I growled. I ripped my head back, trying to head-butt Trunk, but he evaded my blows. Jude smiled as if he'd accomplished some mission only he knew. His eyes rose to meet Evan's, and she matched his gaze with a glare.

"I've seen a handful of rich pricks joyriding out in the Wildlands, but never one dumb enough to bring his woman," Jude said, his eyes locked with Evan's. His words were all mine. "Tell you what, my friend. I'll give you a chance to make a smart decision. A deal. I'll return the woman to you if you do something for me."

"Fine—what is it?"

Jude put his hand on Gator's, lowering the knife from Evan's neck. He claimed her from the older Feral and shoved her against the hood of the UTV. He spoke with deathly calm as he jerked her hands behind her, pulled rope from his back pocket, and bound her wrists.

Evan's eyes met mine. Terror flared in their depths along with something that looked like an apology. Which made no sense. I should have protected her. This was my fault.

"About a mile or two north of here, a clan of transitorios has set up camp. You know what this is?" Jude asked.

I nodded. A band of transitorios had rescued me and Twain in the Wildlands, nursed us, and taken care of us. They were people who'd been exiled or had chosen to leave the Citadel or sanctioned communities like El Jardín. They banded together for safety, creating families and building transient communities. The Conq's regime forbade them from building permanent homesteads. Some had tried, but the Guardia had routed them, burning their villages to the ground. They existed in perpetual motion to avoid being torn apart.

"The chief of this clan is Ambrose Brego. Tall guy with long black hair. Has the biggest wagon in the caravan, usually at the front," Jude said.

I'd never heard of the guy. "Okay..."

Jude cinched Evan's bonds and tugged her off the vehicle. He draped an arm around her shoulders. "Go to the camp and find

Brego. He's got a stash of gold coins in his wagon. Steal them and bring them back, along with his horse."

"Done," I said, ready to finish this.

He cocked a slow smile.

"I'm not finished yet, friend," he said. "That knife hidden under your pants leg? You're going to plunge it into Brego's heart. Kill him. Bring me his scalp as proof. Oh, and grab us some food while you're there. We haven't had anything decent to eat in a while."

"You can't be serious," I said.

"Oh, I'm very serious," Jude said, caressing Evan's neck. "Very."

She jerked away from his touch, but his arm tightened around her shoulders.

"His life or hers," Jude said. "It's real simple. Do this, you get her back."

I had no choice. "Okay."

"That's a good man. A smart man."

"You'll let us leave then, unharmed?" I asked.

"Of course," he said, in a way that signaled the opposite. "Now, my friends and I have places to be. Meet us here at dawn, and we'll make the exchange."

I hesitated. "I want a guarantee that Evan will be safe and unharmed. No one will touch her."

"We're *not* monsters," Jude said, half his mouth quirking up into a gruesome smirk.

That wasn't even close to a guarantee, but his word was useless. I knew that. I also knew had no choice.

"Fine," I said, though every bone in my body screamed against it. I didn't want to let Evan out of my sight. Nightmare images of what they might do to her flashed in my mind. But what choice did I have? They'd kill me and still keep her if I refused. Or kill her, too. At least this way I could buy us time, find a way out of this disaster.

"Go that way," Jude said, pointing north of the road. "It's pretty much a straight shot."

He signaled to his men. They sauntered toward the forest like they hadn't a care in the world. Evan's terrified eyes lingered on mine as Jude dragged her with him.

"Everything's going to be fine," I said, willing her to believe it. Knowing she wouldn't. Knowing full well Jude had no intention of ever freeing her.

The Ferals disappeared into the trees, and I dashed for the back seat of the UTV. I rummaged in the hidden compartment until I found the Tagget. Darkness was falling, time slipping through my fingers. As quietly as humanly possible, I followed the group, chasing Evan's white shirt like a lighthouse in the dark. I didn't want to lose track of her, and I had one shot to get this right.

I powered up the Tagget and aimed it at her bright spot in the distance. I pressed the Launch button, and the beacon sailed into the air. Evan flinched at the impact, drawing her shoulders together, and looked around. I cursed under my breath. The propulsion mechanism needed work, but right now, it didn't matter. All that mattered was being able to find Evan no matter where they took her, and now I could. I lingered in the darkness, watching the Ferals march her away. Letting her go felt like bleeding out. A coldness settled in my bones as hope hemorrhaged on the forest floor.

It cost all my resolve to walk away. I backtracked to the UTV, put it into neutral, and started shoving it toward the forest. I couldn't leave it on the road for the Guardia to find. I stowed the vehicle in the bushes and covered it with branches, camouflaging it from sight. Then I walked back to the road to get my bearings.

The sound of an engine stilled my blood.

I didn't wait to see who was coming. I ran. Behind me, car doors opened and slammed shut. Footfalls crunched in the earth, pursuing me into the tree line. I pushed harder, even as my lungs protested. Moments later, arms came around my torso and tackled me from behind. I fell beneath the weight of someone bigger than me. It was like a boulder had dropped on me. I grunted and tried to breathe.

I don't have time for this shit.

My attacker rolled me over, and our eyes locked. We both froze. "What the hell are you doing out here, *Guy?*"

My Scythe of Thorns contact stooped over me, dressed in black military field dress, an assault rifle slung over his back. *What the hell?*

"I could ask the same of you, *Rod.*"

Footsteps pounded closer now. Rod looked over his shoulder and back to me. "You say a word about knowing me, and I will fucking end you right here," he said.

"Likewise," I half growled.

My Scythe rebel contact was a damn Guardia soldier. *How?* I had no idea if the man would turn me in, if he was a true rebel or an infiltrator, a spy sent to expose and rout the Scythe. I hadn't trusted him before, and now I trusted him even less. I was beginning to regret every decision I'd made in the last few weeks.

Rod yanked me from the ground by one arm. His strength surprised me. He could have tossed me halfway to the road if he wanted. Three Guardia soldiers filled in around him.

"Colonel Tresick, we didn't see anyone else," said one out-of-breath soldier.

Colonel? What the hellfire fuck? What game is this guy playing?

This was even worse than I could imagine. An epic fiasco on my part.

"You see anything else suspicious?" Tresick asked.

"Nothing yet but the downed tree," the soldier replied. "Looks like someone cut it down. Bates and Woodford are moving it off the road."

Please don't let them find the UTV. If they confiscated it, I was a dead man. Luther was a ruthless Sink boss, and if his vehicle went missing, there would be hell to pay—for me and Mac both. As it was, I needed to get the UTV back to the Citadel and repaired before Luther's pickup date arrived. Time was slipping fast like water through a sieve.

"This one's a tourist," Tresick said. "A thrill-seeker hiking the Wildlands like an idiot."

The soldiers laughed, but the colonel was studying me like he was puzzling something out. Like he'd noticed something he hadn't before. I wasn't wearing a disguise. I hoped to the highest heights he wasn't figuring out who I really was.

"Good luck with that," one of them snorted.

Tresick pinned me with his glare. "You'd best hurry back to the Citadel, city boy," he said. "I'm sure you have more important things to do than wander around and gamble with your life. Wouldn't want anything unpleasant to happen to you."

The unspoken message was clear. My life—and Twain's life —were on the line. Along with anyone else Tresick had discovered was important to me. Did he know about Evan? Simone? Did he know who I really was? I'd gone into this situation knowing far less than I should have.

"Of course, Colonel," I said.

"Don't let me see you out here again," Tresick said.

"Got it."

"Let's move out," he said to his men. "We need to get back to the Citadel."

The three soldiers strolled off, but Tresick lingered a moment. When his men were a few paces ahead, he turned on me. I spoke first.

"I'm on schedule," I said.

"I don't know what you're up to out here, and I don't really care, but you're running out of time. I won't abide loose ends, and I don't make empty threats. Remember that."

Tresick stalked away, disappearing before I had a chance to reply.

I bolted. I had no time to waste. That was clearer than it had ever been. I reached the transitorio camp within minutes, stopping at the first hint of firelight through the trees.

The transitorios had arranged their wagons in a protective circle in the forest clearing. The camp resonated with life, people talking and laughing, moving about. The uncanny sense of déjà vu struck me harder than I could have imagined. I'd once lived among a group of people like this one. They'd helped me and healed me, and now I stood outside this community like a predator.

I scanned the perimeter, picking out the sentries. The camp was well guarded. I'd have a better chance breaking inside after midnight, while everyone slept, but I knew what I had to do, and it couldn't wait a second longer. Every minute I hesitated was another minute Evan remained in danger.

Creeping through the forest, I circumnavigated the camp. I kept going until I found the biggest wagon, a mini wooden cabin on wheels, complete with windows, full-sized door, and stairs leading to the threshold. Beyond the wagons, a gathering of men lounged around a campfire. Laughter sprinkled their conversation, and the aroma of roasted meat wafted into the woods, making my stomach growl.

I crouched, watching for the sentries to look away. Days passed in the minutes I waited, but then it happened. The guards glanced away from my position at the same time. I rushed forward, dropped to the ground, and rolled beneath the nearest wagon.

"What was that?"

"You hear it, too?"

I lay on my stomach behind a wagon wheel, pulse crashing through my veins so loud I feared someone might hear it. The sentries patrolled between their posts, rifles at the ready.

"Anything?"

"Nothin.' Probably a possum."

"Or skunk. Better watch out, man, or Martha won't let you in the wagon tonight."

"It'll take more than a skunk to keep me outta our bed."

While they laughed, I slipped from hiding and sheltered between two wagons, gathering my courage. I took a deep breath and stepped into the circle, approaching the gathering of men as if I belonged there.

The tall man, the one with long black hair, saw me first. He reclined in a chair, boots stretched out in front of the fire, holding a steaming mug. His eyes caught mine as I raised my hands in the universal symbol of surrender. One by one, the voices around the fire died as they watched the smile fade from the tall man's face.

"I'm looking for Ambrose Brego," I said. "Someone wants him dead."

23

EVANGELINE

*N*ight descended in the forest. A bright half-moon hung low in the sky, shadowing me like a guardian angel that could offer no salvation.

We walked for a long time through the dark, the men jerking me to my feet when I stumbled, shoving me when I walked too slow. Laughing when I fell face-first in the dirt. My jaw throbbed, and a dark ache had lodged in my head. Gator hobbled behind me, poking my back with a stick. There would be a reckoning with him at some point, and I could feel my luck slipping away.

After a while, we reached a clearing where a fire bloomed in the dark. Dirty tarps hung between trees, forming makeshift tents around the fire. Two men stoked the blaze, roasting a rabbit on a spit. The smell was incredible, and my stomach spasmed with hunger.

As we entered the campsite, someone shoved me, and I tripped over a root and fell, landing inches from the fire pit. Gruff laughter burst from all sides.

"Enough, Gator," Jude said, grasping my arm and hauling me

to my feet. He was not gentle. "Men, we got a friend staying with us tonight," he said.

"She ain't no friend," Gator grumbled. "She's a prisoner of war."

Jude turned on Gator and punched him in the jaw. The old man went to his knees, and Jude swung his boot into his belly. The man grunted, spewing blood, and keeled over, groaning.

Jude leaned over the Feral and ran a finger through the blood on his mouth. He drew an X on the man's forehead with his bloodied finger. "Her fate is not yours to decide," he said. "Touch her again, and I will put a blade through your forehead. Got it?"

Gator nodded. That wasn't good enough. Jude kicked him again. He yelped.

"Do you understand?" Jude repeated.

"Yes! I get it."

"Trunk, secure the woman," Jude said.

I backed away. It was pointless, but my body didn't trust reason.

Trunk snatched a knife from his belt as he approached. "Please, make this hard," he said. "That's how I like it."

I froze, afraid to encourage him. The big man spun me around and pushed me against a tree. His knife slid between my wrists, sawing the rope until my hands flew free. The relief was so sudden, I didn't think. I shoved past him and fled. Shouts flew up behind me, but I ran, hard. I wove between the trees, sucking in desperate breaths. Thick arms snatched me from behind. Trunk lifted me off the ground and hauled me back to the clearing. I kicked and clawed, but Trunk only laughed.

"That's it, girl," he said. "Fight me. I'm getting all horny."

The blood drained from my body, the fight along with it. I was suddenly cold all over.

"Don't stop now," he said, dropping me next to a tree at the edge of the clearing.

"Stop playing with your food," Jude called. He sat by the fire, eating a rabbit leg and smirking.

Trunk grabbed my wrist and looped a new rope around it. I yanked my hand free. His big paw claimed my wrist again, squeezing so hard I was sure it would snap. I resisted again, but Trunk held fast, securing the rope with ease. His hand splayed across my chest as a grin stretched his lips. He pushed me against the tree, then whipped behind me and set about tying my hands behind the trunk. I panicked, screaming and jerking, tugging my hands despite the pain. The rope bit into my skin.

"Damn it, woman, you're a firecracker," Trunk hooted. Even the thrill in his voice failed to still me. I couldn't do this. I couldn't abide being powerless. I'd never survive this night. I had to find a way out of this.

Jude came to Trunk's aid. His fingers clenched my neck and pressed me against the tree. His face hovered inches from mine. He did not speak a word, but the threat was clear. I stilled, despite the fight thrumming through my veins.

Trunk took quick advantage.

"Got 'er," he said, appearing from behind the tree.

Jude didn't move. He stared at me, his hand pinning me. After several long moments, he nodded ever so slightly, as if arriving at a decision, and released me. His fingers latched on to my ponytail holder and tugged the band, freeing my hair. It fell loose around my shoulders. Jude smiled and then walked off without another word.

A tremor coursed through me. His behavior frightened me more than being punched.

I stood against the tree as the minutes stretched and the Ferals went about their business, eating, taunting each other, bragging about their crimes. The men passed around a brown jug, and as the night dragged on, their laughter grew sloppier, their stories bigger, their insults meaner. They forgot me, and I was glad for it. I slid down the tree, wincing at the pull on my arms, and sat. I searched for my angel moon in the sky and thought of Rafe, praying he was safe. Pushing away thoughts of him killing another human, because of me. I closed my eyes and tried to erase it all from my mind.

The spill of liquid nearby startled me. Bear stood a few feet away, a stream of pee spattering the ground, the brown jug at his feet. I snapped my head around, sorry I'd looked. He chuckled and, seconds later, lumbered over and stooped in front of me.

"Poor thing. You must be thirsty."

Bear hauled the jug to my mouth and tipped it up. I couldn't squeeze my lips closed fast enough, and liquor seeped past, blazing a stinging trail down my throat. Most of it spilled down my chin and soaked my blouse. I sputtered and coughed, gagging. Liquor settled in my stomach like hot coals as my eyes watered. The Ferals cackled.

"That girl can't hold her liquor," one of them yelled. "Give her another go!"

Bear was happy to oblige. I shook my head, evading the bottle, but Bear grabbed my hair and wrenched my head back. He tipped the liquid to my lips. I pinched them closed, and the liquor poured down my face and onto my shirt.

"Don't be like that," Bear grumbled. His breath stank of alcohol and decay. He grabbed my cheeks and squeezed, forcing my lips apart. He tipped the jug again, and this time the liquid streamed between my teeth. He let it flow, forcing me to gag and swallow. The alcohol scorched my tongue and throat. Fire coursed through me, warming my belly. My head began to buzz.

"Stop!" I spit the word out and shook my head, the effort making me dizzy. Bear laughed and forced another round down my throat. I swallowed a big gulp and sputtered, spitting the rest out.

"Look at that, you messed up your nice shirt," Bear said, wiping his hand slowly down my chest. He stared at the wet cloth clinging to my skin, and his breath hitched. I squirmed but couldn't move out of reach. I kicked my feet, panicked, pushing myself against the tree and wriggling my way into a standing position. The buzzing in my head intensified, and I teetered sideways. My arms scratched painfully against the bark as I righted myself, but I didn't care. I wanted as far from him as possible.

Bear's face darkened, like I'd taken his toy. He stumbled to his feet. "Where you goin'?" he said, eyes dropping to my breasts. He reached for me.

"Get your hands off me!" I hiked my knee into Bear's groin, hard. He hollered, and his fingers tangled in my blouse, jerking as he buckled. Buttons popped and flew everywhere, leaving my shirt gaping open and exposing the bra beneath. "Get away from me!"

I screamed over and over, kicking Bear repeatedly, determined to keep him at bay. He was so drunk, he fell in the dirt. But then he came to his senses, and his biggest sense was fury. He lunged with his fist raised.

Jude caught Bear's wrist before his blow landed. "Enough!" he said.

Bear dropped his fist, and he scowled.

"Can't no one have a little fun?" one of the men at the fire pit muttered. Jude gave him a silencing glare. He shoved Bear toward the fire ring. Bear left, grumbling every step of the way.

Jude eyed me again. It was unnerving.

"No one touches her unless I say so," he said. The men grumbled around the fire pit. Jude whipped his head around, his glare pinning the group.

"No one. Understood?" His words were a menace. His men agreed with more fervor this time. Jude's attention returned to me, his eyes taking in my gaping shirt. His hands reached for me, and I flinched. His gaze moved to my eyes, staring me into stillness.

His fingers latched on to my shirtfronts and tugged them across my chest, covering me. His hands roamed lower, and I gasped as he tucked my shirttails into my waistband, anchoring them in place. His fingers lingered on my stomach, his eyes on mine.

The next instant, he was gone. Only then did I notice the thrashing of my heart, the heat of fear trembling inside me. Or maybe it was the liquor. My lips felt numb, my head light and dizzy. Everything was fuzzy. Everything except for Jude's words.

"Stay away from her," Jude said as he sauntered toward the campfire. "I know a man who'll pay a fortune for her, but he won't want her spoiled."

My knees buckled, and I sank to the ground.

THE NIGHT STRETCHED SLOW before me. My racing heart jumped at every sound. After his men devoured the rabbit and emptied two jugs of liquor, Jude brought me a few scraps of meat. He stuffed the bits into my mouth, allowing his fingers to linger on my lips longer than necessary, wiping where there was nothing to wipe. He grinned at my discomfort and forced more alcohol down my throat. My head swam with the stuff. I twisted away from the bottle, but Jude wound his fingers in my hair and forced it down.

Finally he left me alone and slept with his arm tossed over his eyes. His men lay sprawled around him, their snores drowning the low night sounds. Bear, who'd been assigned watch, was currently slumped against a tree, snoring the loudest.

I leaned against my tree, struggling to stop the forest from spinning. I was drunk. There was no denying it. My stomach churned; my body floated on waves that didn't exist. I wanted to sleep, but the last shreds of my rational mind kept shouting to stay alert. It wasn't safe to sleep. The alcohol won in the end. My eyes grew heavy. I closed them, and the world mercifully ceased swerving.

Then the nightmare came. In the darkness, Gator's face loomed in front of me. His body straddled mine, pinning my legs, and his disgusting hand clamped over my mouth, blocking the scream rising in my throat. I choked on the smell of his carcass breath, the stink of his sweat. Bile surged, searing my throat. His fingers mashed hard, flaring pain in my bruised cheek and tender lip.

That was how I knew it wasn't a nightmare.

The other men slept around the fire. No help in sight. Gator was going to kill me. Drunk, soaked in alcohol and dirt. Alone. This was how it would end.

I screamed against Gator's hand. He clutched my throat, squelching the sound and strangling my breath.

"No one's going to help you," Gator whispered. "I'm going to kill you. I don't give two shits about selling you. No one gets the best of me. No. One. I own you now."

His hand squeezed harder. Tears pushed at the corners of my eyes. Simone's knife clung to my leg, out of reach and useless.

"You ain't getting away this time."

I thrashed under Gator's weight, to no effect. His face muscles tensed, and his cheeks reddened as he pressed harder. The blood pooled in my face. My skin felt like it might burst, as blackness sparked the edges of my vision. Terror fought through my drunkenness and spiked hard in my belly. I gasped for breath, but none came.

Only a growing gray darkness. Swallowing me.

24

RAFE

$\mathcal{F}$ ive seconds after approaching the campfire, I realized my plan was woefully inadequate. This transitorio camp was armed to the teeth. I found myself flat in the dirt, hands bound behind my back, surrounded by men with firearms aimed at my head.

Perfecto.

The black-haired man strolled forward, arms crossed, and eyed me with amusement. His clothing was a notch above his companions. He wore a clean white shirt with a green cargo vest, brown pants, and polished boots planted a foot from my nose. I'd found Ambrose Brego. It had to be him.

"To be clear," I said, spitting dirt out of my mouth, "I'm not the one who wants you dead."

"That so?" Brego said, leaning toward me.

"Yeah," I said. "However, in the interest of full disclosure, you should know I do have a knife strapped to my ankle, but I have no intention of using it on anyone here."

"Not that you're in position to do much harm, Mister..." he said.

"Roldan. Rafael Roldan."

Brego nodded at his men. Two of them hauled me to standing while a third patted me down rather intimately. He liberated the knife from my ankle strap, snorted at the size of it, and tossed it onto the ground, then continued probing until he came across the Tagget.

He studied it, brow crinkled, and handed it to Brego.

"Don't look like a weapon," the frisker said.

"It's a tracking device," I said.

Brego turned the device over in his hands, frowning, before stuffing it into his pocket. My one link to Evan was now buried in a hostile stranger's pants. Great.

"So, you're not here to murder me," Brego said. "Why are you here? Why risk your life? You should have been shot before you even made it out of the woods."

Brego's glare skewered his men.

"To give you something you want," I said.

He cocked a grin. Hands bound, circled by henchmen, and pockets emptied, I lacked a clear bargaining position. "That's a big presumption. What makes you think you know what I want?"

I explained what had happened with the Ferals on the road, what Jude had demanded. Brego's men murmured in agitation.

"Them's the animals that killed Ben," said a young man. Brego held up a hand to silence him.

"I can lead you to a nest of Ferals. Straight to the camp of your enemy," I said. "They won't know you're coming. You can deal with them as you see fit."

"You tracked the Ferals to their camp?"

"That device in your pocket will lead us right to them," I said, then explained how it worked.

"Then we rescue your friend?" Brego said. "That's what you really want."

"Of course it's what I want. But you want this, too. You want justice for what these Ferals have done to you, to your people.

You're a threat to them, or else they wouldn't demand I do their dirty work for them. How many have you lost to them already?"

"I don't care to lose more by following a stranger into an ambush." Brego crossed his arms. His eyes hardened.

"You don't trust me. I get it. You're wise to be cautious. But think of this—if I'd wanted to harm you, I would have crept into your camp and slit your throat while you slept. I've proven I could do it. You only caught me because I wanted you to catch me."

Brego's scowl deepened more than I thought possible.

"Look, if you do this, it will help me. No doubt," I said. "It will also help an innocent woman who is in danger right now while we waste time debating. But if you do it for nothing else, do it for yourself. For your people. These Ferals will come at you again. If I fail, they'll find another way, and if I can sneak in here, so can they."

Brego's men bristled, faces puckering like they'd swallowed a spoonful of dung. I wasn't making any friends here, but I didn't care.

"How many of your people will be lost?" I pushed on. "How many women and children? It's a risk either way. Go with me now, you have the advantage. You're on the offense. You're in control of what happens."

"Sounds to me like you'd be in control. Could be a trap you're leading us into," Brego said.

"I ain't following this idiot," the man who frisked me said. "He got his woman taken in the first place. Who goes into the Wildlands alone, unprotected like that?"

The man's associates muttered in agreement. He hit where it hurt. I should have planned for an ambush. I had placed too much faith in the notion we'd be exposed for only a brief period of time. It had been stupid of me. Lethally stupid.

"Look, I've survived in the Wildlands before," I said, trying to reclaim the conversation. "It's not my first time fighting Ferals, but these animals have gotten bolder. They would have ambushed the first Imperial convoy that passed their way. I think they were waiting for one and got us instead. In the past, they would have never challenged the Guardia, and you know it."

The men remained quiet. Brego eyed me as if he could discern the truth beneath my skin.

"Think about it," I said. "They know where you are. They told me exactly where to find you. They know what you have worth stealing. One way or another, they're going to come for you."

I paused, letting my words sink in.

"Do you fight on your turf, when you're not expecting it, when you have a camp full of women and children to protect? Or do you take the fight to them? Catch them unguarded? End the threat on your terms?"

Brego squared his shoulders and lifted his chin to stare me down. "Take us to the ambush site. Prove to us what you say is true, then we'll talk."

The transitorio leader gathered a dozen men, not willing to weaken his caravan's defenses by sending more. I hoped the UTV was still there, or we were screwed.

We marched at the speed of molasses, loud as a stampede. It made me want to jump out of my skin. If we kept going like this, the Ferals would hear us coming from a mile off. Still, I had little choice. I walked, hands bound, as Brego scrutinized me and our surroundings. Before long, we reached the road. The pine tree had been moved from the path, but the saw marks in the trunk proved it had been no accident.

"I pushed the UTV into the woods over there."

"Show me," Brego said, and I did. He and his men uncovered the vehicle, taking in the shattered windshield and the crushed front bumper.

"Lift the bench on the back seat," I suggested. "You'll find belongings for two people."

"Averill, check it out," Brego said. The man who'd frisked me leaned into the vehicle and lifted the seat. He dug out two bags and opened one, Evan's rucksack. He drew out the dress Evan had worn the day of the Expo and inspected it. Setting it aside, he rummaged again, pulling out a book.

"Women's things," Averill said, showing Brego.

"Those belong to Evan. Satisfied?"

"Not until we're finished," Brego said.

"Fair enough. Can we go now?"

"How far to the Feral camp?"

"Give me the tracking device and I'll tell you."

I twisted to display my bound hands, inviting Brego to liberate me. The man studied me, deliberating. Finally, he removed my knife from his belt.

"If this is a trap of some sort, there will be no mercy."

"Understood."

Brego sliced through the rope, freeing my wrists, then handed me the Tagget. I powered the device on, and the screen glowed with a lone flashing dot on a map.

"There you are," I whispered, relief swelling in my gut. I fiddled with the device, and a line materialized, connecting with Evan's location. Hope stirred inside me. She was closer than I'd thought.

"A mile, maybe a bit less. We're close," I said, showing Brego the display.

"Let's get this over with," he said, then handed me my knife.

We marched again in silence, following the line on the screen. The men grew serious, their footsteps becoming muffled with caution. The night noises of forest creatures swelled in the quiet. We moved through the trees until the screen indicated the camp loomed less than a quarter mile ahead. I showed Brego the map. He nodded.

"Torches out," he said. His men snuffed out the lights, throwing the forest into darkness. My eyes adjusted as moonlight illuminated the trees in a milky grayness.

Brego motioned us onward. Minutes later, light glowed in the distance. We'd found her.

Brego gave his men commands with his raised hand, and they fanned out in silence. The men began circling the camp and waiting for the signal to attack. In the clearing, a campfire burned low. Shabby bodies lay askew around the fire, sleeping. No one appeared to be keeping watch. Brego raised his palm, a signal to wait as he surveyed enemy territory.

A scuffle in the shadow of the camp snagged my attention, and my heart turned to ice. There she was, tied to a tree. A Feral crouched over her, fingers digging into her throat, choking the life out of her.

I ran. My arms and legs worked without conscious thought, my grip tightening around my knife. Guttural instinct kicked in, raw and furious. I had no idea if Brego had signaled to attack or not. I didn't care. I closed the distance in seconds. My vision tunneled to one thing. I slammed into the Feral, knocking him clear of Evan.

We crashed to the ground, the impact knocking the knife from my hand. The Feral writhed beneath me like a live wire. I straddled him, raining blows on his face. His fingers, no longer on Evan's throat, clutched my own now. Jagged nails dug in hard, but he couldn't get a strong hold. I pounded harder, letting every ounce of fury channel through my arm and into the man's flesh. The pressure on my neck lightened. My knuckles grew slick with blood. His or mine, I didn't know. I didn't care. My fist shrieked with pain, but I couldn't stop, wouldn't stop. Chaos loomed all around me, screams and shouts and gunfire, as fighting overtook the camp. Beneath me, the Feral's fingers loosened and his hands fell slack across his chest, and still, I couldn't stop.

"Rafe…" Evan's voice filtered through my rage. I froze, my ruined fist poised to strike again. The man's eyes remained closed, his body limp. My chest heaved, and my gut twisted at the bloodied lump beneath me, at what I'd done. Never before had I lost control like this.

It was horrifying. It was liberating.

I rushed to Evan. Averill was cutting her loose, and I scanned the area for danger. The attack was over. Feral bodies lay scattered around the fire, bloodied and unmoving as Brego's men meandered around the camp.

Evan's freed arms fell limp at her sides. She tilted, then tumbled over. I caught her and lifted her up. I cradled her face, studying her for any injuries.

"You came," she breathed, her voice raspy. Her eyes locked on mine as if trying to convince herself I was real. A bruise purpled her face, and her hair tumbled loose and disheveled. Her shirt gaped open, buttons missing.

A shiver rolled up my spine.

Evan's hands came up between us. She fisted my shirt and tugged me close. Her lips touched mine. I stiffened, even as heat stirred in my belly. Her lips moved over mine with a hunger that stoked the urge to respond in kind, to replay what we'd done at Blythe's house. I tasted liquor on her lips and recoiled. She reeked of it.

I tilted her face up and looked into her eyes. They were glassy, dazed.

She was wasted.

"Dios mío, what did they do to you?" I said. "Are you hurt? Did they—"

"I'm fine," she said, though swaying slightly.

Something moved to my right. The Feral I'd left unmoving on the ground charged toward us. I shoved Evan behind me and heaved my arm up to block the incoming knife.

My knife. The bastard had my knife.

The Feral rammed me into the tree, and something sharp sliced into my side. He dove again. I blocked him, knocking the knife from his grasp, but his body slammed me, his shoulder bruising my ribs. I grunted and tried to shove him off. He struck my jaw twice in rapid succession. I collapsed beneath him, stunned as he mounted me and pinned my arms with his legs. I watched through a fog as he plucked the knife from the ground. I was trapped, waiting for the killing blow.

It never came.

The Feral howled, and his torso arched. His hands groped for the nape of his neck. Evan hovered behind him, a wild look in her eyes. I wanted to yell at her to run, but I couldn't speak. Shouts rang through the trees, and suddenly Brego's men surrounded us, pushing Evan from view. The men hauled the Feral off me. Moments later, a gunshot thundered in my ear. The Feral fell to the earth, blood blooming from a hole in his forehead.

Evan pushed through the men and dropped to her knees beside me. "Oh God, Rafe, you're hurt." She touched my face with tender fingers.

"I'm fine," I said, struggling to sit up. "Just got the wind knocked out of me."

Pain sliced through my side.

"You're bleeding," she said. Her worried eyes tried to focus.

Brego kneeled next to me.

"Did you get them?" I asked, gasping at the pain.

"No thanks to you, charging off like an idiot," he said. "We got eight. Two cowards ran into the woods. We gave chase, but they escaped. Now lie still while I take a look."

Brego unbuttoned my shirt and peeled it back. Evan inhaled sharply and covered her mouth.

"Gash on your side. You'll need sewing up. Does it hurt anywhere else?" he asked.

"Only when I breathe," I joked, then regretted my levity as pain shot through me again.

"Likely a cracked rib. You'll live," he said. "We'll bandage you up until we get back to camp and can get you stitched."

I motioned for Brego to draw nearer, not wanting my next words to be overheard. "You need to help Evan," I whispered. "They got her drunk."

He laughed long and hardy. "I wouldn't worry too much about your woman, Mr. Roldan," he said. "She was sober enough to save your life. She's the one who stuck a knife in that bastard's back."

Evan stared at me, unfocused, then swayed to the side and puked.

25

EVANGELINE

$\mathcal{M}$y skull felt like a fifty-pound flour sack bursting at the seams. I fought to open my eyes and then wished I hadn't. I shut them as nausea swept through me, bearing a vivid memory. My fists sinking a knife between a man's shoulders. His unholy scream. Blood on his jacket, on my hands. Doubling over and throwing up.

I remembered little after that. We'd walked for a month of Sundays, the forest a blur, my mind fuzzy and unfocused. I couldn't recall how or when I'd gotten here, wherever *here* was. Just endless walking, constantly stopping to rest. Rafe needed to rest. He was hurt.

My eyes flew open.

Rafe lay by me, asleep, his face tilted toward mine. Bandages wrapped his bare chest. Bruises darkened his face, and his lip swelled around a cut. I'd dragged him into my problem, and he'd gotten hurt because of it. I wanted to wipe his injuries away, make them disappear. The warmth radiating off his skin caressed my own, stirring a swarm of butterflies low in my belly, and I had the irrational urge to touch him, to lose myself in him like I had the night of Blythe Damling's party. The sensation jostled another memory. My lips on Rafe's lips.

I kissed Rafe again.

I'd grabbed him and pushed my lips to his. He hadn't kissed back.

My face flushed red, and I pushed to sitting. My head howled in response. I ached all over. My jaw was sore, and my throat burned. I rubbed my forehead and glanced at Rafe. He'd come back for me, and I'd rewarded him with a drunken kiss. An unwanted one. Embarrassment flashed through me, hot and ugly.

A dark green tent sheltered us, lit by a lone oil lamp. It was dark outside and quiet, either early morning or night—I couldn't tell. Beneath us, a pallet covered the ground, layered in blankets and pillows. Food, water, and bandages waited on a low table nearby. Our bags slumped near the tent opening.

I stared at the angry red marks circling my wrists and shuddered. Bits and pieces of memory kept hitting me like punches: being dragged back to the tree, dirty hands touching me, my bound arms, being powerless to stop any of it. The ghost of their hands lingered on me even now. Fingers ripping buttons loose. Touching my stomach. My chest. My lips.

I glanced down to find a man's shirt covering me. I tucked my knees to my chest and lowered my head as a sob built in my throat.

A tender hand touched my arm, and I startled at the contact.

"Hey, there." Rafe's voice sounded groggy.

I dashed tears from my eyes before facing him. "How are you feeling?"

"Like I was run over by a transpod full of lead turnips."

I smiled, though joy felt far from me. It was a wonder Rafe could joke through the pain.

"What happened?" I hesitated. "Things are a bit fuzzy."

"Nothing to worry about," he said. "We're safe, and I'm the

proud owner of a few stitches and maybe a cracked rib. Nothing permanent."

"I was stupid to think this would work. I'm so sorry."

"Hey," Rafe said. He tried to sit up, but pain flashed through his eyes, and he lay back down. "This is not your fault," he said.

"It is," I said. "You wouldn't be here if it weren't for me. How can I bring Juni out here? We were almost killed. She can't survive something like this. I can't even go home. My father sees us like this, and he'll never let us leave again." My voice grew more panicked as I rambled on.

"This is a setback, nothing more," Rafe said. His hand stroked my arm, a touch that soothed and left me wanting more.

"We'll wait a couple of days for the bruises to fade, and then we'll go to El Jardín. We'll come up with a plan."

"Wait? You mean...go back to the Citadel?"

"No, not without your sister. Right now, we're in a transitorio camp. We're safe."

I had no idea what a transitorio camp was, but I knew our circumstances weren't that simple. "I can't keep asking you to risk your life for me and my family."

Rafe's face softened. "Evan, you never asked for anything. I made the choice to insert myself into your situation."

"Why?"

His eyes clouded, and he paused, as if unsure how to explain. He sighed. "The Conq is a monster. He's had more than five hundred years to build a better world, but all he does is hurt and manipulate people. I've seen it, experienced it. What he's doing to the Empire is not only wrong, it's evil. He's harming, neglecting, even torturing and killing his own people," Rafe said quietly. "I decided a long time ago I wouldn't stand by and watch anymore. I've made it my life's mission to do whatever I can to counteract the harm he's doing, to undermine his tyranny, to shake the security he's achieved at the expense of others. To help people get a foot up on a better life. The Conq's ways mean people like your sister have no chance to survive. I mean to change that every chance I get."

"Most people are too afraid to challenge the Conquistador."

"Rightfully so."

"But not you?"

"He's already taken everything from me once. I survived."

I cocked my head in question. There was history there.

"What happened?" I asked.

Rafe's eyes grew distant. "I did something that displeased him. He banished me to the Wildlands when I was sixteen and left me to die there."

"How could anyone do that to someone so young?"

"I was old enough to know better, old enough to take my punishment like a man."

"What could you have possibly done to earn a punishment like that?"

"It's not important," he said. "It's not something I'm proud of, but I more than paid for it."

It was clear he didn't want to go into detail. We sat without speaking, the nighttime noises pushing through the thin veil of our tent.

"I was incredibly lucky it was you who took me and not that other man," I said, breaking the silence.

His brow crinkled in understanding, and he simply nodded. He could have said *I told you so*, but he didn't.

"Thank you…for saving me that day and yesterday. Was it yesterday?"

"It was. You slept all day. You needed it."

I blushed and looked away.

"They kept forcing liquor down my throat," I said. My voice shook.

"I know."

I heard a grunt. Rafe pushed up onto one elbow and reached

for me. His fingers touched my arm, sending goose bumps swimming across my skin.

"It wasn't your fault. None of it." The pain flared in his eyes, and his face strained.

"Rafe, you need to lie down. You shouldn't move." I pressed my palm to his chest and applied gentle pressure until he gave in. I attempted to withdraw my hand, but he covered it and held it against his him.

"I'm sorry I let them take you," he said. "I'm sorry they hurt you. It should have never happened."

The warmth of his skin, the beat of his heart under my palm sent my thoughts scattering. My insides melted and pooled low in my belly. Did he remember my kiss? Of course he did, but he was too kind to mention it. My cheeks ignited with fire. I wanted to look away, but I couldn't. Rational speech abandoned me.

"They didn't...they didn't..." I began. Memories of that night sliced through my thoughts. I couldn't stop the shiver rolling up my spine. "Their leader made them stop touching me. He said..."

My breath shook as the knot of fear grew in my stomach.

"He said he didn't want me spoiled," I said, dropping my gaze. "He wanted to sell me."

Rafe squeezed my hand. His fingers touched my chin and lifted my face so our eyes connected. "He can't hurt you now," he said.

"He's dead?"

His brows furrowed in a look that was part empathy, part regret, and I knew the answer. It crushed me.

"I'm sorry, Evan. He escaped."

EVANGELINE

*L*idia Cabrini was a no-nonsense woman. She wouldn't take no for an answer and wouldn't leave our tent without me. I followed her out and froze. A caravan of wagons—most bearing wooden homes of different sizes and shapes—circled a massive camp. Tents and tables and chairs studded the field inside the circle, along with random campfires. Horses grazed in a nearby rope pen. People milled about everywhere. The wagons looked like the ones I'd seen on the way to the Citadel. The violence of that morning flashed through my mind, and I couldn't reconcile it with the lightness of what lay before me, the feel of home.

Lidia barked the word "Come," and I started. She marched through the bustling camp, and I hurried to keep up. We passed clusters of men arguing and laughing, children chasing each other and squealing, women bent over laundry buckets, and old women gossiping in rocking chairs with knitting needles in hand. A knot of homesickness tightened in my belly. I should have been home right now.

Lidia stopped at a large wagon bearing a small wooden cabin painted in faded blue. A young woman about my age waited by the stairs leading to the cabin entrance, and she greeted us with a smile. A smooth mound bulged from her thin frame. She was with child. I gaped at her and stumbled over a pine cone. If things had been different, I could have been like her. If my mother hadn't died when she had, I might have been married to Dominic already, whether I'd wanted to or not. I could have been carrying his child. I might have never left the farm. And there would have been no hope for Juni.

"Mind your step," Lidia scolded before addressing the young woman on the stoop. "Gabby, what are you waiting for? Get in there and get the water going."

The younger woman frowned and rushed inside the cabin, and Lidia shooed me after her.

"Welcome to our bathhouse!" Gabby said. "It's not much, but it gets the job done."

Inside the sparse cabin, two metal tubs lined the roughhewn walls with a privacy curtain draped between. Each tub had a small wooden stool beside it for sitting or stowing belongings. Shelves bearing linens and soaps filled the back wall. Gabby pointed me to the tub on the left, where a hose extended from a hole in the wall into the basin. She grabbed a lever next to the hose and pumped. Water sputtered and then flowed into the tub.

"How..."

"It's pumping water from the stream on the other side of the tree line," Gabby said, pride bursting in her smile. "It's cold, but it's clean."

"Get on with it, then bring her to the chuck wagon," Lidia said, scowling from the doorframe.

"Yes, Madre," Gabby said. Lidia closed the door and disappeared.

"She's your mother?"

"Oh, no," Gabby said. "She is the matron of our clan. The elder woman in the camp."

I gaped at her. "She's Mr. Brego's wife?" The woman was too old for him.

Gabby laughed. "Uh, no. He is our patrón. Our leader," she said. "He's not married. He was. Once. But his wife died in childbirth. It was so sad. The baby died, too."

Gabby's eyes flicked to her belly. I wondered if she had a midwife like Nina to help when her baby came.

"I'm sorry," I said.

She shook off the worry clouding her eyes. "It was a long time ago. Come on—grab a bar of soap off the shelf and hop in the tub. Madre Lidia will be angry if we take too long."

Gabby plopped down on the stool on the other side of the privacy curtain as I undressed. I was grateful. I didn't want her to see the Conquistador's brand on my shoulder. My face burned thinking about it. How I'd been marked as property. His property.

I folded my clothes and placed them on the stool before grabbing soap, a washcloth, and a towel from the shelf.

"How's the water?"

I dipped my toe into the tub and squealed. It felt like ice.

"You get used to it," Gabby said. Her laughter chimed like a song.

I climbed in and dunked my head under the water. It was like jumping into a cold stream on a hot day. It stole my breath away.

"I never knew anyone except Ferals lived in the Wildlands," I said between chattering teeth. "How do you survive out here? It's terrifying."

The soap smelled like lavender and rose. I lathered the cleanser in my hands and scrubbed my hair with the suds.

"We protect each other. From childhood, we learn how to protect our camp and how to fight. We move constantly. That's as much for the Ferals as it is for the Conquistador. He's forbidden settlements that are not his own. Some clans tried to build towns, but the Guardia came and burned them to the ground."

"That's horrible. Why not live in one of the protected farms?"

My skin was turning purple from the chill, so I quickly moved onto scrubbing my body.

"Some of the transitorios came from the farms," she said. "Tossed out for the smallest of things. But mainly there are too many of us. The settlements feed and supply the Citadel and some of the sanctioned coastal cities. They don't need all of us for that. We would be a burden. At least that's the way I heard it explained."

I finished bathing, dried off, and put on my mother's dress. Cold water dripped from my hair, dampening the fabric, sending chills along my skin. The bath refreshed me, but my body ached from the abuse it had taken. Not even the cool water could wash that away.

"You live a life of freedom few in Florida would ever dream of," I said, stepping from behind the curtain. She handed me a hairbrush, and I tugged it through my hair. "You're brave to live it."

Gabby pondered that. "Maybe. I don't know. I think any life in Florida has its own danger."

"You may be right."

Hair brushed, tub drained, and bathhouse cleaned, we walked to the chuck wagon, moving at an easier pace than the one Lidia had set. As we walked through the camp, Gabby questioned me about my life and how long I'd been Rafe's "woman."

"I'm not his woman," I said, blushing. "He's more of a friend."

I'd never called Rafe a friend before, but I didn't know how else to describe him. We'd been thrown together by circumstance, and I'd been lucky circumstance had tossed me to someone who was honorable, who was kind when I'd done nothing to deserve it. If that wasn't the definition of a friend, I didn't know what was.

Gabby grinned knowingly. I cocked my head as if irritated, but against my will, a smile crept over my face.

When we reached Lidia, she had one hand hooked in the mouth of a spotted bass, the other gripped around the hilt of a filet knife, slicing beneath the fish's mottled skin. "Took you long enough," she said.

"Sorry, Madre," Gabby said.

Lidia laid her sharp eyes on me. "I delivered water, linens, and fresh bandages to your tent. Help your man get cleaned up and dressed before dinner," she said. "Change his bandage and check his wound. If there are any signs of redness or fever, let me know."

Her directness rattled me. I wanted to tell her Rafe wasn't "my man," but her tone left little room to object. In the end, Rafe needed tending. Of course I'd do it. I nodded.

"After dinner, start packing," she said. "We're breaking camp tomorrow."

"What?"

❦

I THREW the tent flap open and charged inside in a panic. I stilled, my desperation melting the moment I saw him. Rafe sat upright on the edge of the pallet, hair soaked, water dripping down a face cramped with pain. His bloodied bandage lay on a low table next to a basin of water.

"Are you all right?" I asked. My eyes darted to the stitches on his side, the dried blood on this stomach.

"Perfecto," he gasped.

"Here, let me help you."

I knelt and took the washcloth from his hand, then dipped the cloth into the water and rinsed it. My eyes flicked to his, and

I hesitated, uncertain about touching him—touching his bare skin.

"Thanks…" he said.

Fire radiated across my cheeks, and I dropped my gaze. There was nothing left but to get on with it. I drew the cloth across his flesh. My touch was timid, trembling, a whisper. My stomach knotted as heat flushed across my skin. Rafe tensed beneath my touch.

"Sorry," I said, withdrawing. "Didn't mean to hurt you."

"You didn't." His body relaxed, though with some effort.

I skimmed the cloth across his skin, wiping away blood and dirt in tender strokes. I focused on my hands, trying to ignore the intimacy of the moment. Trying to forget what my father would say if he found me alone in a tent with a half-dressed man. Touching him. Wondering what it would feel like if nothing separated my flesh from his. A wayward thought scratched its way into my head.

I was a grown woman, and what I did was none of my father's business.

Silence stretched uneasy between us. I glanced at Rafe, thankful he couldn't read my thoughts. His eyes fixed on me with a strange intensity. His gaze dropped to my mouth. Without thinking, my eyes trailed to his. For a moment, I couldn't move. I imagined touching his lips, tracing them with my fingertips. With my mouth.

I felt dizzy, shaken with the want of it.

I had to do something, say something to break the spell, or I wouldn't be able to stop myself, and that would not be good.

"Lidia says they're leaving tomorrow," I blurted. My voice trembled from the tiny earthquake moving inside me. "Breaking camp and going south."

"I heard."

"What are we going to do?"

Left alone in the Wildlands, we'd never survive. Rafe was in no shape to fight, and I couldn't protect both of us.

"We've got options," Rafe said. "We can stay here, fix the UTV, and finish the trip on our own. We lose the protection of the transitorios, but we're not far from your home. The safest option is to go with them. They're willing to allow it."

Go with them. Turn away from home. The idea of traveling farther from home, deeper into the Wildlands, felt wrong. Like turning my back on Juni, watching her life slip away.

Rafe's fingers touched my cheek, and I drank in his eyes. They were full of compassion. And certainty. I wanted to believe him.

"I don't want to prolong this any more than we have to, but the alternative is too dangerous," he said. "We'll travel with them, fix the UTV, and get you home as fast as we can."

"How far? How long? Can we trust these people?"

"If they wanted to harm us, they would have already," Rafe said.

"So, we'll be safe while we're with them, but eventually we have to leave," I said. "We'll be farther away from El Jardín than ever. How will we make it back?"

He squeezed my hand. "One day at a time, Evan," he said. "We need to go with them. It will give us time to heal, to plan. Time to do some convincing."

"Convincing?"

Rafe cocked a mischievous grin.

RAFE

*B*rego had waited a day and half before demanding answers. Having no other option, I'd offered up as little as I could. I'd told him about escorting Evan from the Citadel to El Jardín—a story which demanded more truth than I cared to share. But to remain in Brego's camp, I'd had to spill the swill, including how a Citadelian was familiar with the Wildlands. I'd wanted to tell Brego my past was none of his damn business, but in my current state, that wouldn't fly. There were people in the Wildlands who knew me from my youth, so I needed to stick as close to the truth as possible.

"I was thrown out of the Citadel when I was young. It was... for something stupid. Instead of executing a teen outright, the Empire did the next best thing and banished me to the Wildlands," I'd told him. "I survived, thanks in large part to a transitorio camp much like yours. They cared for me, sheltered me. Not too far from the Citadel, I became separated from the camp during a Feral raid. I made it into the Barrio, and a family there took me in."

He didn't need to know about Twain. He didn't need to know we'd both been banished for stealing from the Conq.

From my father. We'd tried to set up our own black-market lemonade stand, selling pilfered Fount water instead of lemon water. Our first con had been a childish gambit, and I'd roped my best friend into the action. It had been fun while it lasted. It had also been stupid beyond reason. We'd had no idea the water lost potency the farther it got from the source. Citizens of the Citadel hadn't taken kindly to being swindled for glorified pond water. It had been my fault the Conq had exiled Twain to the Wildlands. It had been my idea.

"You're one lucky man," Brego had said. He'd asked about the transitorio camp.

"I came across them somewhere south of the Citadel. Their patrón was a man named Sam Bautista. You know him?"

"I know all the patrones," he'd said. "We gather our clans together twice a year for council."

Sam was a gruff but fair man. His wife, Belinda, had a tender heart. They'd been unable to have children but had adopted Phillip, a boy orphaned by a flu outbreak. Belinda had convinced Sam to take me and Twain into their care after the transitorios had found us wandering in the Wildlands, hungry and battered.

"How are Sam and Belinda?"

A range of emotions had crossed Brego's face.

"What happened?" I'd asked, straining to sit up.

"Belinda's gone. Ferals took her and the boy. They found her days later in the forest, butchered. Never found the boy."

I'd rubbed my face, as if it would dull the pain.

"Dios." My voice had cracked. I couldn't believe Belinda was dead, that she had suffered so much at the end. She'd probably died trying to protect Phillip. I could see her doing that.

"Yes," Brego had said. "You can pay your respects in person at the council gathering."

That was when I'd known we were in, that Brego was allowing us to stay amid the safety of his clan's numbers. That was how we'd ended up here, on a wagon, moving south through the Wildlands, away from our original destination.

Time felt like a noose around my neck, drawing tighter the farther we traveled from El Jardín, but without a functioning UTV, we had little choice. I had over two weeks left to finish the Wreckus. I could still make it home in time to make my deadline. If only I could convince myself that was true. It had to be.

On route to Council Springs, Evan chatted with her new friend in the driver's box. Reins dangled loosely in Gabby's fingers while the horses did the rest, following the wagon in front of them. The two laughed and shared stories while Gabby's husband, Seth, sat next to me. From the roof of their wagon home, we surveilled the passing landscape armed with crossbows, ready for any threat. It had taken some convincing, but Seth had tethered our UTV to the rear of the couple's wagon. It had only cost me a pair of night-vision goggles. They would serve him well when he was on patrol duty.

Gabby had readily adopted us, and though leery, Seth had allowed us to hitch a ride at her urging. He was a man of few words, not that I minded. I didn't need to make small talk or contend with a barrage of questions. Evan and I had had our fill of those at dinner the previous night. I'd forgotten how boisterous and busy the transitorios could be. They were a sociable crowd. They loved to talk and tell stories, to dance, play music and sing, to hug and kiss. It was overwhelming for someone who preferred quiet and was not fond of being touched. Not by strangers.

Laughter bubbled up from below. Evan smiled as she recounted spilling a steaming pot of stew on a bunch of field hands. It was a rare hue of smile, at least in the time I'd known her. Pure, untroubled, and joyful. Beautiful. It helped distract me from the aches and pain rattling my body like an old man.

"We have a healer on our farm named Nina," Evan was saying. "She's our midwife. She'd tease me, said I was too clumsy to be a healer. Said with my luck, I'd stitch up the wrong thing and let my patient bleed out."

"Oh, that's awful!" Gabby gasped.

"I don't think she meant it," she said. "Nina made me her apprentice, and I was happy to learn. I want to know how to take care of my family and friends."

Evan's compassion would make her a good healer. My thoughts drifted to the previous day. To her tending my wounds, bathing me with gentle hands. Her touch had lit my skin on fire and stoked something heated and hungry in me. It had taken everything I had not to grasp her and cover her with my lips, with my body. When she'd slept next to me, I couldn't get her out of my head. I'd watched her in the low light, her brow furrowed, her face flushed from sleep. I'd wanted to pull her close until her body molded to mine in the dark.

Her effect on me was unfathomable. Except for Twain and Simone, I never let my guard down with anyone. Intimacy was not part of my world. Never had been. Never expected it to be. Was I willing to let her change that?

I rubbed my face and forced myself to stop staring at her, stop obsessing over what I couldn't explain. I didn't need these thoughts sidetracking me. I needed to concentrate on finishing this mission, then go home and complete Tresick's project.

Colonel Tresick.

I couldn't shake the dread over discovering who he was. Either I was in deeper shit than I imagined or the scales had been balanced and we both stood with proverbial pistols aimed at each other. He held my fate in his hands, but I had his, too— for now. The longer it took to get home, the more the scales tipped to his advantage. I couldn't afford this delay, but we had no choice. Going it on our own was just too risky. That was why I needed to persuade Brego's clan to escort us to El Jardín, and then usher Evan, Juniper and me to the Citadel. It would be the only chance we'd have to convince Evan's father to let the child go. I was sure of it.

I glanced at Seth sitting next to me. "How much longer?" I asked. We'd broken camp at daybreak, and the sun was now beginning its slow descent into night.

Seth peeked from beneath his wide-brimmed hat. He was red haired and fair skinned and had to shield his flesh from the harsh Florida sun. "Close. Maybe thirty minutes."

That makes twenty, I thought. Twenty words from the man since we'd departed this morning. I suppressed a smile and resumed my vigil.

Half an hour later, a commotion arose at the front of the caravan, and a horn blared in the distance. Panic flashed across Evan's face, and I lifted my crossbow.

"Easy," Seth said, nudging my crossbow down. "We're here."

That made twenty-three.

THE MEETING GROUND was a wide expanse next to a freshwater spring the clans called Council Springs. Seven transitorio clans positioned their caravans in two concentric arcs next to the crystalline water, leaving a vast open space in the middle. Sentries claimed positions around the perimeter for first watch. Inside the clearing, men and women erected tents, set up tables and chairs, and lit campfires. In time, hundreds of clan members began mingling and welcoming each other like old friends. It felt familiar and yet so far removed from what my life had become.

Evan watched in wonder. "They seem so happy," she said as she helped set up our tent.

"They are," I said. "As long as they keep traveling, they're pretty much left alone, to live as they wish."

It felt good to move, to burn away the disquiet in my gut, but the long ride and setting up camp had left me winded. My ribs pulsed with a constant ache. I pushed through it, hoping Evan wouldn't notice. She did. After a brief argument—which I allowed her to win—she took charge, relegating me to holding poles as she secured the tent in place. Afterward, I let her unpack while I went in search of my past.

I found Sam deep in conversation with Brego. Sam's eyes lit with instant recognition.

"Hola, mi amigo," I said. "¿Qué tal?"

He drew me into a bear hug full of warmth. It was such a comfort, I ignored the stab of pain in my ribs.

"¡Ah, mijo, gloria a Dios! You're alive." He held me out, studying my face. "Where is Twain?"

"Safe and sound and at home. We both made it, thanks to you."

"You can't imagine how happy that makes me," Sam said.

"I'm sorry we had no way to let you know, and"—I loosed a breath—"I'm sorry about Belinda and Phillip."

The big man was speechless. All gruffness melted under the warmth of memory. He nodded, too broken to speak.

Brego clapped a hand on Sam's shoulder. "The council of patrones will meet tonight to address the Feral problem," he said. "They're growing bolder, picking off our people one by one. It's time we put a stop to it."

EVANGELINE

*T*he night was on fire. Everywhere I looked, campfires lit the darkness, sending sparks into the black sky, washing faces young and old in warm light. Men, women, and children were dressed in their best clothing, faces washed, hair combed. The women, even the older ones, let their hair hang free, entwining wildflowers into thin braids cascading down their backs or crowning their heads. Gabby braided wild violets and viburnum into my hair. I looked like a fairy from one of Juniper's storybooks.

The evening began with a huge feast, and each clan contributed something special. Brego's clan supplied the mulberry wine. Bautista's group served something called jabalí asado. Rafe said it was wild boar, something that reminded him of a roasted-suckling-pig recipe he'd loved as a child. Five other clans joined the gathering. One brought a salad made with dandelions, blackberries, and watercress. The rest contributed bread, fish, and a honey cake that melted on my tongue.

Rafe introduced me to Mr. Bautista as we sat down to dinner. The men traded memories as we ate, and I filled my belly listening to their stories. Rafe and Twain had been known for playing pranks on the clan matron. Twain had gotten caught once and had to wash the old woman's undergarments as punishment. Bautista had taught the boys to fight and throw knives, and his wife had had to force the boys to bathe, threatening them with more "women's work" if they refused.

The stories were joyful, but the weight of Belinda's absence laced every memory with a bittersweet taste. Still, the man's pride in them was clear. He spoke about how protective they'd been of Belinda, how the boys had designed and built a wagon bench to make rides less bumpy. They'd rigged a ceiling fan so the Bautistas could be cooled with a few pumps of a lever inside their cabin. Rafe and Twain had fed off each other, inventing ideas for improvements, perfecting and building them together. Like their minds had been two parts of one whole.

I could have listened all night, but soon dinner ended and the music and dancing began. And drinking. Sprinkled with lots of hugging and kissing among family and reunited friends. For the first time in a long time, I felt safe and happy.

Rafe and I settled by a campfire, where an old man played a lively tune on fiddle, accompanied by a boy on a drum. People clapped along as others danced, their faces red from laughter and exertion. It reminded me of home, how the crew would sometimes sit around the fire at night, play music, dance, and sing. I couldn't help but smile at the joyfulness all around. Even Rafe wore an unguarded smile. Gabby and Seth were in the middle of it. Seth held his wife in his arms, twirling amid the dancers, his eyes locked on her smiling face like no one else existed in the world.

Bautista stepped in front of me and held out his hand. "Vamos, amiga, you have to dance on a night like this."

I looked to Rafe for help. It didn't feel right to refuse, but I wanted to shake my head. I'd only ever danced with my mother or sister. Once or twice with my father. Never strangers. Never with another man. It wasn't done in our community.

Rafe had a weird look on his face. "What happened to you? The Sam I used to know would rather snack on scat than dance," he said.

"Things change, mijo. You can either fight it or go with it. I'm going with this one," the patrón said.

He snagged my hand and swept me from my seat. Then we were dancing, skipping and hopping into the crowd of dancers as the music beat a rhythm around us. I had no idea what I was doing, but I tried to keep up and avoid stomping my partner's feet.

"That's it! You got it," Bautista said.

I searched for Rafe, hoping for rescue. He watched us, his face dimpled by a big, goofy smile. Slowly, the terror of what I was doing fizzled, and joy filled its place. By the time the song ended and Bautista brought me back to Rafe, I was breathless with delight, with the joy of letting go.

"Thank you, Mr. Bautista," I said. "I think I needed that."

"It's Sam, and it was my pleasure."

The music slowed and the drum disappeared, replaced by the easy strum of a guitar. Seth pulled Gabby close, and the two swayed together, gazes locked in a wordless poem of adoration.

"That's your cue, mijo." Sam snagged Rafe's arm and hauled him up. Rafe winced and his face drained of color as pain roiled through him.

"Eh, lo siento," Sam said, but he didn't let go.

"What—"

Before Rafe could finish a sentence, he'd placed my hand in Rafe's.

"Dance with your woman," Sam said.

"She's not—"

"I'm not—"

Sam interrupted, placing a hand on both our shoulders. Rafe's hand lingered in mine, and I didn't mind a bit.

"As I said before, things change." Sam grew serious, his gaze locked on Rafe's. "I learned that the hard way when I lost you and Twain. When I lost Belinda and Phillip. For a long time, I didn't want to go on. I couldn't see a reason. But Belinda wouldn't let me be. I'd see her in my dreams, reminding me life is what you make it. It's about seeing what you have standing right in front of you that's good and perfect. It's about embracing the blessings of this life, this day, this minute with all you have. Look at the two of you—how in this messed-up world, you found each other."

Sam patted Rafe's bruised cheek, and his eyes softened. "You have so much to enjoy right in front of you. Don't waste any time ignoring it," he continued. "You never know when it might be taken away. Now, go, dance. Enjoy each other."

He nudged us into the fray. We stumbled a step, then stood like idiots, struck speechless. Couples whirled in lazy circles, shifting around us like water around a boulder in a stream. Sam's words sounded like Gospel, and I wanted to shout *Amen*, but I was nothing more than an obligation to Rafe. I stared at our entwined hands, embarrassed, holding my breath in a useless effort to smother the fluttering in my belly. I could no longer deny that I cared for Rafe. The feeling was like nothing I'd ever known, and I hungered for more. Which made it even more painful, knowing he didn't feel the same.

Rafe lifted our twined hands and tucked them into his chest. His hand slid around my waist and drew me close. The tenderness of the moment felt different from the frenzy of what happened between us in the Citadel. Felt deeper. The heat of his body and the clean scent of his skin melted my resolve. My heart thudded deep and hard in my chest. Rafe swayed to the music, pulling me with him. I couldn't believe he was going along with this. I laid a cautious hand on his shoulder and looked up. His thoughts were as unknown to me as the bright moon above, but the way he looked at me sent tremors through my body.

Rafe stopped moving. The music played on, and the dancers blurred around us. His hands cupped my face, and a thumb caressed my bruised cheek.

"You are good and perfect," he said, and the world around us disappeared. There was only the two of us and the frantic beat of our hearts against each other. Rafe lowered his head, and his lips touched mine, soft and questioning, as if we'd never touched before. As if waiting for an answer.

The answer was yes.

I opened myself to him, pressing back, parting my lips in welcome. Our arms entwined, pulling our bodies together until I didn't know where I ended and he began. His touch was sweet relief; I almost cried for the joy of it.

Shouts and cheers erupted around us, shattering our tiny world. We broke apart, and my face glowed red like hot coals. All around us, couples clapped and raised their cups, cheering us on. I was mortified. I was giddy. I couldn't help but smile.

Sam raised his mug and grinned. "To love!" he shouted. He tilted his cup to his mouth and drank deeply.

29

RAFE

The night had grown quiet. Most campers had passed out or turned in for bed. The morning sun was sure to bring a few bleary eyes and late risers as the revelers shook off their overindulgences, but for now, a scattering of hardy folks still lingered by the campfires, talking in low voices. Across the field, Evan and Gabby reclined side-by-side against a log, deep in conversation. Firelight danced on their faces. Seth slumbered with his head on his wife's lap, a hat over his face. I'd been dragged to the council of patrones. Brego wanted me to share what had happened to us, but I had other thoughts on my mind. Like that kiss. That moment with no pretense, no outside forces pushing us together.

Truth be told, I'd been struck like a match. Once blackened and cold, now engulfed in flame, and I liked the taste of that fire. I'd burn to ash just to feel it again. All I wanted was Evan, in our tent, breathless beneath my touch. I wanted...well, I wanted many things, but they would have to wait. I tried to refocus on the conversation at hand.

The seven patrones and their seconds clustered around a

campfire, admiring their Feral problem. Admiring because so far, we'd only gotten as far as one-upping each other about how brazen the Ferals had become. The attacks were growing in scope and audacity. A few years ago, five Ferals working together would have been considered unusual. In the last year, some had seen as many as ten working in tandem. My father had been hell-bent on finding a drug that would create the perfect soldier. Was this the result? More failed experiments released into the Wildlands to live out their days as unchecked monsters.

The patrones continued their chatter, but the conversation had yet to pivot toward a solution.

"They've learned our security measures," said Marcus Jessie, clan leader from the southern region. "Our sentries can't stop them."

A long silence stretched between the patrones. No one could refute it. I myself had proven how easy it was to walk into a camp unimpeded. Exercise a little patience and a lot of caution, and bingo—a hole emerged in the clan's vigilance.

"So, what are we to do?" The question came from Isaac Sain, a clan patrón from the Gulf Coast. "I could put every man I have on the perimeter, and it wouldn't be enough."

No one had an answer. The eerie calm of the night infused their silence with unease.

"What if we could hear them coming? Some sort of early alarm?" Sam asked. His words stirred something in my brain. I leaned forward, listening, waiting for the idea to unfurl.

"Maybe it's that simple," he said. "We set trip ropes in the forest. They'll never see them in the dark. We'll hear them coming."

The men grumbled in agreement, but I was onto something. Something that could serve two purposes—keeping the clans safe and helping Evan and me finish our mission. The clan leaders bandied about ideas on the best booby traps, but I was lost in working out my idea.

A scream pierced the silence. *Evan.*

Brego moved before I understood what was happening. Across the clearing, a Feral clutched Gabby by the hair and hauled her across the log. Brego rushed toward them, and I bolted after him.

In the distance, Evan yanked a log from the fire. Feathery flames engulfed one end, and she swung the wood at the Feral dragging Gabby. Evan missed. She growled in frustration, running after him, and swung again, this time connecting with the side of his head. He howled and dropped Gabby. His hands pounded the fire sparking in his matted hair. Seth claimed his wife and pulled her to safety.

I was several feet behind Brego when movement caught my eye. Ferals streamed into the camp and fanned out. One paused and pointed a crossbow at Brego.

"Brego! Watch out!"

I lunged at Brego, knocking him to the ground as a bolt pierced the earth beside us. Sharp pain stabbed through my chest. My wound had torn open, and my ribs were on fire. Brego rolled to his side and heaved his dagger. It landed hilt-deep in the Feral's belly, and he sank to the ground, screaming.

Across the clearing, Evan tangled with another Feral. He jabbed his knife at her and swerved to evade her firebrand. Seth shielded Evan's back, his pregnant wife tucked between them, as he defended himself.

I scrambled to my feet, ignoring the pain, and ran full tilt. I crashed into Evan's attacker, grabbed his wrist, and knocked his knife free. The collision was excruciating, but something deeper drove me on, numbed me to all but the need to protect. The Feral resisted, and I landed an elbow to his jaw. His head popped back, and he staggered. I went after him again, punching him until I could hardly breathe. Rage poured into my fists, white hot and satisfying. My knuckles burned, but I pummeled the Feral until he dropped to his knees and fell to the dirt, bloody and unmoving.

Swinging around, I searched for the next threat. A Feral dashed into the forest, his hands pounding his head, trying to snuff out the flames in his hair. Evan had gotten another one. Seth chased him but stopped as soon as he disappeared into the woods.

I scanned the camp. Clan members roused from their beds stirred around the circle, armed and ready to fight. But the fight was over, the last of the Ferals fleeing into the darkness.

Evan embraced Gabby until Seth returned, and Gabby latched on to him like a drowning woman clinging to dry land. I gathered Evan into my arms and held her tight to my chest, kissing the top of her head. She clung to me, shaking. The pain that had become oblivious during the fight came flooding back, and it nearly stole my breath.

"I was so stupid. I didn't have my knife. I left it in the tent." Evan buried her face in my chest, and her words came out muffled.

I tilted her face toward mine. "Shh... You were a madwoman with that log," I whispered. "Remind me not to make you angry."

One side of her mouth lifted, even as tears rimmed her eyes. I kissed her, and her lips melted into mine with a trembling tenderness. A profound relief flooded me. She was safe, unharmed, and here with me. I drew her closer, and she sucked in a sharp breath.

"What's wrong? You hurt?"

"It's nothing," she said, cradling her hands against her chest. "Some burns on my hands. Seems I haven't learned my lesson about playing with fire."

I took her hands and turned them over. Her swollen skin radiated red heat.

"I didn't notice it at first."

"You are amazing," I said, kissing her forehead again. "We'll find some ointment and get you fixed up. No blisters so far. That's a good sign."

"Everything all right?" Brego joined us. He gave Gabby a tender pat on the cheek.

"We'll be fine after a little doctoring," I said. "She burned her hands."

"Looks like you might need some tending, too," Brego said, nodding to my side. A patch of blood spread where my wound had reopened.

"A mere scratch. I'm fine," I lied.

"I owe you a thanks," he said. "Second time you've saved my life. I may have to keep you around as a bodyguard."

"Thanks, but I'm already guarding a body."

"Indeed you are." Brego grinned at Evan, and she blushed.

He quickly changed topics. "They stole a horse and some of the food stocks," he said. "Bastards tried to steal an entire chuck wagon. The attack on the women was a diversion. We were too fast for them, but Abraham's injured pretty bad—got a knife to the back. The healer's tending to him."

I shook my head in disbelief. I'd just met Abraham Kabbara, one of the patrones. "Will he be all right?"

"Don't know. His healer's good, but only time will tell."

"You ever thought of combining your clans?" I asked. "You'd have strength in numbers. There had to be at least twenty Ferals tonight. I've never known that many to work together. That's easy enough to defend against with seven clans, but traveling alone?"

"There used to be clans the size of this gathering, but the Conquistador didn't like it," Brego said, his eyes glazing with a distant memory. "Now they're scattered to all corners of the Empire. It may be a conversation we need to revisit. We have other business in the meantime. At first light, we're tracking down those Ferals, teaching them a lesson. Strike us, we'll strike back twice as hard. You up for joining us?"

My body screamed against it, but there could be no other answer.

"Wouldn't miss it."

30

EVANGELINE

*B*rego's healer re-sewed the stitches on Rafe's side. She looked at Rafe's ointment and said she could offer nothing better for my burns. In the tent, Rafe dabbed my wounds with tentative fingers, easing the greasy substance over my damaged skin, his touch soothing more than my burns. He wrapped my hands in clean gauze and cradled them in his.

We sat face to face in our darkened tent as the weight of what happened settled between us. A night of unimagined joy and utter terror.

"I'm never going to be able to sleep," I said. "I keep expecting a Feral to climb into our tent at any moment."

"I wish I could say that won't happen," Rafe said. "But the patrones increased the sentries outside, and the likelihood of a repeat attack tonight is slim."

"But not out of the question."

"No."

"I don't want you to go tomorrow," I said. "You're injured."

I knew asking him to stay was useless, but I was scared. I didn't want to lose him.

"I have to go," he said. "We're gonna need their help. I've got to give them every reason to be charitable."

"I'm scared our luck is going to run out," I said. "I couldn't take it if something happened to you."

I already felt responsible for the death of one person. I couldn't bear to be the cause of another. Was I a danger to every person I cared for?

"I'll be fine," Rafe said.

We both knew he couldn't make that promise.

He gave me a small smile and tucked a strand of hair behind my ear. Then he leaned forward and kissed me. Warmth flooded my body. Every nerve woke. My fingers wove into his hair as I inched closer. His arm slid around my waist, and he lowered me onto the pallet. Rafe broke the kiss and peered at me as if memorizing every inch of my face. He caressed my hair, my cheek, and traced the line of my jaw with his fingertips. His touch was like a salve to my soul, filling an emptiness I'd never realized existed. His caress consumed me. I couldn't think. I could only want. I wanted him to touch me everywhere. I wanted him pressed against me. I wanted his lips on mine. I never wanted it to end.

"Rafe…"

He paused. "Say that again," he said, his voice rough with want.

"Rafe."

His lips swallowed the word as they met mine. This kiss was different, filled with an urgency, a frightening need, alight with heat. I trembled with the same fire. Rafe nudged my lips apart, and his tongue found mine. He moaned at the contact and pressed the length of his body to mine. My flesh melted to liquid flame. My body had never felt like this before. Rafe's lips trailed to my neck, kissing the curve between ear and jawline. His hand skimmed the curve of my breast, and something between a gasp and a moan escaped my mouth.

Rafe pulled away abruptly as if my flesh had burned his lips.

"What's wrong?" I asked, breathless.

Rafe's blue eyes sparked in the low light. He was so beautiful.

"Nothing," he said, stroking my cheek. "It's just—I'm having a hard time keeping my hands off you."

My body and my brain were at war. My body wanted to give Rafe free rein, but my mind screamed caution. I wasn't ready for more, much as I wanted it. We'd already crossed a line that would never have been breached had I not left El Jardín. Unmarried couples were never left alone, never spent the night together, never kissed under any circumstance. I knew what was expected in my old life. Everything was different outside the garden walls, and while I still clung to my modest values, I couldn't feel wrong about what was happening between us. I didn't want to tempt my resolve, though. Or his.

"We should probably get some sleep," I said.

"We should."

Rafe inched over and lay down, leaving me cold where his warm body had been. He groaned as his body reminded him of his injuries.

"Come here," he whispered. I moved closer, and he put his arm around me, pulling me tight to his body. I lay my head on his shoulder and placed a hesitant hand on his chest. The sound of his breath and the beat of his heart under my palm quieted the turmoil inside me. Wrapped in his arms, with the taste of his mouth fresh on my lips, I drifted off.

It didn't last long. I awoke, screaming, with a nightmare digging its claws into me. In the dream, Rafe and I had been lying next to a campfire, lost in a kiss, when the camp flooded with Ferals. All of them had looked like Jude. Dozens of Judes had rushed us. One dragged Rafe off me, while a second hauled me to my feet and trapped me in his arms. One Jude hooked Rafe in a chokehold, cutting off his breath. I'd thrashed in the other Jude's grasp, screaming, but I'd been utterly helpless. I could only watch the life drain out of Rafe as each passing minute robbed him of air, and his face flared red, then purple. His eyes had swelled with panic, his arms and legs flailing fruitlessly.

No! I'd screamed until my throat had gone raw. I awoke screaming the same thing.

"Hey, I got you." Rafe stroked my hair and kissed my forehead. "It was only a dream."

"It was Jude. I dreamed he attacked our camp, and he was choking you. I couldn't get away. I couldn't help you."

"Shh. I'm here, and we're safe."

I couldn't stop trembling. Rafe gathered me against him.

"It feels like he's out there, waiting for us to make a mistake," I said. "I can't get him out of my head."

"If I ever get my hands on him, I'll make sure you never have to worry about him again," he said. "We're going to be all right."

"I don't want to be afraid."

"Evan, you're one of the bravest people I know. You're like the fire you keep touching. Strong and fierce. Full of light," he said. "And I'm here. As long as I'm around, I'll do everything I can to protect you. I'll do everything I can to make sure he never touches you again. Or I'll die trying."

"That's what I'm afraid of."

31

RAFE

$\mathcal{T}$he Feral I'd beaten to oblivion had survived. That didn't stop me from wanting to beat the shit out of him again. He'd attacked Evan and tried to nab Gabby. These Ferals were making me rethink my anti-murder stance.

Someone else couldn't let go. The patrones had given Abraham's son the lead on interrogating the prisoner. Likely an unwise move. Anthony Kabbara was more apt to kill him than gather useful information.

The Feral was an average-built man with wild brown hair and a tangled beard matted with blood. One eye had puffed into a blue-black slit. The side of his face was swollen like a balloon, his flesh mottled with dirt, blood, and bruises. My knuckles bore bloated scabs from his first beating. More than a dozen transitorios had marched the man into the woods and strung him from a tree by the wrists. Anthony had abused his gut so much, the Feral had puked on himself.

Now Anthony pushed a sweaty lock of hair out of his eyes and got in the man's face. "I'll ask you again. Where are the Ferals? Where is your camp?"

The Feral spat in his face. A glob of saliva and blood splatted below Anthony's right eye and trickled down his cheek. He slugged the Feral in the balls and strolled away, wiping spit from his face. The Feral screamed and began raging, growling and thrashing. Anthony wasn't done. He pointed a hunting knife at the prisoner's balls, the tip slicing into his filthy pants. The Feral grew still.

"Oh, do I suddenly have your attention?" he asked. "Let's see if this will loosen your tongue."

Before the Feral could say a word, Anthony pushed the knife deeper, breaching his flesh. The Feral howled.

"I'm taking your balls next, one at a time," Anthony said.

"Stop! I'll tell you. I'll tell you everything."

"That's more like it. Spill, or I will."

"Camp's two miles to the northwest," the Feral said.

"How many were here last night?"

"Twenty-three."

The clan had killed nine Ferals in last night's raid, and the prisoner made ten. That left thirteen.

"More at the camp?" Anthony asked.

"No, we was all here."

Brego had kept quiet until now, but the math wasn't adding up.

"Twenty-three?" he asked. "Against seven clans? That's a suicide mission. You lost half your men. Why risk it? Whatever you stole wasn't worth it."

The Feral kept his brutalized mouth shut. A wicked grin curled his lips.

"What's in it for you?" Brego asked.

He remained silent, staring the patrón down.

"My friend asked you a question," Anthony said. His knife slashed the man's arm, and the prisoner fought to stifle another scream.

The Feral growled. "It's simple. The more we attack, the more we get."

That made no sense. There was little payoff in attacking hundreds of people with a raiding party that size. There must have been something more.

"Not this time, you filthy bastard," Anthony said. He grabbed a handful of the Feral's hair, jerked his head back and planted a knife at his throat. "Let's kill him and go find this camp."

"Anthony, put your knife away," Brego said. "He's going to lead us to the camp. If he fails to do that, I'll let you have him."

In the end, the Feral's intel wasn't necessary. The stolen horse had left a trail through the forest. That along with boot prints from a dozen fleeing men. Twenty of us covered the distance in little time. The daylight was barely an hour old when Seth came across the camp while scouting ahead.

"One awake, on watch," he whispered upon his return. "Six outside sleeping, maybe more inside tents. Camp's about a hundred fifty yards ahead."

Brego patted his shoulder. "Let's go."

We'd gone about two-thirds of the way when our prisoner started yelling. Not much of a yell with a gag plugging his mouth, but effective enough. Shouts rose from the camp. So much for a surprise attack.

Anthony snarled with rage and lunged at the prisoner. His knife carved into the Feral's windpipe. Hands tied, the Feral could do nothing to stop him. The muted screaming stopped as the man folded to his knees. Anthony knifed him in the stomach, and he collapsed, writhing until he could no more. Anthony spat on him.

"Come on!" Brego shouted.

We ran. By the time we reached the clearing, one Feral was fleeing into the forest on the stolen horse. I was almost certain it was Jude. The rest bolted on foot. Brego fired his gun at the Ferals. A bullet struck home, and one tumbled to the ground. We pursued through the forest, but the Ferals had too much of a head start. We returned empty-handed.

"Shit!" Anthony yelled. He kicked a log sticking out of the fire pit, sending a shower of sparks skyward. "Son of a bitch."

"Brego, you need to see this." One of Kabbara's men poked his head out of a big tent. I followed Brego into the shelter.

"What the hell?" said a man who came in behind us.

The tent was stockpiled with food, booze, and weapons, along with a few scattered sleeping pallets. Crates of oranges, potatoes, bread, and dried meat were stacked against one wall. Countless bottles of liquor lined the other wall. We found no firearms but plenty of crossbows, hatchets, and knives. And a Convo—my Convo—sitting atop a crate. I tried to power it up, but it was no good. The device had taken a beating.

My heart sank. I had no way to contact Twain, to let him know we'd been delayed. To warn him about Tresick. The colonel would check to see that I'd returned to the Citadel as commanded. Twain had no idea what was coming his way, and I could only hope the man didn't take my absence out on him. I had to get that Convo fixed, fast.

"Where on God's green earth did they get this?" Brego asked, scratching his beard.

"This is more than a camp raid would provide," said the man who'd alerted us to the cache. "The other tent has more of the same."

"You think they raided one of the Conquistador's deliveries?" I asked, pocketing my Convo.

"It's possible. Too bad we can't ask our prisoner," Brego said. He studied a can of beans, then returned it to the pile, shaking his head. He didn't linger long on the why of it. "Let's pack everything up. Seth, take three men and go back to camp for a wagon. We'll need it to carry these supplies home."

The men scrambled on the clan leader's orders.

"Brego, I need to talk to you," I said. Now seemed as good a time as any.

"Please, call me Ambrose. You've earned my friendship."

"Thanks. I hope you feel that way because I have a big ask."

"Oh?" Ambrose cocked an eyebrow.

"It's inconvenient, but I can make it worth your while."

"Inconvenient? How inconvenient?"

"Depends on how flexible you are. It shouldn't cost you more than time and patience, but I can repay your generosity."

"I'm listening."

"I thought of a way to make your camp more secure," I said. "I can help you protect your clan."

This time Ambrose lifted both eyebrows. "Go on. You have my full attention."

32

EVANGELINE

a week had passed since the attack on our camp, a week that felt like a lifetime. I'd had little to do but pitched in wherever I could. Nighttime, nestled in Rafe's arms in the quiet of our tent, was the only time the nothingness did not threaten to overwhelm me. When I did not feel drowned by the minutes and seconds of my sister's life draining away.

Rafe had worked feverishly to repair the UTV and his Convo. He'd convinced Brego to escort us to within a mile of El Jardín, wait while we fetched Juni, and then ferry us to the outskirts of the Sink. In return, Rafe promised to build a security system for the camp perimeter, something fueled by sunlight that would send a silent warning about intruders. He had sweetened the deal with ten pairs of night-vision goggles. Everyone wanted a pair after seeing Seth's in action.

Brego was taking a leap of faith. Rafe could promise the moon and then disappear forever once behind Citadel walls. But that wouldn't happen. Rafe had proven himself true, and his actions made Brego trust him. It was a good thing. We had few alternatives, and none of them were good.

"We're getting close," Rafe said. We'd climbed into the UTV

at the transitorio camp as the sun settled on the horizon and were now barreling through the Wildlands. Headed for home. I gave Rafe a small smile as the wind whipped my hair around my face. It was all I could manage with the terror building in my belly.

Minutes later, Rafe drove into a tangle of scrub and cut the engine. Beyond the scattering of trees, El Jardín's wall rose up, tall and imposing. I chewed my nails while we lingered, keeping watch until full dark. Under the cover of night, we began walking. That was when the rain came, a torrent that soaked the ground within minutes. By the time we reached the wall, the stream had swelled beyond its banks. I scrambled through brush and muddy water to find my hole. I pushed against the stone, and it gave way without a fight.

"We're in luck. No one fixed the loose stones," I said.

As if leaving the door ajar. Perhaps on purpose.

Rafe stood watch while I knelt in shallow water and clawed the stones away. We belly-crawled through the hole and came out on the other side. I quickly refilled the hole and wriggled out of the brush.

I wiped mud from my soaked skirts. "It's late, so most everyone is settling down for the night, but the watch is somewhere out there, patrolling the grounds."

"Let's hope the rain covers our tracks," Rafe said, pushing dripping strands of hair out of his eyes.

We trudged to the heart of the garden, to my home, without seeing another soul. I stared at my house, teeth chattering. My skirts clung to my legs, wet and heavy with muck, but my appearance was the least of my worries. I couldn't breathe, couldn't settle the frantic beating of my heart.

Rafe touched my arm. "You're shaking."

"I'm worried about what happens next."

"Me, too."

His arms came around me. I latched on to him, buried my

face in his chest, and found comfort in the heat of his body, the scent of rain on his skin. He caressed my wet hair and said nothing, and it was exactly what I needed.

Across the yard, weak light radiated from the living room. The rest of the house appeared dark and still. It had taken so long to get here, and now that we'd arrived, I was scared to take the last step. It was ridiculous. What I'd wanted for weeks stood within sight, and yet I knew this wasn't my happy ending, not yet. Would my father forgive me for what I'd put him through? Could I convince him to let Juni go? The faded bruises on my face would do little to sway him. I needed to assure Pa we had a plan to keep my sister safe.

Rafe's strong hands covered my cheeks and lifted my face to his. "Come on. Time to leap with the leopards," he said. His words caught me off guard, and I snorted in the rain.

He smiled and bent to kiss me. Under the canopy of the Conquistador's orange trees, while the rain poured from above, his lips danced along mine, long and slow. His kiss tasted of promise. He was with me, no matter what.

We sprinted across the yard and mounted the stairs hand in hand. Rainwater dripped from our clothes, so we wrung out them out as best we could and wiped our feet before creeping inside the kitchen. The room smelled of cooking grease and soap—smells of home. In the dark, a haze of candlelight slanted across the threshold to the living room.

Rafe followed, quiet and patient, as I crossed the room and stopped at the doorway. My father sat in his armchair, eyes closed, his head propped on his palm, a *Farmers' Almanac* splayed open in his lap. Even in slumber, his face scrunched in worry. The creases of his cheeks and the corners of his eyes slanted downward, anchored by some heavy weight. My chest tightened, and my brows drew together. I'd missed him. I'd hurt him. But I couldn't bring myself to regret what I'd done. Not if it meant Juni would live.

I rushed to my father and dropped to my knees. I touched his hand.

"Pa." The word came out wrapped in cobwebs. I cleared my throat and said it again.

My father jolted in his chair like he'd been doused with a bucket of cold water. The almanac toppled to the floor, and his hand jerked toward the candle on the side table. I snatched his hand before it could make contact.

"Evan?" Pa stared at me like I was a ghost.

Realization came like a whisper of something I'd half known all along. I was not the same person who'd left weeks ago. My home had once felt as comfortable as my own skin. It was different now. I was different. I was something more, something stronger. Someone who longed to make her father happy but was no longer held hostage to that desire. Someone who could set her own rules, see to her own wishes.

My father's palm warmed my cheek. His gaze registered the bruising on my face, and his eyes crinkled in sorrow. "Oh, Evan…"

I layered my palm atop his and smiled. "I'm all right, Pa."

My father swallowed me in his arms. His heart hammered against my chest, and his body shuddered from silent sobs. It startled me.

I pulled back. "Pa, is Juni—is she…?" I couldn't finish the sentence, couldn't voice the worst possibility.

"Yes, angel. She's stubborn like you. Kept insisting you'd come back. Even when we…when we… She never doubted you."

Pa's face hardened and he clutched my shoulders. "Evangeline Marie, what were you thinking? How could you be so careless? You could have been killed. We could have… They could have taken everything from us."

"Pa, it's late. We can talk about this after we've both had some sleep, but you need to know I did what I set out to do. There's a way to cure Juni. I…we found a way."

Anger flickered in my father's eyes, but it dimmed a fraction at the spark of hope in my words. Something behind me caught his eye, and the anger gusted full gale. He'd spotted Rafe.

Pa flew from his chair, shoving me behind him. "Who are you? What are you doing here?"

"He's with me."

I stepped from behind my father and motioned Rafe over. I met him halfway and faced Pa.

Horror filled my father's eyes. "Sweet faith, what have you done, Evan?" Pa eyed Rafe with murder in his eyes.

"Señor Lovette, I'm a friend of your daughter. My name is Rafael Roldan." Rafe extended his hand.

Pa furrowed his brow and crossed his arms.

"Pa…"

"My daughter doesn't have friends outside this farm."

"Pa, I met Rafe in the Citadel. He helped me out of a bad situation, more than once. Please, be nice to him."

My father rounded on me. "Be nice? *Be nice?* Evan, no one in the Citadel lifts a hand to help anyone unless there's something in it for them. What does this *friend* expect from you? What did you have to pay him for his help?"

I flinched at my father's twisted accusations. "Nothing!" I said. "He's asked for nothing, but he's repeatedly risked his life for me, and he's risking it again being here."

"And risking ours as well, may I remind you," Pa said. "Evan, tell me you didn't go through with the Obligors Expo. Tell me you didn't sell yourself to the highest bidder."

I withered, like a bloom parched by the sun. I couldn't admit that I'd done just that.

"Your daughter is not part of the Obligor program," Rafe said. He stepped forward, shielding me like a scrap of shade under a blazing sun. "She is a free woman and doesn't owe anyone anything. You're right about the Citadel, but I'm one of the few who doesn't think that way. If I did, you would have never seen your daughter again. I've seen people swallowed up by that city more times than I can count."

The color drained from Pa's face. "What do you want?" His voice sounded almost pleading. "There's no way you'd risk the Wildlands, risk breaking into the Conquistador's property, out of the goodness of your heart. What could you possibly want from us?"

Rafe hesitated, as if warring with an answer. "I'm sick of watching the Empire chew up and spit people out like yesterday's garbage," he said. "Evan convinced me a life was at stake. I couldn't stand by, not when I knew how it would end. I don't want anything from you. Except for discretion. I ask you not to share my presence with the Guardia."

Pa's face blazed with disbelief.

"Rafe is the only reason this works," I said, palms held out. "We can't get Juni into the Fount without his help."

"No!" He grasped my shoulders. His burning eyes bore down on me. "You're not taking Juni anywhere. You might as well kill her now. Have you lost all sense?"

"Pa?"

A small voice came from the hallway. Pa's shoulders slumped, and he released me. At the end of the darkened hall, Juni stood in the shadows, her tawny hair scattered, Chickles dangling at her side.

Pa hurried to her and knelt, inviting Juni to climb into his arms. "Look who's home, sweetheart," he said, returning to the living room.

Juni lifted her head off his shoulder. Her cheeks were rosy from sleep, but dark circles rimmed her eyes. She caught my eye, and her face bloomed with light.

"Evan!" Juni squirmed in Pa's arms until he released her. I dropped to the floor and caught her, pulling her into my arms. She locked around me, and I melted, cherishing the feel of her embrace. This...this was what it was all for. This beautiful, brave little girl who held my heart the way no one else did.

"I've missed you so much, Junebug." Tears pressed at my eyes, but I pushed them back.

"You were gone so long."

"I know. How are you feeling?"

"Okay, I guess," she said. "Did you really go to the *City-del?* Pa said you did but I can't tell anyone."

"I did. This is my friend, Rafe," I said, pointing. He gave her a warm smile and a small wave. She waved back using one of Chickles's wings instead of her own hand.

"Rafe came to help us," I said, drawing her attention back. "Can you keep that a secret, too?"

"I don't tattletale," she said, giving me the sternest look she could muster.

"I know. You're a good sister. Now, we need to get you back to bed. You need your rest." I stood, clutching Juni. My sister relaxed in my arms, and a peacefulness came over her face. "I'm going to put her to bed. I'll be right back."

Pa leaned forward and kissed Juni on the forehead. "She won't be able to sleep now that she knows you're here unless you're with her," he said. "Go lie down with her. Sleep there tonight. We'll talk more in the morning." He eyed Rafe for an uncomfortable moment. "Your friend can sleep in your room. The last thing I need is Nina or Dominic walking in tomorrow morning and finding a stranger on the couch."

My stomach clenched like a fist. How would Dominic have taken my absence? I'd walked away from our betrothal without a word. I'd been familiar with another man. I'd never meant to hurt him, but I hadn't asked for him either.

Pa caressed my cheek with the most tender of touches. Something unspoken passed between us. Regret? Apology? Maybe some combination of both.

I glanced at Rafe. He nodded, letting me know he wasn't going anywhere.

"Go on, now. I'll take care of your friend," Pa said.

"That's what I'm afraid of," I said, shooting my father a withering glare. I told Rafe good night and hesitated to leave. It felt wrong to abandon him to my father's ire.

"I'll be fine," he said.

I carried Juni to her room, and she nestled next to me in her bed.

"What was it like? The city? Was it scary?" she asked, petting Chickles's fabric feathers in the quiet dark.

I sighed as weariness crept into my bones. Juni was wide awake.

"It's a big, beautiful place," I said. "You can see the ocean from the city."

"Oooh. I want to see the ocean. Did you see the people?"

"I didn't meet too many people, but most were young and beautiful—or they looked that way."

"Where did you sleep?"

"Juni, shhh… I'll tell you more tomorrow, but you need to sleep."

I played with her hair, stroking long and slow, trying to coax sleep into her tiny body.

"Is the Fount for real? Can it stop you from being an old lady?"

"Juni, come on. Sleep. I'll tell you this—I didn't see anyone who had gray hair or wrinkles."

And it can heal, but only those who can afford it. People who lived in the Barrio or on farms or who traded in the Sink were out of luck.

"Like magic," Juni said, her words wrapped in a yawn.

"Shhh… Close your eyes." I flipped onto my side to face my sister and threaded her hair behind her ear. She curled into a ball and fitted herself into the curve of my body. Her warmth radiated through me, and I relaxed for the first time since we'd left the council gathering.

I closed my eyes and sleep crept through me. Juni's tiny, half-asleep voice nudged me awake again.

"You scared me."

My heart folded in on itself.

"I'm so sorry, little bug," I said, kissing the top of her head. "I didn't mean to. I wanted to find a way to help you get well, to see if we could get you into the Fount."

"Did you?"

"I think so. We need to discuss a few things with Pa."

"Rafe is handsome."

I smiled in the darkness. "Yes, he is."

"Are you going to marry him?"

The question startled me. I'd long dreamed of what it would be like to have my own family, children of my own, and for so long, I'd been resigned to marrying Dominic, whether I loved him or not. But leaving home had changed everything. That kind of life was beyond my grasp. A life with Rafe? It was crazy to consider. He didn't live a life meant for family, but the plain truth was I didn't want my time with him to end. Even now, his absence lay heavy on my heart.

"Juni, hush. Go to sleep."

A handful of minutes passed in silence. My sister's breathing deepened, and her body relaxed into a peaceful slumber.

At least one of us would get some sleep.

RAFE

I tried to unclench my fists as Evan disappeared down the hallway. Tried to tamp down the urge to smash her father's face for his insinuations, for disparaging everything his daughter had endured to protect their family. I wanted to shield her from his storm. I wanted to hold her and kiss her good night, but that was impossible with Papa Bear standing between us like a disgruntled gargoyle.

The living room suddenly felt suffocating, too small. The light from the single candle tossed odd shadows across the walls and darkened Lovette's eyes.

"You should be proud of her," I said. "She's gone through a great deal to keep your family intact. To save your daughter's life."

"You have no idea what we've been through to keep this family intact," he said. "Don't pretend you know us. You don't."

I straightened. "I've known your daughter long enough to know she's a fighter. She would do anything to protect the people she loves. Family means everything to her."

"You think I don't know that? She's always had her mother's

instinct. Always fought for what she thought was right. The problem is she acts without considering the costs."

"How could saving the life of someone she loves not be worth the sacrifices she's made?"

"There are always consequences, things she doesn't consider," Lovette said. "I see the way she looks at you. She's already jumped off that cliff. But what she doesn't see, what she doesn't consider is what you're going to cost this family. You might be the one who tears it apart for good."

Lovette stalked off, leaving me shaken with his version of a truth bomb.

"Your room's there," he said, pointing to a door in the darkness. "Stay there."

I grabbed the lit candle from beside Lovette's chair and found Evan's room. Exhausted as I was, I was too angry to sleep. Too disjointed. I had no idea how we would resolve this thing. It was out of my control, a scenario that didn't sit well with me. I preferred maintaining control over my destiny. I lay in bed all of two minutes before I rose and started pacing.

Evan's room contained a single bed draped with a handmade quilt. A chair next to the window held a sewing basket with a cross-stitch project and a half-finished dress. A stack of books sat on the narrow nightstand, including a book of love sonnets, with an inscription that was way too personal for my eyes.

I read it anyway.

Someone, likely her father, had scrawled a note on the inner cover: *Helene, you are a gift from God. The words in this book cannot match my feelings for you, but I will try each day of our lives to show you the depth of my love. Like the roots of the orange trees blooming beyond our window, my love for you grows deeper day by day. Love, Gabriel.*

Lovette had poured out his heart to his wife in the folds of this book. His outpouring roused a nagging ugliness in me. Envy for a depth of love I'd never known and rarely witnessed. I tried to shake the feeling, but it needled. Life doled out love and affection by inconstant degrees, and it had been stingy when filling my cup.

There was little else to explore. A small chest with a minimal stock of clothing. Drawings tacked to the wall, including a small stick-figure sketch of two people holding hands in a stream. That was it.

I finished exploring and lay on the bed, staring at the ceiling. Sleep hid from me. I yearned for Evan, the press of her body next to me, even as I fretted over the mess I'd found myself in. Time had never felt so aggressive. I needed to do something, anything to assuage the hostility in my brain.

I popped out of bed and pulled my Convo from my pack, along with my tool pouch. I'd been close to repairing it, but the UTV had taken precedence. I grappled with fixing the device for nearly an hour before I was able to power it on with my body heat. My heart raced as a raw static noise filtered through the speaker. I swiped a call button that would send a wake-up alarm to Twain.

"Come on, come on," I muttered.

Agonizing seconds passed before I heard him.

"Rafe, where the hellfire fuck have you been?" Twain said. His cursing betrayed how upset he was, but his voice still felt like a light in the darkest night.

"I know. I'm sorry, man," I said. "We were ambushed, and the UTV wrecked."

I gave him a shortened version of what happened, including the run-in with Colonel Craphole.

"Tresick may come looking for me," I said.

"He was..." Twain's words cut in and out, but I caught the gist. Tresick had paid him a visit.

"Mierda. I'm sorry I put you in his crosshairs," I said. "I'll come back as fast as I can."

"We both knew the risk and—" Twain's next words were lost in a burst of static. He tried again. "I'll do as much—"

Damn it. I had no idea what he was saying, but whatever it was, he was trying to reassure me, calm me where no calm could be found. That was his way.

"I don't deserve you," I told him.

"No, you don't. Your penance is toilet duty for an extra year."

That came in loud and clear. I could almost laugh, but the stakes were too high. I was about to respond when the light winked out on the device, and it went dead. I almost threw the Convo across the room, but I couldn't afford to damage it any more than it already was.

I set it aside and lay down on the bed. At some point, I snoozed, but how much it was hard to say. It felt like minutes, but it was near dawn when I woke. The faint scent of coffee lured me out, and I went in search of it. I found the coffee and a sour, middle-aged woman.

Lovette had clearly filled her in on my presence. I could only imagine what he'd said. The woman eyed me with a potent brew of contempt and suspicion. After years in the Citadel, it was jarring to see a woman marked by wrinkles with white streaks usurping her blonde hair.

I sat at the kitchen table, watching the nameless woman skitter around preparing breakfast. She eventually permitted me a cup of coffee, but the exchange looked as if it pained her. At that point, I didn't much care. I'd have climbed over a dozen venomous vipers for a steaming mug of caffeine. My head ached from sleep deprivation. I attempted small talk, but the woman refused to engage. So, I sat there in the awkward silence, defiantly sipping my coffee.

The back door creaked open and slammed shut. Lovette paused on the stoop to stomp dirt from his boots. Mud smeared his cheek and pants. He aimed a scowl at me but said nothing.

The woman paused kneading a lump of dough. "Cup of coffee?" she asked.

"Yes. Thanks, Nina."

Lovette tugged his leather work gloves off and tossed them onto a side table. He sat in the chair opposite me, and Nina placed a steaming cup in front of him. He didn't touch it. Not right away. He simply stared at me, his face inscrutable, showing neither anger nor kindness. He sat for several long moments studying my face, and I let him. I wouldn't give him the satisfaction of knowing he unnerved me. Few people elicited that type of response in me, and I'd be damned if I let him know he was one of them.

"Why do you look familiar?" Lovette finally asked.

That did it.

All my nerves withered to jelly and pooled in a cold puddle in the pit of my stomach. I wasn't wearing a disguise. He was scrutinizing my real face. We'd never met, but maybe he'd seen the Conq before. Did my father and I look that much alike?

I kept my face calm and hoped he couldn't sense my unease. "I have no idea," I said.

"When are you leaving?" Lovette asked.

"That's up to Evan."

"You're not leaving with Juniper."

"That's for you and your daughters to decide. I'm not forcing anything, but you should know our window of opportunity for a safe return is short."

"You're not taking Juni."

"I hear you."

"You cannot have both my daughters," Lovette said. Pain rose in his eyes like a tidal wave that would drown him. His stone facade threatened to crumble, but he wouldn't allow it. He held himself in check. All except his traitorous eyes.

"I don't want to take anyone from you," I said.

It was true. Yes, I wanted Evan, but I didn't want to. I knew it would have to end. We came from different worlds, and we belonged in different worlds. Whatever had grown between us would not last. If I'd ever doubted it, last night had reinforced it. The reunion with her family had made it clear. Her family was her world. She had risked her life for it, and this was where she belonged. I could see that now, as much as it pained me.

But I didn't belong here. That was also clear.

"You already have," Lovette said.

"No, I haven't," I said, setting my coffee cup down a little too hard. Hot liquid splashed my hand, but I was tired of being painted as the villain. After all I'd risked, I couldn't swallow his recriminations anymore. The anger swelled inside me. The lack of sleep wasn't helping.

"I haven't done a thing to you," I said through tight lips. "I've tried to help your daughters, to help your family, so I'd appreciate it if you stopped treating me like the enemy."

Nina dropped a dish into the sink, and it rattled as she tried to still it. I guess she wasn't accustomed to someone mouthing off to her boss.

Lovette's cool demeanor faltered for a moment before sliding firmly back into place. "Mr. Roldan, you have no idea of the customs and rules of this community, so I'll grant you may be unaware of the harm you have done. Let me ask you this. Have you kissed my daughter?"

What the hell? Why on earth would that matter?

I didn't answer. Answering was a trap.

"I'll take that as a yes," he said. "Have you held her in your arms?"

"What does that have to do with anything?"

"Have you lain with her?"

"Have I what?" After all we'd been through, all we'd survived, *this* was what he was worried about? "You've got to be kidding me."

"This is no joking matter, Mr. Roldan," he said.

"What exactly are you trying to say?"

"In our community, physical contact between men and women is forbidden until after marriage. Relationships are carefully cultivated, and our rules call for purity and fidelity at all times."

This was insane.

"Have you no regard for the danger Evan put herself through for you and Juniper?" I said. "I would think you would be more concerned about that, that you would be grateful she is alive and in one piece and home. But seeing as you're not, let me reassure you. Your daughter has done nothing wrong, and neither have I. I assure you her virtue is intact."

"There you are wrong," Lovette said. "In our community, touch is an intimacy not tolerated outside the sanctity of marriage. If you kiss her, you claim her. No one else here will. She was promised in marriage to a member of our community, but not anymore."

I was speechless. Evan was engaged. She'd never said a word about it. What's more, in her father's eyes, I had defiled his daughter. We had never made love, but we might as well have. Evan was a fallen woman. No one would have her for a wife. Not here. Did she know?

"That's ridiculous," I said. "You're saying because she kissed someone, she'd doomed to live the rest of her life as an old maid?"

"Our rules and customs are not ridiculous. We don't live according to the sloven ways of the Citadel where anything goes. We live according to God's word, with order and respect for each other's boundaries," Lovette said. "You two have crossed a line that cannot be uncrossed, as much as I wish it were different. The man she should have married will not have her now, nor should he be expected to have some man's seconds." He glared at me. "Five hundred years of a Lovette stewarding this farm will come to an end. So don't tell me the two of you have done nothing wrong. You have taken one daughter from me, and you'll not take another."

Lovette's calm had finally cracked, and his voice hardened with every word.

"She's not leaving you. She will come home to you when this is over. She is still your daughter."

His voice grew quiet. The pain returned. "No, she is not mine. Not anymore. Even if an exception could be made, she can't stay here anymore."

"You're going to banish her over a kiss? What kind of father are you?"

"This is not my choice. It was hers," Lovette said.

"This makes no sense." I wanted to shout, but I could see it was pointless.

"The Guardia came two weeks ago. They'd been told to keep an eye on our family—worried someone else might get sick, even though Juni's cancer isn't contagious. Even with the doctor's clearance. Paranoid tyrants," he said, scowling down at his hands on the table. "Evan was gone. They wouldn't accept any excuse for my inability to produce her. I had no choice. I couldn't jeopardize our home, our safety. She gave me no choice. I told them she died in an accident. Everyone except those in my closest circle thinks she's dead and buried." He glanced up at me, a storm in his eyes. "There's no way she can come back."

"Oh, Pa, no…"

Evan stood in the doorway, her hand over her mouth, her face pale. Her knees buckled.

34

EVANGELINE

*P*a had declared me dead. I could never come home again. How could this be? All I'd ever wanted was for our family to be whole and healthy, like it used to be.

My fingers tingled. Black spots floated before my eyes. My legs went numb and melted like ice in a fire as I sank to the floor. Rafe scooped me into his arms and carried me to the living room. My father loomed behind him, scowling at the way he touched me.

Rafe settled me on the couch and wiped a mess of hair from my face. "You okay?" he asked.

"No."

Pa gripped his arm and pried him away. Rafe pulled his arm free and glared at my father before stepping aside.

Pa sat on the low table opposite me. "I'm sorry, angel," he said. "There was nothing I could do."

"Pa, there must be a way." I was desperate. I'd been prepared to barter years of my life for Juni's, but I'd thought I'd be able to come home eventually.

"I don't know how to fix this, Evan. Wish I did, but I don't. When you made the choice to leave, you made choices for all of us, intentional or not. I did the only thing I knew to keep us safe. I'm sorry."

I buried my face in my hands and pressed back tears. "No," I cried into my palms. The word spilled from my lips over and over again, rising like an angry wave until the lone syllable crashed one final time.

Pa grasped my arms and leaned in. "Hush, angel. Juni will hear."

"I don't care," I said, my words hardening, spewing from a place beyond thought and reason. "This has to be for something. Everything we risked, everything we went through. If I'm to be banished for what I've done...if I must give up my home for the rest of my life, then let it be for something. Let me finish this. Let me take Juni where she can be healed."

"Evangeline, no. You take her from this house, you might as well dig her grave while you're at it. It will kill her."

"You keep her here and it will do the same," I spat back. "At least give her a chance."

My accusation jarred him. He was speechless for a long moment as hurt dashed through his eyes. Then he shook his head.

"You never think things through, Evangeline. You decide with your heart and reason be damned. Look where it's gotten you, where it's gotten us," Pa said. "Even if she survives the trip, what makes you think she can come home? It'll be your situation all over again. How will I explain her absence?"

I opened my mouth to respond, but I had no answer. My righteousness drained away, leaving me cold. He was right.

"Angel, you've done enough," he said, sighing. "I love you for trying. Your heart is in the right place, but you dream in a world that doesn't exist. We belong here, not the Citadel. Right or wrong, the luxuries of that life are not for us. We've been fortunate to have a safe home, right here. God only knows what will happen with Juni, but at least here, she's safe. She can be at peace whenever God decides to take her."

"I made a promise. I told Mama I would take care of her," I said. I'd tried my best to shoulder our mother's role to make up for her absence.

"Angel, I'm the parent, and it's my responsibility to take care of you, to protect you both, not yours," Pa said. "Your mother would have never wanted this. She would have never asked you to sacrifice your life like this."

"This isn't protecting anyone."

He waited a beat, tamping down his anger. "Look, you can stay here a couple of days, but let's not fight during the time we have left together."

I looked to Rafe. He was staring at the floor, arms crossed, his lips pressed in a tight line, like he wanted to say something but held his tongue. Nina hovered in the doorway, eyes soft with sympathy. I'd hurt her, too, and it was the last thing I wanted to do.

The silence lingered painfully long until her voice broke through the cloud of anger.

"Well, right, the biscuits should be ready, if you all would like to come to the kitchen," she said. "You can help yourselves. I'm going to take some to Dominic."

Realization dawned on me. In my absence, Nina had filled in to help my family, feeding them, looking out for Juni. She'd probably told Dominic to stay away this morning. I didn't deserve her kindness.

My father disappeared into the kitchen. Conversation over. My stomach burned hollow and cold. I was anything but hungry. Rafe and I exchanged a look, and in his gaze, I found a spark of comfort. I wished I could bury myself in his arms. We followed without speaking, without touching.

The day passed in a slow haze. Before breakfast had ended, Rafe had given my father an edited version of our journey. I couldn't bring myself to make polite conversation. Pa knew about transitorios but had never met any. He'd journeyed to the Citadel twice as a teenager, making deliveries when his father had managed El Jardín, but he knew little about the city.

After breakfast, Pa had buried himself in his duties. He and Nina had checked in throughout the day, reluctant to leave us without a chaperone besides Juni. The day had stretched on, uneventful apart from the levity of being with my sister again. Yet even as we'd played games and read together, I'd felt the gravity of time slipping away, and with it, every chance we had of saving Juniper.

That night, we sat in the living room like the weight of the world wasn't pressing on us. Rafe was losing his third game of checkers to Juni, playing on a handmade board with painted rocks for game pieces. I sewed buttons onto a dress for my sister. Pa pretended to read his almanac as he eavesdropped on the game.

"Hey!" Rafe protested after Juni leap-frogged three of his pieces in one move.

"You're not very good at this. Didn't you never play when you were a kid?" she asked.

"Certainly not enough," Rafe said. He winked at me.

Juni held her arms up in victory and gave him an evil grin. Her small win felt like something larger than it was. She'd missed out on so much in the last few months, it was a glimpse of her old self. It passed far too soon, and she had to lie down on the couch as a wave of tiredness crept over her small body.

Outside, music flared to life. The crew was enjoying an evening around the fire pit, as they often did when the night wasn't too cool or too hot. Where we would've been if things were different. Laugher and song filtered through the curtains, but Juni didn't stir, didn't even look outside to watch. She used to dance all the time, her bare feet stirring up dirt like a dust devil. Even when there'd been no music, she'd move to a melody that had existed only in her head. So much of the girl she had been was slowly draining away.

I had to find a way to make Pa understand. A dark thought crossed my mind. What if I stopped asking for permission and just left with her? Hadn't I done that when I'd left home the first time?

I shook my head and glanced at Rafe out of the corner of my eye. He'd sank back in his chair and was flipping through one of my father's almanacs. He represented so much of how my life had changed in these few weeks. I'd run away from home, kissed a man—repeatedly, lied and stolen. I'd crossed so many lines and violated so many rules in this quest, I could no longer call myself a rule follower, and I was weirdly comfortable with that. But directly defying my father's wishes and stealing his child was one line too many. I would not cross it.

Shouts of joy filtered into the living room.

"They're celebrating," Pa said. "Marta delivered her baby this morning."

"Babies are gross," Juni said. "They poop their britches."

Rafe snorted from behind the almanac.

"That was you once," I said. "I changed your poopy britches many a time."

She ignored me and peeked between the curtains. "Pa, remember when you danced with Mama? And Evan and me? That was fun."

Pa's eyes clouded in sadness. "I remember, sweetheart," he said, his gaze meeting mine. "Those were some good memories."

We sat in silence, letting the music fill the quiet. Juni slid my *Grimm's Fairy Tales* into her lap and began flipping the pages. I concentrated on the needle moving in and out of the fabric in my hands. I didn't want to remember those times. I didn't want to recall a tradition that had gone cold.

Minutes later, the music grew louder and the crowd clapped along to a jig, pounding out a lively rhythm. Juni tapped her book, and her leg twitched beneath her lap blanket. One corner of her mouth angled up in an unconscious half smile. I glanced at my father, and he, too, softened with a small smile. He tossed his book aside and stood up. The move was so sudden, I almost stabbed myself with the needle.

Pa offered me his hand. "May I?" he said. The tender gesture made my chest swell with bittersweet emotions.

"Of course." I put my hand in his palm.

He twirled me around the living room, dodging chairs and tables as he matched the rhythm pouring through the window. The ever-present weight on my chest lifted a little, and I couldn't help but smile. Pa held me after the music stopped, and I laid my head on his shoulder, relishing the comfort of strong arms that had always kept me safe and warm. The next time I left, that haven would disappear.

He whispered into my ear, and his words dissolved me.

"I love you, angel, always," he said. "You and Juni matter more to me than anything else in this life. You'll always be my angel, no matter what happens."

35

EVANGELINE

he morning sun had yet to rise, but I couldn't sleep. I felt like a bug captured in amber, stuck and unable to move forward or back. But the minutes were ticking down to the time I would be forced to move, to leave home and never return. I couldn't stay in bed, tormenting myself with thoughts that led to nowhere. Pulling on my robe, I slipped out of my room and stole into Rafe's. He was wide awake, tinkering with his Convo in my bed.

"I don't know what to do anymore," I said, voice inches from breaking. Rafe climbed out of bed and held me. I latched on with a fierceness that verged on desperation. He caressed my hair and said nothing.

"My father was right," I said. "I'm reckless and stupid. I don't think things through, and people get hurt."

Rafe peered into my eyes. "That's not who you are, and anyone who thinks so is an idiot. You care more than most people, and you do something about it."

"No, you don't understand, my mother...she died because... because of me."

"That can't be true."

I couldn't meet his eyes.

"Evan, what happened?"

"We...we were moving crates of fruit from the back acres. I had the reins. The horses startled—I'm not sure why, but they took off. I couldn't control them. I couldn't stop them," I said, keeping my eyes low. "The wagon hit a ditch and rolled. It crushed her. I couldn't handle the horses, and my mother died because of it. It was all my fault. Now I've dragged you into this and put you in danger, and it's for nothing. I'm a curse."

Rafe's hands cupped my face, and I finally glanced up at him. Something feral passed through his eyes, a fire burning fierce. "Evan, you are not responsible for your mother's death," he said. "It was an accident. Freak accidents happen all the time, and this was one of them. It was a terrible, tragic accident, but you are not responsible for her life or her death, and whoever made you feel that way is lying to you."

I fixed my gaze on him, raw hope welling inside me. His words felt like absolution. Words I hadn't realized I'd needed to hear. It didn't change the grief I still felt or the fact that I'd gotten Rafe into this position.

"You've risked so much for nothing," I said. "I don't know how to convince Pa."

"We'll think of something."

I hoped he was right. We were running out of time.

"I can't ask you to keep sacrificing for me and my family. Once this is settled, I promise I won't be a burden anymore."

Rafe studied my face, his brows softening with sympathy. His hand circled my neck, and he kissed me. His thumb wiped a tear from my cheek as our lips melted together. My fingers raked his hair and drew him closer until our breaths stirred as one. My hand skimmed down his back, and I pressed into him, relishing the hardness of his muscles. I craved more of him, and the thirst terrified me. Thrilled me.

Rafe pulled away, breathing hard, like it was an effort to

remove himself. He caught my hand and stared into my eyes. "Whether Juni comes with us or not, I'll see that you find somewhere safe to land. I'll work out something. I don't want you to worry."

Confusion pushed past my desire.

"You'll be safe. I'll make sure of it. That's all that matters," he said.

What was he saying? Was he done with me? Was he ready to wash his hands of me?

Something sharp and jagged pressed into my chest, and I freed my hand from his. I was so tired. So tired of others deciding what would happen with my life.

I stepped back, letting distance fortify me. "I don't need you to plan my life for me, to decide what's going to happen when this is over," I said. Beyond anger, something strange was building inside me, something new. A sense of strength pushing against the barb in my heart. "I can figure my life out on my own. I am not helpless, and I never have been," I said. "I can build a life of my own, and I don't need you or anyone else to do it for me."

Rafe opened his mouth and reached for me, but I held up my hand to stop him. We stared at each other, hurt and resolve simmering between us.

I turned my back on him and slipped out the door. His words stung. I'd thought he cared for me, and maybe he did enough to help me find a new home, but not enough to be with me. I'd thought his heart had enough room for me, but it didn't. It was as closed off as ever. The sting of rejection settled in my stomach like a brick, but something else was dawning inside me.

I'd spent most of my years living the life someone else had designed for me. I didn't have to do that anymore, and I didn't want to. I didn't have to live by the boundaries someone else built, by rules that no longer made sense. In the last few weeks,

I'd discovered there were other ways to live and thrive in this world, and I would find my own path.

I crept down the darkened hall. I didn't want to climb into bed and wake Juni, so I decided I'd wait out the sunrise on the couch.

"Have you no shame?"

His voice boomed from the shadows, and I froze.

Dominic stepped forward and blocked my path. His shirt was untucked and wrinkled, his hair mussed like tossed hay. Gray shadows circled his eyes. Gone was the neat and orderly man I knew. Something wild had taken root.

I tugged my robe tight around my chest. "Dominic. What are you—"

"How could you do this right under your father's roof? Sneaking around like a whore in the night."

"What?" My face flushed with heat. I willed my thudding heart to slow, but Dominic's sudden appearance, his fire-poker words shook me. I deserved his anger, his disappointment, but not this. I'd never seen him behave like this.

"Stealing into his room? Did you spend the night with him? Let him touch you?"

"I slept with Juni," I said, anger freezing to steel inside me. "Not that it's any of your business."

I moved to step around him, but he blocked my way. His hands gripped my shoulders and pushed me against the wall. His face loomed above mine, too close. "It is my business. You were meant to be mine. My wife. Now you've ruined it. Defiled yourself and shamed your entire family."

"I belong to no one. My father made you a promise. Not me. There is nothing between us. I've known you my whole life, but I barely know you, and you never even asked what I wanted. So, no, I don't want to be your wife. I never did. Now take your hands off me."

I pushed at his hands, but his fingers dug in. A shimmer of

hurt passed through Dominic's eyes, and for a moment, I regretted my stab of anger. But then he laced his fingers through my hair, pulling the strands into his fist until it hurt.

He lowered his forehead so it touched mine. "Gabriel promised we would marry. He promised this place to me, with you, his blood, by my side. You were supposed to be mine."

Dominic clenched my cheek, and his mouth pressed against mine.

"Stop!" I shoved Dominic's chest hard, and he staggered back, releasing me.

Suddenly Rafe pushed between us. I hadn't heard him come out of his room.

"Back off," Rafe said. "Leave her alone."

Dominic swung at him. Rafe blocked his blow and threw a punch into his gut. A whoosh of air escaped Dominic's mouth and he grunted, doubling over. Rafe shoved him.

"You bastard. You corrupted her. She was mine." Dominic rushed at Rafe, knocking him into me. Rafe's shoulder blade rammed my mouth, and I tasted blood. His broad back smothered me as Dominic pushed him.

Suddenly Dominic was wrenched away. "That's enough." My father's gruff voice brooked no argument.

Rafe twisted to look at me. "You all right?" His finger wiped blood from my lip.

"What the hell is going on?" Pa asked, yanking him away as well.

We all glared at each other in the cramped corridor, no one answering.

My father cracked the silence. "Dominic, what are you doing?"

His foreman stared at his feet.

"I trusted you when I told you about Evangeline being home. Maybe I shouldn't have. Explain yourself."

"I'm sorry, Gabriel. I had to see her," he said. "I wanted to know why. Why she threw our future away."

"Dominic, this isn't about you or some dream you had about us being together," I said. "Everything I've done, I've done for one reason. To save Juni. This has nothing to do with you."

"If it's about Juni, then why did I find you coming out of his room?"

"What?" Pa's face burned crimson.

"It's not what you think," I stammered. "I was in there for a few minutes, just to talk."

Rafe interceded. "We've done nothing improper, so you can both get your minds out of the gutter."

"She's been with you for weeks. You appear all too familiar with her. No man touches a woman like you did unless he's married to her," Dominic said.

"You had her backed up against a wall with your hands all over her—and not with her permission, I might add," Rafe said. "How does that fit into your rules?"

"You did what?" Pa looked at his favored worker with disbelief. Dominic had no answer. His eyes fell to his feet again.

"Go back to your cottage. We'll discuss this later," my father said.

Dominic spun around to leave but stopped and pointed at Rafe. "She is yours now, whether you deserve her or not," he said, words cemented with hate. "You're expected to make it right. It's your duty to redeem her in the eyes of God and marry her." Dominic's eyes flicked to Pa, looking for confirmation.

Rafe's face paled. I could swear he leaned away from me. It was the barest of movements. My father said nothing, but his silence confirmed his agreement.

After a standoff both awkward and silent, Rafe stepped back. "I came here to help your daughters, nothing more," he said to my father. Then he looked at Dominic. "My rules are not your rules. I didn't sign up for your brand of crazy."

Rafe pushed through the two men and stormed down the hall. The back door opened and slammed shut. I was speechless. None of these men who supposedly cared for me stopped for even one second to consider my thoughts on the matter. What I wanted didn't matter. Well, it mattered to me, and I would not be forced into anything. Never again.

My father turned on my former betrothed. "Go home, Dominic," he said.

He obeyed without arguing, his shoulders folded in on himself.

Next my father aimed his attention at me, disappointment in his eyes, a look he wore all too often. "I'm not done with you, but I need to go stop your idiot friend before someone sees him."

Pa stalked off. He was crossing the living room when an alarm sounded, paralyzing him mid-step. The alarm signaling inspection.

Panic darkened his eyes. "Get your things and hurry."

Pa disappeared into Rafe's room as the alarm blared in the courtyard. I ran to Juni's room and grabbed my belongings.

"What's going on?" She raised her head from her pillow and rubbed sleep from her eyes.

"A routine inspection. Go back to sleep, and remember— Rafe and I were never here."

"What if they find you?" Juni's voice quivered in the darkness.

I knelt next to her. "Just act normal. They have no idea we're here."

I hoped that was true.

"I have to go." I caressed Juni's cheek and hurried into the hallway.

Pa waited there, his arms filled with Rafe's possessions. "Follow me," he said. I had no idea what he planned. There was no place to hide.

In the kitchen, Pa yanked open the pantry door. It was a terrible idea. A closet would be searched if the Guardia decided to be thorough. He fiddled with something behind a shelf of jarred green beans. There was a click, and Pa pushed. The pantry's back wall pivoted to the side, giving way to a small dark space. A hidden room. Light from the kitchen illuminated shelves lining the narrow space, sparsely populated with more jars of food and bottles of wine and spirits. A knife and pistol perched on one shelf, a wooden box on another.

"What on earth?" My jaw hung open, and a stab of betrayal flitted through me. My father had hidden this from me. What else had he been keeping from me?

Pa tossed Rafe's belongings inside and motioned me into the room. "Quickly."

I stepped inside and stared at my father.

"Stay put until I come for you. Don't make a sound."

A second later, the wall slid back in place, and the darkness consumed me.

I stood with arms full of my belongings, my heart thumping in the dark. My mind reversed through the last few moments until I felt sick.

Rafe had run off, fled to get away from me. The first mention of marriage, and he'd run. I sank to the floor and allowed silent tears to flow.

Marrying Rafe was the last thing on my mind, but even before the confrontation with Dominic, he'd begun to distance himself. The thought of marrying me had been the last straw. Fine. I didn't want to marry him or anybody else, and my father could go jump in the creek if he thought he would force me to do such a thing. Pa had been blessed to marry a woman he loved heart and soul. How could he demand anything less for me? I wouldn't accept that.

Inside the hidden room, light filtered beneath the pantry door, exposing the faint outline of shelves. I paused to listen for sounds in the house. It should have been empty except for Juni, who I hoped had fallen back to sleep. Silence. No one was here.

I slid a large box from one shelf and removed the lid, straining to keep quiet. The scent from the box nearly flattened me. It was the scent of my mother, clean cotton and homemade lavender soap, flashing through me in bits and pieces of memory. A hug in the kitchen. Sitting in her lap reading. Walking through the orchards with baskets of freshly reaped strawberries. *My God.*

I pressed one of her dresses to my nose and buried my face in the cloth. I drank in the lingering scent of her. The scent of home, of comfort, love. I could almost imagine her right next to me. It was bliss. It was agony. I searched the box, finding more dresses, a few pieces of simple jewelry, a book, letters…all mere crumbs from a life that had been so full. A life I missed so much.

Why had my father kept these things from us?

I finished exploring the box, finding a small bag of pesos and not much else. I leaned against the shelves and waited. I didn't want to think about Rafe, how much his rejection hurt, whether he'd been caught by the Guardia. So, I put my mind to something useful. I prayed for Rafe's safety. I prayed for a way to see this through. I prayed for my father's broken heart. The petitions came spinning out of my mind in the dark, floating wordless up to God. Every difficulty, danger and heartache that existed in my world I tossed heavenward, praying for redemption and rescue. An indescribable peace came over me as I opened my heart and unleashed my faith. It made no sense, but there it was.

A sudden burst of voices pierced the silence. Boots boomed on the wooden floor. I froze, afraid to breathe. I waited, listening. Beyond the pantry, chairs scraped away from the table as soldiers filled the seats. Pots rattled and clattered on the stove. Someone was cooking for Pa's guests. *Oh great.* This would take a while. But it also meant they weren't searching the house.

They hadn't found Rafe. They would have been torturing him or tearing the place apart to find accomplices if they had. Rafe was safe. He had to be.

I jumped at the sound of someone opening the pantry door. For a moment, I thought I'd been discovered, but I heard a familiar throat being cleared. Pa shuffled into the pantry and scuffed a shelf as he drew a jar from its perch. The door closed behind him, and I was alone again.

The Guardia were not going to search the house. I was safe. Pa was safe. Juni was safe.

Juni is safe.

My eyes opened wide in the dark, and I sat forward.

I knew exactly what I needed to say to convince Pa that we could pull this off.

36

RAFE

I stormed out of the house, not sure where I was going or why. The first whispers of light dawned in the distance, painting the farm pink and gray. The farmworkers would soon be rising. I shouldn't have fled out here. It was reckless. I knew that, but I couldn't stand to go back inside. The pit I'd dug since attending the Expo kept getting deeper. I was drowning in it. I'd only wanted to stop Evan from being broken and abused. I hadn't signed on for a lifetime commitment, for upending all my plans and endangering everyone I loved.

I made a beeline for the orchard, dashing for cover. As I reached the trees, a screeching alarm blasted through the courtyard. Moments later, a Guardia SUV appeared, zooming up the main road toward the house.

Hellfire and fuck me.

I ducked behind an orange tree. My eyes made a quick circuit, seeking a decent spot to hide. I could *not* get caught. Not again.

Farmworkers poured out of bunkhouses and cottages, filling the courtyard. The chaos was the best distraction I would get. I waited until the car passed and crept among the orange trees to a live oak camouflaged in Spanish moss. The workers assembled in neat rows before the main house, while the Guardia exited their vehicle. I heaved myself into the tree and hunkered down among the branches, trying to decipher what was happening.

Roughly thirty workers assembled in the courtyard. Dominic joined the front row. The workers had been caught off guard. Some buttoned their shirts and yanked on boots as they ran, but most still sported nightclothes and serious cases of bedhead. Lovette met the four Guardia on his porch, nodding to the men and exchanging a few words. One guard descended into the crowd and began trolling the rows, looking the workers up and down with contempt. A woman at the end of one row yawned as the guard approached. He crunched to a halt in front of her, scowling. The guard said something, and she failed to answer.

"I said, 'Am I boring you?'" he shouted, his face jutting inches from hers. The woman shook her head, eyes bulging in her pale face. The guard popped her in the mouth with a gloved fist, and she fell to the dirt, a cry spilling across her bloodied lip.

I shouldn't have been surprised. I'd witnessed cruelty worse than this, but I never got used to it. Bloody apes. I wanted to level every one of them, leave them writhing in the dirt. But I could do nothing.

Lovette wiped his face and looked away. There was nothing he could do either.

The goon inspecting the workers finished his perusal and returned to his comrades. Then the Guardia conferred with Lovette once more. The steward nodded and called over three workers. He sent the trio to the barn on some mission, then addressed the rest of the assembly, speaking in a loud voice. "Good morning, friends. Thank you for your promptness. You are free to go and carry on with your work assignments. Thank you."

Lovette's eyes made a quick scan of his surroundings. I

forced myself not to move, not even when he opened his front door and allowed four armed Guardia into his house. Into the house where Evan was trapped.

The clearing emptied, but I waited to see what happened. When the soldiers exited Lovette's house half an hour later like nothing was amiss, the knots in my stomach loosened. I'd never felt so impotent, hiding in a tree like a scared cat while a woman was beaten, while Evan hid inside her home. Intervening would have been disastrous, but my brain called it like it was. I was a coward. Perhaps in more ways than one.

I didn't want to go back into that house. I wanted no part of a shotgun wedding. Thinking about it made my blood boil. I cared for Evan, but I wasn't about to be forced into anything. Marriage had never been in my plans. It wasn't going to happen. It couldn't.

I slid down from the tree and began walking. The soft loam cushioned my footfalls, and the orchard shaded my way. I retraced the steps we'd taken days before, walking until I reached the wall by the stream. I sank down and sat there, staring at the water, arms draped over my knees.

What am I doing?

I had no idea.

"Dammit, Twain, why are you always right?"

I could have used his wisdom right now, but I'd left my half-functioning Convo in my room.

I sat for a long time, wallowing in self-pity and righteous anger. It was ugly, I knew. But sometimes you had to simmer in your own funk before you could put it behind you and decide what came next.

The sound of a horse in the distance called me back to the present. I scrambled to my feet and shoved myself into the shrubbery, branches scratching my face and tugging my clothing. Tossing stones aside, I opened the hole in the wall and scurried through, drenching half my body in the stream. I peered through the hole, waiting, counting the seconds ticking by.

A horse stomped through the stream, splashing water in the quiet. Its rider slowed and walked the horse in a circle in the clearing. Had Lovette come looking for me?

"Whoa," an unfamiliar male voice said. He dismounted and stood hidden behind his horse, silent for long seconds. Then came the unmistakable sound of a zipper opening, piss hitting the dirt. I'd never been so relieved to hear someone taking a leak.

Seconds later, the rider swung into his saddle and trotted off.

I closed my eyes and willed my heart to slow. Was I actually scared of Lovette? I'd lived through worse than the likes of him. He was no Conquistador. He wasn't my father. Or Bane. Yet I had no doubt he'd come after me, and it made me want to run even more.

If Lovette wasn't going to let us save his child, maybe it was time to turn for home. There were other lives I had to protect, and I didn't have time to play his games.

I peered at the forest in the distance like it held the secrets of the universe. It was only a dash away. I didn't deliberate long. I made the dash.

EVANGELINE

*T*he sun had set, and Rafe had yet to return. Doubt settled over me like a gray cloud. If he didn't come back, none of this would work. Everything would be for nothing. I'd be trapped in this house the rest of my life, living in a closet behind the pantry. Juni wouldn't have a chance, and neither would I.

After the Guardia had left, Pa released me from the closet. His eyes snagged on the open box on the floor, and his expression soured, as if I'd opened a Christmas present too early. He'd frowned and left in a wake of cold silence.

Pa had made the rounds of his workers, something he always did after an inspection. He liked to check on them, reassure them. He knew how much the Guardia's visits rattled them, even when nothing happened. Later, he'd made rounds in the outlying areas of the farm. It hadn't been his shift on security, but he'd gone anyway. He'd been searching for Rafe, likely trying to prevent someone from stumbling across him. Whatever the reason, he hadn't shared it with me. He refused to talk to me.

I'd distracted myself doing the dishes and spending precious time with Juni. I'd braided her hair, and we'd read stories together, leaning against each other's warmth like old times. I sewed. I paced. Each time Pa had stopped by the house, he'd been alone. Rafe was nowhere to be found. My stomach was a tangled mess. What if Rafe had left for good? What if he was already home? That was what he wanted, to return to his old life. He'd never wanted any of this. My father's stubbornness had sent him fleeing before he could be chained to another duty he'd never wanted.

Some fine man you brought home.

They were the first words Pa had said to me all day. It'd been late in the afternoon, and he'd finished his rounds. He'd tossed his boonie hat onto the kitchen table, grabbed a mug, and filled it with water from the tap, downing its contents in two big gulps. I hadn't responded. Nothing I said would change what he thought of Rafe. He'd slammed the mug onto the countertop, retrieved his hat, and stomped outside.

I didn't see him again until nightfall. Rafe still hadn't returned.

Dinner was iced in silence. Bellies stuffed with tension, no one was hungry. After dinner and dishwashing, I perched on the living room couch waiting, and still Rafe did not come.

My father's anger grew with the passing of the hours, simmering in silence below the surface. Finally, he went to bed early, leaving me alone with my withering hope.

38

RAFE

*A*s soon as I made it outside the walls of El Jardín, I unburied the UTV and drove through the maze of trees to the transitorio camp. Half a dozen men trained their weapons on me as I approached the perimeter. I called out to them.

"Rafe, nice to see you again," Averill said, lowering his weapon.

I climbed out of the vehicle and asked after Ambrose. Without Twain to keep me sane, Ambrose was the next best thing, a man with a pragmatic grasp on the way of the world. Averill pointed me in his direction.

I found Ambrose in the middle of camp, outside his wagon. He was leaning over a wooden table, sketching on a large map with a pencil. He glanced up at the sound of my footsteps.

A smile dimpled his face. "You made it back! Where's Evan and the little one?"

Suddenly my boots looked exceedingly interesting.

"What happened?"

I met Ambrose's eyes but couldn't think of what to say.

What was I doing? I didn't want to go back, didn't want to go forward.

"Are the girls all right?"

"Yeah, yeah. They're fine."

Ambrose didn't ask the next logical question. He waited for me to explain. I squirmed under his scrutiny. Then I confessed.

"I left them."

Still, Ambrose said nothing. He drilled me with his eyes, and I withered like a kid under a parent's knowing stare. Guilty. And well aware of it.

I blew out a deep breath and dived in. "Lovette—Evan's father—he wanted me to marry her. It didn't appear he planned to give me a choice. I lost my head and bolted."

Ambrose's brow creased, as if sorting through something in his mind.

"I know how this looks," I said.

"What do you plan to do?" he asked.

"I don't know."

Ambrose tossed his pencil onto the map and leaned his hip against the table. He crossed his arms over his chest and gave me a long, hard look before quirking his mouth in a half smile. "So let me get this straight. The man who single-handedly dared to infiltrate my camp a couple of weeks ago, who pushed me to attack a pack of Ferals, desperate to save this young woman... the man who repeatedly risked his life for this woman, and others, mind you...this man is fleeing a marriage demand? This is not the man I've come to know."

"It's not funny. You don't understand. I'm not marrying anyone, no matter who it is."

Ambrose scrunched his face in disbelief. "You're more afraid of marriage than death?"

"No! That's not it."

"Then what is it?"

I groaned and turned away.

"Don't you love Evan?"

"I care for her, yes."

"My friend, you love her. You're deluding yourself if you think it anything less."

He couldn't have been more wrong. I wasn't capable of love. Not like that.

"I only know I won't make a vow I can't keep," I said. "I can't —won't—shackle myself to anyone, ever."

"You have been given the wrong idea about marriage," Ambrose said. He circled me so I could not avoid his face. "When you love someone, marriage is not a cage. It's freedom, it's joy. It is the strength to face the world together."

"In my experience, familial relationships tend to come with a steep cost."

"Everything worthwhile requires something of you. But cost? Not with the right person. How can it when the heart has freely given itself away?" Ambrose said. He retrieved his pencil and resumed sketching on the page.

I stood there and watched. I couldn't argue his experience, but neither could he argue mine.

"So, what happens now?" he finally asked. "You have two choices. What will it be?"

The options were simple: Keep going and be home before sunset. Leave all this behind. Finish the Scythe of Thorns job and be done with it. Or go back to El Jardín and see this through. Find a way to avoid getting hitched, duck the Scythe a bit longer, and keep my promise to Evan.

I knew the right thing to do. Twain's voice in my head and that nasty little tug in the pit of my belly were broadcasting the answer loud and clear. I wouldn't be able to live with myself if I failed to keep my word to Evan, if I let that sweet little girl die when I could have done something to prevent it.

We'd figure the rest out.

We walk the fire together. And rise from the ashes together.

We'd make this work.

As for what else Ambrose was suggesting...I wasn't going there. I pushed it from my mind, not ready to face it, let alone put a name to it.

I paced, and Ambrose watched, his mouth quirked on one side.

"Stop grinning," I said. "You know exactly what I'm going to do."

"Now that's the man I've come to know."

"Lovette's the hard part. Besides the marriage thing, he's like a bull about his youngest daughter. So far, we've not been able to convince him to allow Juni to leave. He's certain it'll kill her, even though not doing so would surely result in the same thing."

The man had one more chance to say yes, and then I'd be out of time. I had to return to the Citadel and finish the Wreckus. Six days remained until Tresick's deadline, and it wasn't just my life on the line. I had to protect Twain, too.

Ambrose's face clouded with a calculated look. He put down the pencil and dropped a hand on my shoulder. "You're making the right choice," he said. "Now, come, let's get some coffee. I have an idea that might help with your future father-in-law."

He grinned, enjoying this a bit too much.

"Very funny."

39

EVANGELINE

"*E*van, wake up."

A voice stirred my sleep. Fingers brushed stray hairs from my face. I jerked awake and shrank into the couch cushions.

"Hey, it's me."

I blinked sleep away and focused on the man kneeling before me. "Rafe, thank God," I said. "You're safe. I was afraid I'd lost you."

Rafe dropped his head. "I'm sorry," he whispered.

"No, don't. Dominic...my father... I'm not... They can't make us do anything."

Relief and guilt swam across his face. "None of that's important. I'm here, and I'm going to do everything I can to help Juni reach the Fount," he said.

I leaned toward him, hope rising in my chest. "I think I came up with something to help my father change his mind," I said.

"Really? Me, too."

"You did?"

"Yeah, I brought backup."

He pointed toward the kitchen. A tall man stood in the

shadows of the doorway. He moved into the circle of candle-light and smiled.

"Mr. Brego!"

"Please, call me Ambrose."

There was no need to wake my father. Our voices had drawn him out. He froze at the threshold to the living room, his eyes wild and wide. His hands curled into fists, and his face went stone cold.

He opened his mouth to speak, but Ambrose snagged his attention. Pa stepped back, unawares. His face paled, as if he'd seen a ghost.

"Gabriel, it's good to see you," Ambrose said.

"Ambrose, is that you?"

"It is. You have a lovely daughter."

What? How on earth did my father know Ambrose?

"What are you doing here?" Pa asked.

"I'm here to help."

"Pa, how do you know Ambrose?"

My father ignored me. "What the hell is going on?" he said. "Best I can tell, this idiot has chosen to endanger us again by stealing another person inside these walls. Ambrose, you know if the Guardia finds you here, they'll kill you. They'll kill me for harboring you."

"Calm down, Gabriel. No one is going to get hurt."

"Easy for you to say. I have a family to protect."

"As do I," Ambrose said. "Why don't we sit and talk this out."

My father rubbed his forehead. His mouth pinched in defeat. As someone used to being in control, the constant shocks were wearing at him.

The four of us gathered around the kitchen table. I made chamomile tea and served everyone a cup. The half argument, half conversation stretched on for a long time. Ambrose repeated our plan to smuggle Juni under the protection of his transitorio clan. Ambrose's mere presence gave the idea more weight than it had coming from me or Rafe. Why, I didn't know. Still, Pa refused to allow it.

"Gabriel, you can come with us," Ambrose said. "Deliver Juniper safely to our caravan, and we can take it from there."

My father paused at the idea. He thought long and hard. Finally, he shook his head. "I can't do that. You know I can't leave here."

"The Guardia was just here. They never return the next day. Never. Tomorrow is your last chance. We can do the same when we bring her back, healthy and hale."

That silenced Pa. The idea shook his resolve. I could see it in his eyes.

"But the Guardia will eventually return, and she will be gone. How do I explain how I lost another daughter?"

I'd been holding my tongue while the two of them argued, but Pa's question jarred me back to my discovery.

"Pa, you won't need to explain anything," I said.

"'Course I will."

"No, you won't. They aren't checking on Juni. They didn't before the doctor's visit, and they didn't today. Think about it. They don't care about her anymore."

I could see the truth sink in. He studied me, looking for a way to counter, but he couldn't.

"They'll never know she's gone."

The struggle played out in my father's face. Pa knew we had a good plan, but he didn't want to chance it.

"Please, let us do this."

My father put his elbows on the table and buried his head in his hands. We sat there watching, waiting.

"Pa?" Juni came to my father's side and tugged on his sleeve. He drew her into his lap. Her face was pale, her eyes wide. How long had she been listening? "Pa, I wanna go."

"Oh, angel."

"Please, can I go?" She steeled her small shoulders. "I'll be good."

My father surveyed the expectant faces fencing him in. He drank in the sight of Juni like it might be his last.

"I need to think on this," he said to her. His message was meant for all of us. "Let me sleep on it, and I'll let you know in the morning. It's late. This one needs her rest, and so do I."

Pa leaned over to kiss Juni's forehead, then sent us to bed, assigning Ambrose to my bedroom and Rafe to bunk on the couch. I tucked Juniper beneath her blankets, the mystery of how my father and Ambrose knew each other unsolved. As I changed into my nightgown, I heard them in the hallway, speaking in hushed voices.

"I do trust him." It was Ambrose's voice. I put my ear against the door to listen.

"Well, I don't," Pa said.

"He's proven himself. He saved my life. Evan is alive today because of him."

"There must be some ulterior motive. No one sacrifices like that for people they don't know unless they have something to gain."

"Look, I don't know the whole story, but the only motive I see is the desire to protect your daughter and help her. He loves her, though he won't admit it to himself."

Loves me? Impossible. Rafe was tired of being responsible for me. Yet the thought sent a spiral of butterflies through the heart of me.

"If he loves her, then he shouldn't have run. He's ruined my daughter and refuses to marry her."

"Stop being such a prude, Gabriel. Remember what it was like with Helene," Ambrose said. "Don't push them on the marriage thing. They love each other. I've seen it, but if you force them into something they're not ready for, you'll destroy that. You of all people should know how much love matters. You had the best."

A quiet fell between them as it dawned on me that Ambrose had known my mother, too.

"I did. I know," Pa said.

"Sleep on it, my friend."

They parted, disappearing behind closed doors. I sank into the bed next to Juni. She was already sleeping, her chest rising and falling with her tiny, humming snores. Sleep wouldn't come to me. My head was too full of Rafe, of Juni, of the prospect of a miracle. Of what the future would hold once the sun rose tomorrow.

PA FOUND me in the predawn darkness. I lay wide awake with Juni curled into me, staring into the shadows as if they would foretell my future.

"Okay," Pa's voice whispered over his tiny daughter.

I held my breath, scared he would change his mind. Scared he wouldn't. The burden of his trust doubled the ever-present weight on my chest, but I would gladly bear the load. For Juni. For him. For me.

I would not let the dread that had shadowed me ever since my mother died drown me. My love for them would buoy me through any storm.

Pa grew quiet, watching Juni sleep. Pain flooded his eyes. "I can't deny her a chance to live a normal life. A long, normal life," he said. "It's all I ever wanted for the both of you."

"It's what I want for her, too. I believe with all my heart it's the right thing to do."

"I don't know what's right anymore, how to protect the two of you," he said. "My worst fear is that you'll leave and I'll never see either of you again."

I wanted to promise that wouldn't happen, but I couldn't. Life wasn't bound by the promises we made. The only guarantee I could give was that I'd do everything in my power to come back, to bring both of us back.

My sister was giddy when she heard the news.

"I can't wait to see all the fancy people," she said. "Do they got a princess?"

We gave her the rules for the trip: No excitement, no overexertion, rest as much as possible. The responsibility for Juni's well-being settled on me like a load of bricks. I'd not been able to save my mother, and maybe her death hadn't been my fault, but I could do this. I could change the outcome this time.

We spent the day getting ready. Half an hour before midnight, we gathered in the living room with our packs. Juni clung to my father, sleep tugging her eyes, her mouth curved with a groggy joy. Pa took a long look at her and sighed before heading out the back door. "Let's go, before I reclaim my sanity."

My father carried Juni the entire way. At first, she was so happy to be outdoors that she perched upright in his arms, drinking in the landscape, the sapphire sky, the blanket of stars. I'd missed seeing her smile so much. Soon, she tired and slumped onto Pa's shoulder, passing in and out of sleep. It was well past her bedtime.

Rafe and I had spoken little during the day, but now I caught him watching me as we walked, considering me, searching beyond skin and bone to something deeper. What was he looking for? I was an open book to him. He knew everything about me that mattered.

Before long, we arrived at the break in the wall, the same place I'd started my journey weeks ago. There was no crawling through the muck for this trip. My father had brought a spare key to unlock the iron gate across the stream. Ambrose waded through first, scouting for soldiers. Pa came through last with Juni. A smile glimmered in her eyes at the first glimpse of forest beyond the wall. Tonight was a great adventure for her, and if this worked, she'd have plenty of carefree times in her future. That was my hope and prayer.

My father was a different story. His eyes hardened as he surveyed the unprotected landscape.

"This is foolish," he muttered. "I have lost all sense."

Still, the moment Ambrose broke for the woods, my father followed him into the dark. Rafe's hand slipped loosely around mine, and he pulled me after them.

40

RAFE

*W*e arrived at camp in the deep dark, as fireflies danced in the shadows. Juni's tired eyes sparked to life, following the tiny lights in the forest and drinking in the encampment like it held untold magic. Lovette scrutinized the gathering, begging to find a reason to change his mind, but he hadn't retreated yet.

Ambrose insisted Evan and Juni bed down in his wagon. He bunked outside his home, spreading blankets next to me and Lovette. Evan's father squirmed in his bedroll until Ambrose rolled over and groused at him. He finally settled and grew silent. I lay there listening to the night sounds gather around us, sleep beyond me. Exhaustion sank into my bones, but I could only stare at the sprinkle of stars peeking through the treetops. I tried to clear my mind.

No dice.

I was a prisoner freed from bondage, still haunted by the sins of my past. Evan saw a miracle on the horizon, but my mind foretold misery. Every foot we retraced placed me one step closer to the Conq's palace. A place to which I swore I'd never return. If I was caught, if anyone recognized me, it would cost my life. But damn it, I was going. I wasn't going to let dear old Papi and his minions' bloodlust and depravity stop me from saving this kid's life. From keeping my word.

Beyond the fear, beyond the doubt, beyond the danger, there was simply Evan. What would happen to her when this was over? Our lives had been woven together in a way I could never have imagined when this had begun. The shared threads of experience bound us, one to the other, like the cords of a rope. I cared. I wanted more than what my old life had held. I liked having her near. I wanted her safe. Who else would ensure that? Certainly not her father.

At some point, I fell asleep. It lasted a few blinks, or so it seemed, and then the camp was coming awake, the morning sounds rousing me from sleep. I woke to find Lovette glaring at me like I was the spawn of hell.

To be fair, he wasn't far off.

Or maybe he was contemplating offing me in my sleep. Hard to tell which brand of scowl it was.

Gabby and Seth came bearing a breakfast of sweet breads and apples. They doted on Juni, and the girl marveled at Gabby's baby bulge. Gabby flattened Juni's small fingers on her belly, and the girl stared wide-eyed, giggling, while the baby kicked. There was nothing like inviting someone to feel an alien squirming in your belly to cement a new friendship.

Dark circles rimmed Juni's eyes, but she had no patience for fatigue. She was fueled by joy at the world she'd been missing. She was fearless. Like her sister.

Evan munched on a warm biscuit and drilled Ambrose about his connection to her father. Ambrose was former Guardia, part of a quartet that had inspected the farm when Lovette's father had been steward. After a year of regular inspections, he'd had enough. Like all the Conq's Guardia, his squad had dished out its share of cruelty, but Ambrose was not one to raise his hand without cause. He'd refused to humiliate and beat the workers.

One sweltering summer day, a worker had fainted during an inspection. She'd been with child, early in her pregnancy, overcome with heat and fear. Her husband had rushed to help, and the Guardia had pounced on easy prey. The quad leader, a man named Rufus, berated the woman as she'd lain on the ground, called her lazy and worthless. The husband had tried to explain about the pregnancy and the heat. Rufus said if it was too hot, he could fix that. He'd grabbed the woman's dress and ripped the front open, baring her to the entire assembly. The husband had become enraged and lunged at the guard. That was all the justification Rufus needed. He'd kicked the man to the ground and shot him, repeatedly, until he'd lain in a bloody heap.

Later, as the squad filled their bellies at Lovette's table and gotten loaded on liquor, Ambrose had slipped outside to take a piss and never come back. As the squad readied to leave and shouted his name, Ambrose had been sneaking through the orange grove. That was where he'd run into Lovette. When Ambrose continued to ignore the drunken calls, Lovette realized what he was doing.

"He had every reason to report me, but he didn't," Ambrose said.

The young Lovette had brought him home and stashed him in a secret room behind the pantry, where he'd stayed until the squad had given up and left. Two nights later, the trio had reappeared, sober and angry, and turned the garden inside out looking for their missing comrade. By that time, Ambrose had already disappeared into the Wildlands.

"My father did this?" Evan was stunned.

Ambrose nodded and smiled.

"Well, that explains it," she said.

"Explains what?" he asked.

"Explains where I get my tendency to go out on a limb."

Where she'd learned to help others at her own expense. Lovette couldn't see how much she was like him.

Ambrose laughed, then excused himself to prepare his wagon. It was time to move on.

The rest of the clan began tearing down camp and hitching horses to their wagons. Lovette collected the breakfasts dishes and took them to the chuck wagon, then returned to Ambrose's wagon. He scooped his youngest daughter from her perch near the campfire and clutched her tight to his chest. Her arms came around his neck in a loose embrace. The man's big hand stroked Juni's hair as he whispered into her ear. The young girl leaned back, put her tiny hands on his lined face, and said, "Love you, too, Pa."

For a moment, time stopped. Dread sunk into my gut, as if I'd witnessed a final parting. I shook the thought away. That would not happen. I would not be responsible for fulfilling Lovette's darkest fear. I would see her healed. I would see her back in his arms.

Juni dropped a noisy kiss onto her father's cheek, then wriggled in his hold, arms extended toward me. I raised an eyebrow. Evan and her father stared at me as if I'd grown a second head. Juni impatiently flashed her fingers. I hesitated for only a second. I reached for her, and she wrapped around me like she belonged there. Lovette's face burned red, and his fingers clenched into fists. Evan tried and failed to suppress a smile. She slid her hand into his, and his fingers relaxed into hers. He gathered her into his arms, crushed her hard against him, and kissed the top of her head.

"I'm begging you to be careful," he said. "You two are all I have."

His eyes locked onto mine as he spoke. His glare anchored me like an oath. One I accepted.

Ambrose broke the tension. "Gabriel, they're in good hands," he said, putting a reassuring hand on Lovette's shoulder. "We'll take good care of them."

Lovette nodded and held out his hand. The key to the gate lay in his palm.

"Bring them back," he said.

I gave a single nod and scooped up the key.

Moments later, the wagons were moving. Lovette stood in the clearing, arms crossed, his face a scowl. For the first time since meeting him, I hoped I would see him again—and soon.

§

THE NEXT MORNING, everyone was cleaning up breakfast and packing to move on. Juni lobbed a pine cone at my head and missed.

"Come on, you can do better than that," I said, zigging and zagging in front of her. "Hit me, right here." I pointed to my forehead. Juni giggled and cocked her arm, hand loaded and ready to fire.

A buzzing sound echoed through the camp, something not of the Florida wilderness, and I froze. The hairs on my neck stood at attention as the camp grew quiet. A pine cone struck the side of my head, but I barely flinched. Evan paused with a soapy skillet in her hand as the sound grew louder.

"Everyone stay calm," Ambrose shouted. "We keep our cool, and everything will be fine."

"Stick with me, Juni," I said, taking her hand and tugging her over to her sister.

"Is that...?" Evan couldn't finish the sentence. Her eyes were the size of plates.

"Yeah, a Guardia truck, maybe two." I grabbed her soapy hand, then towed both girls into a throng of transitorios. Gabby and Seth squeezed in beside us.

My heart was seizing. If Colonel Tresick was among the approaching Guardia, I wasn't the only one in danger. I couldn't let him discover that Evan and Juni were with me.

"May I?" I said, pointing to a bonnet dangling from Gabby's neck. She untied it and handed it over without question. I slid the bonnet over Juni's head and tied it loosely beneath her neck.

"We're part of the clan. Relax, and don't do anything to draw attention." I squeezed her shoulder. Evan pulled her to her chest and wrapped her arms around her. We stood shoulder to shoulder, so close I could feel the heat emanating off her.

Three Guardia trucks halted outside the ring of wagons. A dozen soldiers emerged from the vehicles, rifles slung across their chests. They pierced our circle of safety as Ambrose greeted them.

"Welcome," he said, arms spread wide. It was a gesture of hospitality, but I knew better. Ambrose wanted no misunderstanding as to whether he was armed or not. "To what do we owe the pleasure?"

"We're here for an explanation."

The voice came from somewhere behind the soldiers, the owner of it unmistakable. Worse than Tresick. I edged to the left, shielding myself from view behind a tall man with a wide straw hat. Evan mirrored my movement, sliding behind the woman in front of her.

"Commander Bane," Ambrose said. "I'm not sure what you mean."

The Commander appeared from behind the wall of soldiers, hands clasped together like a scolding schoolteacher. "Our drone surveillance indicated a large gathering of transitorios south of here several days back."

Drones? Since when had they been using drones? How much had they seen of our movements? The puddle of unease in my belly spread into a chasm.

"And that concerns you why?" Ambrose asked. "We've adhered to the Empire's parameters."

"That may be," Bane said. "But our intelligence has uncovered recent attempts at treason and assassination. We executed a rebel for his crimes against the Empire, and we are well aware a thriving trade exists between the Barrio and the transitorios. When that trade extends to treachery, we will no longer turn a blind eye."

A muscle twitched in Ambrose's jaw as he warred with a response. "How about not turning a blind eye to Ferals who've been murdering your citizens unchecked in the Wildlands?" he said.

Bane prowled forward, nose to nose within Ambrose's personal space. The patrón didn't flinch, didn't yield.

"You forget yourself, vagrant," Bane said, his temper even. "You answer to me, not the other way around. Search their wagons. Bring me anything suspicious."

This was not good. They were going to find the UTV. They were going to find us. The Guardia always left the transitorios to their own devices. They never bothered with them. Why raid us now? What did they know? Did Bane know who Ambrose was?

Eight soldiers peeled off and began tearing through the wagons. Evan vibrated next to me, and I had the urge to comfort her, but I didn't dare move.

"What exactly do you expect to find? My people have done nothing wrong. We have followed your edicts to a fault," Ambrose said.

"Is that so? So, you weren't conspiring with other transitorio patrones to overthrow the Conquistador?"

"What? Are you mad?"

"Why else would you be gathering the clans so often?" Bane said.

Ambrose stared at the Commander, eyebrows creased with disbelief. "You twist and pervert every beautiful thing in this Empire," he said.

"Watch your tongue, or you'll be spending the rest of your

life in the Calabozo," Bane said, as simply as if he were remarking on the nice weather.

Ambrose took a deep breath. "We have no interest in what goes on in the Citadel," he said. "We gather for community. To enjoy one another's company. To share a meal and conversation. We gather so our young people can meet others and find matches outside their own bloodlines. We meet to celebrate life."

"How sweet," Bane said. His next words were interrupted by a pair of soldiers barreling into the clearing.

"Commander, sir, we found this," said a blond soldier with a bad sunburn. He displayed the night-vision goggles I'd given Seth. "And a UTV tied to one of the wagons."

One eyebrow on Bane's head raised, and his lip curled in amusement. I clenched my fist until my nails dug holes in my flesh. Every muscle coiled tight from head to toe.

"Intriguing," he said. "Who do they belong to?"

Next to me, Seth shifted on his feet. The quiet stretched thin. I couldn't raise my hand and confess, but if I didn't someone else was going to pay the price. After everything this clan had done to protect us, I couldn't let that happen.

"They're mine," Ambrose said before I could.

No. No, he couldn't take the fall for me.

"Where did you get these?" Bane asked.

"I found the UTV along the road to the Citadel. Looked like the vehicle had been ambushed and abandoned. The goggles were inside the vehicle."

Not too far from the truth.

"And you took them?"

"You find a treasure in the Wildlands, you take it," Ambrose said. "Law of the land. Ferals started it, we adopted it."

Finders keepers was indeed legal in the Wildlands, but that wouldn't stop Bane from arresting someone if he was feeling cranky. He was always feeling cranky.

"What's your name, vagrant?" he asked.

The entire clan grew still. Sweat broke out across my forehead, and a shudder ran down my back.

"Brego," Ambrose said.

Bane considered him. "That name sounds familiar. How long have you been patrón of this clan?"

"Coupla decades," he said.

"I see." Bane continued to stare at him, like he was weighing his options, which flavor of ruination he'd visit on these innocent people. Finally, he turned his back on Ambrose and rejoined his soldiers.

"We have been investigating each of the transitorio clans that participated in this gathering," Bane said. "Fortunately for you, your stories match. But know that we are watching you. Any act of treason, any threat against the Empire will be dealt with swiftly and severely. You have been warned."

"You have nothing to worry about with us, Commander," Ambrose said. "I assure you."

"Never trust the word of a vagrant," Bane said, then commanded the solder at his right. "Confiscate the UTV."

We were so fucked, and so was Mac.

PART IV

WHAT THE WATER GAVE ME

41

EVAN

*C*reeping dread had bounced back with a vengeance, mashing on my chest, and the more innocent people I dragged into this quest, the heavier it got. We'd lost Mac's UTV. The UTV that was meant for Luther, a Los Reyes boss in the Sink. As we approached the Citadel's outer wall near sunset, it felt like we were beggars at the door, bringing nothing but trouble.

Traveling with the caravan had been slow going compared to zipping through the Wildlands in the UTV. During the two-day trip, Rafe had repaired his Convo and reached out to Mac, warned him about the situation, and arranged to have the gate opened to allow us inside. Then he'd given the Convo to Ambrose so we could contact him for the return trip. We'd said our goodbyes and left Ambrose's clan a mile back. Averill, Seth, and two other transitorios—all armed—accompanied us, a precaution against Feral attacks. Without the UTV, it was the best we could do for a half-hour walk through the Wildlands.

Rafe had carried Juni on his back for the first twenty minutes, quiet and lost in thoughts. Right now, she was draped on my shoulders, quietly murmuring words of awe as the massive city came into view. I wished I could enjoy seeing it through her eyes, but I couldn't stop fretting about what Luther was going to do when he found out what happened to his vehicle.

We reached the gate, and it cracked open, enough for us to squeeze inside. It was dark as night beyond the opening, no one in sight. Goose bumps rose on my skin.

"Thanks for looking after us, guys," Rafe said, shaking Seth's hand. "Safe travels."

"You, too," Seth said, giving him a small smile.

Juni's arms tightened around my neck. Her heart raced against my back.

"Breathe, Junebug. I got you."

Rafe caught my eyes for a moment. There was fear there, the same trouble burning in his eyes as the day the Ferals had ambushed us. The next few moments were out of our control, and he knew it. But I also knew he would do whatever it took to protect us. I nodded, offering what little confidence I could spare. Rafe stared into the darkness and led us inside.

The gate sailed shut behind us with little noise, snuffing out the sunlight and throwing us into darkness. Rafe froze and drew me close.

"Mac?" His voice bounced on the stone walls and fell in the quiet. Suddenly a lantern flashed on. A figure stepped out of the shadows and grabbed Rafe, yanking his hand free from my arm. The man was huge, with arms the size of small tree trunks.

Juni screamed. Her child-sized shriek pierced the air and echoed off the walls. She gasped for air as I scuttled away. Rafe struggled against his attacker.

"Luther, please. Stop!" Mac's voice rose above the commotion, pleading as two men restrained him.

Luther trapped Rafe in a headlock, and his face reddened as the big man's grip tightened.

"Eh… Ev…" My sister couldn't draw enough breath to say my name.

"Hold on, Juni." I sat my sister on the ground and began rooting in my bag.

Then I heard a click and a cold voice close to my ear. "Stop right there," a man said. "Hands up. Slowly."

A short man with a handlebar mustache placed the cold muzzle of a pistol against my temple. Juni's gasping wheeze screamed in my ear.

"I'm all right, Junebug. Calming breaths."

I raised my hands. The mustached man snatched my bag and showed it to Luther.

"My sister is sick. She can't breathe. She needs the medicine in that bag," I said.

The man looked at the bag, then at Juni, surprise registering on his face.

"Luther," Rafe grunted. "Please, she's just a kid."

"Please," I begged as Juni continued to gasp for air. "She can't breathe!"

Luther signaled to his men. More lights in the tunnel flickered on, and he stalked closer, with Rafe wedged in the crook of his arm. The red in Rafe's face deepened, but Juni's face was losing color.

"Juni!"

I didn't think, just moved. I pulled her into my lap. Her panicked eyes sought mine.

"Please, I need her medicine," I said, fighting to keep my voice calm. I stroked Juni's hair and glared at the men holding my friends hostage.

"Give the woman her bag," Luther said. Mustache Man tossed my pack. It landed at my feet. I tugged the bag open and collected the tin of ointment. My hands shook as I tried to unscrew the lid.

"Here, hold 'im." Luther shoved Rafe into the mustached man's hands.

"Let me," the big man said, stooping and taking the tin from my hand. The container disappeared in his massive palm. His fingers twisted the lid, and the smell of eucalyptus and lemon drifted into the air.

"Here." He handed it back and waited. I scooped a glop of the ointment and rubbed it under Juni's nose. I spread more on her chest.

"Slow, deep breaths, Juni," I said, catching her eyes with mine. "Focus on me. Forget everything else. Slow, deep breaths."

I repeated my reassurances over and over, caressing her hair. Everything faded until it was the two of us and this one thing. After long minutes, a blush of color rose in Juni's cheeks and her muscles unknotted. I closed my eyes in relief and bent my head to hers.

"What's wrong with 'er?" Luther asked.

"She has a growth in her lungs," I said. "Sometimes she has trouble breathing. It's been getting worse."

"Hmm," he said as he stood.

Again, I didn't think. I clutched Luther's hand. "Thank you," I said.

He tapped the tip of my nose and winked.

"Now, as for you, you thief." Luther stalked to Rafe, fisted his shirt in his beefy hand, and shoved him against the wall. "I'll teach you to steal my property."

"Luther, please, the Guardia confiscated your vehicle," Mac said. "They stole it from you."

A bruise circled Mac's eye like a storm cloud, and his lip was busted and crusted with dried blood. I shuddered at the damage he'd suffered because he'd helped us.

"They stole it from him," Luther growled. Rafe said nothing, taking the abuse like he deserved it. He didn't. Horror sank into my heart as Luther unsheathed a knife from his waist and aimed for Rafe's stomach.

"Stop! Please!"

Luther's fist halted at the sound of my sister's small voice.

"Don't hurt him, mister...please," Juni said, her head heavy against mine. "He's helping me."

He hesitated, his hand suspended mid-strike. His face remained clenched in rage, his lips parted in a gap-toothed scowl. "Little lady, I got to teach your friend here it ain't right to steal. No one lays a hand on my property," he said. He gave Rafe a shove against the wall for emphasis.

I rose from the dirt, pulling Juni behind me, where she clung to me. My heart pounded in my ears as I edged toward Luther. Mustache Man aimed his gun at me, but I kept going. Rafe shook his head with the tiniest of movements, but I needed to fix this. I couldn't let him kill Rafe. I stood next to Luther, so close I could smell sweat and the clinging grease of a fried fish dinner.

"Please, sir," I said. "This is my fault. Rafe is helping me and my sister. I couldn't get her here without him."

Luther eyed Juni, who peeked out from behind my hip. I couldn't say the words he needed to hear—that Juni would die without his help. I couldn't say it out loud, not with her right beside me. I glanced at her, and the words stuck in my throat.

Mac did it for me.

"I told you. That little girl needs medical care, the kind you can only get in the Citadel," he said. "Without it, she'll die."

I flinched at his words. Juni did not. At such a tender age, she'd come to accept what might happen. It broke me.

"You saw what happened to her," Mac said.

"Shut the hell up!" Luther's words bellowed in the cramped space.

"We had every intention of returning the vehicle—and

repairing any damages—before you took ownership," Rafe said. "I'm truly sorry."

"I can't let something like this slide," Luther said. "There must be consequences."

Juni slipped from behind me and placed her little-girl fingers on his muscled forearm. "Please, mister, let him go," she said.

"Ah, hell," Luther muttered. He re-sheathed his knife, and relief flooded my core. Luther cocked his fist and slammed it into Rafe's face. His head snapped sideways, and his body slumped to the ground. Juni shrieked, and I pulled her against my stomach.

Luther stepped over him and dusted off his hands. "Mac, I expect a new vehicle in six months, or there will be hell to pay," he said.

"Of course," he said.

Rafe groaned and rolled over. I smoothed Juni's hair in a calming gesture, then dropped next to him on the ground. I cradled Rafe's face and wiped blood from his mouth. He blinked dazed eyes and pushed up onto his elbows.

"As for you," Luther said, pointing at him. "You live on one condition: You owe me. Some day in the future, I will find you and you will do something for me. Whatever I ask, you will do it. Fail me, and I'll make you wish you were dead."

"Understood," Rafe said, his voice hoarse.

"Now get out of my sight before I change my mind."

42

RAFE

*U*pon returning to the Phoenix Nest, Twain hugged me like he hadn't seen me in a hundred years. This was longest we'd been apart, managing life and survival without each other. We'd been inseparable for more than half our lives. I'd missed him, too.

"Life gives you lemons, and you stir them in a pot and make a crap stew," Twain said.

I cocked an eye. "Something like that," I said. "Sorry I spilled some on you."

"You should be," said Simone, who was kneeling and greeting Juni like she was a celebrity. The girl was starstruck, eyeing Simone as if she were Taylor Swift, if Juni had known who Taylor Swift was. People in the Wildlands tended to know little about pop culture. "Whatever happened to having a backup plan and a backup for the backup?"

"Believe me, I know," I said, wincing at the pain in my jaw. Luther hit hard. Hard enough that I'd seen stars.

I was so tired of being a punching bag, but I was a lucky bastard. Los Reyes were known for a particular flavor of justice, and it wasn't much different than what the Conq dished out.

Luther had been ready to gut me. If Juni hadn't charmed the beast, who knew what would have happened? But now the beast owned me. He'd come for his due, and I'd have to answer the call, no matter what he asked. My hole just kept getting bigger.

"Hey, man, should I call Carlton?" Twain asked. "Your face looks like a mud puddle."

"I feel like a mud puddle," I said, stretching out on the couch. "I'll be fine."

Twain disappeared and returned bearing an ice pack, ibuprofen, and a glass of water.

We caught up over the next hour, Evan filling in the details while Juni played with a basket of toys Simone had bought for her. Twain and Simone nestled together on the love seat, a new familiarity lingering between them. Something had happened between them during our absence, and it was about damned time. Simone's hand settled on Twain's knee, and she watched him speak with a look on her face I'd never seen before.

I wanted to be happy for them, but I couldn't kick the sense of mounting dread. I had two days left to finish Tresick's device, or I'd be on another hit list. Then there was the impending trip to the Fount. Phantom memories kept resurrecting like zombies. Getting caught sneaking into the Fount. Being imprisoned in the Calabozo. Being tortured, beaten, and left for dead in the Wildlands.

In short order, I would revisit the scene of my crimes, venture to where I'd lived the darkest hours of my life.

Evan's voice interrupted my thoughts.

"Come on, Juni, let's get you settled for the night," she said.

"We should be going, too," Twain said.

"Going where?" I asked, though I already knew the answer. "Don't you live here?"

Twain had the gall to give me a sheepish look. "I may have been spending my nights elsewhere in recent days," he said. I swore he was blushing.

"He means my place," Simone said. "And you can wipe that smug look off your face."

I didn't know my face muscles were capable of looking smug at the moment, but I couldn't help but smile. They both deserved to be loved, deeply.

Simone gathered her things, and Twain motioned me aside.

"Tresick's been by twice," he said. "I showed him the device and promised him we'd make deadline. He's a ferocious sort of goliath. Big on the threats."

"I noticed. I have no idea how that's going to happen," I said. "I'd planned on having two weeks to finish it, not less than two days."

Twain clapped a hand on my shoulder. "I've made some progress on it," he said.

For the first time in weeks, I felt a ray of hope.

"You've been working on it?"

"Yup. Remember the whole *walking the fire together*?" he said. "I was familiar with the research, since I stole it, but I could only get so far. Hardware's not my thing."

It was better than no progress at all. Way better.

"Twain, if we pull this off, I'll do toilet duty the rest of my life," I said. I would have grinned at him, but there was still work to do.

"That's a deal I can get behind," he said.

Twain and Simone left, and for a few minutes, I was alone with my thoughts circling the drain.

Evan returned bearing a fresh glass of water. "She's already asleep. The day wore her out."

"I can relate."

Silence lingered awkwardly between us.

"I'm glad your friends aren't mad," Evan said, handing me the glass.

"Hard to be mad after hearing what happened."

"Maybe," she said. "But I'm not sure they'll ever forgive me for putting you in danger."

Ten feet of space separated us. I felt the tug to go to her, like a wave pulling a boat out to sea. I stayed where I was.

"We both entered this willingly. You're not to blame for anything that happened. We can't own other people's bad behavior."

"I know, but I don't want anyone to get hurt, for the harm to outweigh the good," she said. She crossed her arms and hugged herself as if suddenly cold.

"No one can ever guarantee that," I said.

Evan nodded. Silence stretched to the point of discomfort. I deposited the glass on the coffee table.

"Try to sleep," I said. "I've got some work to do tonight, and tomorrow will be busy."

I skirted her, close enough to catch a hint of lingering sunlight on her skin, fresh like the forest air. I hesitated for a fraction of a second, fighting the urge to pull her into my arms. I couldn't look her in the eyes. I would surrender if I did.

I moved. Her hand caught my wrist.

"Thank you for coming back for us," Evan said, her voice choked with emotion. I removed her hand from my wrist and squeezed it reassuringly. Then I let it drop and rushed to the safety of my workshop.

I worked until my eyes struggled to stay open, until I broke a vital part trying to wedge it into place. I almost screamed. I didn't have time for another trip to the Sink. I went to bed angry and exhausted and barely slept.

TWAIN AND SIMONE were back early the next morning, carrying an armload of boxes.

"I botched your progress last night," I said to Twain. I explained what happened, and he raised his eyebrows.

"I broke the same part—twice," he said. "I procured some spares while you were gone, just in case."

"You're a miracle worker," I said, but I had no time for relief. Tresick expected the device to be delivered sometime tomorrow, and the next Immersion ceremony was six days away. We had to act fast to set up our fake identities, arrange travel, and book an Immersion. We were pushing it, getting approved for entry into the Fount.

"I know," Twain said.

"Good, 'cause I still need a miracle to pull everything off," I said.

"You mean *we*. We need a miracle," he said. "You're not alone."

"You are my miracle," I said. "I'd never have survived this long without you."

"We save each other." He chucked me on the arm and headed for the kitchen.

We game-planned what needed to happen next while eating Evan's crepes. They weren't like the torrijas I'd loved for breakfast growing up, but they were homemade and that made them something to savor. Twain had been working on our fake identities, and all that was left was to program our biogloves and retinal masks. Once that was complete, we'd book our Immersion and travel.

A few hundred tourists visited the Fount each year. The Conq doubled the price for foreigners, but it didn't dissuade the wealthy visitors, and thanks to the cash we got for Blythe's jewels, we could afford it. More would visit the Fount if the Conq allowed it, but he guarded Florida's most valued asset jealously. The Floridian regulars to the Fount were known to the Citadel. We'd have to play the part of travelers from America.

"I have a surprise for Evan and Juni," Simone said after breakfast, her eyes bright with delight. Evan raised her eyebrows.

"How much do you know about the protocol for the Fount?" Simone asked.

"Not much, other than the travel situation," she said.

"After you clear border security, you'll arrive at the Imperial Hotel, where Fount guests stay. That evening you'll attend the Fount Ball."

I groaned, loud. Twain gave a half cackle from where he was rinsing our breakfast dishes at the sink and putting them in the dishwasher. I suddenly wanted to throttle him.

"We get to dance?" Juni asked.

"Sí, it's tradition. A ball always happens before every Immersion ceremony," Simone said.

"Yay!" The girl did a little chair dance, waving her fork like a magic wand.

"Is the ball required?" Evan asked. She couldn't mask the horror on her face.

"Only if you want to avoid drawing attention. Everyone goes. It's expected."

"I have no idea what to do at a ball," she said.

"Don't worry—I'll give you and Rafe lessons. You'll need to know the customs, the dances."

"Dances? No, really."

"Take it easy," Simone said. "You'll be well prepared. This is for you." She handed a small white box to Juni, who promptly tore off the lid and lifted out a light blue ballgown bursting with chiffon.

"Wow..." Juni said. "It's so pretty."

"Why don't you go and try it on," Simone said. Juni was moving before the last word came out of her mouth.

Evan laughed, and a genuine smile stretched across her lips. I loved that smile. I didn't want to love that smile.

"This is yours," Simone said, pushing a larger box across the counter to her.

"You've done too much," Evan said.

"Open it. Go on."

Evan lifted the lid and withdrew a crimson silk gown. She gasped and covered her mouth. "It's beautiful."

"Try it on," Simone said. Evan looked at her in disbelief. "Go on."

Evan slid off her stool and held the dress up, letting the folds of its skirts fall to the floor. It was strapless, with a fitted bodice and long flowing layers. She'd look like a queen in it.

She disappeared down the hallway but reappeared moments later, the dress clutched to her chest, her face pale.

"What's wrong?" Simone asked.

A sob choked her throat, and she buried her face in her hands. Simone flew to her. Her delicate hands came to rest on her shoulders. "Evangeline, what's wrong?" she asked.

Evan continued to sob. Finally, Simone forced her hands from her face.

"What is it? Talk to me." Her eyes attached to Evan's, unwilling to relent without an answer.

Evan unbuttoned her blouse, pulled down the collar, and bared her shoulder blade.

Simone gasped. Twain dropped his dish in the sink.

My father's mark was etched into her skin. His crest, his symbol, his claim.

"What. The. Hell?" It was all I could think to say.

My Convo buzzed on my wrist. I ignored it, staring at the tattoo. It kept buzzing, an urgent, annoying wake-up alarm that no sane person would use during the day unless it was an emergency. I looked at my wrist. A message blared in red.

Koi pond. Midnight.

My time was up.

43

RAFE

*T*urned out building a device while you're pissed off could be quite productive. I couldn't decide who infuriated me more: Evan, for not telling us about the tattoo. Or the Conq, for his disgusting arrogance in marking people as his own.

My father had branded Evan, stitched his mark into the fabric of her flesh. Sinking my attention into the work allowed me to funnel my anger and frustration into finding solutions that had seemed impossible days before. Twain joined me in the workshop, and together we finished the Wreckus shortly after midnight. On the wrong side of the finish line, but still finished nonetheless.

"Be careful out there," Twain said. Concern wrinkled his brow and darkened his eyes. The handoff could be uneventful, or it could be a trap. I still had no idea if Tresick was the real deal or a Guardia spy.

"I'll be back," I said, tying my black running shoes. I hoped it was the truth.

I threw on a ballcap and pulled the backpack loaded with

our offering onto my shoulders, and then I disappeared into the night.

Forty-five minutes past midnight, I found myself alone at the koi pond, searching the darkness shrouding the surrounding trees. No lights shone, except the pale moon dancing off the night-blackened water. I stood there like a sitting duck, steam building in my chest with every passing second. Ten minutes passed. Had Colonel Crankhole been here and left, or was he playing me? Either way, I was done being a pawn in his games.

I turned to leave and almost bumped into the man. Tresick stood outside the archway to the koi pond, lurking in the shadows.

"What the hell?"

"You're late," Tresick said.

"I'm here." I sighed. "It's next to impossible to force invention to bend the knee to deadlines. Why are you hiding in the bushes?"

"Wanted to make sure you hadn't brought company," the man said. He towered over me, flexing his brown arms in the moonlight.

"I was half convinced this was a trap," I said. "What kind of game are you playing?"

"The kind where you've discovered my identity, and I've figured out yours. *Miguel.*"

My heart stopped. Dread scorched my stomach. This guy was a colonel in the Conquistador's Guardia, and I was a dead man. He knew who I was. He knew I was the Conq's son and that I had no business being in the Citadel. My recklessness had finally caught up to me, and I would pay for it with my life.

I backed up. I didn't even realize I did it until Tresick said, "No need to run. I know who you are, and I don't care. It can only help our cause."

"I'm going to need you to explain. Are you a Guardia spy or not?"

"Not. If anything, I'm spying on the Guardia, doing what I can to minimize their damage," he said.

"Then why the fuck were you threatening to kill me and my friends? That's the kind of vile shit the Guardia does."

"That man they executed in the arena after the Expo? He was the Scythe's leader. He had nothing to do with any assassination attempt. That was someone who went rogue, someone who was tortured to death giving up our leader's name," Tresick said. "The Conquistador will not tolerate opposition of any kind. He murdered our leader, a man who died protecting every one of us. I didn't know who you were. I had to make sure you were legit. Once I realized who you were, I had to know you were on our side. What exactly are you hoping to do? Take over for the old man?"

My face screwed up in disgust. "I have zero desire for that," I said. "I simply want the man dethroned. I want his tyranny to end."

"Then we are on the same page," Tresick said. "Things must change."

We stood in silence, staring at each other, seeking the truth of each other's words.

"You have something for me?" Tresick finally asked. He held out a hand, and I transferred the backpack to his custody.

"There's no way to test it without doing damage," I said. "But based on everything we know, it should work. I recommend giving it a trial run somewhere inconsequential, if such a place exists."

"We've got a plan," the colonel said. "Something that your father will not consider a direct threat."

I nodded.

"How much do you know about hacking?" Tresick asked.

"Some, but I'm no expert," I said. Twain was the authority on all things related to programming, but even with this newfound truce with Tresick, I refused to offer him up to help the Scythe with a cyberattack. If I'd learned nothing over the past weeks, it was that those kinds of decisions had to be made together.

"I can ask around," I added.

"One more thing," Tresick said. He hesitated. "I meant what I said in the Wildlands. You have information about me that no one should have. If I were a smart man, I'd kill you right now, but I don't want to do that. But if you betray me, I will come for you, and I will take out every person you care about right in front of your eyes."

My skin went cold. I glared at the man.

"I have no interest in mutual destruction," I said. "You keep my secret, I'll keep yours, but if you keep threatening the people I care about, then we're done. I don't work with people who put my family at risk."

"I think we understand one another."

THREE DAYS LATER, I was ballroom dancing. Simone insisted on teaching Evan and me for the Fount Ball. She partnered with Twain to demonstrate. We were supposed to mirror their steps as she counted the beats, but I still couldn't stop thinking about the tattoo, about what was coming next.

"You're crushing my fingers," Evan hissed through clenched teeth. I dropped her hand and retreated. My temper had abandoned me. I needed to get my shit together.

"Come on, Rafe," Simone said. "This is important."

"What's important is not keeping secrets from people trying to help you," I said.

Carlton couldn't remove Evan's tattoo. He'd masked it with a semipermanent, flesh-colored patch, invisible to the eye, but the brand was still there, woven into Evan's skin about an eighth of an inch deep. A scan of the tattoo confirmed it carried more than mere ink. Data was embedded in her flesh. Data that detailed our transaction at the Obligors Expo. Our names and addresses were fabricated, but our digital images were not. I wore a disguise, but if the Conq's minions studied my photograph too long, it was possible they could recognize me.

Twain had tried to fry the data, but nothing worked, and nothing would short of lasering a big hole into Evan's shoulder, and that would be akin to raising a red flag.

"I'm sorry," Evan said. "I've never stopped being sorry."

Her lip trembled, but I could not find it in myself to back down.

"Your secret puts us all in danger. Everyone you said you were trying to protect."

"I know. I'm sorry. When it happened, I was so shocked, so ashamed, I...I wanted to forget about it, and I did. I had no idea I'd be in a situation where anyone would see it."

"You won't be," Simone said. She dropped Twain's hands and placed a placating hand on my shoulder. "Rafe, you've already chewed Evan out over this. You and I both know it wouldn't matter when she told you. There's nothing that can be done about it beyond what Carlton's already done. It's not her fault she was branded."

I closed my eyes, drew in a deep breath. It did nothing to calm me. Everything she'd said was true, but my heart thrashed at the thought of my father catching us. At things beyond my control. At what my old man had done to Evan. I knew she wasn't to blame, but I couldn't find a path to rational thought.

"Would you have helped us?" Evan asked, her voice small. "If I'd told you back then? When it happened?"

Her question gutted me. I knew the truth without thinking. *Yes.*

I remained silent, letting silence damn me. Evan waited, her brows knit together.

"If this changes nothing, then what is it?" she asked. "There's something you're not telling me. You were ready to walk into the lion's den with me, and *now* you're spooked?"

Twain and Simone exchanged glances and waited for me to tell her.

I couldn't.

She would never look at me the same way again. She would only see the stain on my soul, the truth that marked me as damaged and complicit. Corrupted.

"What is it?" Evan asked. Her gaze darted between me and my two lifelong friends. She edged back like a cornered animal.

"Whatever it is, you all know it," she said, hand covering her mouth. "I'm so stupid. I told you everything. You know everything about me and my family, and you've been hiding something from me. Lying to me all this time. God, I thought I'd learned better."

Twain touched her arm, and she twisted away.

"You need to understand what's on the line," he said, his tenor appeasing. "If Rafe is recognized, he'll be arrested. He'll be executed. He won't get another chance. That was made abundantly clear when the Guardia tossed us out the first time."

"I don't deserve anything from any of you—I know that. But my sister is my responsibility. Mine. If you don't trust me, and I can't trust you to be honest with me, then this is all for nothing."

The room fell silent, thick with words left unspoken.

"She's right." Simone broke the standoff. "You're about to attempt the most dangerous con of your life, Rafe. You know the price of failure," she said. "Your life, her life. Juni. She deserves to know what she's walking into."

I rubbed the space between my brows and stared at my shoes like they held the answer to life's deepest mysteries. Guilt battled with anger. With understanding.

Suddenly Evan was in front of me, shoving my shoulders. "You came back for us," she said, fire burning in her eyes. "You could have left, but you didn't. You came back. So, finish what you started. Tell me the truth, and we'll finish this or we won't. I will not risk my sister's life on anything less than the truth."

Her eyes pinned me where I stood. I never backed down from a challenge, but I didn't want to tell her the truth. I didn't want her to see the real me. I wanted to remain her protector, her friend, her savior. I didn't want to be someone less. Someone unworthy. Someone monstrous.

For years, my friends had reassured me I had nothing to be ashamed of, but I knew different. I could almost feel the pollution running through my blood. A DNA of depravity knitted in the fabric of my being. I'd lived that life once, made choices that shamed me to this day, but now I spent every day trying to claw free of that legacy.

I knew the truth. Remnants still coursed through my veins. They always would. I was still corrupt, a criminal, just like my father.

Evan squeezed my hand and pinned my gaze. "Talk to me."

"Evan...I've never lied to you."

She dropped my hand and looked away.

I captured her chin and steered her face to mine. "I never lied to you, but I purposely did not tell you the full truth of who I am," I said. "I'm about to tell you something only Twain and Simone know."

And now Tresick.

"It's a part of me I've tried to erase, ignore, deny, but it's part of me whether I like it or not."

I sucked in a deep breath and dived in. No turning back now.

"The Conquistador is my father."

Evan wobbled as if her knees had liquified. Her palm spread

over her chest like a shield, and she bent over, bracing a hand on her knees, sucking in air.

I laid my hand on her back and bent to her ear. "Breathe."

She recoiled from me, held her hand up to stop me from touching her again. "Don't," she said.

I could see the thoughts running through her mind. My father was the boogeyman parents warned their children about. Every cruelty in Florida boiled down to this one man. His edicts set the course for countless lives he'd never met, and those who did cross his path often ended up in prison, as slaves, or dead. No one crossed this man. No one. Not even his son.

And that was exactly what we were about to do.

"We...can't...do this," she said, between strangled breaths.

"Evan, calm down."

"No, I won't calm down," she said. "I may have a reckless heart, but even I know this is madness."

"Listen, this is nothing new. We've lived here for years, right under his nose. It's why we wear disguises. The old man thinks I'm dead, and we've worked hard to keep it that way."

Her eyes were full of fury. She had every right. I'd been furious about the brand on her shoulder, but the detail I'd withheld was so much worse.

"How could you keep this from me, knowing what we were about to do? After everything we've been through, everything I shared with you, you didn't trust me?"

"No, I mean yes. I...I don't tell anyone. It's not something I'm proud of."

"Your friends know," she said, gesturing to Twain and Simone. "I thought I meant something to you. My entire family's lives are on the line here, and you left me in the dark. I trusted you, and you betrayed that trust."

Her arrow hit the mark, wounded me, but anger welled up in my blood.

"Might I remind you my life is on the line, too," I said, taking a step toward her. "I'm risking everything for you. Does that mean nothing?"

She closed her eyes. She couldn't argue. That was the one thing that had always been true. Everything I'd done since meeting her had been a threat to me and everyone I cared about.

"Why?" she asked, voice breaking.

It was Twain who answered.

"We all know the risk we take each day, existing inside the walls of the Citadel," he said. "We believe people like Juni deserve a chance at life as much as anyone. That's why we do what we do. That's why Rafe is taking this chance."

"The palace was your home," she said. "They'll recognize you. Why would you even consider this?"

"I was a skinny teenager when we were thrown into the Wildlands. I look nothing like that kid, and the disguises do the rest."

She stood there, visibly shaken, eyeing me as if I were a stranger. "It will never work."

"I was in the same bar as my father right before I met you," I said. "Twenty feet away. He never noticed me. Most people are invisible to him. If we're careful, if we follow the plan, it'll work."

"This is madness." She looked to Simone and Twain.

"It is," Simone said. "But Rafe is good at what he does. We all are. Rafe wouldn't do this if he didn't think he could pull it off."

"Ta-da!" A small voice came from the hallway, and Juni glided into view, arms outstretched, blue ballgown draped unzipped off her shoulders. She twirled in her new favorite outfit, a bright smile on her face. She'd barely taken the thing off since Simone gave it to her.

Evan mustered a fake smile and hugged her sister.

"You're so beautiful!" Evan said, glaring at me over Juni's

shoulder. Her eyes still swam with fear and doubt. She wasn't convinced.

"Wait here," I said, then rushed from the room. When I returned, I handed her a box and grabbed a chair.

"What is this?" she asked, standing.

Beside her, Juni began twirling again, oblivious. Simone snagged the little girl's hand and tugged her toward the hall. "Come on, let's go figure out how to style your hair," she said, smiling at Juni. The kid followed, grinning all the way.

I opened the box in Evan's hands and withdrew a pair of hair clippers. "I want you to shave my head."

"What? No, I can't."

"It's not hard. Turn it on and run it over my head. I won't be completely bald."

She stared at me, not moving.

"No one in the Citadel has ever seen me without a head of thick black hair."

Carlton had worked magic on my facial bruising, but I'd still need to cover the remnants with makeup. Shaving my head would perfect my disguise.

Twain piped in. "With that beard, some colored lenses, and no hair, you'll be near impossible to recognize."

"Exactly. Come on, Evan. Let's get this over with."

She found the On switch and flipped it. Her hands shook as they combed through my curls, and the connection sent a shock of warmth through my belly. It had been so long since we'd touched each other, it opened a well of yearning inside. I placed a hand on her hip and drew her closer. Red heat rushed up her neck.

"You're not going hurt anything," I whispered. "It's hair. It grows back."

Evan pushed the clippers through the hair above my brow. Thick clots of hair tumbled to the floor. The room fell quiet, marred only by the clippers' hum. Did she hate me now? Did I care? Maybe this would make it easier when this was over and we had to go our separate ways. But somewhere deep inside, I knew the truth: I did care. I didn't want her to hate me.

"Promise me one thing," Evan said, pausing. "Whatever happens, make sure Juni gets home. That's all that matters."

"We'll take Juni home—together," I said.

I prayed I was right.

44

EVANGELINE

I couldn't stop staring at the wedding band on my finger. The circle of metal was the only thing real about this whole situation. The marriage was fake. Our names were fake. The man in the front seat of this Jeep was a fraud. How could I have been so careless? I'd known Rafe had secrets, but I never could have imagined this. I'd be walking into the Conquistador's palace with the Empire's condemned son. With my little sister and a mark on my skin I couldn't erase. This was beyond unwise.

But what choice did I have? We either moved forward or my sister died.

I toyed with the wedding ring and repeated our fake names in my head to distract myself. Joseph and Elizabeth Johnson—that was who we were now.

The Jeep barreled ahead, headlamps piercing the dark. Stale air blew through the open top, mussing the hair I'd carefully sculpted into a bun this morning. We were sneaking out of Florida, driving through a tunnel dug deep into the earth, pushing into a foreign land.

America. The United States.

A smuggler named Harley drove, trading jokes with Rafe, most of which involved my fake husband's shaved head. Rafe looked like a different person, a stranger—which was, of course, the point. I'd never felt more distant from him, and it made my heart hurt. In the days after his revelation, we'd barely spoken, and part of me was good with that. Another part, the traitorous part, wanted to run into his arms and block out the rest of the world. Despite his deception, he was still here, braving terrible consequences. For me. For us.

In the back seat, Juni snuggled into me. Her tiny fingers dug into the fabric of my dress, and I caressed her shoulder until she dozed off. After more than two hours, we reached a wide area in the tunnel. Harley steered the Jeep to the side, got out, and unloaded our luggage.

"Take the stairs over there," he said. "You'll come out in a barn. The limo's waiting outside. It'll take you to the transpod station."

"Thanks, man," Rafe said, clasping hands with the smuggler. He'd had already paid the man, but he filled Harley's palm with a wad of pesos.

"That's why you're my favorite customer. Holler if you need me."

Rafe grabbed our bags, and I held Juni's hand as we climbed the stairs and stepped onto a landing next to a door. Faint sunlight filtered beneath the door, along with the scent of hay and earth. Rafe leaned in close, listening. He eased the door open, peering through the crack before pushing it wider. Dozens of hay bales filled the barn and not much else. Beyond the barn, a long black vehicle waited.

"Wait here a sec," Rafe said. He approached the car with caution. A tall man in a black suit and hat folded out of the car and greeted Rafe. They shook hands, and Rafe motioned me forward. I led my sister outside, into the brightness of an American afternoon.

We stood in another realm.

According to Rafe, America was a free country. He said it wasn't perfect, but people had a voice and could choose their leaders. They had more opportunity to choose the kind of life they lived. They had a better chance of getting help if needed. I never knew places existed where people lived with freedom and choices. That hadn't been part of our lessons growing up.

The driver opened a rear door and motioned us inside. I glanced at Rafe, and he nodded. Juni and I ducked inside and sank onto a smooth cushioned seat. The interior was huge. A small area with crystal glasses and a decanter filled with amber liquid sat to one side. A glass window separated us from the driver, offering privacy.

Rafe slid in next to us, and the driver closed us in. Seconds later, we were moving. I reworked my hair into a smooth bun and began re-braiding Juni's hair.

"Is it far?" she asked.

"No, Annie," Rafe said, calling Juni by her fake name. We were getting used to our pretend names and needed all the practice we could get. "It's about an hour away."

The car fell quiet as the countryside floated by. A black-topped road stretched before us, surrounded on both sides by trees. It stirred up memories of traveling the dirt road leading to El Jardín...and the ambush. I cleared the thought from my mind. Ferals didn't exist in America. Of course, there were dangers on this side of the border. The dark side of the human soul existed everywhere, but I had no reason to believe we'd be ambushed and kidnapped again. I hoped.

Juni laid her head in my lap and fell asleep. The trip, the newness of everything exhausted her. The cure couldn't come soon enough.

Rafe stared empty-eyed out the passenger window.

"Why didn't you leave Florida?" I asked, breaking the silence. "In America, you wouldn't have had to hide."

His brows furrowed above a haunted gaze. "Florida's my home. The people I care about are there. Plus, I can't sabotage the Conq from America. I can't help anyone that way."

"Your father."

Rafe searched me, his gaze seeking something beyond my words. What, I didn't know.

"Why didn't you tell me? Did you think I would turn you in?" I asked.

"No... No, it wasn't that." He hesitated, trying to frame his thoughts. Finally, he shook his head and asked, "Would you want to admit it if the man was your father?"

He has a point.

"Not if he'd done to me what he did to you."

"I deserved it," Rafe said.

I looked at him, forehead wrinkled in disgust. "You were a kid, Rafe. No kid deserves that, especially not from the person who's supposed to protect him."

"I was a punk, and I abused the position I was in, took advantage of people. I took what wasn't mine to take."

"What could a teenager steal that would deserve a death sentence? He had to know the odds of your survival were slim."

"Oh, he knew," Rafe said, his jaw tightening. "I stole water from the Fount, tried to sell it to desperate people."

You don't steal from the Conquistador.

"Oh."

"Yeah, like I said, I'm not proud of it."

Something wasn't adding up, though. Why was an adolescent plot cause for such severe punishment? In fact, how was that different from what was happening right now?

"How is that different from what the Conquistador is doing?" I asked. "Sounds like you got that idea from your father."

Rafe recoiled as if I'd slapped him, turning to face me. "I am nothing like him."

"That's not what I mean. When we're kids, most everything we do is shaped by the people around us, our parents most of all," I said. "We learn by watching what they do, and we mimic it in our thoughts and actions. Only when we grow older do we see the world more fully and learn to live by our own hearts and minds. I'm learning that more and more every day. What you did, you learned from him."

I paused, holding his gaze. "But you are not that boy anymore. Anyone can tell you're not like him."

He had a heart, a big one. His father had a shriveled lump of coal for a heart. Rafe was not to blame for his father's choices, just like I was not to blame for the circumstances that led to my mother's death. I let that truth finally settle in my head, let my heart release the guilt I'd clung to for so long.

Rafe looked out the window again, shame written across his face. I reached across the seat and squeezed his hand. He looked at our hands on the leather fabric.

"Most people would have run, Rafe, fled to America," I said. "Looked out for themselves. You didn't. You stayed where it mattered. You are not him."

Rafe nodded in silence and removed his hand.

We rode the last hour in raw silence. The driver stopped in a parking lot and lowered the privacy window.

"We're here," he said.

RAFE

*C*ustoms was a breeze. The border agents imaged and accepted our passports without incident. Our biogloved hands and masked eyeballs scanned effortlessly, and the transpod ride was routine. Underground transportation carried us straight to the Imperial Hotel, the official outpost of the Conq's palace and gardens. We would stay here until tomorrow, after sunset.

In a little over twenty-four hours, I'd be back inside the palace. I tried not to think about my last time there. I'd been young and naive then. Pretty much a reckless, self-absorbed idiot. An education in the Wildlands tended to cure that brand of stupidity.

Our transpod ascended to an interior reception area in the Imperial Hotel. The room was cavernous yet strangely intimate, capped by an arched ceiling of glass and marble. Blue sky blazed beyond the roof, and warm sunlight filtered inside, illuminating a large oak tree at the far end of the room. An iron love seat with white cushions dangled from one of its branches, and a murmuring waterfall spilled into a nearby pond. Off to the side, a crystal-and-silver chandelier that resembled an exploded star hovered above a curving, marble staircase. The room was empty, save for a tall man dressed in a spotless white suit, blond hair slicked into tight control.

"Welcome, Mr. and Mrs. Johnson, Miss Annie." A tablet in his hand displayed the photos from our passports. "I'm Lucien, your concierge."

Lucien motioned with his fingers, and three hotel staff appeared from nowhere. They relieved us of our baggage and offered refreshments, vintage Moët & Chandon Dom Pérignon for the adults, a cherry nectar for Juni. Evan wriggled her nose as fizz floated up from the crystal flute. I smothered a smile as she sipped the bubbly and resisted the urge to pucker her lips. Juni sipped her drink, and her eyebrows peaked in delight. She swallowed a large gulp, draining the glass in a matter of seconds.

"Can I have some more?" she said, wiping the red juice from her lips with her forearm. Red stained the area above her upper lip.

"Maybe later," Evan said, wiping at Juni's mouth with a napkin. Which did no good.

Lucien cleared his throat, smiled politely, and said, "If you'll follow me."

He led us along a corridor dotted with a scattering of ornate doors. At the end of the hallway, he passed his hand over a panel next to a carved mahogany door. The entrance clicked open. "The door is programmed with your biometrics, so you may enter the same way," he said.

Juni's eyes widened as we crossed the threshold, and her mouth opened but no sound came out. Evan marshaled her expression like this sort of luxury was commonplace. I'd forgotten what it was like this deep into the Conq's world. Everything pristine and shiny. Perfection to mask the ugliness. Comfort to cloak the inhumanity.

Our suite was a study in sunlight and white. The sitting

room held white couches and plush chairs draped in ivory chenille blankets and pillows. Two bedrooms branched off to reveal expansive, fluffy beds. Crystal vases stuffed with peonies and orange blossoms dotted every open surface, along with bowls of fresh fruit, chocolates, and beverages, including an impressive selection of Spanish wines. Floor-to-ceiling windows lined the far wall, and a light breeze stole through a set of open doors crafted of crystal and iron tendrils. Beyond the patio, a private flower garden was in full bloom.

Lucien explained the room's features and how to summon him should we need anything. Evan swiped a palmera from a silver plate when he wasn't looking and gave half the cookie to her sister. I tried to swallow my grin as Lucien began reviewing our itinerary.

"You'll travel via horse-drawn carriage. I'll collect you when the carriage arrives," he said. I'd been zoning out, but now he had my full attention.

"No transpods?"

"Except for the Conquistador's, of course. Another way to secure our most precious resource," Lucien said, smiling. "Only one way in and out."

"Of course," I said, offering a reciprocal smile. Transpods used to come and go from the palace all the time. Back then, it had been easy to sneak in and out of the place. Ol' Papi had finally wised up. Leaving us few options should the need arise.

"You'll also need to go through security, so bring your documents with you," Lucien said.

Security? The Scythe of Thorns must've had the Conq on the defensive. When I was a teen, protocol had dictated that if you made it as far as the Imperial Hotel, that was all the clearance you needed. Now we had to survive a second screening. Could this get any worse? Returning to the scene of my crimes was beginning to feel like an anchor dragging me under.

Lucien babbled on while claustrophobic thoughts trashed my mind.

Breathe. You can do this.

"He'll be here momentarily," the concierge said.

My thoughts snapped to attention. "Sorry—what?"

"The doctor will be here momentarily," Lucien said. "As you know, children are not permitted to partake of the Fount, except for dire medical purposes, such as Miss Annie's cancer diagnosis. The Fount viceroy approved your daughter's Immersion on the condition that one of the Conquistador's approved doctors complete a visual inspection and take a blood sample first. He'll be here any—"

A gentle knock came from the doorway. Yet another hurdle. The Conq had to ensure whatever the kid had wasn't contagious. Didn't want to risk tainting his precious Fount.

Lucien excused himself and admitted the doctor. I tried to hide my relief when Carlton entered the room. Juni had a spooked look in her eye. I scooped her up and whispered into her ear, "Don't worry. He's gentle, but remember—you're Annie, okay?"

She grabbed my head and maneuvered it so she could whisper into my ear, "Okay." I swallowed a grin. She was a cute little nena.

"May I introduce Dr. Carlton Shires. He's one of our very best," Lucien said. We each shook his hand, even Juni, who remained wary.

"Well, I'll leave you to it," Lucien said, before slipping out the door.

"If you'd bring Annie over here, I'll take a look," Carlton said. I gave him a puzzled look but did as he said. Juni settled onto one of the couches, and Evan drew close, putting a reassuring hand on her shoulder. Carlton opened his bag. He retrieved a MedScan and passed it over Juni's tiny frame. As he did so, he whispered out of the corner of his mouth, "Consider the entire place bugged. The Guardia is paranoid as hell."

In a louder voice, he said, "Annie, you're doing great. This won't take much longer."

Good to know.

Carlton talked Juni through the rest of his exam, finishing by taking a small blood sample with the MedScan. The prick to her finger elicited a tiny squeak out of Juni. "That's the worst of it," he said, patting her hand. The doctor took a moment to review the results and compared them to Juni/Annie's medical file on his tablet.

"Well, looks like everything's in order," Carlton said. "Her bloodwork and vitals match the information we have in the medical file your doctor provided. Your daughter is fit to be cured."

The doctor packed his equipment into his bag and started for the door. "My best wishes, Mr. and Mrs. Johnson," he said, giving us a wink as he left the room. The door had barely shut when Juni disappeared out the patio doors.

"J—Annie, stop!" Evan chased after her.

On the far side of the garden, Juni bent to catch her breath.

Her sister kneeled before her and grabbed her by the shoulders. "You can't run like that," she said. "Take some deep, slow breaths before you have a problem."

Juni did as commanded, then snatched Evan's hand and tugged her into the garden. Even as I lost sight of them, their words and laughter floated to me, light as a sunbeam. I sat on the patio, listening, reeling from everything that had happened in the last few days. The look of betrayal when I'd told Evan my darkest secret. The compassion warming her eyes when she'd told me I was nothing like my father. The relief I'd felt at those words.

Juni ran up to me, paused to catch her breath, and handed

me a dandelion puffed with seeds ready to break loose and fly away.

"Out of all the beautiful flowers in the garden, she picked the lone weed," Evan said, laughing.

"It's for you to make a wish," Juni said, handing me the stem. "You blow on it and make a wish, but you can't tell us, or it won't come true."

Warmth spread in my chest.

"Thank you, Annie," I said. "Why don't you help me blow on it? We can both make a wish."

We puckered our lips and blew. White, fluff-topped seeds abandoned the stem, floating on the air, but a few remained. We blew again until they were all gone, and my wish drifted out into the ether.

I'd never wished for something so hard in my life.

46

RAFE

*I*mmersion night arrived like an earthquake in my gut. We boarded an open-air, horse-drawn carriage as the sun shed its last light. The driver followed a path that meandered through an expanse of grass encircling the massive palace complex, the heart of the Citadel. Dressed in twilight, the palace's imposing stone walls and turrets appeared soft around the edges, enchanted. The towering doors swung open to admit the caravan, and our carriages came to a halt.

"Please have your documents ready for inspection," our driver called to us. "We'll have you inside in no time."

I clenched my fist, half-tempted to jump out and flee into the gathering darkness.

No one will recognize you.

I kept repeating it in my head, willed it into being. My hair was gone, and a salt-and-pepper stubble beard covered my chin. A light application of glued-on creases mimicked emerging wrinkles, and brown lenses masked my blue eyes. Tortoiseshell glasses further distorted my identity. No one would recognize the boy imprisoned in the Calabozo so many years ago. That kid had been dumped in the Wildlands and was dead and rotting in the underbrush.

The minutes ticked by like a time bomb, and then we were at the guard post.

A soldier in red-and-black military dress stood outside the guard hut and approached our carriage. "Papers, please." He held out his gloved hand.

I handed him our docs and scanned the other soldiers lingering behind him, half expecting to see Tresick in the wings. The man was like a shadow, popping up where least expected, and I didn't want to explain to him what I was doing here. I didn't want him to know about Evan or Juni. The less he knew about the people I cared about, the better.

The soldier studied our passports and our faces as I squirmed inside. Tresick guessing my identity had me rattled. I felt naked and exposed.

Our driver hopped down from his perch and opened our carriage door. I tried not to panic. They'd done this for the carriage ahead of us, and nothing had happened.

The soldier mounted the small set of stairs and pulled a handheld device from his belt pouch. "Your hand, please," the soldier said. He scanned my palm, and I hoped he couldn't see my hand trembling.

"Please remove your glasses," he said.

Oh shit.

I did as commanded. The soldier held the device up to my right eye and pressed the Scan button. He moved to Evan next, and the tightness in my stomach eased, just barely. Juni struggled to keep her eye open, but after a couple of tries, the soldier managed a passable scan. He descended the carriage steps, and our driver waited for approval to move on.

Without a word, the soldier disappeared inside the guard hut. The driver and I exchanged a look, and his eyebrows raised in concern. The soldier definitely hadn't done that for the previous carriage. My heart started to pound, harder, like a prisoner demanding to be freed of its cage.

The soldier reappeared and climbed back into our carriage.

This is it. We'd failed. I'd failed. In that moment, I no longer cared about what happened to me. I was terrified for Evan and Juni.

"For the brave little miss," the soldier said, producing a lollipop from behind his back and presenting it to Juni.

For the love of Dios. This was the first time in my life that I'd witnessed an act of kindness from one of my father's soldiers.

"Thank you, mister," Juni said.

The soldier smiled and left our carriage. "Have a pleasant evening," he said, waving us on. I felt like puking.

We joined roughly fifty visitors for the evening's festivities. Dressed in haute-couture gowns and tuxes, most were clutching to their youth like it was their last dollar. We enjoyed a grotesque banquet of food before being ushered into a small ballroom. Guests flooded the dance floor as waiters circulated with flutes of champagne and trays of sweets. A scattering of Guardia stood among us, including a few high-ranking members, so noted by the silver bars studding their red coats. I didn't recognize any of them. A relief, but a small one. The night was young.

The only thing distracting me at the moment was Juni. The kid's eyes were afire, despite the gray circles beneath. The night was like a fairytale for her, not the horror show exhuming ghosts in my head. I swept her around our corner of the ballroom, and she giggled, a sound sweeter than music. Carlton had sent a nurse to the palace to watch over Juni, and the woman had allotted her one dance, her scowl barring any argument. She was our shadow until Immersion time, assigned to stick with Juni until the ball ended. Carlton trusted her, so I trusted her. Didn't mean I had to like her.

The song ended. Juni smiled a big, expectant smile and

wobbled on her feet. I caught her, steadying her, as Nurse Isabella appeared from the sideline to reclaim her.

"That's enough, Mr. Johnson," the nurse said. The big woman scooped Juni into her arms as if lifting a feather. I couldn't help thinking she needed a name that matched her formidable personality. Something like Helga or Ursula.

"The young lady needs to sit and rest."

"Thank you, Isabella," I said, my grin strained. "I think I know how to take care of my own daughter."

"Indeed," she said, pivoting and carrying Juni off to a nearby couch without waiting for a reply.

Evan hooked her arm through mine. "I think Juni is a bit scared of her," she said.

"I think I'm a bit scared of her," I said, glancing at my fake bride. That one simple action stirred a visceral reaction that nearly knocked me to my knees.

Evan's arm draped across mine like it was the most natural thing, and she gazed into my eyes with depthless hope and affection. There was fear there, to be sure, but the light drowned it out. I'd thought I was going to lose her and Juni during the security inspection. What I felt looking at her now was more than that.

We had traveled here side by side, dined together, and danced a few requisite songs, but in this moment, it was like stepping out of time. Like seeing her anew. She stole my breath. Something sleeping shook awake inside me.

I'd lost her at El Jardín. I realized that now. I'd pushed her away. She'd brought a shitload of trouble into my life, but she'd also brought something priceless. She'd gifted me joy, something I'd never truly experienced before. Her light had melted the fortress around my heart, and I'd let her in. But then I'd shoved her back out and rebuilt my walls. I'd kept her locked out ever since.

But now...now I saw her again. Saw the beautiful, empathic,

headstrong woman beneath the disguise. She wore the crimson gown Simone had picked for her—with shoulder caps added for peace of mind. Her honey hair was dyed black and swept into an elegant updo, baring her lovely neck. Her green eyes shone crystal blue. We'd given her a couple of wrinkles, a few of strands of gray, makeup to camouflage her youth. Enough to bear up the illusion of her as Juni's mother. None of it dimmed her radiance. She was stunning.

She was so much more.

Evan had transformed a lifetime's worth in the matter of a few weeks. Recklessness diminished to mindfulness. Naivete steeled into newborn confidence. Wild hope tempered into reasoned promise.

I lifted her hand to my lips and kissed it. A deep blush rose in her cheeks, and her eyes flushed with pleasure. I looped my arm around her and pulled her against me, never taking my eyes off hers. We moved to the flow of the music as everything else disappeared. Nothing and no one else existed but the two of us. It felt so damn good, holding her again, ignoring the world. Falling into her once more.

I realized something. I wanted more. I wanted her all to myself—needed it. I glanced at Juni. She was tucked into Isabella's lap, studying a book. She was content, safe. Now was my chance. I danced us to the edge of the floor and kept going, slipping through a pair of open doors to the darkened garden beyond. It was blessedly empty.

Evan laughed, and the sound was like falling into paradise. A sound I'd missed, I craved.

"What are you doing?"

"This."

I cupped her face and kissed her. Her lips tasted of strawberries and champagne. Her fingers gripped my jacket, and she pressed her body into mine, opening to the kiss.

I kissed her breathless.

I kissed her until I came to my senses. Until I realized I didn't want this to end. Whatever this was, when this whole ordeal was over, I didn't want her to leave. I didn't want to tuck her away somewhere safe. I had no idea what the future held, but I didn't want a future without her.

"I'm sorry—for being an ass, for keeping things from you," I said. My chest heaved, greedy for air. I could feel Evan's heart drumming against my own.

"It doesn't matter," she said.

"It does."

"I can't be mad at you, not after I've asked so much of you."

I touched her cheek. "No more apologies. I'm not doing this because I think I have to. I care about you."

Evan covered my hand with hers and smiled. "I couldn't ask for more," she said.

"Yes, you can. When this is over, I want you to stay. I want you with me. Whatever that means, whatever that takes, I want to be your home. You can have as many of my tomorrows as you want."

"Rafe." My name was a wisp on her lips, a spark lighting my chest.

Words tumbled out like instinct, like they'd always been waiting there. It took voicing them to realize they were true.

"I love you, mi corazón," I said. Something I'd heard my father say to my mother many times. Only now I understood its true meaning.

A tear escaped down Evan's cheek. I wiped it away.

"What's wrong?"

She squeezed my hand and smiled. Her hand trembled in mine. "Nothing. I never thought... I didn't think..."

Evan paused, drawing a breath, and staring into my eyes. Her hand touched my cheek. She said the next words without hesitation: "Rafe, I love you, too."

I gathered her into my arms and kissed her again. Her arms

wrapped around me, and we held on, lost in the depths of each other. Nothing in my life had felt more right than this moment. I could almost forget where we were.

A bell chimed in the ballroom.

I looked at my beautiful Evan. "It's time."

"Oh…" She smiled like the sun.

"In less than an hour, she will be healed, and we'll be together, heading home."

"Thank God," she said.

I was thunderstruck by her radiance, by the hope shimmering in her eyes. I bent to brush her lips, and she smiled into the kiss. I tucked Evan's hand in my arm and escorted her into the ballroom. I glanced at her again, drunk on her confession, on her afterglow, and collided with another guest. Champagne splashed out of the man's flute and onto his cuff.

"For God's sake, man, watch where you're going. Look what you've done."

My body went numb at the sight of him. His hair was thicker now, and his body had put on a few pounds. His beady eyes glared at me, and for a moment I thought he recognized me. His unseeing gaze was full of contempt, but not recognition.

"My apologies, sir," I said. "I'd be happy to have the staff secure you a new jacket."

"Forget it. We've no time," he growled.

His eyes darted to Evan, and my blood went cold. His gaze lingered a bit too long, skimming the length of her. She held her ground.

"Of course. Enjoy the Immersion," I said, ushering Evan away.

"Was that—"

I cut her off and whispered into her ear, "Jerome Blackwell. He's the one who tried to buy your Obligor contract."

47

EVANGELINE

*J*erome Blackwell. I remembered the hunger in his voice as he'd bid on my Obligor contract. He knew Rafe, knew enough of his secrets to condemn him. So far he'd yet to recognize us, but even if he did, it would be self-destructive to expose us. My body shook, and I didn't know if it was because Rafe had told me he loved me or because I was terrified of being caught. Maybe both.

We lost sight of Blackwell as the crowd exited the ballroom. We collected Juni, bid her nurse farewell, and joined the throng. A palace official dressed in flowing white garments led us to a changing room and provided Juni with a plain blue tunic. Inside the small wood-paneled room, I tugged the dress over her head.

"I can't wait to tell Pa about the castle," she whispered. "And the chocolate. That was the best."

"Shh… You can't talk like that. Remember who you are. Your pa is waiting right outside the door."

"I *know*."

"As soon as you get into the Fount, go underwater and take a big drink. Swallow as much as you can. Okay?"

"Okay."

Juni twirled in the tunic, and I pulled her into my arms and gave her a bear hug. "I'm so happy for you, Junebug," I said.

"Me too...Mama," she said.

The word was a bittersweet ember in my heart. I kissed her forehead. "That's my girl."

We rejoined the crowd in the corridor. Buzzing voices mushroomed in the enclosed space as I held Juni's hand, trying not to fidget. We were so close. I wanted this to be over, for Juni to be healed, for life to find whatever normal the next day brought. I was ready for the day when we no longer had to fight so hard. When I could spend my days in Rafe's arms, unafraid and free.

A white-robed man approached. He was tall and thin, with old gray eyes on a young face. "Mr. and Mrs. Johnson?"

"Yes," Rafe answered.

"If you'll follow me."

We fell in behind him, and two Guardia peeled off from the crowd and followed. My limbs went numb, as terror spiked in my stomach. Rafe squeezed my hand and nodded ahead of us. A man in a tuxedo and a red-haired woman in a blue tunic also had a pair of guards trailing them. Every group was the same.

We walked for so long that Rafe had to carry Juni. We passed areas with leather couches and stained-glass lamps, a music room filled with instruments and chairs, at least two libraries stacked floor-to-ceiling with books, dozens of rooms behind crystal or dark-paneled doors. The palace was huge, with every comfort imaginable. Every room was a work of art. I couldn't imagine Rafe running the halls as a boy, finding warmth and comfort inside these walls.

At last, the crowd filtered into a large room marked by decorative steel columns arching to the ceiling. Silvery metal vines spiked from the columns like tree branches, supporting a clear glass roof. Pedestals bearing white candles filled the empty spaces, illuminating the room in a soft, ivory glow.

An attendant mounted a small marble dais and raised his hands to silence the crowd. "The Water holds time at bay, brings the ages to heel," he began. "We are…"

"The Empire Eternal," the guests replied.

"We are…" he said, louder.

The guests' replies were thunderous: "The Empire Eternal."

The echoing voices died down, and he continued.

"Esteemed guests, welcome to the Fount. You are about to experience a miracle beyond imagining. Ordinary water holds the power to cleanse, to slake your thirst, or, in its darkest nature, to suffocate, erode, and destroy. Only water from the Fount has the gift of eternal life. The power to heal. To cure the disease of aging. To subdue time itself," he said. "You receive this gift by the grace of our sovereign, El Conquistador. Conqueror of time, divinely appointed Guardian of the Fount. You have partaken of his hospitality and enjoyed the pleasures of his house. Now, you enter his sanctum. You are to show the utmost respect for this holy place."

The attendant stared us down, a solemn look etched into his timeless features. "Keep to the path. Touch nothing. Remain silent and follow your attendant's directions at all times. The time has come. Breathe in and find yourself renewed. Your guide will escort you the rest of the way at your appointed time."

A set of glass doors with steel accents opened, and the first guests proceeded into the darkness beyond. The remaining visitors stood in place or settled into one of the seating areas. We waited in silence. Juni rested her head on Rafe's shoulder. She looked exhausted, tiny and thin in his big arms. Tension stretched across Rafe's brow as he stared through the doors, digging up unwelcome memories. I squeezed his arm, offering an anchor to his storm. His trance broke, and he gave me an unconvincing smile.

Our attendant beckoned us to follow. Rafe and I exchanged a look for courage, and then we passed through the doors.

It felt like falling...and not knowing where or if the ground existed. My stomach swooped. My senses came alive.

A wilderness was growing inside the towering palace walls. Tall trees and flowering bushes flanked a path adorned with tiny mosaic patterns of every color of blue imaginable. The patterns swirled and twined like the currents of a river. Thousands of lights twinkled in the forest canopy, and fireflies winked in and out in the dark depths. Mushrooms and moss glowed luminescent on the forest floor. Along the walkway, warm flames flickered in ornate steel lampposts. The air was warm and soothing, the light breeze scented with jasmine and lilac. The rhythmic humming of tree frogs and katydids filled the quiet.

This land was ancient and beautiful. Lush and mysterious. Unlike anything I'd ever seen.

We followed the line of guests and escorts, winding through the forest for many minutes until the path became a cobbled walkway laced with moss. The canopy changed to light purple as we entered a tunnel of wisteria. The dangling flowers tickled Rafe's head, triggering a shower of petals. Juni giggled, and I couldn't help smiling. Our guide walked on in dignified silence. At the end of the tunnel, we slipped into something not of this world.

Something had shifted in the air. It was nothing visible, but my body reacted, stirring at its touch. It felt like falling into a caress. I breathed in deeply and at once felt calm. Purified. Peace, like a sun-gilt river, flowed through me. I laid a hand on my chest and felt the warmth run through me, soothing the anxiety there.

Juni lifted her head from Rafe's shoulder, and her gaze swam across the scene before us. "Wow," she said.

My heart sang at the wonder in her eyes.

In the distance, the stone path encircled a large pond fringed with ferns, ancient trees, and scatterings of purple-and-white flowers. The Fount. Its water was an unnatural color of blue, alive with light, like a summer sky infused with starlight. Radiant silver sparks floated from the calm surface, swirling into the dark night. Light from the Fount illuminated the Spanish moss in the forest, transforming them into frayed shrouds swaying in the shadows.

Beyond the Fount, about fifty yards into the tree line, stood a towering, boxy structure with lights burning bright behind glass walls. The silhouette of a man appeared in one of the windows, watching.

Rafe slowed his pace and grew still. He had the wide-eyed look of a horse spooked by a snake in the grass.

"What's wrong?" I asked.

Our guide halted and peered at us. The guards were closing the space behind us.

"Um, my arms are getting tired," he said, eyeing our attendant.

"Here, let me take her," I said, gathering Juni into my arms.

Rafe took my elbow to motion us forward. His hand was shaking.

We entered the stone circle behind another group. The guests lined the platform while their escorts floated to the rear, allowing space and privacy. On the far side of the circle, stone steps descended into the shimmering water. They ended in a submerged landing next to a statue of a woman with one arm stretched high, water flowing from her palms. She was etched in stone but wore a crown of golden roses atop her head, with spikes radiating like a sunrise.

A blonde woman descended the stairs. She could have been in her thirties, maybe early forties. At the water's edge, a man in a dark blue robe offered her a hand and gave instructions. She placed her palm in his and descended the steps. As her feet sank into the water, her mouth opened and her eyes bloomed in wonder. She hurried down until she was neck-deep in the water. A small sound of ecstasy escaped her mouth and echoed across the water as she leaned back, and the Fount claimed her.

The woman floated beneath the surface, the blue tunic rendering her almost invisible in the clear blue waters. A warm light radiated from her body, like a sun buried beneath the waves. After several long seconds, the woman surfaced, gasping and glowing, her face and eyes clear and joyous. Soaked from head to toe, her face shone with a new youthfulness, as if age and worry had never touched it. She now looked my age, early twenties.

The blue-robed man offered a hand to help her out of the water. She hesitated, then glanced up the stairs and at once began picking her way up the stone steps. My eyes followed hers, and I stepped back without thinking, ice flooding my bones.

The sentinel standing half-hidden by the guests was dressed in the same crisp red uniform he'd worn the day he'd taken a whip to my back.

"Do you see him?" I whispered. "Commander Bane."

Rafe inhaled sharply. "It'll be fine," he whispered. It sounded like he was trying to convince himself. "I was a skinny, floppy-haired teenager the last time he saw me. No way he recognizes me."

"He's the one who flogged me," I said.

Rafe's eyes flew to me. He leaned toward my ear. "Does he know what Juni looks like?"

I paused, thinking. "Probably not. She was a toddler the last time he saw her. He wasn't there for her evaluation."

"Just relax and be confident. Remember—act like you belong here."

I wasn't so sure, but I nodded. Rafe leaned over and kissed

Juni's head in a show of fatherly love to cover our conversation. He stroked her hair, and her eyes drooped under his touch.

Attendants escorted the blonde Immersee from the Fount area, and the next guest stepped on deck, a short man with gray-speckled hair and a paunch. The line shifted forward, and as it did, a new nightmare came into view. Jerome Blackwell. A beautiful brunette with sparkling diamonds around her neck had her arm draped through his. His ticket into the Fount, most likely. Blackwell or his girlfriend was next in line, and he stood near Bane. I prayed he wouldn't look our way, wouldn't recognize us.

He looked.

I averted my eyes too late. When I glanced his way again, he was watching us, lips puckered in puzzlement.

"He's staring at us," I whispered. I could feel his eyes boring into me. I shivered in the warm air.

"Shift Annie to your other hip and block his view."

I hoisted my sister to the opposite hip and turned. Juni leaned into my neck and whispered, "I'm scared."

I died a little inside. What had I gotten her into?

"It'll be over soon," I said, faking a confidence I didn't have. "Just stay calm and remember to drink the water when it's your turn. Got it?"

Juni nodded.

Across the way, the paunchy man climbed out of the water, his face a mask of ageless bliss, his gray hair now deep brown. Now it was Blackwell's turn. He'd stopped staring at our little family and taken position on the other side of Bane. Two groups waited ahead of us, not counting Blackwell. We were so close.

Blackwell hovered at the top of the stairs, seconds from an experience coveted by millions of people the world over. Yet his eyes drifted to us again. I saw the moment recognition caught in his eyes. Surprise shifted to anger—to thwarted desire.

"Dear God, Rafe, he knows."

"Ostia puta," he cursed.

We were too close to let something like this stop us. Juni was alert now. She knew something was wrong, and her breaths were coming harder, approaching full-on panic mode.

"It's okay," I said, stroking her hair. "Rafe, we have to get her in the water."

"Not yet," he said, putting his arm around me, as if comforting a nervous wife. "Blackwell can't prove a thing. He outs us, he outs himself. He has as much to hide as we do."

Across the pond, Blackwell bent toward Bane, lips moving, eyes locked on us. Then he pointed right at us. Bane's eyes followed. Rafe was wrong—Blackwell had nothing to lose. We couldn't report him without endangering our friends. He couldn't accuse Rafe without condemning himself and his cousin, Carlton. He could, however, report everything he knew about me, an Obligor who had no business being here.

"God, help us." I sank into Rafe's arm and tried to think. I had to get Juni into the Fount.

Bane stalked in our direction, and Blackwell followed like the bully he was. We were out of options. We had come too far for this to happen. We were inches from the Fount, and yet Juni's chance at a miracle—at a normal, long life—was about to be ripped away by a stranger.

This couldn't happen. I couldn't let it.

My sister wheezed in my arms as Bane drew closer.

I knew what I had to do. There was no choice. Calmness swept over me, the kind that surfaced when you came to a decision, made peace with it, and were ready to move.

"Calm breaths, my little bug," I said, stroking Juni's hair. I looked to Rafe, and my words flooded out, sure and heartfelt. "Rafe, I love you. No matter what happens, please make sure Juni gets out of here. Take her home. Keep her safe. Thank you —for everything."

"What are you talking about?"

I tried to step away from him, but his arm tightened around me. I could feel his heart hammering against my skin.

"Let go," I whispered, but he put his lips to my forehead and whispered back.

"Don't move. I've got this."

"Pardon the interruption," Bane said as he approached. Everyone was watching. A handful of soldiers edged closer, a wall of red and black behind their Commander.

"Good evening," Rafe said, holding out a hand. Bane shook it and studied him. "Is there a problem?"

"This man has made a very serious accusation," the Commander said. "He seems to think your wife is an Obligor."

"I've no idea what that is," Rafe lied. "Who is this man?"

"That's irrelevant," Bane said. He withdrew a device from his belt and held out his palm. "Please present your palms."

This was good. Our palm scans had already passed the test multiple times. Still, Rafe faked his displeasure as Blackwell hovered behind Bane, a smug grin on his face.

"We are US citizens," he said, offering his hand. "We came through the border yesterday without incident, and you are frightening my daughter."

Bane cocked an annoyed eye at Rafe, unaccustomed to being challenged. "She'll live," he said, scanning Rafe's palm. Satisfied, he held out his hand for my palm, and again, my fake identity cleared without issue.

"Are we good?" Rafe asked.

"I'm telling you I bid on that woman a little over a month ago," Blackwell said.

Rafe's fingers tightened at my waist. He would have throttled the man if he could have gotten away with it. Maybe worse.

Bane pivoted on Blackwell, and the creep retreated, chastened.

"You will be quiet, or I will throw you out of here myself," the Commander said. He nodded toward a soldier, and the man grabbed Blackwell's arm and pulled him away. A small part of me relaxed. Maybe Rafe was right—we were going to be fine. But then Bane twisted his attention back to us.

"One last thing," he said. "One can't be too careful. Madam, if you'll please bare your left shoulder."

No. No. No.

Rafe pushed me behind him and straightened. He stood practically nose to nose with Bane. "I beg your pardon. My wife will not undress for you or anyone else in his cursed place. This is an outrage."

Suddenly hands were on me, yanking me from Rafe's shelter and pushing me and Juni toward the Commander. Another soldier grabbed Rafe's arm and secured him.

"Keep your hands off my wife," he said, his voice low and guttural, like a wolf bracing to attack. Juni began to cry.

The soldier ignored Rafe and yanked my sleeve, baring my shoulder and nothing else. The Conquistador's mark was camouflaged, the flesh-colored patch unseeable.

"Nothing there," the soldier said.

I jerked away from him and hugged Juni tight. "Get your hands off me," I said, shaping my embarrassment as outrage.

They had nothing on us.

"This is a disgrace, and that man should be arrested for causing my wife and daughter such distress," Rafe said, pointing at Blackwell. "We didn't pay more than a million pesos to be insulted like this. I demand my daughter be permitted her Immersion immediately. Can't you see what you've done to her?"

Juni's little chest heaved against me and tears streaked her face. I'd never wanted to hurt another being, but in this moment, I wanted someone to bleed.

"You may go free," Bane said, motioning me forward, "after I've scanned her shoulder."

Ice spread in my gut. I couldn't let that happen. If he scanned my shoulder, he'd find the proof to doom us all. We'd be arrested, and Juni would never step a toe in the Fount.

Bane snapped his finger and said, "Bring Mrs. Johnson over here."

I didn't think. I moved.

"Hold on," I told Juni. I ducked and shoved my shoulder into the red uniform coming at me, knocking him back. Bane cursed as the soldier stumbled into him.

I held tight to my sister and leaped into the Fount.

Our twined bodies plunged into the water. Warm liquid wrapped around us, bubbling along our skin. Juni's fingers loosened around my neck, but I barely noticed. I was lost in free fall.

The water was electric, bursting with light, seeping beyond flesh and bone. Light fizzed along my skin and washed through my veins, blazing through my body. The sensation sank heart-deep, soothing as a cool breeze on a perfect night. Every ache and hurt vanished. The water whispered through me like the answer to every heart's desire, like a sunrise in my soul. All pain, doubt, and fear erased in one weightless moment. I was free, healed, whole. Mind, body, and soul.

Juni released me, and the change jolted me. For the first time, I noticed my lungs thirsting for air. I clutched my sister's hand. I had to deliver her to Rafe. He could save her. I knew it in my bones.

I drew Juni to me and kicked in the water. My feet tangled in the layers of my ballgown, threatening to anchor me, but I couldn't panic. The Fount wouldn't allow it. I held Juni in one arm and paddled toward the surface with the other.

We broke through the veil of water and into chaos. Rafe was restrained and surrounded by half a dozen Guardia. They lined the platform, kneeling and grabbing for us, shouting. Bane stood off to the side, barking orders. It was clear the soldiers were meant to capture me without touching the water. Even now, the water was off-limits to all but the most privileged.

Juni tightened her arms around me. "Evan," she said, her voice trembling. Her heart pounded, chest rising and falling rapidly, but she was breathing without trouble. Her eyes were clear, her face flush and healthy, dark circles gone. My heart lifted at the realization.

It had worked. My sister was healed.

I kissed the side of her head and hugged her to me. "I'm going to hand you to Rafe," I said. "I want you to run. Both of you. Do what he says, you understand? You have to get out of here."

"No!"

I ignored her and paddled to the edge, straight to Rafe. He shook loose from his captors and stooped at the edge of the water. I hoisted my sister up as she clawed at me, desperate to hold on. Sobs poured from her lips, but I blocked everything out. I locked eyes with Rafe, evading the soldiers' clutching hands, and pushed Juni into his arms. Guards grabbed at me, but my skin was slippery with water, and I dodged back from the edge.

"Go!" I yelled. "Please!"

Rafe stared, wide-eyed, as realization sank in.

I was staying. I was begging him to run—without me.

"No..."

I couldn't hear him, but his lips formed the word and his head shook. Juni squirmed in his arms, reaching for me, and he struggled to hold his ground, to hold her while the crowd surged around him. While soldiers tried to haul him away.

I swam to the edge of the platform and raised my hands to the soldiers flanking Rafe.

"Arrest them!" Bane shouted to his men. His voice shook Rafe back to reality. He stood as two soldiers stooped and grasped my hands.

I squeezed their hands and kicked off a stone pillar beneath the platform. I yanked hard. The soldiers toppled, one landing on top of me. We folded beneath the water. Peace flooded through me once again, and I let go, allowing gravity to take me.

More bodies plunged into the water...one, two...three, maybe more. I didn't care. I'd live in this moment as long as my lungs could stand it.

A soldier seized my arm and tugged me through the water. His arm ringed my neck, and he paddled for the surface. I floated like a dead log, neither helping him nor hindering him. I let him drag me, praying I'd given Rafe and Juni enough time and distraction to slip away to safety.

By the time we surfaced, gasping for air, the platform had descended into a whole new level of madness. Soldiers and guests were pulling people out of the water. People were shouting and pushing. Bane was nose-to-nose with another soldier, yelling in his face. I scanned the scene, but Rafe and Juni were gone.

Thank you, God. Please, set them free.

Rafe knew the territory, and he would keep Juni safe. That was what I told myself. My sacrifice would be worth it. It had to be true.

"Get her out of there. Now." Bane's voice rose above the chaos. He was pointing a me. I shivered despite the Fount's blissful cocoon.

The soldier holding me side-swam to the edge of the platform, to where the Commander and dozens of Guardia had crowded out the guests. Uniformed arms lunged for me. I lost count of the number of hands digging into my arms and legs as the mob dragged me from the water. The soldiers hauled me in front of Bane, my gown and hair soaked and dripping on the stones. The Commander stared me down, seething with speechless anger.

When he found his voice, it was sharp as a knife. "If this weren't a sacred space, I'd cut you down where you stand. How dare you?"

I lowered my eyes in submission. What could I say? What I'd done was worse than stepping out of line at El Jardín. Much worse. I should have shown remorse, begged forgiveness, trembled in fear. But my spirit was flush with the Fount's miracle—and more, a bittersweet relief.

We'd done what we'd set out to do. My sister was healed. She was with the person I trusted more than anyone to get her home safely. What happened to me now was beyond my control. I had to be brave enough to face it.

Bane snatched my arm and whirled me around. He placed his scanner on my left shoulder and pressed a button. I closed my eyes, waiting for him to discover the evidence of my deceit. It was over now. He'd find out everything.

Run, Rafe. Please.

Silence followed. My heart ticked like a clock gone mad.

Bane stalked over to Blackwell. His brunette friend was trying to pull him away, but it was too late.

"There is no evidence to support your accusation," the Commander said. "You have made a mockery of this sacred ceremony, and for that you will be punished. Guards, take him away."

Relief swelled in my veins. Bane had found nothing. The last proof that my Obligor contract had ever existed had been washed away by the Fount. The last evidence of my ties to Rafe were gone. My flesh was free of the Conquistador's disgusting mark.

"No, Commander, please. You don't understand," Blackwell began begging, but Bane ignored him.

He prowled back to me, vengeance smoldering in his eyes. The consequences of my actions would be swift and brutal. My knees buckled, but too many hands held me aloft, fingers digging bruises into my skin.

"Get this piece of filth out of here."

48

RAFE

This was all wrong.

Every curse word imaginable rushed through my head.

Dammit, Evan.

We had to run. There was no other option, but abandoning Evan to those vultures felt like stabbing myself in the gut. She'd wanted me to flee. Her eyes had radiated with apology and resolve as she'd yelled for me to go.

How could I leave her? Run like a coward?

Cold reality dictated she wasn't making it out. Staying would only endanger Juni, and the odds of me surviving capture were zero. Evan had hauled those soldiers into the water to buy us time. I couldn't waste it.

Along the platform, soldiers abandoned their guests and crowded the edge, craning to reach Evan. Juni wailed and strained for her sister, her voice drowned amid the shouts of soldiers and guests. The Guardia crowded in, nudging Bane to the side as he bellowed orders. I followed Evan's lead and began body-slamming soldiers into the water, along with anyone else in my path. Bodies plunged and water splashed onto the platform, buzzing along my skin. More soldiers pressed in, and I inched back from the mayhem, ducking behind soldiers and guests as they concentrated on pulling people out of the Conq's precious Fount.

I could only imagine him watching from his abode in the Fount Garden, steam pouring out of his nostrils like a raging bull. I glanced at the window where he'd been standing, but it was empty. My father was nowhere to be seen.

I needed to disappear, but Juni was wailing like a banshee. I pressed my lips to her ear. "Juni, be quiet," I growled. My tone was harsh, but it worked. The girl startled and grew quiet. "Your sister wants us to escape. We can't do that if you're fighting me and screaming."

I backed into the trees bordering the platform. The distraction I'd stirred up wouldn't last long. They'd notice we were missing and come looking.

"We can't leave her," Juni said, her voice tiny and broken.

"I know. I don't want to, but we must."

She buried her face in my neck and shook with silent sobs. The Fount water from her tunic soaked into my shirt and tingled where it touched my skin, dredging up the crime that had started everything. I pushed the thoughts aside and shifted further into the shadows.

Something hard pressed into my back, and I stilled.

"Why do you keep showing up where you have no business being?"

The familiar voice sent chills down my back. I turned. Tresick sheltered behind a tree, a dazer aimed at my midsection. The Conq prohibited most weapons in the Fount Garden, but soldiers carried dazers with enough electrical power to flatten a cyclops. Twain and I had gotten our hands on one as teens and taken turns knocking each other out. Once had been enough. I didn't want to repeat that painful lesson. Plus, a dazer hit would likely kill a tiny thing like Juni.

"I keep asking myself the same thing," I said.

"You are such a loose end," Tresick said. "I should kill you right now."

Juni raised her head and locked eyes with the man. He straightened and took a step back. He wanted nothing to do with harming a child. I could see it in his eyes.

Chalk another one up for Juni, the giant slayer.

A voice crackled on the colonel's Convo. "Male subject fled with child. Unit five pursue."

Tresick's eyes flicked beyond me. "I assume you know a way out of here?"

I nodded.

"Then you'd better take it. Don't make me regret this."

That was all the permission I needed. I hurried past the soldier, then paused.

"Please protect her," I said, leaving out Evan's name. Even now, I didn't want him to figure out who she was, where she'd come from.

He glanced at Juni again and shook his head. "I'll do what I can, but I can't save her," Tresick said. "That's out of my hands."

Footsteps pounded nearby.

"I'll try to misdirect them. Go!"

I ran. As a boy, I'd known these woods like the back of my hand, and I let muscle memory take over. There was one escape route no one knew except me and Twain. At least there had been, years ago when I used to sneak around the Fount grounds on a regular basis. I shifted Juni to my back, and she latched on to my neck as I bolted through the woods.

Soldiers appeared to my left and shouted at us to stop. Like that would happen. I pressed harder, put some distance between us, but I couldn't outrun them. I fled until I reached the old oak tree. It was an ancient, sprawling thing with a shallow hole in one side. The tree was five feet wide, with heavy, drooping branches. I sprinted beneath a limb and ducked behind the trunk. Footfalls pounded in the distance, and branches cracked as the soldiers crashed through the forest.

I knelt and settled Juni inside the trunk's hole. "Stay here until I come back. Don't make a noise. Don't look out," I whispered.

As I peeked from behind the tree, I spotted two soldiers approaching our hiding spot, dazers drawn. I had one shot at this.

I waited until they passed and hurled myself at them. I rammed the nearest soldier, and both men fell like dominos. The three of us toppled to the ground, me on top of the Guardia sandwich. I throat-punched the closest soldier. He clutched his neck and gasped for breath as I searched for his weapon. I snagged the dazer from a pile of leaves, scooted off the soldiers, and aimed.

A jagged blue line of electricity spewed forth and nailed the nearest soldier in the chest. His fists curled into claws as his body arched, and his eyes rolled to the rear of his head. The soldier beneath him quaked as the electricity penetrated the top soldier and jumped to him. It only took seconds. I released the trigger, and both men fell slack.

I didn't wait to see how long the dazing would last. I collected the second dazer, tucked it into my pocket, and found Juni. She was curled in on herself, rocking. Not weeping, not making a sound, but crying out with her whole body. I felt like a steaming pile of dung as I scooped her up. There was no time to comfort her. We weren't out of the woods yet.

The Fount was secured inside a mini fortress. A wall surrounded Florida's most precious resource, with only one door for visitors, another door for the Conq, and no windows. The only other entrance was a secure transpod tunnel to my father's private residence inside the Fount Garden. As teens, Twain and I had exploited the transpod tunnel by digging a long shaft into the garden. Our escape hatch had allowed us to enter and exit the Fount grounds undetected whenever we'd wished. We could make our way anywhere inside or outside the palace by using service tunnels and a master key I'd swiped. Fortunately, fleeing the Fount didn't require a key.

Our escape hole originated beneath a massive boulder midway to the western wall. It took longer than I liked, but I found the rock and the gap beneath it.

I set Juni on the ground and knelt before her. "Okay, kiddo. I'm going in first. Then you come after me, and I will catch you. Got it?"

Juni nodded, tear-soaked eyes glued to me. In her wet dress and dripping hair, she looked like a deflated balloon, but her eyes were clear, her face flush with healthy color.

She'd been healed.

At what cost? It was too much.

I dropped to my hands and knees, lowered to my belly, and edged into the gap. My feet bumped something hard, and I crawled out. I activated the flashlight on my Convo and ducked my head inside to see what I'd bumped against. A long metal pipe traversed the hole, blocking the way into the shaft. That hadn't been there before.

"What the f—frost?" I stopped myself from cursing in front of Juni.

A small trickle of water leaked from the pipe. I touched it and felt a familiar tingle. Fount water was leaking from a pipe running beneath the garden grounds.

What the hell?

That pipe had no business being there, but I had no time to contemplate why it was. I needed to find a way out, and this wasn't it. That left one option. One shitty option. The transpod tunnel running directly to the Conq's house.

"Change of plans," I said, pulling Juni onto my back. "We're going to that big house over there. We need to be extra careful.

There will be people there, and they can't see or hear us, or we'll get caught. Got it?"

The girl buried her face in my neck. I took that as a yes.

By now, the forest was flooded with soldiers. Their calls rang through the trees. I was counting on the Guardia thinking I'd never go near the Conq's house. Only an idiot would do that, right?

Yeah, that was me.

I picked my way through the forest, watching for the red uniforms that shone like beacons in the night. Narrowly missing several. Finally, I reached the bamboo hedge at the rear of my father's house. The three-story manse towered into the trees with translucent glass walls, giving the illusion the house and forest were one. As usual, it was lit up like a birthday cake, radiating light every direction.

Beyond the hedge, a wide stone veranda held a small bathing pool marked by a trio of sleek waterfalls and a vine-covered pergola with a fireplace and seating area. A narrow, stone-lined stream wrapped around the entire house, connecting with the backyard pool as well as an infinity pool at the front of the house. This was my father's private retreat, and the man was big on water.

Everything appeared to be abandoned. It was late, so most staff would be home and in bed, but the Conq was a notorious night owl. Maybe he'd gone to check out the disturbance at the Fount. Maybe he'd stopped watching the ceremony and had no idea it had taken place. I had no way of knowing. I searched for signs of life, anyone who might notice us crossing the patio. Security cameras spied from all over the place, but I was counting on no one actively monitoring the feeds, otherwise we were screwed. I had no other options.

I made a dash for it.

I zipped through the bamboo, jumped the stream, and ran under the pergola to the glass door. I peeked inside and found an empty kitchen. Dread settled in my belly. It couldn't be this easy. I twisted the doorknob. It was locked. Of course it was.

There was a retinal scanner nearby that could unlock the door, but it was unlikely my eye impression remained in the device. I looked around the yard. We were running out of time. It was worth a try.

"Hold tight, Juni," I whispered. I fished the retinal mask out of my eye and leaned close to the scanner. I pressed a button, and the device activated. Seconds later it beeped, and the door clicked open.

"You really should update your security, old man," I muttered as I eased the door open. The stairwell to the transpod tunnel lay a few feet away. I glanced around the pristine kitchen and down adjacent hallways. Again, I saw no one. I tiptoed to the stairwell and down the first flight.

Footsteps sounded in the kitchen above me. I put Juni down and motioned for her to run downstairs. She didn't question my instructions. She fled, and I lost sight of her as she turned a corner. I followed but stopped at the second landing. I lifted my dazer, waiting to see if anyone trailed us. Boots tapped on the stairs in rapid succession. I saw the soldier two seconds before he spotted me.

It was one of the Conq's private bodyguards, dressed in bulletproof black, armed to the teeth, with an automatic pistol in hand. I zapped him before he could aim. The electricity connected in the flesh above his collar, and his eyes rolled skyward. He collapsed and his gun skittered down the steps. I lunged and caught the man before he could make more noise.

I was tempted to leave the bodyguard where he was, but if my father or anyone else discovered him, they'd fire off every alarm in the place. I hauled the soldier over my shoulders in a fireman's hold. His weight almost sent me to my knees, but I steadied myself and baby-stepped down the stairs, breathing heavily.

I froze at the sound of a familiar voice.

"Cooper? You there?"

Papi.

His voice rumbled from somewhere above, possibly the stairwell entrance. Every adolescent nightmare from my past bubbled to the surface, even as something deeper inside me yearned for the father he'd once been. Years ago, when my mother had been alive with her angelic face and lilting British accent. What would he do if I climbed the stairs and embraced him? The little boy in me wanted nothing more. The man I'd become knew better.

For several moments, no one moved. It was so quiet, I could almost hear my father breathing. Then the floor creaked as he took a step.

It was over. He was coming.

I would daze him, too. Didn't matter that I had a two-hundred-pound gorilla slung over my shoulders. I waited, holding my breath, ready to pull the trigger.

He never came. The Conq retreated and his footsteps faded somewhere deep inside the house.

Screw it. I wasn't carrying this dead weight any farther. Time to get the hell out of there, and fast. I eased the soldier to the steps, retrieved his gun and any ammo he had, and pocketed them. I jogged down the stairs on silent feet until I reached the darkened tunnel. Juni waited there, her arms hugging her tiny, trembling body.

"Good job, kid," I said. "We're almost free."

I towed Juni through the underground passage toward the service exit, but then I stopped. The Conq's transpod sat right there. The one vehicle in the entire Citadel that could not be tracked. It was a safety measure for the Conq, and I was going to take full advantage of it.

"Come on," I said, tugging Juni toward the vehicle. We climbed aboard and settled into the plush swivel chairs mounted in front of the control panel. Papi's transpod reeked of luxury, with high-end finishes, soft carpeting, and a fully stocked bar. I resisted the urge to pour myself a shot of his aged whiskey. I could have used some liquid courage, but there was no time. I powered up the engine and pushed the Launch button.

We shot through the tunnel, the transpod headlamps pushing away the darkness in front of us. The security gates slid seamlessly open before us, and we sailed through. I held Juni in my lap, caressing her hair as numbness set in. As the crack in my heart deepened the farther we fled from Evan. As anger filled the crevice.

After nearly half an hour, I stopped the transpod near a service platform in the tunnel. I programmed the vehicle to drive another thirty minutes, and we waited on the platform as the autopilot engaged and the transpod faded in the blackness.

I activated my flashlight and knelt next to Juni. "You're doing great, kiddo," I said. "We're almost there."

"What about Evan?" Her eyes were teary and tired. It broke my heart.

I stared at the ground and swallowed the anger in my throat. It should never have had to come to this.

"I'm sorry, Juni," I said, looking into her eyes. "I want her here, too, but this is what she wanted. Come on."

I pushed on the door to the service exit, and we left the tunnel behind.

We were safe. Minutes from home. Freedom.

As we walked in silence, images of Evan assaulted me. I'd left the woman I loved to the wolves. They would tear her apart, and it was my fault.

Forgive me for not protecting you.

They would rip her to pieces and find out everything. I'd failed her. Failed my friends. Destroyed everything.

Juni and I were safe, for now. But not for much longer.

It was only a matter of time before the Empire figured out who I was, before they tortured the truth out of Evan.

I had to get home. I had to warn Twain and Simone. Scuttle the only home we had and flee.

Yes, we were safe in this moment, but our running had only just begun.

I would not run forever. No, I'd come back, and if Evan survived, I'd free her or burn the whole place down trying.

49

EVANGELINE

*M*y body was a thing I barely recognized. Lying on the cold stone floor in a ruined ballgown, my flesh ached with bruises from the hands of faceless soldiers. Even so, my soul buzzed with a shadowy, lingering calmness, an undeserved remnant of bathing in the Fount. The anvil that had sat on my chest since my mother's death was gone, vanished like a bad dream. I could breathe. Without fear, without regret.

I'd been in this dark cell for hours, shackled to the wall with heavy chains. The place stank of urine and mold. Moans and cries from other prisoners seeped through the floor-to-ceiling bars from unseen places. The cell across from me was empty. I was utterly alone, haunted by faceless voices. I'd cried myself dry, first with relief and then uncertainty about whether Rafe and Juni had escaped, about what might happen to my family if Bane recognized me.

But I couldn't bring myself to feel sorry for what I'd done. My sister was healed, and she had the chance to live a full life now. It was on Rafe and my father to make sure that happened. For me, it was over. If Bane demanded a hand for stealing a tangerine, what would be required for stealing an Immersion? I didn't want to die, but I couldn't see another way for this story to end.

Sometime in the night, I fell asleep. I startled awake at a sudden clanging at my cell door. Two soldiers waited as a third unlocked the door and ushered them inside. I bolted upright and scuttled away, as if I could run from them. The tallest soldier yanked my cuffed hands toward him, sending a bolt of pain through my wrists. He unlocked the cuffs, and they dropped to the floor in a noisy clatter.

"Let's go," he said, groping my arm and hauling me off the floor. Another soldier cinched a new pair of shackles around my wrists.

This was it. This was my death march. Justice came swift in Florida, and payment had to be made. I resisted the urge to claw at the soldier, bite him, do whatever it took to fight my way free.

My fighting time was over. There was no way out of this.

I let the soldier manhandle me down the dank stone corridor, up a flight of stairs, and through several corridors of a stark building. I had no idea where I was or where they were taking me, only that it couldn't be anywhere good.

We halted before two large doors made of a dark, shiny wood. The soldiers knocked and received a command to enter.

Commander Bane stood inside an elegant office, before a massive, dark wooden desk. A man sat behind the desk, and his angry eyes struck me in a way I didn't understand. He was well dressed in a suit and open-collared shirt. His black hair was cropped short on the sides, wavy on top, and his blue eyes captured my gaze and wouldn't let go.

I was too caught up in the man behind the desk to see it coming. Bane slapped me hard across the face, sending me to my hands and knees, dumbstruck.

"How dare you stare at our sovereign?" he said. "You will kneel before him in your shame."

I stayed down, trembling, afraid to look up. My cheek throbbed, and my ear rang from the blow. The tang of blood spilled across my tongue. I heard movement across the room, and suddenly the Conquistador stood in front of me. The man stooped, cupped my chin with a gentle hand, and lifted my face to meet his gaze.

"What I want to know..." he said as he dangled a photograph in front of my eyes. It was Rafe's photo, the one from his fake American passport—shaved head and brown eyes that usually matched those of the man in front of me.

"What I want to know," the Conquistador repeated, "is who are you and what you were doing with my son."

I couldn't help myself. A smile spread across my bloodied lip.

The man who looked like an older version of Rafe scowled, but I didn't care. At that moment, I knew.

They'd made it out.

ACKNOWLEDGMENTS

Fount and Fortune has been a labor of love for many years, and I can't say "thank you" enough to my family and friends who've supported me, believed in me and cheered me on throughout the process. To everyone who kept asking when my book was coming out, thank you! Your interest and curiosity kept me going. To my readers, if you've made it this far, thank you for being one of my supporters and taking this journey with me.

To the first people who read my novel, especially in its preliminary stages, and provided insightful feedback and encouragement, thank you from the bottom of my heart: Linda Harris, Katherine Hanselman, Donna Burd, Rose Guildenstern, Amy Jo Odubhaigh, Kimberly Cooper, Maria A. Eden and Neff Rodriguez. Thanks to Elizabeth Arway for her marketing and website advice and ongoing support. My gratitude also goes out to Emanuel Flores and Michelle Hill for helping with my Spanish phrases.

To Hannah Morgan Teachout, thank you for your insightful editorial assessment which helped me strengthen my storytelling and character development, bringing my characters' arcs to whole new levels. To Mandi Andrejka with Inky Pen Editorial Services, thank you for your incredible attention to detail, helping me clarify my writing and flesh out pieces I hadn't even realized were missing. Thanks also to the extremely talented

K.D. Guthauser at Story Wrappers for my beautiful and captivating book cover.

To my husband, Bill, my children, my parents, my entire family and my dearest friends, thank you for loving and supporting me and showing me anything is possible, and dreams are worth pursuing. I'm so thankful for all of you. GLYSDI.

THANK YOU!

THANKS FOR READING MY BOOK. I hope you enjoyed it! Reviews are incredibly important to reach other readers. If you enjoyed this book, please take a few moments to leave a review, even if it's one or two sentences. Good places to share your review include:

- Your own social media accounts
- Amazon and other online booksellers
- Review sites such as Goodreads, Fable, and The Story Graph.

I appreciate your support so much.

WANT TO KNOW WHEN MY NEXT BOOK IS OUT?

Sign up at mickeyschoonover.com and follow me on Instagram at @AuthorMickeySchoonover.

ABOUT THE AUTHOR

Mickey Schoonover has been making up fictional stories for most of her life, writing fantastical tales in the margins of her days as a reporter, editor and public relations professional. Fount and Fortune *is her debut novel. Find me online at mickeyschoonover.com or on Instagram at instagram.com/authormickeyschoonover.*